SAMURAI
AWAKENING

April 15th,

Jess:
I know you hate my advice, but this time try to take it: Never get on a plane. There's no way to know where you'll REALLY end up...

—David

An excerpt from an unsent letter to his sister, later added to the Matsumoto archives

SAMURAI
AWAKENING

Benjamin Martin

TUTTLE Publishing

Tokyo | Rutland, Vermont | Singapore

DEDICATION

To the people of Kitadaito Island, Japan
and
Gail Bernstein,
the teacher who taught me to write.

Published by Tuttle Publishing, an imprint of Periplus Editions (HK) Ltd.

www.tuttlepublishing.com

Copyright © 2012 Benjamin Martin

Library of Congress Cataloging-in-Publication Data in process

ISBN 978-4-8053-1228-5

First edition
16 15 14 13 12
10 9 8 7 6 5 4 3 2 1   1205RP

Printed in China

Distributed by

North America, Latin America & Europe
Tuttle Publishing
364 Innovation Drive
North Clarendon, VT 05759-9436 U.S.A.
Tel: 1 (802) 773-8930
Fax: 1 (802) 773-6993
info@tuttlepublishing.com
www.tuttlepublishing.com

Japan
Tuttle Publishing
Yaekari Building, 3rd Floor,
5-4-12 Osaki, Shinagawa-ku,
Tokyo 141 0032
Tel: (81) 3 5437-0171
Fax: (81) 3 5437-0755
sales@tuttle.co.jp
ww.tuttle.co.jp

Asia Pacific
Berkeley Books Pte. Ltd.
61 Tai Seng Avenue #02-12,
Singapore 534167
Tel: (65) 6280-1330
Fax: (65) 6280-6290
inquiries@periplus.com.sg
www.periplus.com

TUTTLE PUBLISHING® is a registered trademark of Tuttle Publishing, a division of Periplus Editions (HK) Ltd.

CONTENTS

—

THE MATSUMOTO ESTATE

April,

What is nothing? If you really think about it, can you imagine nothingness? Not black, white, or any other void, but complete non-existence? If you are one of the rare ones, if you can grasp that slippery idea, then maybe you will begin to understand what it was like...

He was still not sure how it had happened. Even when his sister got in trouble, David had been able to avoid fighting. Bleeding from at least five different injuries was a wholly new experience, and with the broken bones in his hand, he was having an absurdly bad day at the end of an incomprehensibly bad month.

From the front seat of the black Mercedes, Yukiko passed another critical eye over him as he pulled at his uniform collar. His Japanese clothes never fit him quite right. With a slam that rocked the whole car, Masao Matsumoto closed the driver's door. As usual, his host father was impeccably dressed in a traditional kimono and the sleek sedan came to life with a quiet purr.

Within seconds, the car was tearing along a maintenance road through the forest behind Nakano Junior High. Masao bit off a string of quick Japanese as they raced through the blind turns of the darkening forest road.

"Masao would like to know what happened," Yukiko said in perfect English. His host mother sat as serenely and composed as ever in her brightly colored clothing despite the high speed driving. Unlike Masao, her kimono was bright and colorful, with an array of light flowers that enhanced her delicate features. To either side of him, his host siblings Rie and Takumi slid into him with each turn. He was sure he looked strange plopped down between the stunning pair. David was bruised, bloody, and stuffed between two diminutive thirteen-year-olds that could have been on the cover of any sports magazine.

"Uh," David said. Masao turned around to look at David, which was extremely frightening given the trees rushing by. In a desperate attempt to get Masao's eyes back on the road, David spoke quickly. "I ran into a couple of third years."

Rie leaned over him, unleashing a quick stream of Japanese at Takumi, who merely shrugged in reply. Yukiko smiled, encouraging David to continue. Luckily, he knew the twins would have no idea what he was saying. Their grasp of English, even after a year of studying it, was about as good as his nonexistent Japanese.

David told her about the fight. He had caused the third years' team to lose, again. They had not picked him, instead, their teacher Mr. Shima, had assigned him to the team as a kind of handicap. David had done his job a little too well. His chronic lack of coordination was something he had almost considered a blessing back in the Phoenix desert, where the hot summers made running any distance painful. In Japan though, his apathy towards sports had become a liability.

They had found him behind the gym after school. The three boys were older than David's thirteen years, and full of hard-coiled muscle. He had smiled weakly and looked for the twins, but somehow they had been separated on the way to meet up after school. He was sure it was no accident.

The anger and hate on the oldest boy's face had been easy enough for him to understand. He tried to bolt, but they surrounded him in a close circle almost instantly. Then the pushing began.

As usual, he did not retaliate as they bounced him from bully to bully. He had tried to stay calm, to take it. He hoped that if he did not give them a reaction, they would soon grow bored and leave him alone.

In a lull, the oldest boy, Koji, caught David's eye. He stood there for a minute as two of his friends closed in behind. When Koji smiled, it was a smile he had seen before in Arizona. It reminded him of a boy who liked to pull the tails off lizards. Koji held up the picture that David had brought in for a report on his family. The one picture he had of his whole family, still together. Though David could not understand his words, Koji's eyes were clear enough.

It was like a switch, they had found the one thing that could set him off. The chance Koji could ruin the one picture he had of his mother released a torrent of fire with him. He broke. The weeks of frustration, loneliness, and rage blurred in his mind as his body reacted without thought. Screaming, David had lashed out, his hand striking Koji square in the chin.

Pain had washed through his hand and arm as he fell to his knees in agony. Koji, unfazed, took the opportunity to throw a few quick punches of his own before kicking him the rest of the way to the ground. The boys had laughed, then rolled him down the hill to the forest's edge and left him there, curled in a ball around his broken hand.

Takumi and Rie had found him a few minutes later, still crumpled on the ground, crying like some elementary student. The shame was almost worse than the pain. He wanted to disappear. Rie helped him up, and the pity in her deep almond eyes had been almost more unbearable than his hand. Takumi had stood apart. It was a first to see his host brother so calm at school, and then David saw his eyes. A new and dangerous element in them made David shudder.

It took a while for Masao and Yukiko to get there after Takumi's call. They had driven in through the forest. David was not sure if they had done it to save him the embarrassment of having to walk through the school, or if they simply wanted to avoid creating an incident. Whatever the reason, he was glad.

David stopped talking and the car skidded out of the forest onto a much larger main road. Yukiko had already set his hand. From her serene and formal dress, you would never know she had been a nurse. David tried to remember his own mother, but his memories of her had faded into a distant shadow. He was a toddler in the picture. Jessica was a newborn. The images of her faded even as he tried to grasp at them. In the front, Yukiko began translating David's story into Japanese.

David recognized the road as the main street between Nakano and Himeji. Not far from Japan's inland sea, the Matsumotos lived on an estate just outside of Nakano town, which was in a valley surrounded by tall mountains. It reminded David of a smaller, greener version of home.

He had left his sister Jessica, and his father Dr. Matthews, nearly a month before on a whim to study in Japan. A last minute opening in the exchange program had had him hustling to prepare in time to leave for the beginning of the Japanese school year in April. A month ago, David had driven down the road with excitement. Now he felt defeated, not just by the boys, but by Japan. He had tried, but nothing he did had helped him worm his way into any group. Most of his classmates had written him off when they discovered he only snowboarded, poorly. At the Estate, the Matsumotos had been welcoming and friendly, but only Yukiko spoke English and the rest of them kept to themselves.

Masao turned the car onto a narrow, but well maintained dirt road. They had arrived at the Estate. Without the spring sun, the trees were old and foreboding. The forest seemed more of a barrier to David than the ancient stone wall that came into view when the car skidded around the long drive's final curve. Sliding along the seat brought David back to the present. He was in an alien land and could barely say hello.

The Estate's wall rose like a dark cliff. Rough in design and old with lichen, it was still elegant in its own way. A huge gate stood in the center of the road. Wide enough to let two cars through simultaneously, it was welcoming and imposing at the same time. Two huge wooden doors covered the road, while stone and wood supported the overhanging roof above. Tiered eaves with elegant curves and dark clay tiles bespoke their ancient purpose to repel rain and arrows alike.

As the car approached the gate, Masao finally slowed. Although he had seen it many times over the last month, he was still struck by the view as the heavy doors parted.

Beyond the gate, the main house rose before them, a single level with a tiled roof. As with the outside gate, the Matsumotos' main house followed traditional Japanese design. With both wood and modern materials, it was a seamless combination of functionality and art.

Behind the House was the Estate's jewel, a Japanese garden complete with brook, pond, and stone bridge. Each miniature tree had been shaped into specific, asymmetric designs. Rocks and boulders were strategically located along with grasses and flowers. The pond wove through it all, fed by the brook, tying the separate elements of the garden together. It was both more beautiful and yet more alien than anything David had seen before.

The garden was flanked by the Estate's other two main buildings, creating a kind of open-ended square. When he had first arrived, Yukiko had shown David the dojo and workshop. She had explained that the Matsumotos were both sword makers and masters of kendo—the Japanese martial art focusing the use of swords. The Estate also contained a few other odd buildings, sheds, and mysteries David had yet to explore.

He spent hours of his free time sitting among the garden's trees, trying not to worry about his little sister and father. Jessica was probably busy keeping their eccentric father from blowing himself up with his latest experiment.

'But I'm not there to keep *her* out of trouble. Maybe that's why I swung at that bastard Koji.' David thought as the gate's doors closed behind him.

As the car pulled around the front of the house, the old man David knew only as Grandpa came out to meet them. He stood tall despite his advanced age. His jet-black hair lightly streaked with gray, Grandpa had a ready smile and an energy that made him seem far younger than his eighty-five years. When they had first met, David had thought him only in his early fifties. It had taken him nearly two weeks to figure out that *oji-isan* was not a title or even his name. It was Grandpa in Japanese. The old man smiled, radiating gentleness and a deep but secret wisdom as he walked forward to meet the car.

"よかった、おじいさんは ちょうど 準備が終わったところ だ," Masao said in his usual fast Japanese. As usual, David struggled and failed to comprehend a word. Masao tended to be clipped and direct, his words aimed with precision, especially when at his children. To David's surprise, Masao turned around again in his seat and stared at David. Beside him, the twins froze. "ダビッド君は日本のこと分からないな．明日から　手ほどきしよう."

Luckily, Yukiko was nearly always ready to interpret. As a nurse and she had been required to study foreign languages and her English was impeccable. She was constantly trying to make David feel more comfortable. After a few more words between her and Masao, she turned to David.

"David, do you want to see something special tomorrow?" Yukiko asked.

"Sure," he answered. It was not often that the Matsumotos extended invitations to him, and he had noticed extra work going on around the Estate the last few days.

"Grandpa has just finished his preparations to begin a new sword. As part of that process, tomorrow morning we will have a ceremony at the Matsumoto shrine. Please come." Yukiko smiled as warmly as ever. "It's nice to be able to invite you to a family event few outsiders have ever seen."

David smiled. The pain from his hand and bruises momentarily forgotten, he looked out at the lively old man. David never knew if Grandpa understood him. He always stared until David broke down and attempted Japanese. Although he had only known him for a short time, and did not speak the same language, Grandpa made him feel like part of the family.

"とても　面白いですよ．君はこの儀式を見る初めての外国人だよ," Takumi said. Takumi occasionally tried to use the English he had picked up during his first year of junior high, but normally just settled for speaking his usual quick Japanese. When David gave one of his usual stares of incomprehension, Takumi added a lot of gesturing. Rie was a bit more helpful as she generally tried to speak more slowly.

"ダビッド君、いっしょに　行こうか," Rie added, opening the car door. The twins were interesting. Unfortunately, the language and cultural barriers had kept David from getting to know them. As they got out of the car, David felt another twinge of loneliness. He missed having his sister around. She was two years younger and often annoying, but Jessica knew him better than anyone else did.

Rie reminded him of her a little bit. Shorter than David, she was thin and willowy, yet had a grace and strength born from constant competition with Takumi in both martial arts and school. With long black hair and deep brown eyes, Rie had her mother's looks and poise, yet giggled at the strangest moments. Takumi, with jagged short black hair and wearing a badminton shirt, looked like he had just stepped out of a sports wear commercial. Strongly muscled yet still lean and lithe, Takumi was a study in contradictions. Serious at the Estate, he remained confident and driven at school, but was also as entertaining as any of their classmates.

David slowly slid out behind Takumi. He was taller and wider than the twins, with skin that had never tanned since he had preferred staying indoors in Arizona. In school and town, his skin, hair, and lack of Japanese were all obvious signs that singled him out as a gaijin, a foreigner. In Japan, being a gaijin literally meant you were an "outside person." It was not only David's looks that set him apart. David hated how he seemed to lumber along, his lack of coordination all the more apparent next to the twins.

As heirs to the Matsumoto name and Estate, Rie and Takumi both practiced kendo every morning. As junior high school students in Japan, they were expected to participate in afterschool activities as well. Since Nakano was a relatively small town that meant sports. Both Rie and Takumi played on the school badminton team. The confidence and ability they possessed from their martial arts and sports activities came out in every step they took. Takumi had invited David to both activities, but David preferred sleeping in as late as possible.

After a week of David replying, "Maybe tomorrow," Takumi had given up. Rie had more luck, introducing David to badminton with an almost grim determination on weekend afternoons. With plenty of time to sleep in, David was far more willing to go outside and hit a shuttle around behind the dojo.

"ちょっと待ってダビッド君," Rie called from the car as David limped for the house. His own name at least, though "Japanized" David understood. Stopping to think, Rie screwed up her face into a mask of concentration, until, giving up she turned to her mother. Yukiko hefted her shopping bag and a quick stream of Japanese flowed between them before an elegant pivot of her head brought him back into their conversation.

"The day before a ceremony, Rie and Takumi must help prepare," Yukiko said. "Unfortunately, only the Matsumotos and their apprentices may do these things. Rie says she is sorry that they were unable to stop the students who hurt you. Shall we go have a better look at your wounds before I start dinner?"

Guiding David to the main door, Yukiko stopped to give an elegantly low bow to Grandpa. Smiling warmly, Grandpa seemed to ignore David's disheveled state as he slapped his shoulder, jostling David's hand. With a laugh as David blinked through the pain, Grandpa joined Masao and the twins as they walked around the left side of the house for the workshop.

That night David lay awake for a long time. He looked around his darkened room, considering his life.

'I can't believe how strange the Matsumoto's reactions always are,' he thought as sleep eluded him. 'They all but ignored the fight. I wasn't grounded or in any trouble. Back in the States, I probably would have been expelled.'

Anger surged again within him. David had recovered his picture, but it was dirty and scratched. Koji would pay for that.

'Not with my family,' he thought. Even as his rage solidified into a hard knot of determination in his chest, the shame of his injury froze it to a brittle shell.

Alone in the back corner of the main house, David was in the only four-walled bedroom. His refuge and island of western culture now seemed an isolated prison cell.

'And the twins would probably rather die than be seen with me,' he thought as sleep finally claimed him.

THE SHRINE

April,

Is it not funny how connected existence is with anticipation?
If you do not know about something, if it does not exist for
you, then there is no anticipation. Yet that double-edged feel-
ing hunts us, drives us…

Yukiko woke David early the next day. After checking his
splinted hand, she left him to dress. David's sluggishness from
having to wake early on a Saturday morning stayed with him
until the red flames of sunrise erupted through the trees behind the dojo. The sun's rays glittered along the pond and
awoke the main expanse of the Matsumoto forest into a bright
green sea. A solitary path through the trees began at the edge
of the garden, where two old stone pillars rose on either side of
the path to support the two massive curving beams of etched
stone. The torii gate's obvious age and simplicity lent it a mysterious air even in the clear morning dawn.

　　With Yukiko beside him, David passed under the gate and
followed the winding path north. Along the way, smaller foot-
paths branched off to places he had never been. David only
ventured into the forest with Yukiko, so he had only ever seen
the vegetable garden. At the end of the path, a small clearing

strewn with boulders met the base of a tall mountain. On the far side, a small stone Shinto shrine rose out of a hollow in the mountain. Although man made, the shrine was so old it seemed natural, as if it belonged among the scattered boulders.

Warm spring sunshine pervaded the area, making it hot despite the early hour. The rest of the Matsumotos were already at the shrine, but they waited for David to recover from the walk.

The shrine was a curious thing. A small house made of stone was set upon a pillar of rock carved from the mountain. From the pillar's base, stone stairs descended to the clearing, where Takumi and Rie helped Grandpa adjust his robes. Looking back, David noticed a fused mass of metal before the shrine. The jagged edges had been carefully laid upon a small wooden altar.

"What's up with the metal?" David asked. He was immediately sorry he broke the calm silence in the clearing as everyone turned towards him. Despite his embarrassment, he was awed by the way the metal caught the green tinted sunlight and threw it back in an array of gray.

"The purpose of this ceremony is to… bless the metal on the shrine. It will become a new sword," Yukiko answered quietly, her poise relaxed as always even through the difficult English. "The metal has been prepared to look as if it came from a meteorite, in memory of how the first Matsumoto sword was created."

Finished with their preparations, the twins and Masao joined David and Yukiko. Meanwhile Grandpa, bowed and ascended the two meters of steps to the shrine. In the full garb of a Shinto priest, he wore a long and voluminous white robe accented by a tall black cap. In one hand, he held a wand made of cut white paper, folded into zigzagging tendrils that flew about with his every movement. In his other hand, he held a small brown paddle.

As David watched, Grandpa began to chant in a low voice. The sound was unlike any Japanese he had heard before. It was older, more simplistic, yet refined. He had no idea what it meant, but beside him, Takumi watched the old man intently, his mouth moving slightly as if trying to recite the words himself. Grandpa alternated waving the paper wand, bowing with the wooden paddle in front of him, and pacing back and forth in front of the shrine. David frowned. The meaning of Grandpa's words was lost on him. Just as with everyone else over the last month, he was expected to listen attentively to another boring speech without the slightest clue as to its meaning.

Unlike at school, where he would just zone out right away, David made an extra effort to keep his attention on Grandpa. David liked the old man, but unable to follow what he was doing, the heat and humidity soon began to weigh on him. His eyes strayed from the shrine, following the brooding trees around the clearing as his thoughts flowed back to the previous day's fight.

'Why can't I break through their walls? It's like all of Japan is trying to keep me from understanding. Yukiko probably brought me here to make me feel more included. Her and Grandpa are all I have here,' he thought.

As his eyes and mind wandered, the dark greens and browns of the forest shifted just perceptibly, and a golden patch wavered through the tall ferns above him. David blinked. When he looked again, the forest was as it had been. Then he returned his attention back to Grandpa and found the golden hue again. Larger than before, and mingled with black streaks, the colors were brilliant against the dark browns and greens of the forest. David focused on the spot, the colors resolving into the black and gold stripes of a giant head. A large graceful tiger peered through the forest, its eyes intent, and ears alert. David watched as it slowly crept though the underbrush, angling for the shrine.

David completely forgot the ceremony, captivated as he watched the tiger move gracefully through the ferns. For an instant, David thought of the Matsumoto twins and their surreal agility. He had often watched them wishing he too could move as smoothly and confidently as Takumi, as gracefully as Rie.

'What's a tiger doing in Japan?' David thought. 'And why isn't it orange?'

Although the incongruous thoughts made David blink to clear his vision, the tiger was still there. Its tail flicked languidly through the air and he almost convinced himself that he was dreaming.

'After all, why would a giant tiger be stalking through the trees above the shrine?' David shook his head, trying to clear his mind. The movement brought the tiger's bright gaze on him, sending waves of primal fear rolling through David's body. Time stretched as his heart struggled to beat, and then the golden eyes flicked away in dismissal. David managed one jagged breath. The massive head turned, and the tiger's full attention focused on Grandpa. Black lips peeled from ivory fangs to form a hungry snarl.

"Takumi!" David hissed, trying to get the boy's attention. "A tiger… Takumi!"

Afraid the tiger might not be a figment of his imagination, David pulled on Takumi's sleeve. When that did not work, he grabbed the boy's muscled arm, pointing frantically. He finally succeeded in getting Takumi to look at where he was gesturing.

"何？　ダビッド君　静かにして！" Takumi said harshly. He put his finger to his lips and turned back to watch Grandpa, adding only "Shh!" when David continued to stare and babble at him in surprise. Although David could not understand his words, Takumi's face said, "Catch the hint, I was ignoring you."

When he turned back toward the shrine, the tiger was much closer to the old man. It crouched, every muscle tightening as it shuffled its legs beneath its long powerful body. David had watched enough Discovery Channel back home to know what would happen next. It was like watching a deer just before an attack. The tail swept over dead pine needles as the tiger's whiskers twitched. The only problem was that there was no deer, and the huge golden tiger had its sights set firmly on Grandpa.

David felt panic rising within him. Grandpa was in danger. David started moving before he realized he had made a decision. As he ran forward, the full power of the beast's muscles unleashed in a surge of motion. David moved quickly, as he had the time Jessica had followed a dog into the street, up the steep incline next to the stairs. The tiger sped forward, using the high ground to its advantage as any hunter would.

'I'll never make it,' David's mind screamed in despair, the panic sapping his energy even as he willed himself forward.

Looking up, the world slowed as the tiger landed and recoiled, preparing for the last jump. As his mind sped up to deal with the flow of adrenaline, David became aware of the tiger's loose furred skin rippling over powerful muscles. He could see every sharp edge of the tiger's white fangs, every bristly hair between deeply ancient eyes. As his opponent gathered its last bit of energy, David's heart seemed to pause again at the anticipation he saw in the feral golden eyes.

David surged forward. As he leapt, Grandpa clapped his hands twice and stepped back. The old man bowed low, and the last image David saw as his momentum carried him over Grandpa's back was the gaping, fang-filled mouth of the giant tiger.

As the buzz in his ears grew louder, David realized that he was lying down. Most of his body felt numb, as if submerged in ice. He tried to take a gulp of air, only to find his lungs did not respond. The wave of panic that swept through him threatened to push him deeper into his subconscious, but the incessant buzzing refused to let him sink into oblivion.

Slowly, David locked onto a pain that cut through the numbness and buzzing.

'If the tiger ate me, how come I hurt so much?' he thought. He focused on what he remembered of his body and finally decided that his chest hurt. More specifically, his heart burned, as if someone had ripped it out and replaced it with molten metal. As the heat seared through him, an intense agony far, far greater, suddenly overcame the hell in his chest. He tried to scream out as burning lances pierced his mind, but his deadened body provided no outlet. His consciousness filled with a strange voice, each word surged through his mind with a ripping bolt of pain that shook his core.

'*You tried to save him,*' the voice said. It was deep, with a haunting edge. Every word was a scalpel that cut harshly at David's mind.

'Of course. Grandpa is...' Pressured by the force of the voice's presence, David fought to make his thoughts coherent. He groped in the abyss as his consciousness was ripped apart, his own thoughts stripped away to be examined even as he grasped for them.

'*You have no idea what you have begun. Take care of the young one,*' the voice said as it faded away. A long roar of pain reverberated through him, and then he agonizingly faded back into unconsciousness.

Hours later it seemed, the buzz returned. The memory of the agony faded even as the noise resolved itself into words and familiar voices.

"Is he alright? He stopped shaking," asked a high girly voice.

"Aside from the shirt there's no blood," a kind voice said. So similar to the first, yet more mature and refined, it was familiar. He knew the voice.

'That sounds like Yukiko,' David managed to think.

"What about the metal? It's gone. Why did he run forward?" asked an excited male voice.

"Look, his eyes are moving," Yukiko said. David felt two practiced fingers check his pulse. "His breathing has calmed down as well."

'Yukiko,' thought David. Opening his eyes, the bright glare was blinding. As his eyes recovered, he took in the blurry images of the Matsumotos standing over him.

"He is awake! David? David!" Yukiko called quietly but intently to him, bending closer to try to rouse him.

"Let's get him to the house," Masao said calmly. With his vision foggy, David could not place him. Suddenly he felt hands digging under him, lifting him from the ground. He was trapped within his unresponsive limbs, unable to react, yet too muddled to care.

The pain in his chest became less pronounced the farther they carried him from the shrine. David's mind wandered, eyes darting as he struggled to control his unruly body. Sometimes he lingered on one of the Matsumotos, sometimes on a rock or bug. Although both Rie and Takumi tried to talk to him, David remained in a daze, unable to respond. As they passed beneath the grey stone torii gate, David jerked abruptly and became as still as the windless trees.

≡

THE MAN, THE METEOR, AND THE THIEF

April,

Even after all those years, nothing prepared us for the pain, so much more powerful than any human could ever know or withstand...

The inside of the Matsumoto's main house was sparse. Each room had mat covered floors separated from the other rooms by sliding doors instead of walls. The tatami mats were firm, like wood, covered with thin straw. A hardwood hallway skirted the outside of the house leaving the tatami rooms in the center. The outside sliding doors were removed to catch afternoon breezes, leaving the house mostly open.

Though he kept his eyes closed, David knew he was laying on one of the portable Japanese beds, called a futon. He suspected he was in the largest room of the house near the low table, with the four Matsumotos sitting and drinking tea. He could sense someone near him by the faint rustle of fabric. Yukiko would be kneeling off to the side, checking him.

"Did what I think happen, actually happen to David?" Yukiko asked. David remained still, not quite ready to will his limbs to move.

"David will have to answer that. I have my suspicions, just as you do, but until we hear from him, who knows for sure?" Masao's words, so easily understood washed over David.

'Masao only speaks Japanese, right?' David cracked his eyes open just enough to see his host father sitting calmly at the head of the table.

"I've never seen anyone sleep so much," Rie said. "I thought he was dead after he stopped moving under the torii gate, but no, just asleep."

David opened his eyes the rest of the way. Finding the ceiling in focus, he tilted his head to look at the source of the voices around him.

"You are in the main house. You had quite an accident. Do you remember anything?" Yukiko smiled kindly down at David, easing some of his anxiety.

Masao quietly regarded David as he waited for his response. David jerked to a sitting position, pushing away a heavy quilt. Seeing Grandpa sitting in his ceremonial robes sent a jolt through his mind that finally focused him.

"Grandpa! You all right? Tiger, it…" David's words came out in slurred Japanese. He worked his jaw in confusion at the difficulty he had forming words. Slowly, he registered the carved wood of the main room's low table.

'I'm back.' David fell back onto the tatami. 'Why can't I… think.'

Takumi and Rie shared surprised glances, understanding each other as only twins could. David had just spoken broken but understandable Japanese. Although limited, his words were the most sophisticated Japanese he had attempted in the last month.

"Can you tell me what happened? Everything from the beginning of the ceremony?" Masao asked casually in Japanese.

In a far off voice, his eyes staring blindly, David began to speak rough Japanese. His words came faster and more fluently than ever before, yet they were still imperfect. David's mind was so clouded he missed the change in his own words.

"Got to the... place. Grandpa... there, ceremony start." David's voice wavered as English thoughts became Japanese words.

Masao nodded politely, throwing a discreet warning glance to Rie. She sat forward, her eyes wide. Takumi merely watched, his eyes flickering occasionally to Masao. Yukiko remained kneeling nearby, quiet but eying Masao and Grandpa shrewdly.

"In the trees, gold. A head. Big gold and black... Tiger. I don't believe it. Tiger move forward, like on TV," continued David.

"He tried to get my attention," Takumi said, his calm breaking a little. "When he pointed to the trees... there was nothing there." Takumi stopped abruptly as both Grandpa's and Masao's eyes fell on him as if sword blows.

"Just because *you* did not see anything, does not mean there was nothing there," Grandpa said, unusually stern. After holding his frown on Takumi for a beat, he smiled and gestured to David. He tried to continue, but as he tried to think past running to Grandpa, he faltered and withdrew into a confused silence.

"But why is he speaking Japanese?" Rie asked. Her thoughtful frown and curious eyes were riveted on her father. Her expression was one David had seen many times over the last month. When she did not understand his English, she often looked at him the same way, as if trying to figure him out through simple observation.

"Japanese? Why you speak English?" David stared dumbly, as he tried to work past the mental fog slowing his speech.

"You just said that in Japanese..." Rie's voice cut off abruptly after a sharp look from Masao.

David shook his head. He clearly understood everything said to him, but it was like walking under water to get each word out. He stood, staring at the people around the room.

"David, sit down," Masao said lightly. Ignoring him, David took a step back. His vision flickered then cleared. Suddenly, his mind was sharp.

He saw not the Matsumoto's house, but a time and place he could not recognize. Around him, David saw the rough gray of old rock cliffs rising around him. He felt hard stone under him, smelt salt on the air. A figure caught his attention. It was barely visible, its features blurred by both darkness and fire. As the thing before him rushed forward, David jumped back in fear, catching his foot on the outer sliding door's track. He fell before Takumi could reach him. Rolling back off the veranda to the ground outside.

When David finally re-awoke, his head throbbed from both his fall and the incident earlier in the day. Opening his eyes he saw the Matsumotos sitting around the table, waiting for him. Although now in their usual house clothes, the sun was still visible through the northern doors.

"Good, you are awake. I know you are having a hard time," Masao said. Although he attempted to be comforting, an edge to his voice bespoke his impatience. "Let me ask you a question, and then we will tell you a story that few have heard."

David sat up, rubbing his sore head. His mind felt clearer, his vision sharp. He easily recognized the five Matsumotos and even smiled. Grandpa was there, and after a month living with him, David trusted him implicitly. Even with the language barriers, he had felt Grandpa's concern for his well-being. He also knew Masao could not be rushed.

"Have you ever heard of the *Kojiki*?" Masao asked.

"Is that Japan history book?" David asked in reply frowning at his own imperfect words.

"The *Kojiki* is one of the first two books ever written in Japan," Yukiko said. "It was written after the events to help solidify the Emperor's position. Most historians today consider it more mythology than fact. Masao and Grandpa will tell you what really happened. Do not worry. Your questions will be answered."

"Our ancestors roamed the land in small nomadic groups," Grandpa began, using the same voice he had used earlier that morning. Unlike at the shrine, however, David felt his attention pulled to Grandpa's every word. "There were no villages or farms, and thus Japan was not a unified country. The historians will tell you that this was because the people of the time did not understand how to farm, and that they could only live off gathering or hunting. There is a deeper, darker secret. The *true* reason the people of Japan could not unify.

"In days long forgotten, evil walked freely through the land. It took many forms, some of which we still know and talk about today, though as a caricature of the real danger they possessed. Of the many spirits and monsters in Japanese legends, the worst were those that did not hunt alone."

As Grandpa spoke, images filled David's mind as if in a waking dream. Monsters and animals, unique in their grotesque appearances and horrifying visages slid through his vision like a half remembered nightmare, then as if the nightmare became aware of him, the images slowed. David saw beautiful humans walking amongst a group of Japanese gathering berries. In a blink, those same beautiful people were suddenly savage. One of the monsters seemed to rip the very life out of its prey, while others became giant wolves and devoured the screaming people.

"The *ōkami* were vicious crosses between spirit, man, and animal that roamed the land stalking the young," Grandpa continued. "The demons were even worse."

David saw giant red monsters with flaming weapons attacking travelers on an old dirt road. In another flash, he saw whole towns destroyed. The demons reveled in the destruction and grew in power with every person they destroyed.

"Yes, *oni*, were especially dangerous. And then there were ghosts, both good and bad that ran amok," Grandpa whispered, his voice compelling.

A small boy lost and alone in a forest was guided to safety by a translucent apparition that could have been his mother. Another flash and David was outside an ancient hut, people in rudimentary clothing screamed and ran as the building shook.

"Together the ancient monsters made it impossible for our ancestors to stay in any place for long," Grandpa said. "And there were far worse things than those."

Takumi and Rie hung on the elder Matsumoto's every word. David could not understand how Grandpa did it, but the visions became ever more real. The twins shared a look that told David they were surprised Grandpa was sharing the story with him.

"It was in the ancient world of chaos and evil that a man named Ninigi lived," Masao said, taking over for Grandpa. David detected something similar about their voices. Whatever it was that Grandpa had, Masao had it too, yet in a different way.

Masao's words transported David. Just as with his vision of the island, David was in another place. He saw a lone hunter walk through a bright young forest. His clothes were rough and simple. He carried a bamboo staff cut to a point on one end. At his side was a rough metal knife. Suddenly the hunter looked up and a light streaked across the sky. The earth shook as a meteor impacted and set a patch of forest ablaze.

The man worked his way towards the dying blaze and found a small crater. Looking in, David saw a fused mass of metal. Clasping the knife at his side, the man smiled triumphantly. David followed along as Ninigi took the metal to a man in a small hut filled with odd tools. Ninigi talked and argued with the man, eventually showing him the metal. David could hear Ninigi ask in ancient words for the ironsmith to create a peerless weapon for him, something to banish evil. Thinking hard the smith finally agreed to the attempt. Together, they took the iron to a shrine and began a ceremony much like the one David had just seen at the Matsumoto Estate.

Grandpa stared intently at David as Masao spoke. To David, briefly seeing through the vision to reality, it felt as if Grandpa was staring through him, into his soul. He was suddenly afraid of what the old man might see.

"It was a summoning ceremony, performed at a small wooden shrine in a clearing before a stand of tall mountains." Masao gestured past the sliding doors in the back of the room to the garden and torii gate beyond. "The smith hoped to summon forth a god to imbue the metal with the ability to defeat evil. We call our gods *Kami*. They are the spirits that inhabit and protect objects, animals, and sometimes people. By the time preparations for the ceremony were complete, word of the metal had spread, and another man also desired Ninigi's prize."

The Estate disappeared and David emerged into a dark forest. A man dressed all in black slipped through the night. By his furtive glances and secret steps, David knew he was a thief. Silently, he followed the thief as they approached the familiar mountains. When he arrived at the edge of the clearing, the thief crouched, watching the smith in his simple priest's robe.

Chanting softly, the smith asked a Kami to come forth, imbue, and purify the metal. The thief smiled and withdrew a small stone blade. Caught up in the scene, David tried to warn the smith. As if called, Ninigi rushed forward to stop the thief. The two men met with the clash and ferocity of old rivals.

Spinning away from his opponent, the thief slashed the smith's robes. Turning on the priest with raised knife, the black robed man smiled his victory.

From behind, and with a mighty heave, Ninigi pulled the thief back just before the knife could connect. Ninigi lost his balance and fell. The shrine exploded under the weight of the two men. The thief's eyes locked onto the jagged metal sticking out of Ninigi's lifeless form. Shaking, the hooded figure ignored the smith and backed away until he was lost among the trees.

David's mind suddenly awoke with fresh memories, visions from within. Images flashed so quickly he had difficulty understanding the torrent before his eyes. The perspectives all seemed wrong somehow. He was next to a giant lake, then running through a forest, on a mountain, then in darkness. The river of images suddenly slowed and he was left looking at Ninigi again. The old mountain clearing warped and he was before the Matsumoto shrine. The morning's events played in slow motion as if from outside his body. He watched as, missing Grandpa, he crashed into the shrine.

Quietly, David's hand reached up to where he had been pierced by the metal. His heart burned as if remembering the agony his mind could no longer recall. Then, just as fast as it had come, the pain was gone. David searched himself quickly, expecting to find a jagged chunk of metal sticking out of his chest.

"Do not worry David, you are quite well," Yukiko said, her tone calming him only slightly.

"What happened to shirt? Where I get this one?" asked David, nearly frantic.

"It's one of Takumi's, I, uh, changed it for you." Rie smiled sweetly as David turned red in embarrassment. Rie looked to Masao for permission before continuing. "Don't worry, here."

David caught the thrown shirt. Sure enough, in the center was a large hole through both sides.

"Does this mean he's a…" began Takumi.

"Let us finish," Masao said, pointedly glaring at Takumi. His son remained silent, but threw a superior, knowing look to Rie.

"When Ninigi crashed into the shrine and died, the *Jitsugen Samurai* were born," Masao said with a final, hard look at Takumi to ensure his silence. "Ninigi's sacrifice during the summoning ceremony allowed a small part of the Kami that had come at the smith's summons to enter him. The separated bit was not much, but the instant it left the old Kami it became a new awareness. Weak as it was, it bound itself to Ninigi, saving both of their lives.

"It was not the first time a Kami had entered a human, but it was the first time a youngling had. The new Kami combined with Ninigi to create one new being.

"Since Ninigi's sacrifice was selfless, and Ninigi was without evil, the new god was able to meld with him, rather than dominate him. The elder Kami spoke to him, asking Ninigi to protect the new Kami. Eventually, he named her Amaterasu after the sun."

"Over time, Ninigi and Amaterasu grew together, both learning from the other," Grandpa said, leaning in and squinting at David. "As the first Jitsugen Samurai, they began to drive evil out of Japan. They started small, destroying the beasts and demons that threatened their friends and family, allowing them to grow and flourish. As Ninigi and Amaterasu grew in strength and wisdom, they turned their powers to the good of the rest of Japan."

"With evil on the run, Ninigi began to bring the separate nomads together," Masao said. "Eventually, Ninigi's descendants became the Emperors of Japan. Whenever evil has returned to Japan, a new Jitsugen Samurai has risen again to fight it."

"I thought that was all just a bedtime story. I could probably tell that story by heart, but I didn't think it actually happened," Takumi said.

"How do you think my father taught me the old histories? Bedtime stories." Grandpa smiled at Takumi. Takumi glanced at Rie as they both nodded in understanding.

"The smith, what name?" asked David quietly as he made the connection between the story and himself. Outside the sun sank below the southern edge of the house.

"Matsumoto Toru," Grandpa said. The pride that radiated though him left no doubt as to the accuracy of his words. "Ninigi charged our family to keep the secret of the Jitsugen Samurai. As he neared death, he knew evil was far from completely destroyed. He suspected others might come after him to fight evil. Our family has done as he requested ever since. We still live where the first was created. We train in ancient kendo and keep the histories alive. A few Matsumotos have even been Jitsugen Samurai, though mainly we stand ready to help the next generation. You, David, can be a Jitsugen Samurai."

David sat in stunned silence, looking to the twins. Rie was unusually quiet and refused to meet his eye. Takumi sat stiffly as if all his muscles were locking him into place. David laughed aloud. He laughed as he had not laughed since coming to Japan, with a complete lack of restraint usually reserved for the stereotypical foreigners on Japanese television. He laughed with the frantic, nearly panicked thought that the Matsumoto elders might *not* be joking.

"David there is a choice you must make," said Grandpa gravely. "A Kami sacrificed some of itself for you. If we do nothing you will gain the abilities of a Jitsugen Samurai over time. You do, however, have a choice. If you want, we can stop that process, but you will be nothing more than you are now. If you wish to be a part of something more… you may embrace a new destiny."

"I know you will think what you will for now. It is much to take in. Whatever you choose, you must say nothing of what we have discussed here today," Masao said sternly. He appeared to grow suddenly, even as the room around him faded into a sudden dusk. "David, you must speak only in simple Japanese, and repeat none of our secrets. The new Jitsugen Samurai's greatest ally is stealth, for if all evil attacked a Samurai by himself, he would surely fall. Takumi and Rie, you two have studied our ways all your lives. Do not fail your duties. I need iron bound promises… now."

Takumi bowed low, Rie looked like she was about to start screaming but instead suddenly placed both her hands in front of her and bowed as gracefully as anyone David had ever seen. Yukiko smiled encouragingly, lending her usual strength and poise to the tense situation. David sat stiller than the rest, yet was the first to speak.

"Sure," he said slowly, "Sure. I'm not believe you, so who believe me? I promise won't tell."

David spoke more to himself than Masao, his mind drifting far away from the tatami floored main room of the Matsumotos' house. He thought about his sister, his father, and even his mother. He thought about his life until that point. It was not until he could name the emotion driving his thoughts that he finally relaxed. It was hope. He might not believe them, but he wanted to.

NAKANO JUNIOR HIGH

April,

Back then, I was imprisoned by a total lack of sensation. I was alone in an abyss of nothing. I knew something was missing, but I could not lock onto what it was...

With a groan, David stumbled out of his room. His mouth was dry, as if he had been hiking Phoenix's North Mountain without water. Just outside his room, Takumi caught him before he could ram his head into one of the hardwood support pillars.

"Wow, you're finally up. Good, you can grab breakfast with us," Takumi said almost formally. David stared dumbly until he recognized Takumi in his *gi*, the outfit he used for martial arts. Takumi steered David toward the kitchen. Since that was where David wanted to go he let Takumi guide him.

"Dad asked me to come get you. He took a break from his research. They've spent the last two nights looking into the old writings about the Jitsugen Samurai. They don't want to miss anything important in your training," Takumi said in a low voice.

"Wait, so that wasn't all a dream," David rasped. Then Takumi's words fully registered. "Two nights? It's Sunday isn't it?"

Takumi shook his head. David grabbed at another post. His eyes widened in shock as his hand made contact. It was completely fine. There were no bandages and no pain. In fact, David could not remember any pain from his hand after the accident.

"My hand!" His shout alerted Yukiko, who found him staring wildly at Takumi. After she explained how the accident had healed more than just the damage done by the metal, and after he pinched himself trying to wake up, she led him on.

'Could all of that have really happened?' he asked himself.

An instant later, he was sitting next to Rie. She refused to look at him as she ate one of Yukiko's breakfasts of fish, rice, egg, and miso soup. When she came back in from the kitchen, Yukiko checked David over with a practiced eye, and then while they ate, hovered protectively. Her concern and thoughtfulness drove his last doubts from his mind.

"Are you sure you do not want any more soup? Rice?" Yukiko asked. When he shook his head, mouth full of rice, she continued, "Well I am glad you are feeling all right. Go get ready for school or you will all be late, and remember, use only the Japanese we have been working on in your tutoring sessions." Yukiko rushed David out, sending him off to his room immediately after finishing his breakfast.

David was soon outside the Estate, walking along the wooded drive with Rie and Takumi. The walk reminded David of his first day of school, only a week after arriving in Japan. On that day, he had left the Estate and sweated along after the twins through Nakano town. David had been caught off guard by the strange signs, new sights, and multitude of uniformed students walking along with as many incoherent conversations. With his new ability to understand the Japanese around him, it was like the first day all over.

David listened in on the twins' whispered conversation. With each step away from the Estate, Takumi became less intense, and Rie seemed more her regular energetic self. With a full day of sleep to clear his head, David was easily able to discern the twins' Japanese.

'I'm even thinking in Japanese now,' he thought. The mental leap helped him to understand why he had thought the Matsumotos were speaking English. David was so astounded that he missed a dip in the rough road and ended up on the ground in a heap of uniform and bags.

"Are you alright?" Rie asked. Dressed in her white and blue sailor uniform, she appeared over him with the same concern Yukiko always showed him. When he looked to her, she immediately stood and turned away. David just had time to wonder if he had offended her before Takumi was there pulling him up.

"So, yesterday, I mean Saturday really happened?" David asked sheepishly. Brushing off the dust from his black uniform slacks, he struggled to understand what was happening to him. David looked to the twins for answers.

"Yep, it definitely happened," Rie replied, suddenly turning on the boys with a bright smile. Her return to the Rie he remembered before the accident made him sigh in relief. He had not been able to talk to her before, but he had definitely begun to worry the accident would keep him from ever getting to know the twins. "Now we can have a regular conversation! Maybe even get to know each other a little better."

"Right, because he's so concerned about getting to know *you*." Takumi rolled his eyes. Then his hand moved in a blur as he caught Rie's right punch. A low block deflected what David had thought would be a painfully accurate blow. David jaw hung loosely as he stared at the sudden show of martial arts prowess. Although he had been aware of the Matsumotos' training, it was the first time either of the twins had been so open about it in front of him.

"It's a good thing I'm such a nice sister, and didn't kick you," Rie said as she ended her attack and returned her attention to David. "Anyway, yes, it was real, but we can't tell you much more than what you've already heard. Dad refused to tell us more, and I've only heard..."

"Look, like Dad said, secrecy is important, so we can't talk about it except at the Estate," Takumi said. Rie was suddenly very interested in the trees along the path. "You never know who might be listening."

David laughed once at Takumi's words, but the complete lack of reply from his host brother quickly stopped the laugh, turning it to a thoughtful frown. Takumi was deadly serious. Even Rie eyed him with concern.

As they turned off the drive to the main road into Nakano, more students began to filter into the town, all walking from the surrounding estates and farms. On his first day, David had imagined their conversations were about class and work. The students always seemed so serious. As he listened, he was shocked and pleased to hear them talking not about math, but cartoons, games, and the latest competitions.

David was also pleasantly surprised as they entered Nakano at his ability to read the various signs, banners, and flags. He had always wondered what the complicated symbols that the Japanese used for writing had meant. Although he had learned basic writing, he had yet to study *kanji*. Walking into Nakano it was as if he suddenly had an intuitive understanding of it. He smiled to himself as he passed beneath an advertisement for a movie. As they walked, Takumi completed his reversion to school mode, taking on an air more akin to Grandpa than Masao.

"So who do you think will be matched up?" Takumi asked his sister.

"I don't really know, but Tsukasa-sensei better not try and pair me with Natsuki. I didn't like the hints he was dropping." Rie's features darkened as she mentioned one of their classmates. Surprising both of the twins, David interjected himself into the conversation.

"What's wrong with Natsuki... san? You two don't seem to get along, and I always wondered why." David smiled at his ability to speak clearly, and his new understanding of the words people were always adding to names. The mental fog had completely evaporated.

"I forgot you understand what we say now! You're going to be a terror at school. Natsuki? She's just a little back-stabbing, stuck-up-princess, cry-baby, traitor is all," answered Rie, a crystallized smile serving only to darken her features even more.

"They had a falling out a few years ago. She used to train with us until... well things changed when we got to junior high," Takumi said, cringing. David got the hint. Takumi was still friends with Natsuki.

"Now she uses every opportunity to make my life miserable. She and her little pack of friends, you know, Mizuki, Yuka, Kaeda, Yuuto, and Daisuke," Rie added. With the subject on Natsuki, it was as if Rie had forgotten to be awkward around him. David decided to keep it that way.

"Isn't that almost half the class?" he asked as he tried to remember all his classmates.

"Well maybe a third," Takumi said with a strained laugh. "They're mostly track team kids with a few badminton players as well. Mizuki is class rep. She's the leader of the pack. A lot of what Natsu-chan does is to get along with the group."

"You always defend her don't you? I'm going on ahead," Rie said, suddenly speeding up. She was nearly out of sight by the time David and Takumi passed the Police Station.

"So... what happened?" David asked once he was sure Rie would not hear.

"It wasn't just one thing. Right before we entered junior high, Natsuki's father invented some new gadget and suddenly her parents went from so poor they were on the verge of selling their family land to wealthy. Mizuki and her friends started to notice Natsuki. They invited her to their houses, and

Natsuki started going out with them more and more. That's why Natsuki and Rie started to bicker. I think Rie felt left out since our training and other responsibilities kept us from having much of a social life. Anyway, it came to a head one day during kendo practice. Natsuki walked out and Rie has never forgiven her."

"Wow. Yea, that explains a bit of the tension." David shivered.

'I definitely don't want to get on her bad side,' he thought. 'One day knocked out and I'm already seeing sides of the twins I never knew existed.' Before they got too close to school, Takumi pulled David aside.

"Look, I wanted to say sorry I wasn't around the other day. Koji-sempai had a couple of his friends led Rie and me off." Takumi clasped his palms together in front of him and bowed low as he apologized.

More than a little thrown off, David was embarrassed by Takumi's apology. After all, David had broken his own hand. "Hey no problem, right?" David wiggled his completely healed hand in front of Takumi, which actually prompted a laugh.

"Your Japanese is a lot better today, I mean almost perfect. Don't forget. You have to keep using English. You can start 'improving,' but nothing too sudden," Takumi whispered. His dark brown eyes bored into David's.

"Right," David said, "I'll try not to forget." It was hard for David to be concerned about his language skills. He was far too pleased his new ability to let Takumi get him down.

Takumi eyed David skeptically as they crossed the road in front of Nakano Junior High with a group of third years, luckily not Koji's friends. Mingling, they all bowed and mumbled good morning to Principal Yogi and Police Officer Yonamine. Both stood in front of the school welcoming students, stopping traffic at the crosswalk, and otherwise keeping an eye on things. David smiled widely, listening in on the conversations around him, taking in as much as he could.

"Don't forget to dumb down your Japanese. You don't want to stand out any more than you already do," Takumi added a bit desperately as they entered the school.

With the admonition in mind, David felt the same anxiety he felt on his first day. He would essentially be meeting his classmates anew. Maybe this time he would be able to remember all their names. Since he would be able to understand what they said, he might even be able to have slightly more meaningful conversations than just self-introductions.

Walking into the Class 2B room with Takumi, they got the usual round of shouts that David was now able to understand as greetings. The other members of Class 2B were busy preparing for the day. Most of the students stood in groups roughly divided around the different clubs or cliques. The darkly handsome Korean exchange student, Chul Moo Jeong, stood alone. Although several girls threw him hopeful glances, Chul Moo stared out the window. He was tall and strong; with exotic features that seemed to be held back only by the ordinary white top and black pants of his school uniform. The one time David had tried to talk to him, Chul Moo's expression had been so frightening that David now did his best to avoid him. With a sudden enthusiasm David never saw at the Estate, Takumi called to his friends as he pulled him towards the back of the room.

"Hey Takumi! How's life with the gaijin?" Shou asked as David put his bag away. Shou, the most outgoing person in the class, liked to test out new English he picked up from TV shows on David. "How long did it take you to wake him up *this* morning?"

'Great, so Takumi complains about me to his friends,' David thought as he tried not to let it show in his expression.

"Oh, not too long, you know, he's great. David's Japanese is improving *really* fast," Takumi said quickly, trying to derail the conversation before it did any more damage. He threw David a quick glance as David's jaw muscles tightened.

"Hey, that's great, now if only he'd lose some weight and get better at sports. He's been killing us in all the inter-class competitions," Naoto said bluntly. Leaning in close he whispered something that sounded a lot like "Third years" and "Stomped." Takumi's shoulders slumped a little as Naoto laughed. Naoto was the kind of boy that preferred picking David's brain for the English phrases he'd never let Jessica or Yukiko hear him say. Missing David's reaction, the round faced boy retrieved his books for first period.

Attempting to hide the red creeping into his cheeks, David hurried to his desk. The boys' words had stung; he had thought Naoto and Shou were his friends. Distracted, he accidentally knocked into Natsuki on his way, pushing her into Mizuki, the class representative.

"Hey watch it. Oh, it's you. Such a waste of space. You don't even know what I'm saying, so what's the point of insulting you?" Natsuki said in a voice loud enough for everyone to hear. Mizuki and the rest of the girls around them giggled. Before he could stop himself, he eyed her and said, "Jerk."

Fortunately, it came out in a crude form of Japanese that shocked her dumb just long enough for him to slide out of her way. Watching from the back of the room, Naoto and Shou shrugged as they watched the exchange. Usually, David hung around them until the beginning of class.

With only a minute to go, Rie came in followed close behind by a diminutive man with short black hair. Moriyama-sensei was their homeroom teacher. Despite his somewhat odd appearance, he was energetic and easily commanded the respect of his students. David liked how the Japanese used the suffix "teacher" as a sign of respect. It seemed so much more appropriate than using "Mr." or "Mrs." all the time.

"Hey, don't worry about it. They like you, but just haven't really had a chance to get to know you," Takumi whispered. He leaned across the aisle between their desks. "What did you say to Natsuki?" Before David could reply, Moriyama began class.

'If this is just the start, today is going to be a horrible day,' David thought. He dreaded finding out what the rest of the school might have to say about him. He almost wished he could go back to his previous oblivion. Moriyama did not improve his mood when he announced a schedule change for the day. An extra P.E. class would be added in exchange for English. 'At least I'm decent in English class, why couldn't they just cancel Japanese?'

David began their second period worrying about what Rie, Takumi, and all his other classmates thought of him. Luckily, the next period was math. David found that understanding Japanese enabled him to answer all the problems he had been struggling with for the last month. He had already studied the same material a year ago in Arizona. Math was one of his stronger subjects and he had been on an advanced track. Like his father, David had an affinity for math and science, though again like his father he sometimes ignored social niceties in his pursuit of figures. It was a flaw that his socialite younger sister always seemed eager to bring up.

During the class, Tadashi-sensei asked several students to write the answer to their homework problems on the board. Tadashi was the opposite of what David expected for a math teacher. A track team coach, he was nearly as lithe and energetic as Takumi when he was at school. After circling all but one answer on the board, Tadashi called attention to Natsuki's.

"Can anyone tell me why this one is wrong?" he asked.

Surprising everyone, including himself, David raised his hand. After a brief pause, Tadashi called David up to fix the problem. As he rose, Takumi gave him a hard stare.

"This, and Natsuki forgot this," David said, pointing to the mistakes and using only the most basic Japanese. His limitations had the effect of making what would have been a reasonable explanation terse, as if not worth the effort to explain further.

"Very good! Yes, David is correct. Natsuki please be more careful in the future." Tadashi covered his surprise with praise.

David just caught Natsuki's face, seething with resentment as he returned to his seat. Despite himself, David felt a little thrill of satisfaction. Takumi leaned over and whispered with a strained voice, "You just made her look like an idiot in front of the whole class." He was rewarded with several back slaps from the students sitting around him, including Naoto and Shou. It was almost enough to help him ignore the piercing glares from Natsuki and her friends. Takumi looked stoically towards the front for the rest of the class.

David continued to impress teachers over the next two periods, surprising everyone with his sudden participation. By lunchtime, classmates and teachers alike were assuming that David had just been holding back. David also found that if he spoke very slowly, he could get away with more advanced language. He began to overhear whispers. Mizuki and her friends were telling people that he had held back so that he could show off later. The whispers grew to outright gossip when he corrected another of Natsuki's answers and two of Mizuki's in science. Although unhappy about the rumors, Takumi told David not to refute them since it was an easy cover in case he slipped.

五

BADMINTON

April,

Despite awakening isolated, with confused senses that I could only barely comprehend, one thought drove me to fight through the despair: They are coming...

Although the day had gone better than he had expected, David still worried about the afternoon's double P.E. period. He had yet to get used to Nakano valley's humidity and the athleticism of his classmates was intimidating. While there was a wide range of interests among the students, they all seemed to be semi-professional athletes. The only exception to David's avoidance of sports in Arizona had been snowboarding and swimming, two activities that got him out of the heat. David's reluctance had not been just because the sun was so hot it could melt your shoes. He avoided sports because he hated looking like a fool. David had been acutely aware of when people made fun of his father for his eccentric TV persona.

'Of course, I succeeded in making a fool of myself anyway. A least my hand and bruises healed,' David thought with a smile. 'I wonder if I can convince the teachers to let me read instead...'

While thinking of ways to get out of a potentially humiliating P.E. class, David headed off to help clean the school. Unlike back in the United States, Japanese schools generally did not hire janitors. They relied on the students to clean every day after lunch and before school. Fukiko-sensei, the small and sometimes quiet English teacher, had given a thoroughly unconvincing speech about how it helped build responsibility. Her enthusiasm for sweeping aside, David liked her. She had been extremely helpful over the last few weeks. Just as Yukiko had been his crutch at the Estate, Fukiko kept him afloat at school with her nearly perfect English.

'If anyone is going to catch on to my new skills it would be her,' David thought as he took the long way to his cleaning section to avoid her.

After cleaning, David always went with Rie and Takumi during free period. Since they were both on the badminton team, it meant he had to brave the gym's sweltering heat. Even though he was there nearly every day, he had yet to play since there were so many people waiting. Rie had also invited him to the after school team practices, but David usually opted to study Japanese with the Language Club in the air-conditioned library. The only times he had even picked up a racket had been with Rie at the Estate.

David took a seat in the gym while Takumi and Rie went off to play. As he watched the various games, another second year student came over and sat next to him. The student looked vaguely familiar and as he spoke, it took David a second to realize he was speaking perfect English, instead of Japanese.

"Hi, sorry I have not introduced myself before this, but we are in different classes," the boy said. "My name is Chul Soon."

'Ah, so *this* is Chul Moo's brother, great.' David inched away. Chul Soon smiled warmly at David's surprised expression, completely ignoring his move.

"You must know my brother Chul Moo... We are both from Korea, and can speak English, but Chul Moo is not very social. I, on the other hand," Chul Soon said smiling broadly and gesturing to himself, "think we should be friends. Anyway, I have seen you over here a few times, but you never play. Would you like me to explain the rules?"

"Sure." David carefully checked himself, so that he replied in English rather than Japanese. Embarrassed at his initial reaction, David smiled. "I've seen it but don't know all the details."

Chul Soon went through all the rules and basic strategies for David in English. David was impressed with his language skills. Even with his strange brother, it was hard not to like someone so outgoing and friendly. Though David had actually picked up a lot about badminton, he let Chul Soon speak. David was surprised to learn it was actually a British sport, which explained why the students always counted the score in English.

Most of the time, people played two on two. Each player used an oval-headed racked and hit the shuttle back to their opponent's side. Unlike the rare occasions he had seen it back home, here it was fast and exciting. Some of the best students could jump high into the air, smashing the shuttle back towards their opponents with blinding speed. David smiled in spite of himself; Jessica could probably do well here. Although still in elementary school, she could literally run circles around him.

Despite having spent a great deal of time watching the sport, and Chul Soon's explanations, David had long ago convinced himself he could never get through an actual game. The year before in P.E., he had been given a tennis racket with the rest of the first years. He was quickly relieved of it after hitting every single ball out of the court. Thanks to Rie's help and skill, he had not had the same problem while practicing at the Estate, but David felt that might have been more to do with her skill and the feathers on the shuttle.

Before he knew it, the free period ended and people started to leave the gym. Chul Soon said goodbye and left to meet his brother. A group of first year girls giggled as he walked past.

'Apparently he has the same effect on girls his brother does,' David thought. 'Hey, maybe that's why Chul Moo is always so annoyed.'

The only exceptions to the mass exodus were the second years staying for the double P.E. class. Both the 2A and 2B classes would be together, while the other second year class had homeroom. Tsukasa, the badminton coach and shop teacher came in.

"Since Shima-sensei is out today, we will be having a badminton tournament. Please check this list for your teams and then begin warming up." Tsukasa's voice echoed through the gym as he used a well-practiced coach-yell to get everyone's attention. Upon hearing the news, the vast majority of the students erupted in cheers. It seemed only David and Chul Moo were unhappy.

"But I've only played badminton with Rie at the Estate! This will be horrible. I can't play a game. Whoever is stuck with me will be furious," David said, leaning over to Takumi as they walked towards the list. Takumi checked for their names before offering David a grim smile.

"Don't worry, you're with me, I'm good enough for the both of us." Halfway down the list Takumi smiled widely and laughed. "Rie's with Chul Soon!" Takumi handed David one of his older backup rackets and led him away from the crowd forming around the lists.

"What's wrong with Chul Soon? I just met him today," David asked.

"Everyone likes him. It's just that he's so nice... He never goes for winning shots and Rie's really competitive," Takumi replied. "It's going to be fun rubbing it in when we win."

The class began to run around the courts, warming up before stretches. David trailed behind with a few of the less enthusiastic students. In the past, he had felt being towards the back was his own form of social protest against mandatory sports. After hearing other students encouraging the others around him, he was embarrassed for lagging behind. The other slow people here were doing their best, while David had been merely lazy. He tried to pick up his pace, but was soon out of breath.

While the first matches began, David and Takumi went off to one corner to practice. On the way, they passed Natsuki and her friend Yuka, followed closely by Kaeda and Mizuki. Seeing David and Takumi, the girls quickly huddled together. Grinning maliciously, Natsuki craned her head out of the group.

"Aww, sorry Takumi, looks like you'll be last. Too bad you ended up with the gaijin." Natsuki filled her voice with over the top sympathy.

"Better watch your head. He's more likely to end up hitting you than the shuttle," added Kaeda with an evil smile. The four girls giggled as David walked away, attempting to appear as if he had not understood their insults.

"See? He doesn't even know when he's being insulted, how pathetic," Mizuki said, sending the group's parting shot at David's back.

"Don't worry about them. They're just mad you showed them all up. By the way, where did *that* come from?" Takumi asked once they were out of earshot.

"Now that I understand what the questions mean, I can do them," David said after fighting down his anger at the girls' words. "We studied all that stuff last year. I've also spent a lot of my free time helping my dad plan his experiments, so I know a bit about science. I'm sorry you are stuck with me though. Hopefully I won't throw you off."

"Really? That's great!" Takumi's smile went from forced to genuine. "Now you can help me with my homework. That'll more than make up for it if we lose." Seeing David's face fall, he added, "Just kidding. Relax and have fun. Rie says you aren't too bad at hitting the shuttle. I'll show you how it's done."

Takumi's wide grin was infectious. David knew that studying and getting into the right schools were critical to getting a good job. If he could help them study, then perhaps there was a way to even things out. At the very least, he could offer up his homework.

David and Takumi's first match turned out to be against two students from Class 2A. A mixed boy girl team, neither opponent was on the badminton team. With much of David's inexperience compensated for by Takumi's extraordinary ability, they were able to win by a relatively high margin. David even managed to score on a lucky shot.

As the boys grew used to playing with each other, they improved. Each game was more difficult as better players advanced, yet the pair still won their games. David's unconventional shots, due to lack of formal training, threw off their opponents' defenses. After the sixth point David made from hitting the shuttle in when it should have gone out, Takumi started calling David's wild points "gaijin shots."

Takumi's loud shouts and aggressive play were shocking, even after seeing Takumi in class, but he could not argue with the results. In almost no time, they were in the finals. David's heart fell when Natsuki and Yuka joined them on the court for the last match. Seeing the fear in David's eyes, the girls smiled.

"Sorry Ta-kun. No hard feelings when we win, right? Yuka, just hit everything at David," Natsuki said.

"You mean like we did with Rie and Chul Soon? That was such an easy first match," Yuka replied, grinning.

"Don't worry, just play like you have been, and we'll be fine." Takumi calmly kept up a low dialog through all of the girls' banter, attempting to keep David's spirits high.

"Don't let them win, Takumi," Rie shouted from the sidelines. Their matches cut short, Rie and most of the other students crowded around the court to watch the drama play out. Tsukasa took a seat behind David's side.

"As if everyone watching isn't enough pressure, Chul Moo is giving me the evil eye," David muttered as he wiped a bead of sweat from his forehead. Chul Moo stood directly in front of David and stared, his dark eyes flinty.

After a quick rock-paper-scissors match to determine the first serve, Yuka sent the shuttle flying at David. A high serve, David ran back, but hitting it with the edge of his racket sent it flying into the crowd of students. Natsuki's derisive laugh was echoed by her friends in the crowd.

'You can do this, just relax,' David thought, trying to calm down.

Takumi received the next serve low, returning it to tie at one point. With David in the back during Takumi's serves, both Yuka and Natsuki hit their shots high, forcing him to return them. After another shot went wide, Tsukasa shouted to Takumi. Before the next serve, Takumi took his hand and twisted his racket.

"Here, this should keep you from hitting it out. You're doing fine, keep it up," Takumi said.

With his new grip, David prepared to face off against Natsuki's serve. He could feel his heart beating furiously as competing desires to run away or make some kind of spectacular shot to shut up the girls jostled for superiority. Seeing David concentrating so hard, Natsuki laughed and hit a lazy serve high and back, forcing him to scramble back. The result left no one laughing. Nearly stumbling, David swung his racket wildly. Hitting the shuttle dead center, he sent it smashing back into Natsuki's shocked face.

Embarrassed, she composed herself just enough to toss the shuttle back at David for his next serve. Then something happened that David had never experienced before. The crowd cheered him on; he could hear people shouting his name, with choruses of "Gambare" and "Fighto David!" It sent a thrill through him.

The game grew more intense with each serve. David's gaijin shots and Takumi's skill kept the girls on the defensive.

Finally, with the boys ahead, Natsuki dropped the shuttle just in front of the net on David's side. Her victorious smile turned to horror as David flung himself forward. Somehow getting his racket under the shuttle, David sent it back up with just enough force to make it land on the top of the net and tip into the girls' side.

"Ha! How do you like that?" David yelled, still sprawled on the court. The tension brought out the part of him usually reserved for when Jessica got on his nerves. Luckily, the resulting cheer from their win nearly shook the gym and covered his all too appropriate Japanese from all but a few. Clapping and with a wide smile, Tsukasa walked up to the students.

"David, you are going to join the badminton team. I'm sure that with practice and Takumi's help you'll do great. You've got great concentration, fighting until the end like that. I like that in my players," he said seriously. "Besides, you need an after school activity."

While Takumi made a show of trying to translate, Chul Soon stepped in and relayed Tsukasa's semi-invitation in English.

"Do it David," Rie said, popping out of the crowd. "Dad already gave his permission." David took a look around at his classmates watching him.

'It was fun to win, and I like practicing with Rie. Maybe it is time I took up a sport. Jess will never believe me.' The thought of his sister's incredulous reaction decided him.

"Sure, I will," David replied carefully.

"Good, I'll see you a bit later today then," Tsukasa said before turning to Takumi. "Take him through the basics and explain the drills before practice. Anything he doesn't understand he can pick up later."

David ended his first day after the accident so exhausted that he completely forgot to bring up the events of two days before. The games plus drills in the afternoon left him so sore all he wanted to do was crawl into bed. David smiled. He had also made a new friend. Chul Soon had congratulated him after the crowd died down. Before David could make it to his room, Takumi, his formal quiet manner back, caught up with him.

"You know, you insulted Natsuki with pretty much every word you said today. I know you've only been speaking Japanese for all of one day, but there are some things about directness I should probably tell you."

Nearly an hour later, David sat before a computer screen, staring at the blinking cursor, his head nodding. After the lecture from Takumi on how to say things in a more roundabout manner, and the different modes of conversation in Japanese, he was trying to send an email to his sister. With all that had happened in the last three days, he needed a bit of clarity. Unfortunately, Masao had been all too clear about secrecy.

Sighing, he tried to sum up his feelings, but instead wrote about badminton and made vague references to his new friendships. He knew Jessica would be as unsatisfied with his letter as he was, but only hoped she could grasp enough to either ask the right questions, or at least make the right snide comments to get his thoughts working clearly. With a yawn, David hit send and headed for bed.

MATSUMOTO KENDO

April,

That one simple thought drove me to push out from the confines of my mind. To seek the boundaries and claw past them, if only for a chance to escape the approaching doom...

When he awoke, David had a response from Jessica waiting in his inbox. It had simply asked *what happened*? Unable to explain further, he made a few weak excuses and then prepared for the day.

At school, David tried to capitalize on his sudden successes but met with mixed results. Trying to fit in, he attempted to emulate people back home. This resulted in several older students calling him "KY," which he quickly learned meant out of touch, or socially awkward. Moreover, Koji and his friends were sure to laugh every time they saw him. It was clear the entire school knew about his hand. The worst setback was when he tried to apologize to Natsuki. Instead of accepting his apology, which he made in front of numerous students, she was even more abrasive.

"I always thought someone should call Natsuki out for being an uncultured bully," Naoto told him after.

Perhaps because of the problems, the week sped by quickly.

His teachers remarked at his improvement, and after he scaled back his attempts to fit in, the time he spent with his classmates went more smoothly. Shou began taking time to explain things, and Naoto gave him a manga he had finished. Chul Soon even offered to practice badminton during free periods.

David's early evenings were filled with homework and badminton. Thanks to Chul Soon's after lunch practices, David was soon able to keep up with the first years' drills. Though he lost every game he played, most of the team members were encouraging.

Through it all, his impending decision loomed, and Jessica was not content to leave him be. Despite the sixteen-hour time difference, she caught him online after practice one night, insisting he explain what was going on. Although young, she was as strong of mind as anyone he knew. She had to be to check their erratic father.

Very carefully, David finally explained about his impeding choice, without telling her any of the specifics. He attempted to explain how he had to decide if he should take on a new responsibility, or if he should just leave things be.

With a *lol* Jessica replied, "You already know what you will do. So go do it already. That's always been your problem, too much thinking not enough doing. Go for it. I decided daddy is going to take me to Disneyland. We leave next week."

It was surprisingly easy to imagine she had convinced their father that, because of some scientific imperative, they both had to go to Disneyland immediately. With a laugh, David started on his English homework.

Barely into his second month in Japan, the change was dramatic, and not only because he understood Japanese. Back in the States, cliques ruled most schools, but they were nothing compared to the tight-knit groupings developed over years of being in the same classes that pervaded Nakano. David finally understood that the not so vague feelings of isolation he had felt throughout his first month had little to do with his lack of Japanese. The fact that David had not participated or been a member of any groups meant that most of his fellow students had, subconsciously or not, ignored him. The incident with Koji was an extreme symptom of being so different from his classmates. He was also realizing that Koji was rather unique at the school, but for whatever reason nothing was done about him.

With his new language skills, and inclusion in badminton and class activities, David felt as if a veil had lifted and his life had finally begun. Accepted, if cautiously, his life quickly became much fuller. He also noticed a new and strong pressure to conform. With acceptance as a member of a group came responsibility. He was amazed at how easily he could feel bad when he let a team member down, or when he lagged behind.

Among other things, David had difficulty adapting to the separations between each class level. At badminton practice, he was often confused over whether he should be helping prepare for practice or clean up. He knew it had something to do with the social pecking order, but he had yet to figure it out. Most of the time, whenever he tried to help, someone was there to take away the mop or bag of shuttles. Not knowing what to do in the various situations that popped up kept him from integrating as smoothly as he would have liked.

Things began to change on the Estate as well. Everyday David learned something new about the myriad aspects of the Matsumotos' lives, yet there always seemed to be a vast store of knowledge to which he still did not have access.

Although David occasionally tried to talk about the accident, his hazy memories, their busy schedule, and the twins' reluctance to speak about it made it easier for him relegate it to the back of his mind. Masao and Grandpa had made themselves scarce during the evening hours, making it easier to avoid thinking about his impending decision. According to the twins, the elders were off working in the dojo, doing research in the library, and training in the mountains. David was surprised, then, when Masao came into the main room while the three were studying together after Friday badminton practice.

"David, are you well?" Masao asked. He was dressed in his usual house clothes. David thought the yukata made him look as if she just stepped out of a movie. Simple, but stylish, it was a stark contrast to the modern Japan he was beginning to understand.

"I am OK, a bit sore from practice, but I think I am starting to get the hang of things." David did his best to use formal Japanese with Masao, instead of the regular or common forms used around friends. His new language abilities did not fully cover the complicated social and linguistic differences.

"Good, good. David, Grandpa and I would like a word with you. Would you come with me?" Masao asked. Outside, Grandpa sat on the stone bridge above the pond meditating. When they were a few steps away, the old man gestured to a stone bench near the water, David's favorite place to sit at the Estate.

"The time has come for you to make a most important choice," Grandpa said as soon as David sat. "It will be all the more difficult since we cannot explain everything, or even much until after you make your decision. If you choose not to be a Jitsugen Samurai, I will stop the process that will eventually change your life completely. You will lose your new language powers, but will lead a normal life, continuing the path you began when you came here.

"If you choose to be a Jitsugen Samurai, you must do so knowing that it is a great responsibility, and you will have to sacrifice much for it. There will be benefits as well. I must say that Japan needs you, for a Kami would not have made such a sacrifice if it was not so."

David sat for a long time lost in thought. His eyes fell into the black pond before him, the stars bright lights on the smooth surface.

'What should I do?' he asked himself. 'This last week has been the best of my life, yet they want me to be some ancient warrior. I've had no clear path to guide me. No dreams of being president. I've gone from school to school, activity to activity, searching for the one that would hold me. Even coming to Japan was just another way to widen my experiences in the hopes that somehow I'd find a purpose. Can I take the final plunge, commit?'

As he watched the dark pool, David wondered at his thoughts, feeling as if once again he stood on the brink before a fall. A memory of Jessica popped into his head. She stood with his father leaning over a lab bench. If he picked this life, he would leave them behind. Sure, they would still be family, but they would grow apart because of it. 'No matter what, Jessica would not let me get away that easily. She would be disappointed in me if I didn't take the chance.'

Looking up at the Matsumotos, David felt his stomach drop as, in a small voice, he said, "You won't tell me more?" They both remained silent. "I do not know if I can be a Jitsugen Samurai, but I will try."

"So be it," Grandpa said with finality. David finally let go, and jumped.

Back at the main house, David rejoined Rie and Takumi. Nothing had changed, and then again, it had. He suddenly felt as if there was a doom upon him, that he had a destiny greater than anything he could have imagined for himself. The fiery vision he had had before he fell out of the main room came back to him then, and he shuddered in fear. In the doorway, Masao turned back to David.

"David-kun, did you know that both Rie and Takumi practice kendo every morning before school?" Masao asked. David had noticed that indirect questions like these usually led to a request or command of some kind. The use of *kun* after his name was a familiar suffix that served to increase David's unease.

"Takumi invited me, but I was never really able to get up that early. I have always been interested in martial arts, but I just do not seem the type, do I?" David answered weakly. He was embarrassed, and given the discussion he had just had, was afraid his sacrifices were about to begin.

"You will begin training with them tomorrow. You may still not quite believe the story you heard last week, but the training will be good for you." Masao smiled a little then, adding, "In any case you need to learn how to punch something properly. You are a Matsumoto, and *all* the Matsumotos train. Remember: continue to keep what happened last week to yourself. Secrecy is the only protection you have for now." Turning, Masao left the room.

"Protection from *what*," David muttered, and then a thought hit him. "When do you practice?"

"At four-thirty," Rie said brightly. David slumped with a tired look in his eyes.

'She's not quite back to the super energetic girl I remember, but at least she'll look at me again,' David thought. David went back to finishing his homework, trying not to think about having to wake so early. Apparently, he failed to hide his feelings because Rie laughed at his expression. Takumi simply reached over and started copying his English.

David's room was dark, the only sound from frogs in the pond. Compared to the sparse rooms the rest of the family slept in, his was almost cluttered. In deference to David's western upbringing, the Matsumotos had converted the old office at the back of the house into a bedroom. With a western style bed and locking door, the room allowed him a bit more privacy than the rest of the house. Since only sliding doors separated the main house's rooms, the Matsumotos usually walked right through them. Flailing, David tried to hold on as his world suddenly tumbled.

"Hurry up and get some clothes on! It's time to go!" growled Takumi. He had spent the last ten minutes trying to wake David up.

"But it's only four-ten," David said groggily looking at his alarm.

"We start practice at four-thirty but we run before that." Takumi spoke as if he expected David to be completely aware of their exercise habits. "You should get up at four." David simply stared at Takumi as if he had two heads.

"What's going on? It's almost time to take off." Without knocking, Rie came in looking for the pair. David scrambled for his covers.

"Nothing I haven't seen before," Rie said, then she suddenly turned and was out the door again.

"Come on," Takumi said.

Grandpa was waiting in the dojo when David came crawling in at nearly five. Takumi had returned before, while Rie had gone back for him. The dojo had wooden floors, with sliding doors and racks with swords and other weapons. One wall was mostly mirrors with two doors opening into a storage area. Along the far wall, the framed pictures of past Matsumoto Masters solemnly peered down at them.

"I am *not* a runner." David gasped as he pulled himself into the dojo. Just behind him, Rie entered.

"You only ran half a kilometer, if you can call that running," she said. Her tone reminded David of Natsuki for the barest moment. She seemed to catch his look and continued a bit more kindly. "We usually run five K to warm up."

"Go easy on him. I am sure he will be up to your standards soon enough, if not completely blow them away," Grandpa said easily. He sat behind a low table chuckling and sipping tea. "I think for today, David can just watch. Start with basics, slowly, so David can follow, then he can begin tomorrow. David? Have a seat next to me. You will get used to the early hour soon enough."

With David struggling to stay awake, Rie and Takumi went into the rooms behind the dojo to change, emerging in simple tunics and trousers called *gi*. In perfect unison, they began a series of stretches, blocks, kicks, punches, and other moves. While they worked, Grandpa began to explain the purpose behind what they were doing.

"Matsumoto kendo is not what you might see taught elsewhere in Japan. Our style has been handed down from father to son, or daughter, since the time of Ninigi. That is not to say it has not changed. Our family's style includes elements from many other martial arts.

"The core is kendo, or the art of the sword. The sword is an extension of the body, so before a person can learn to use a sword, they must master their own body." Grandpa gestured to the twins as they stepped and blocked accentuating his point.

"The basics you see the twins doing are the prerequisites to weapon basics. Though they have mastered these techniques, they still practice them every day. They are the basic movements you will use in an unarmed fight. Your body must know them so well, that even if your mind is otherwise occupied, you can still react appropriately. By practicing the basics every day, they become second nature. The student becomes correct in form, fast in movement, and accurate in target without having to think about what their body is doing. This leaves your mind open to do other things." Grandpa smiled mischievously, his eyes twinkling at David.

"How am I supposed to do *that*," David said pointing as Rie kicked above her head.

"Do not worry over much. You will grow. You have chosen a samurai's path. The training will not hurt," Grandpa said. "Well... maybe it will, but it will be good for you. It is not all physical training either." Grandpa poked David's temple with a long finger. "We will train your mind just as we train your body so that when the time comes you will be such a Jitsugen Samurai as to make Ninigi himself proud."

Finishing the empty hand basics, Rie and Takumi went to the racks and retrieved heavy wooden swords. Back in the center of the room, they began again with the fluid movements of sword basics. The blocks, attacks, and combinations were adaptations of the empty hand movements David had just seen. They moved slowly and with precision. The twins ended practice with a sparring match. With no protection, and the heavy wooden swords, the twins sprung at each other with a flurry of activity David could barely follow. The whack of wood on wood periodically echoed throughout the dojo as their swords met. Their forms became a blur of graceful feet and flying wood.

David's next week was the hardest of his life. Mornings started promptly at four with being rolled out of bed, all too often literally, by Takumi. After a grueling practice, and a quick Japanese style breakfast of rice with raw egg and soup, David was off to school with the twins. At school, he again had trouble concentrating, not because he did not understand, but because he was so tired from all the new physical activity. Morning practices, P.E., and badminton combined to leave him exhausted and sore every day. He felt constantly on the verge of physical breakdown, but somehow managed to stay just shy of injury. Luckily, his last year's studies kept him up to speed, and his teachers were used to students dozing in class.

As his classmates began to get to know him, David was invited to several free time sports. Although a small school, his classmates played everything from basketball to soccer. Since David usually chose to practice badminton with Chul Soon, and he was so popular, David was soon meeting many new students in other classes.

After school, David spent most of his time with the first years running drills, and learning how to practice badminton. He could follow along without explanation by the end of his second week, and although he was not as fast or accurate, he was not far behind them. Many of the first years had only a month of practice on him. Back on the Estate, David tried to get through homework as fast as possible so he could escape to bed.

One positive note to keep him going was the five-day vacation at the beginning of May known as Golden Week. Similar to spring break back in the States, it was one of the busiest vacation seasons in Japan. Hearing his fellow students talk about their plans, and their excitement, made David all the more eager for a reprieve from his physical training.

"Any plans for Golden Week?" Chul Soon asked after lunch one day. Though it was by now apparent to everyone David understood most Japanese, Chul Soon continued to talk to David in English. "My brother and I are not going anywhere, so if you want to hang out, let me know!"

"Actually, I'm not sure if the Matsumotos have any plans. Guess I should ask," David replied. He had yet to hear anything about the break from the twins, and assumed they would just take a vacation from their training. Exhausted, but looking forward to the expected break, David brought it up to Takumi after studying late Thursday night.

"So what will we do next week? I've heard everyone talking about their plans for break. Shou and his family are going to a hot spring! Chul Soon mentioned he'd be in town if we want to hang out too." David's hopes for a week off died as Takumi paused his video game.

"Ahh. I forgot to tell you. We go on a camping trip every year. You'll come this year too," Takumi said.

"That's great," David said. "I love camping. We used to go up north to the forest every year in the summer to escape the summer heat for a while. I was also a boy scout. I always loved sitting around the campfire, chopping wood, setting up the tents. My Dad would wander around looking for…"

Laughing, Takumi rolled away from his new 3DS and sat up. Rie came in carrying drinks and snacks and set them on the table.

"What are you so happy about?" asked Rie warily. "I don't trust anything that makes him *that* happy," she added to David.

"I just told David we're going to the mountains and he started talking about tents and fires," Takumi said, struggling to get the words out past his laughter.

"Oh, I'm afraid you have the wrong idea, David," Rie said stifling a laugh of her own. "Think of it more like extended training. The three of us will hike out together with just our supplies. Then we will have to evade Dad and Grandpa, find food, survive, and make it back to the Estate on Wednesday."

"What do you mean evade?" David asked, afraid of what the answer would be.

"If they find us, Grandpa and Dad will attack us. Plus there will be traps," Rie said excitedly.

"What about food?" he asked. Although concerned about the other aspects of what Rie was saying, several days without food seemed the most important thing.

"That's what our weapons will be for. It is great practice. And pretty fun too," added Takumi, still struggling to keep a straight face.

"We used to play war games out in the desert with super soakers. Sneaking around and stuff, but that was just for a weekend. We had food and tents. This sounds more like ranger survival training or something." David's brain finally made it into the conversation as he realized just what they were talking about doing.

"We'll be with you." Rie looked away, and then deftly stole Takumi's game, leaving David dumbfounded.

七

CAMPING IN STYLE

May,

In the darkest moments the memories came. The flashes of places and things so ancient as to be nearly as incomprehensible as my alien environment. The visions were a torture, a taunt, a glimpse of what I had been searching for...

Saturday morning David woke in a panic and unable to breath. Two shadows stood over him. One had put a hand over his mouth, while the other pinched his nose. Frightened, David struggled for a breath. Luckily, one of the shadows let go of his nose, allowing him a deep exhalation.

"It's just us," Rie whispered. "Don't say a word, don't make a sound. Just put these on and hurry."

Rie handed David what turned out to be a cross between a ninja's outfit and standard military camouflage. Under Takumi's supervision, he donned pants, boots, a shirt, and a pullover that tied at the sides. The ensemble also included a hood and removable facemask. His new outfit was almost black, but with limited and random patterns of dark green and brown for camouflage.

Outside, the two shadows moved along with David, blending into the dark outlines of trees and buildings. David moved slowly, but he lacked the grace and utter soundlessness that the twins were able to achieve. A trickle of stones kicked out from David's shoes as he stumbled, eliciting a hiss from one of the twins. The trio circled around towards the back of the Estate, avoiding the path to the shrine. Moving through the Matsumoto forest, they quickened their pace until the wall at the back of the Estate loomed before them. With deft movements, Rie scaled the wall and watched as Takumi helped David negotiate a path up the rocks.

"We already disabled the security sensors along the top of the wall. They're supposed to give us a lead, but that's no reason we should tip them off to *when* we leave." Rie spoke in a less-than-whisper that barely made it to David's ears as he pulled himself up and over the wall. Once outside the Estate, they struck straight out from the wall.

"Walk straight ahead. Rie and I will go ahead to check for traps. Your job is to create a trail leading off in a direction we don't plan to follow. Do your best to hide yourself, but don't go too slow. We need enough time to get to a better spot before this afternoon." Takumi was busy adjusting his own pack and clothes as he talked, ensuring one last time that everything was ready.

Takumi and Rie backed away, blending into the forest. Within seconds, David was alone in the unfamiliar wilderness with nothing but a knife, his clothes, and water.

'This is definitely not going to be like camping in Arizona,' David thought. He took a deep breath and reminded himself of the map and compass courses he had done as a Boy Scout.

Steeling himself, he stepped carefully through the rough terrain, his eyes adjusting slowly to the darkness of early morning. Only the barest light from the still waxing moon remained to guide him as his thoughts turned inward.

There were numerous rocks, streams, and thickets to block his way, forcing him in new directions. The land grew ever more rugged and he soon breathed heavily with every inclining step.

Although it was difficult, David walked for hours alone in the forest. The isolation was surprisingly welcome after being inundated with new people and activities over the last few weeks. Along the way he thought back on his family camping trips, of fishing for crayfish he never ate, and exploring caves with Jess following close behind.

David thought of the twins. He was only just beginning to get to know them. Takumi was obviously determined to carry on his family's tradition. He was serious and straightforward, at least at the Estate, yet he laughed and joked louder than Naoto at school. When Rie smiled, she engaged the whole room, yet there was something new about the way she acted towards him since the incident at the shrine. He could not quite name the change, and so shrugged the thought away. After all, the responsibilities of being a Matsumoto hung over the twins, maturing them before their classmates.

'And I just committed to the same life, didn't I? I'll just have to be sure to let myself have some fun and relax. No way I want to turn into Masao,' David thought.

When he finally made it to a dark stand of trees, where he figured it would be safe to take a few minutes rest, David sat down. As he did, the sun began to rise from behind him.

"Well I guess I've been heading west then," David muttered to himself, looking around the dark trees.

"Actually you've been heading north, but turned west about ten minutes ago," Rie said from right behind him. David jumped from his stump in surprise, his head knocking into a low branch.

As he staggered, the branch creaked and fell beside him. David rubbed the painful bump that sprung up and blinked his smarting eyes. Rie steadied him, and then led him to a low stump to sit down.

"Sorry, didn't mean to surprise you, but sneaking around is kind of a habit out here," Rie said smiling. "This should give Grandpa and Dad something to think about. You picked a good spot to rest. We can cover your tracks in the stream just on the other side of those trees."

Once David recovered, they followed the stream, Rie showing him how to shift his center of mass in order to walk without disturbing or slipping on moss. Eventually, they were able to end the trail David had been creating from the start of the trip.

It was an interesting experience just walking through the forest with Rie. They barely talked yet it was the most time they had ever spent alone. The longer they walked, the lighter her steps seemed, the more relaxed her shoulders. She began teaching David how to be truly quiet in the forest.

"Being sneaky is fun," Rie said as she slid past a tree. "If no one knows you are there, then you have all the freedom. Come on, if you thought I was good at kendo or badminton, just wait until you see what I can do out *here*."

Hours later, David was beyond sore and tired as they stopped before another tree trunk near the top of a mountain. From the vantage point, the pair could see most of the surrounding area and nearly every possible approach. The only exception was to the north, where the mountains grew even taller. Being stealthy had made a challenging hike far more difficult. The techniques Rie showed him required the use of rarely used muscles. Despite the jolts of pain in his legs, David was enjoying the trip. As he slid to a sitting position, Rie circled the area.

"This is the place Takumi told me about. It should be a good spot to camp during the heat of the day. We will hunt, then sleep," Rie said with just a hint of uncertainty and concern in her voice.

"Great! I'm..." David's words were cut off as he fell back into a hole beneath the trunk. Once again, he found himself with a hand around his mouth and a shadow whispering in his ear.

"Shh, it's me. You two took forever, I already found lunch." Takumi's voice was dull, muffled by the very small space around them.

Letting David go, Takumi opened up the hole covering just enough to signal Rie. She slid in next to him, and then checked the cover for any marks before shutting them in. The hole under the trunk burrowed back into the mountain for several feet.

"I've been working on this hidey hole for years. I discovered it a while back, but it was too small so I started making trips to widen it out. I've never used it before, so I'm pretty sure neither Grandpa nor Dad will know about it. We probably won't be able to use it again, but I figured now is when we will most need it. There's water stashed in the back. Here's lunch."

Takumi pulled out an assortment of raw fish and some wild mushrooms. In the darkness of the shelter, David could not be sure of what he was eating and was glad for the ignorance.

"We have some dried meat but we need to save it in case we can't find anything later. After all, we still have three more days to go and a fire would give us away immediately," Takumi said.

"You come up here a lot?" David asked between reluctantly convulsive gulps.

"We all do," Rie said from somewhere in the dark. "In order to prepare for this trip and to work on our other techniques, we all spend time in the mountains. Usually we go alone or in pairs."

"Rie especially likes coming out here to play with the bugs," Takumi said. David heard a soft thump followed by a burst of air from Takumi. "I mean she likes coming out here to play with—" David heard another punch and this time a low groan from Takumi. "OK, sorry."

"For now, let's sleep," she said. "We can guard in shifts. David, take the first. We're probably still safe."

"Yea, when you can't stay awake anymore, wake Ms. Touchy up," added Takumi. Soon all David could hear was the slight sounds of light breathing. David settled himself against the moist wall and stared at the entrance. As the minutes crept by, along with far too many bugs, his mind wandered.

'Who would have thought I'd be hiding in a hole with two other teenagers while their parents tried to hunt us,' he thought.

David tried to remember the accident at the shrine. The memory of it was oily, slipping away as he tried to grasp it. So close to a dream, it was intensely difficult to think of it as reality, yet he could speak Japanese.

With no external focus in the darkness of the hideaway, his memories slipped away, his mind playing scenes without his bidding. All his gaijin moments replayed themselves in the dark cave, the instances where cultures clashed and he had made the same mistakes so many foreigners make in Japan.

He nearly laughed aloud remembering the first time he had entered the Matsumotos' house and had almost stepped up to the wooden floor without first taking off his shoes. Grandpa had run at him babbling in incomprehensible Japanese, scaring him so much he had fallen back outside of the house. Helping him up, Rie had slowly shown him how to take his shoes off and place them in a little locker, and had even shown him his own pair of house slippers.

Rie again helped him during his first meal, showing him how to use chopsticks. While some people had used them back home, he had never quite gotten the hang of them. Using hand gestures, she had shown him how not to pass food from chopstick to chopstick. To use the reverse end when eating from a communal plate, and to never stand his hashi in his food. Takumi seemed to enjoy showing David how *not* to use them, but only when Masao was not looking. As the memories played in his mind, David closed his eyes to the darkness.

Drifting, David found himself slinking though a young forest. The perspective wrong, he crept with a curiously smooth and lithe step through low ferns, mere inches above the ground. His ears twitched. There was a scent ahead. Gliding forward, he caught just a hint of gray. Freezing, David crouched, slowing his heart, and waiting for the perfect moment...

David came to pinned on his back, a knife to his throat and Rie's hand over his mouth. She pressed against him, every inch of her body locking him into place.

"Jeeze David! I thought you were Grandpa." She pushed away from him in an instant. "You could have just tapped me on the shoulder. No need to jump me!" Takumi brushed past them as he cautiously checked the entrance.

"It's still light out, though it's later than I thought it would be. David?" Takumi asked.

"I guess I must have slipped off to sleep, sorry!" David said, his cheeks flaming red. He hoped they would not ask for more of an explanation.

"It's alright. Lie down and get a few hours of sleep. We have a long way to go tonight." Takumi took the next watch as Rie laid back down. As he tried to find a soft bit of damp ground to lie on, David did his best to avoid thinking about the dream. Rie shifted beside him. Luckily, his utter exhaustion had him back asleep in minutes.

David awoke hungry, tired, and sore, but soon they were back to sneaking through the forest. He was thrilled to be away from the cloying smell of moss and dirt that had built up with the three of them in such a small space. As they hiked, he struggled, but with the twin's assistance, he kept up. Something about the forest seemed to invigorate him. He had more energy and felt motivated in a way he never had in the dusty desert.

As they walked, Takumi asked him about his life in America. David told them of the hot summers and cold winters. How he had grown up with only his father and sister, and how his father, while brilliant, had the attention span of a two-year-old.

They laughed when he described the popular TV show his father did for kids. He told them about how his sister had learned how to control and guide their father's randomness from a young age, something he had never been able to do.

"I probably would have been in something like the technology club here, but I was not really smart enough. Instead I touched many groups without really being a part of any of them," he said, finishing. Takumi grunted as he cleared a fallen tree in one lithe movement.

Later that evening, the trio began coming up against traps left so that Grandpa and Masao could track their progress. Whenever the trio stopped to rest David spent his watch carving a long stick into a makeshift sword. Although he was not convinced it would be useful, the twins had insisted he have something in case Grandpa or Masao found them. Whenever he slept, his mind seemed to run free, keeping him from getting rest. When he woke, the dreams slipped away. He was unsure why, but he soon developed a fear of sleeping, even though he was exhausted.

The constant relocations and hard surfaces also hindered his attempts to recuperate. Nearly all of Monday disappeared in a haze of sleep deprivation. His only clear memory was the realization that while Takumi often led, this was not his element. Rie seemed to be the one most adept at slinking through the woods and detecting traps. While Takumi was proficient, it came to Rie naturally. Takumi seemed better at the blunt attacks and powering through the forest when they were hemmed in. David realized it was a lot like the badminton games he had seen Takumi play. While he could be sneaky when he had to, Takumi excelled at the straightforward attack.

As Tuesday began, Takumi and Rie began to lead David back towards the Estate. They stopped again during the day, letting David recover somewhat. Waking him as the sun began to set, Rie slid next to David.

"From now on will be the most dangerous," she whispered. "We'll have to pick one of the mountain passes, and will probably be attacked. Stay alert."

His mind clearer from the extra sleep, David nodded. As they moved towards the Estate, the twins detected many lures and traps. Takumi taught David to detect the faint discolorations of the plants and wood that marked them as having been manipulated, letting Rie keep them safe while he taught. The traps set for them were sometimes simple and obvious, to the twins at least. Twice they pointed out nets strung up in the trees with tripwire. Other times, the traps were cleverly hidden rocks set to develop into landsides, or branches set to fling at the heedless adventurer. After seeing so many of the traps, David realized that all they were set to hinder approach to the Estate, but did not prevent anyone leaving it.

As they moved down a hill, a soft flick was all the warning David had before a branch hit him in his face, knocking him back. Simultaneously, the ground beneath him gave way. The twins were just able to jump behind trees as David rolled by upon a bed of loose soil and stones. Exchanging a silent look, the twins hurried after.

八

DANGEROUS SHADOWS

May,

Although, my world was alien, the memories were not. After the initial panic and pain they caused, I recognized them as glimpses into how things should be...

The twins found David sprawled on top of a pile of stones, mud, and dead branches. Hearing them approach, David sat up, groaning from the pain of a hundred bruises. His clothes were covered in leaves and were ragged as if just sent through a blender.

"You alright?" Rie asked in a hushed voice as soon as she saw him, her concern was evident even in the minimal light.

"Yea, I think so," David said, mimicking her. Fortunately, the pain from his cuts and bruises began to fade as he kicked a branch off his leg. "I ended up on top of all this, and it leveled out pretty quick."

"It was designed to not hurt you. This is Grandpa's work. If you can walk, we need to go. Even if we had thrown them off, Grandpa and Dad will be here soon," Takumi said, looking around as if expecting them to jump from the shadows at any instant. From the top of a large rock, Rie's eyes hunted the depths of the night around them.

Jumping from her perch, Rie helped David stand as he brushed the leaves from his tunic. Miraculously, David still gripped his makeshift sword. He checked himself for broken bones, and then gingerly walked forward, glad to find he was whole. He nodded to Takumi.

"We need to move quickly," Takumi whispered. "I'll scout, you two follow." Silently, he slipped off into the night.

Rie rolled her eyes at her brother, and then glanced towards David. "You probably hurt, but I know from experience that you'll be alright. I was caught in a similar trap two years ago." David smiled, feeling a bit better about himself but his legs buckled when he tried to step forward. After a steadying hand from Rie, he took a few tentative steps.

"We need to go much faster," Rie said. She turned to him, and although he willed his legs forward, they moved only minimally. With a sigh, her hand slid down from his elbow and she took his hand. Before David could even register her grip, she was off, dragging him behind. He stumbled along, attempting to match her fluid movements, but failed horribly. A focused killer had replaced Rie. She stalked swiftly through the forest, letting nothing, not even David, slow her down.

After an hour weaving through the forested mountain, David was extremely happy to have the last week of morning runs under his belt. The only rest he got was when Rie paused to listen and check for traps. David became used to the sudden stops so he was unsurprised when Rie jerked him behind a tall tree. His legs rubbery, David collapsed among the tree's roots.

"It's nearly sunrise. Takumi should have checked in," Rie hissed, her words full of venom. "We aren't far from the Estate. Our goal is the shrine. The trip is over when at least one of us touches it. Grandpa, Dad, or both must be between us and the shrine."

Something in her voice made David eye her more closely. The way she fidgeted gave David a sinking feeling.

"How many times have you made it back to the shrine?" David asked quietly.

"Never," she answered. "This is only our second time on our own. Before, mom would always go with us. Get your stick ready, and be very quiet. If something happens, do whatever it takes to get to the shrine. Don't look for me or Takumi." Rie lapsed into silence, watching the night around her. "If you see mom, ignore her too, she's the referee." She turned slowly, observing the entirety of her surroundings. David strained with all his being, willing himself to hear someone approach.

As the first light of morning pierced the sky, David heard Rie yell. He was startled to realize she had left his side. He was far more surprised to find he was excited rather than scared. Just like capture the flag, all he had to do was make it past his enemies' lines undetected. He was encouraged that the rest of the way was downhill. David heard the clash of wood on wood from the direction Rie's voice had come. Hesitating only a second, David turned and hurried as best he could toward the sound.

He emerged beneath a group of ferns just in time to see Rie fall behind a flurry of blows from a man dressed in the full armor of a traditional samurai warrior. As she fell, another taller man came out from the shadows of nearby trees. Takumi was draped across his back.

"She must have left David to draw us off his course. They probably told him to head straight for the shrine," the taller man said.

"Hurry on and try to catch him. If you don't find him, cover the other side. I'll bring in these two and set them up as bait near the shrine in case he somehow makes it past you," replied the shorter man.

Though he could not see their faces, and their voices were barely audible, David recognized the way they moved. The taller man was Masao. Nominally the head of the house he still followed Grandpa's instructions. That meant the shorter man, who had just knocked out Rie, was Grandpa.

David watched as Masao ran off into the forest. A few seconds later, Grandpa revealed some of his strength by hefting both twins. With them secure in his arms, he headed for the Estate. Sliding forward, David tried to use everything he had learned over the last few days to stay quiet. Instead of simply following Grandpa, David strayed out and away from both him and Masao. Based on the rising sun, David figured he was north and a little east of the shrine. As they neared the Estate, David kept to the east.

David finally left the mountains, abruptly entering the forests around the Matsumoto Estate. Turning west, he crept ahead, keeping his pace just slower than Grandpa. As the sun rose higher above him, David saw the Estate's wall ahead. He ran along parallel to the Estate, staying in the tree line until he found the stream. David slid under the Estate's wall where the water flowed through. Big as he was, he barely made it through the small outlet. Luckily, the water had carved into the ground enough so that he could shimmy through on his behind and keep his nose above the water. David poked his head slowly out of the opening. With no movement around him, he crept north through the trees as quietly as he could.

"I could not find him," Masao said, surprising David with how close his voice was.

"He has to be along the western pass, behind the shrine. There was no sign of him along the way back on the east. String up the twins, maybe he will go for the bait," Grandpa said.

"I hope the twins didn't tell him that only one of them needs to touch the shrine for all of them to win," Masao said, unusually grumpy at his inability to locate David.

"It's no matter if they did. Either he will come, or we will have to go find him. Hopefully he did not injure himself. Though if he did... Make the twins look convincing. I will cover the west, he is sure to come from there." Grandpa slid back into the forest.

Masao took Takumi and Rie from where Grandpa had left them. Stringing them up by their hands, Masao began to jab at them with his wooden sword. From his few kendo practices, David was able to assure himself that it was all for show.

David waited for Grandpa to head off into the forest again before creeping up towards the shrine. Finding a concealed spot, he waited and watched. Although Masao continued with his show, his eyes roamed the entire area. After his third pass, David noticed he spent slightly more time watching to the west. He followed the direction, peering into the forest, trying to catch a glimpse of Grandpa's armor.

Yukiko entered the clearing from the shrine path. As usual, she was arrayed in elegantly traditional clothes. She eyed Masao and the twins before taking a spot directly in front of the shrine.

Finally, David caught a shadow move away from the shrine. Yukiko's head twitched toward the west. Checking for Masao in the clearing one last time, David surged forward with everything he had left. He ran, his muscles pumping acidic fire through his legs as ferns and branches threatened to claw him back.

As David moved, Masao twirled away from the twins. A heavy projectile struck just where David had been waiting. From the west, David heard Grandpa hurrying back towards the clearing.

David reached the steps, running up along the opposite side he had run during the shrine ceremony. Grandpa burst from the trees on the far side. David leapt. With his legs stretching back behind him, Grandpa tried one last desperate grab to catch him in midair. His arms flailing, David's makeshift sword knocked into Grandpa's head just as his hand brushed the stone shrine. His smile was cut short as he connected with the hard stone of the shrine's base.

David awoke with a start, his instincts honed to expect trouble at any second. A large quilt hampered his flight. Looking around, David realized he was once again waking up after having been knocked out. Unlike the last time, he was alone in the room. The outside sliding doors were open, showing the last rays of the dusky orange sunset. As David extricated himself from the blankets, Rie came in toweling of her hair. Seeing him awake, she abruptly stopped.

"You're awake! The bath is ready. You were still asleep so I went first… Spend some extra time cleaning up before you get in." Rie hurried to her room.

'So much for an explanation,' thought David, slightly annoyed by Rie's casual reaction to his waking up from being knocked out.

Just as it was taking him time to get used to each of the Matsumotos, it was taking David awhile to get used to Japanese customs. Unlike back home, where he could just shower in the bathtub, in Japan he had to shower outside the tub. It had been an awkward conversation when he first arrived, first with Takumi, and then with Yukiko when gesturing did not work. One tub was used by the entire family, which saved water and heating fuel. Even with the warm spring air, David looked forward to soaking. Four and a half days had left him ragged.

In the shower room, David was surprised to find that his body had changed from the one that had gotten on a plane nearly two months ago. The weeks of sports, running, and the last days of mountaineering had left faint outlines of muscles that had not been there before. He was nowhere near the bone and muscle of his classmates, but he was pleasantly surprised at the effect.

The bath helped drain the tension of the last few days out of him. Only a sudden and ravenous hunger kept David awake long enough to finish and head to his room to change. David's appetite was whetted further when he emerged from his room to the smells of Yukiko's cooking floating to him from the main room. David found the Matsumoto family waiting for him at three low tables piled with a vast banquet.

"You picked a very hard stick," Grandpa said with a severe frown as David entered. After a second, his frown broke and he laughed ruefully as he gingerly touched a bandage on his head. "You're going to have to tell me all about how you got past us."

"He must be starving. Save your questions until after he gets a few bites down. I'm just as curious, I didn't get to go this year," Yukiko said from the end of the table, laughing. "David, go ahead and sit down. Grandpa is just being a sore loser. This is the first year I have had to bandage *him* up."

David sat, Rie and even Takumi gave him big smiles, and then with a customary "Ittadakimasu," everyone began serving themselves from the plates of food. Although he tried to fill his own glass, Rie insisted on pouring his iced tea for him.

Usually when they ate together, each person had several small dishes accompanied by rice. For the feast, however, the dishes were large and varied, allowing each family member to take what they wanted. There were selections of his favorite Japanese foods, spaghetti, and a few other western dishes. After they had eaten enough to sate their initial hunger, Masao called for everyone's attention.

"Tonight is a celebration greater than any we have had before. After every trip, we celebrated the finish, but this is the first year that the newest generation has beaten the previous. David touching the shrine, and Rie and Takumi providing David with the chance to do so, is a great achievement.

"In the past, this would mark the Matsumoto children's entry into adulthood. Nowadays this means that all of you will begin learning our family's deepest secrets. You have proved your ability to protect those secrets. David, having completed your first trip, you should make your own practice sword with Takumi's and Rie's guidance. Once finished, you will have the right to carry and use your sword anywhere on the Matsumoto Estate," Masao said proudly.

"Now, enough talking. Let's eat and celebrate," Grandpa said raising his glass to the young heroes of the evening. "Kanpai!"

David relaxed and enjoyed the night as everyone traded stories about the last few days. David finally came to understand all the rules and purposes as Grandpa and Masao talked about the traps and strategies they had laid. As he had guessed, the whole point was to simulate an attack on the Estate. As the students learned to infiltrate it, they also learned how they could one day defend it. Everyone was particularly interested in David's accounts. Finally, though the night was yet early, everyone retired.

Although he was utterly drained, sleep eluded David for a long time. As he lay before drifting off, the dreams he had had in the mountains came back to him. He felt himself running through the forests and mountains, but with wildly strange perspectives and sensations. The persistent déjà vu was disconcerting.

The rest of the shortened week went by quickly. Chul Soon was disappointed David had not met with him, but was interested in David's trip. After only one morning's rest from training, he was again woken up by Takumi to train before school.

David had a slew of emails waiting from Jess that for once he was able to answer mostly truthfully. She seemed excited by the idea of the trip, but also laughed at the peculiar Japanese customs. Her pointed questions about the time he had spent alone with Rie also unnerved him.

"She's my host sister," was the only reply he could think of.

For the first time ever, David was happy to look forward to just the regular schedule of training. No matter how hard basics or badminton seemed, it was nothing compared to his trials in the mountains.

九

THREE'S A CROWD

May,

The darkness receded, but even as I began to comprehend the world around me, I found new barriers to my freedom. Doors without keys, and windows that would not break...

The next weekend, Yukiko drove David and the twins to Himeji to select a length of wood for a new practice sword. The need to find a fine grain wood of sufficient strength made it more efficient to buy from a dealer than hack down a tree. Once back on the Estate, David wanted to get right to shaping his sword, but the twins had other plans. Takumi soon showed his greatest strength was in working with his hands. Where he might be straightforward in badminton, around the tools and samples of the woodshop he revealed a subtlety and depth of knowledge that was surprising. In the workshop, Rie explained the various wood working tools, then the twins let him practice on bits of old firewood until he got the feel for each one.

From that point on, David spent every evening working on his sword with the twins. Just as every night another layer of wood was painstakingly removed so that the sword within could be revealed, David worked to integrate into school life.

During his first month, many of his classmates had made opinions that were hard for him to break.

Luckily, the twins provided continuous support. They were a critical anchor for him among the various aspects and activities he was attempting. Physically and mentally exhausted from constant changes, David needed something, someone constant among so many differences. Though they did nothing to indicate a problem, David secretly feared the twins might grow weary of him, and he would end up losing his way. As he studied woodworking, David also studied the twins, attempting to emulate the way they moved. At school, he began to mirror the way they talked around their friends.

'I've been far too careless with my words and even actions. If I'm going to be a Jitsugen Samurai, I had better learn how to play the part,' David thought from the corner of the 2B classroom as Takumi moved easily among their peers.

David would have enjoyed the days more if he had slept better. His schedule was demanding. He ended every day exhausted. Worse were the nights. Without exception, they were plagued by the strange dreams that had begun in the mountains, yet when he woke, he could never quite remember them. They left him confused and worn out, nearly more so than when he lay down. The worst part was the feeling of panic and dread that accompanied the nightmares, like a slowly approaching storm he could not avoid.

With the little free time he had, David attempted to escape the constant pressures of his new responsibilities by retreating to his old hobbies. He spent as much time as possible in the library, losing himself in the plethora of new novels available to him now that he could read Japanese. He drank in Japanese history, fairy tales, and manga. For brief periods, the books allowed him to step outside his responsibilities, and focus on a world that was not constantly hammering him down.

In the library, David finally had a chance to get to know some of his other classmates. He saw Tsubasa so often that he eventually asked about his work. Kenta, another of his classmates, tried to wave him off but it was too late. Tsubasa was in the technology club, there to do research. He spent the next ten minutes babbling on about circuits and gears.

Outside of the library, it was so difficult for him to concentrate that he had several more run-ins with Natsuki and her friends. David finally realized that Natsuki was one of the "loud girls." There seemed to be two types in his class. The shy quiet ones would never raise their hand in class or talk to anyone but their friends. When they did talk, it would be with their hands in front of their faces and giggles as their eyes darted around the room. The loud ones on the other hand acted as if they were trying to outdo Naoto for loudness. Natsuki in particular liked to shout across rooms and smack people on the head.

Looking around at his classmates, David was still surprised how different things were from Arizona. He was only recently getting used to what the boys in his class would do when they had to tuck their uniform shirts in. Instead of simply stuffing it in, most boys would just drop their pants all together, smooth out their shirt, and then re-zip. The first time he had seen it, it took him several seconds to realize none of the students had even noticed. It was just how things were done.

Chul Moo was the only other student in the class with less energy. Whenever David took a step out of the throng that was his class, Chul Moo would be there in the opposite corner, staring out the window.

'Is he bored, or does he just hate us all so much he won't even look at us,' David wondered.

Though he was too tired to notice, David was gradually adapting to the demanding new routines. He won his first badminton game during practice, and was even able to extend his morning runs to one then two kilometers. Every day he lost weight from the excessive training and grew a little stronger.

It took David two weeks to finish his practice sword. After he sanded away the last bit of wood, Takumi and Rie finally announced it ready. Rie congratulated him enthusiastically, while Takumi remained more serious and critical.

"It should hold up," Takumi said. "Before you use it, we should seal it. We'll pick some up tomorrow." Takumi's lack of enthusiasm might have weighed on David, but he was finally getting to understand his host brother a little better. Where Rie was almost always outspoken, Takumi, on the estate at least, strove to achieve his father's quiet reserve.

The next day the trio went to their usual Saturday badminton team practice. After changing and warming up with the rest of the team, they gathered around Tsukasa. Unlike during the week where it was mostly drills, the weekends were mostly practice matches. The team rotated through both singles and doubles, changing partners to gain experience. As the team gathered, David noticed Chul Moo enter and sit in a corner.

"What's Chul Moo doing here? I've never seen him during practice before," David asked. Takumi followed David's gaze to the corner, where Chul Moo had taken a seat near one of the gym's windows.

"Who knows? He usually avoids school as much as possible. Maybe Chul Soon dragged him to track and field practice and he got bored," Takumi said. He was cut off as Tsukasa began speaking to the team.

"Today we will start doing things a little differently," Tsukasa called to the waiting students. There will be a mixed doubles competition during the summer so we will start doing mixed teams as well. Find your new partners and opposing teams after I call your name, then begin." After going through most of the names, Tsukasa called David's name, followed by Natsuki's.

"She doesn't look too pleased does she?" David gestured to Natsuki, standing with her friends in a heated discussion, her expression furious.

"I don't know who she hates more right now, you, or Tsu-kasa-sensei," Takumi said. David sighed at his impending plight as Takumi ran off to find his own partner. Annoyed at her scowl, David hesitantly walked over to the fuming thir-teen-year-old.

'Sure I made her look bad the day after I began speaking Japanese, but it's not like I did it on purpose. She acts like my existence is a personal burden on her,' he thought.

"You'd better not suck." Natsuki glared petulantly. It was the only greeting David got before she walked off to a court. David and Natsuki turned out to be stronger than their oppo-nents were, but David's inconsistency kept them from taking an early lead. While the teams played, Tsukasa wandered among the games, observing and making suggestions. From behind, David noticed Natsuki's attention shift as she looked past their court to the windows. Chul Moo was walking from his corner towards their court. Distracted, Natsuki missed her serve.

"Hey! Natsuki!" David called. Her long black hair whipped around as her scowl found him. When she missed his glance at the other team, he pointed. She turned back to the other team stiffly as she realized they were waiting for her.

The game turned fierce as both Natsuki and David took their frustrations out on the shuttle. Finally, one point ahead, David received a shot just above the net that he was able to send smashing right between the other team, winning the game. After handshakes, Tsukasa came over to hear the score and give advice.

"David, nice work, you took advantage of a great opening. Natsuki, you're slipping, get it together or I'll pair you with a first year for the competition," Tsukasa said.

"I can't believe it! Only two shots the whole game and *you* get the credit. So *typical*," Natsuki seethed. She started to walk away only to abruptly turn. Beyond, David saw Rie talking and laughing with Chul Moo. He was so shocked it took him an extra moment to register Natsuki run into him.

"Jeeze you're always in the way aren't you," Natsuki growled. "What's your problem?"

"I can't believe it, you are *so* rude." Natsuki's eyes tightened in anger as she stepped up to him. "You're always in the way, running into me and saying sorry like you didn't do it on purpose. Strutting around as if you own the place, never bowing to anyone. Everyone thinks you're a jerk. Don't look at me as if you don't know what I mean. You've been here for two months and you never bow. I know you speak Japanese. You're so full of yourself!"

After a final scowl, her open palm sent him flailing back several steps before he could even register an attack. Anger surged within him. Despite being raised to never hit a girl, he wanted to punch her, but when he made it back around only Takumi was there.

"What was that about?" Takumi asked, suddenly raising his hands in defense as he took in David's fists.

"Who knows," David said, clutching his hands as he tried to relax.

He made it through the rest of practice without seeing Natsuki, for which he counted himself lucky. After his second game, he had a chance to calm down a bit and think about her words. As he stretched, David watched the other students. Just about everyone bowed at least a little whenever they met someone, and often in the middle of conversations.

'Maybe I have been rude... I don't know the first thing about bowing,' David thought as he met up with the twins after practice.

"Hey Chul Moo finally took off," Takumi said.

"He disappeared again after Natsuki left," answered Rie mischievously. "Apparently he only came because Natsuki had asked him to. He laughed so hard when she missed her shot. I guess he's not too bad after all."

When they got back to the Estate, Grandpa was waiting for them. He smiled in a way David had never seen before. Usually so carefree yet strong, he had a look in his eye that almost seemed on the edge of pleading. His face was so strange, so sad that David immediately assumed something terrible had happened. Before he could react, Rie sighed beside him.

"Where did she go?" she asked. Looking to her, David was surprised to find a smirk on her lips that seemed at once admonishing and conciliatory. It was a look he had seen a thousand times, but on Jessica's face.

"She's gone to Himeji for a seminar. One of her friends became ill and asked her to cover. She left this morning. We survived on ramen but…"

David finally understood. With Yukiko out of town, there was no one to cook dinner. The one time both girls had been gone and the elder Matsumotos had been responsible for dinner they had only managed to make instant ramen that had turned out half-soggy and half-crunchy. Takumi had explained that while all the Matsumoto men had attempted to learn from Yukiko, their cooking always turned out horrendous.

"Of course, I'll make dinner," Rie said.

"Why don't I help you?" David asked.

"Awesome, David-kun makes killer food," Takumi said. He immediately took off to his room.

"Go seal David's sword. You know, work for your dinner," Rie called before he got away completely.

On the Estate, the kitchen was attached to the side of the main house at ground level, not raised like the rest of the house. When he had asked Yukiko about it, she had explained how traditional Japanese kitchens had been outside. Eventually, they had built the more modern version around the old, but it was still separate.

Since his father had usually been busy with his experiments, David had taught himself to cook at an early age. Before the accident and his training had begun, David had often helped Yukiko in the kitchen. David smiled. He was looking forward to the chance to show Rie something he was good at.

Usually Takumi and Rie did everything together, but just like his father, he was useless in the kitchen. David was surprised at how much he enjoyed the time walking to the vegetable garden with her to select ingredients for dinner.

"So what's it like to grow up with the history your family has? I don't even know my grandparents," he asked as he sliced fresh carrots. She turned towards him as the rice cooker beeped.

"What? You mean it's not normal to have an ancient charge to protect and train the heroes of Japan and keep secret its greatest treasures?" Rie laughed but as she looked at him, her smile faltered, as if something about *him* made her uncertain. "We all have our duties. I'll do my part."

"At least I had a choice," David whispered, starting to realize he was not the only one who had to make sacrifices. When Rie finally looked up from her work again, it was with a happy smile, one he recognized as more show than tell.

Takumi, Grandpa, and even Masao praised them for saving them from another meal of badly cooked ramen. As they began to eat, David caught Rie watching him. Her glances reminded him of Jess, how she would look when she was trying to convince herself to do something unpleasant. After dinner, she insisted he go with Takumi while she cleared up. In the workshop, he showed David where his sword lay drying, a fresh coat of sealant already on it.

STRANGER DANGER

May,

Fate is sometimes cruel. But then, if you believe that, you would have to believe in fate itself. I know better...

"You might want to avoid being alone for a while," Tsubasa said as he hefted a heavy pane of glass outside the gym. "Koji-sempai seems keen on the idea of a repeat performance of your fight."

David was still trying to recover after being destroyed in a humiliating singles match with Natsuki, and Tsubasa's passing comment did nothing to help his confidence. With the sun high over Nakano, the twins joined David as the rest of their teammates left the gym. Most of the third years turned together to head to a cram school to study for high school entrance exams, while the rest headed home or to hangouts around town. With the twins, David turned towards the Estate.

Farther into town, a red light struggled to shine out amid the sweltering sun. The Nakano Police Station was a small two-story building that hosted the town's lone police officer, Yonamine, and his family. The lower building was partitioned into an office and a small room that served as a jail cell. David had visited once before to get his photograph taken for his alien registration card.

He was about to ask Rie if their classmate Daisuke was Yonamine's son when his world upturned. He just caught the image of a wiry man in ragged clothes and mangled hair surrounded by a halo of shattering glass as he spun through the air. Two meters away, he landed, his skin burning as it slid against concrete and the falling glass around him. By the time he stopped, Takumi and Rie were both crouched in the familiar Matsumoto fighting stances, blocking the stranger's escape. Glancing around wildly, the tall man's gaze stopped on Takumi. He crouched, as if preparing to rush past him.

"Don't," Takumi said.

The stranger lunged Takumi low, nearly on all fours. Takumi blocked, fending off the stranger's wild blows, keeping him in front of the station. His careful calm broke as the stranger's fist connected, hitting him in the face. With a look of outrage, Takumi let loose a vicious high kick that forced the stranger to roll to avoid the powerful blow.

As David stood up, Rie and Takumi warily converged on the stranger. With a final look at the twins and his surroundings, the stranger lowered his hands as if giving up. Then, with a shard of glass, the stranger was suddenly behind David, the glass pressed against his throat.

"Don't move unless you want to get cut," the stranger growled, his voice strangely and heavily accented.

David froze, terror racking his body. The strangers' voice sent tendrils of fear through his body, like a super charged version of some dread he had felt before, but could not name. Aside from the incident with Koji, he had never been in a real fight before, let alone attacked by a crazy, smelly, violent man. David screwed his eyes shut. Even as fear enveloped him, a new emotion emerged more strongly. It was accompanied by a burning in his chest the like of which he had never felt before. He felt a sudden, driving, need to stop the stranger.

Takumi and Rie inched closer, their eyes darting, bodies shifting as they reacted to every change in the man's movements. Held in his bony grip, David's arms suddenly rose from his sides as his emotions suddenly calmed. Before either twin could react to help David, a large jagged piece of metal appeared before him. It fell, a sharp spike driving into the stranger's foot. Howling in pain, he dropped the glass shard and released David.

David just caught a glance of the metal before it disappeared as Yonamine stumbled out of the station. Bleeding from a head wound, he quickly had the stranger in cuffs. The officer attempted to take him towards the station, but he struggled so much that Takumi had to help carry him inside. Rie watched Takumi and Yonamine struggle with the criminal, and then looked to David.

"We'd better go," she said, sidling up to David.

"I'll need statements from all three of you before you go," Yonamine called. Gesturing with his chin, he asked, "Is he alright?"

"Oh, yes, of course he is," Rie answered as she stepped to cut off his view of David's deadpan stare.

"Better bring him inside," Yonamine said, glancing around at the crowd beginning to form as people noticed the broken glass glittering under the sun. Luckily, none of the passersby had seen the actual fight. "I'll call your parents."

Rie pulled David into the Police Station after Yonamine, Takumi, and the stranger. As they walked, she tried to shake him to awareness, but he remained just as vacant. Inside, the stranger was safely locked away and the three students were given seats around a small table. Finally coming around, David started to speak, but Takumi put his fingers to his lips and then jerked his hand towards Yonamine coming from the cell.

"Let me get you bandaged up while we wait for Matsumoto-san," Yonamine said, indicating Masao would be there soon. He gestured to David, who was bloody in several places from the glass. Dabbing the blood with a bandage from his kit,

Yonamine looked up in surprise. "There are no injuries underneath the blood. Weren't you cut?"

Jerking in surprise David looked to Takumi.

"Uh no, he wasn't. He must have just got some blood on him from the prisoner," Takumi lied calmly.

"I didn't see any cuts on him either. How strange. Are you sure you're alright?" Yonamine asked again, prodding David with his eyes.

David nodded a quick affirmative before his eyes unfocused and he lapsed back into silent thought.

"Maybe it was from me when the stranger popped me in the nose. I must have gotten some on him before it stopped," Takumi said.

Although he sounded far from completely reassured, Yonamine's questions ended abruptly when Masao entered the small office in a suit. His entrance jolted David to awareness, as he had never seen Masao in anything but traditional clothing. Standing and bowing to Masao, Yonamine came around his desk and gestured to a free spot next to Takumi.

"Matsumoto-san won't you please sit," he said. "I have to ask the children about the incident. Before that though, please allow me to apologize and explain what happened. Tea?" At Masao's nod, Yonamine quickly served iced tea for everyone then sat down with a notebook.

"This morning, I brought in Jahangir, the man who broke the window, for questioning after getting complaints about him milling about behind the grocery store. Before I could get more than his name, he clocked me on the head while I was distracted by a fax. Apparently, he jumped through the window, as he must have seen me lock the door. I'll ask the three of you to tell me what happened after that." Yonamine sat back, readying his pen. Masao cleared his throat, leaning forward to preempt the others from speaking.

"David-kun does not speak fluent Japanese, so please let Takumi speak for him," Masao said.

"Of course. Takumi-kun?" Yonamine said.

"Well, like you said, the man came bursting out of the window, knocking into David. He tried to run past me but I, uh, stopped him. While he was trying to get past me, he hit me in the nose. Then he picked up a piece of glass and took David hostage, but David stamped on his foot. You came out right after and got him again. It all happened very fast," Takumi said seriously.

"Is that how it happened?" Yonamine asked, looking between Rie and David. Rie nodded her assurance, but David just stared back blankly. "OK, well, David that was very dangerous. It seems this same person is wanted in another town for burglary. You're lucky he let you go."

'It's strange how people still talk to me as they would anyone else, though supposedly I don't speak Japanese,' David thought. He had finally gotten over the shock of the attack, but he continued his charade of ignorance.

"If there is nothing else, I would like to get them all home. I am frankly surprised no one is taking cell phone pictures for the news already." Masao stood, effectively ending the interview.

"Yes, that should be all for now. Thank you. I do apologize for the inconvenience," Yonamine replied with a bow. Masao led the twins and David out to the car, waiting just in front of the station.

Back in the car, Masao eyed the teenagers in the rearview mirror. David thought of the last car ride just after the fight. He thought it would spark a feeling of déjà vu but without Yukiko, and with Masao in a suit, the whole thing just seemed wrong.

"I thought I impressed upon all of you how important discretion is. What really happened anyway?" Masao asked sternly. All three looked at each other before Rie spoke up.

"It happened just like we told Yonamine-san," Rie said bravely.

"Except I didn't step on him," David cut in, receiving anxious looks from the twins. "A piece of metal fell on his foot and he let me go, but when I looked again the metal was gone. It was so strange. There was such a weird feeling in my chest, and I didn't want to let the stranger get away. I was scared at first, but only for a second, then I just wanted to stop him."

Masao pulled the car off the road and stopped abruptly. Looking back, he gave David a piercing gaze.

"Did either of you see the metal?" he asked. Both Rie and Takumi nodded.

"We both did. The stranger probably went for him since we were in fighting stances and he wasn't," Rie answered.

"The metal appeared in front of David, then fell and hit the stranger's foot," added Takumi.

"So soon… Anything else?" Masao prompted.

"Well David was cut by the glass but he has already healed. We passed off the blood on him as blood from me getting a nose bleed when the stranger hit me," Takumi said.

"He hit you?" Masao asked, seemingly more surprised someone could get the best of Takumi, than at David's lack of injury.

"He was pretty fast and extremely strong, but didn't actually make me bleed," Takumi said defensively.

"Are you saying the metal I saw was real? It was such a strange feeling. Where did it come from?" asked David, still confused.

"It came from *you* David. What you saw was the *honshitsu*, the essence of the metal that impaled you at the shrine, the raw material for a *Seikaku*," Masao said staring gravely ahead as he started driving again.

"But it was just a hunk of metal," David said, confused.

"One of your most basic abilities as a Jitsugen Samurai will be the ability to summon a true sword, a Seikaku," Masao replied.

"Dad hasn't forged yours yet," Takumi said. "Throwing around chunks of metal wouldn't be very practical."

"The accident at the shrine, do you remember it? Has anything else strange happened?" Masao asked as he pulled the car back onto the road.

"Just… Just dreams. It's been hard to sleep lately." David spoke carefully, uncertain how much he should say.

"That is what I thought. There is still much you must learn to protect yourself. Until now I have tried to avoid telling you too much too soon, and I have only told Takumi and Rie enough for them to be able to watch out for you," Masao said as, speeding around a corner, he brought the car onto the Matsumoto drive. "I am glad you are all safe, but secrecy is critical. No more stunts like that in public. It raises too many questions we cannot answer. Takumi, good job covering with the bloody nose story."

"Why did my cuts heal so fast? I was definitely cut by the glass—it hurt." David unconsciously rubbed where one of the more painful cuts had been on his arm.

"It is another benefit of being a Jitsugen Samurai. There are others but they will take time, a long time. The fact that you can summon the metal already is surprising." Masao brought the car into the Estate's circular drive and was out walking towards the dojo in an instant.

KAMI

May,

I finally knew my purpose and understood the danger that was coming. Unfortunately, that did not make waiting easier…

In the dojo, Masao left Takumi and David standing near the entrance and walked off toward the far wall. There, Masao stopped before a rack of famous Matsumoto blades. The ones crafted over the centuries by past masters. Masao's hands glided over the sheathed blades as if feeling them without actually touching them. Choosing one, he lifted it from its place and attached it to his side. Masao turned to the boys, his smile relaxing David.

From the entrance, David heard Rie and Grandpa enter and turned to meet them. Before he could even complete his turn, Masao was suddenly before him. The gleaming blade in his hand whistled through the air as it sliced down towards David's unprotected neck. Again, he felt a sudden inner heat as the metal appeared before him, held for the briefest moment, and then fell.

"David! Open your eyes." Grandpa's kind and mellow voice overrode his fear. David saw Masao standing just before him, frozen. Masao's sword was so close to his neck that he could feel the coldness of the steel, though it did not even graze his skin. Before him, the fused metal shards that had impaled him weeks ago fell through the air.

"*Look* at the metal," Grandpa said insistently.

Masao stepped back in a rustle of fabric. The metal disappeared before it could touch the ground. Sagging in the aftermath of the fake attack, David met Grandpa's eyes. His were the deep brown of the oldest trees in the forest, filled with wisdom.

"Did you feel it? Do you know what it is and where it resides within you?" Grandpa asked in a deep mellow voice. "Look within yourself, think back on Masao's attack."

David wanted to complain, but prompted by Grandpa, he turned his mind inward, searching. Grandpa's tone made David feel as if he already had the answers, if only he could see with the older Matsumoto's keen eyes.

The image of the metal shards lying on the shrine emerged unbidden in his mind. The shrine fell away, leaving only the metal, different from before, more pure. *Honshitsu*. It was a mysterious word, yet it seemed to have substance as it raced through his mind. As he focused on that word, he thought again of the stranger's attack. He remembered the intensity of the sensation. Mentally following the tendrils of feeling through his body, he was surprised to find a place he had never felt before. Within him, where he knew his heart had once been, he felt the cold power of what could only be the essence of the metal shards, the honshitsu.

David's eyes tightened in concentration as he struggled to call the metal forth. After what seemed like an hour, he finally felt something give. His hands flew out as he imagined the metal outside of his body, instead of within. His hands ready, yet uncertain, caught the honshitsu just before it fell out of his reach.

"It is in me. It *is* me," David breathed. He sat. The fused metal mass still in his hands. "I summoned the metal. I can feel it, yet it's almost as if it's feeling me." The mass seemed to thrum lightly with power in his hands.

David stared into the shifting grey facets of the honshitsu. Turning the metal in his hands was like peering into his own soul. His hand wandered up to his chest, to the place where this same piece of metal had impaled him just weeks ago. His eyes asked the elder Matsumotos, "Why?"

"This is the first step in your awakening as a Jitsugen Samurai. It happened much sooner than legends suggested, but since you are so young we do not know for sure how your awakening will progress. The attack may have acted as a catalyst. Whatever the reason, we had to show you that the honshitsu is not only real, but also a part of you. You can, you *must* control it." Masao came forward and sat in front of David.

As Grandpa came to sit with them, David saw a similarity between the men that he had missed before. Although Masao was in a suit, some of the rigidity he had always associated with him seemed to waver, as if it was merely a cloak he used to distinguish himself from his more relaxed father.

"We cannot be sure if your awakening was caused by chance or need. Masao and I have been searching our records, trying to find any precedents. So far, we have had little luck outside the course of an adult Jitsugen Samurai. You must be ready for anything. Now that you can summon the metal's essence, we must forge your sword as soon as possible." Grandpa stared at David with a burning intensity.

"You must master summoning the honshitsu so that we can help you forge your sword," Masao said, continuing for his father. "You must also learn how to wield the sword, which is why you have been training with Takumi and Rie. In the past, new Jitsugen Samurai would retreat here to the Matsumoto Estate to train in secrecy and safety. Your case is different in that you are so young and you would be missed from school. We press you because you are in danger as long as you cannot protect yourself."

"What if I don't want to be a Jitsugen Samurai? I've been in Japan all of two months and I've already died and been taken hostage. I'm not athletic or special. I only agreed to be one because my whole life I've been searching for something and thought this could be it, but..." Worn out by the weeks of strange events and difficulties, David wanted answers.

"We warned you that once you started down this path there would be no turning back, and that there would be sacrifices," Grandpa said slowly. "One of those sacrifices is having to trust in us to guide you. We cannot reveal everything you wish to know... There are things for which you are not ready."

"We're in the dark too, and we've been learning about this stuff our whole lives," Takumi said.

"Yeah, see? Takumi is oblivious, but Dad and Grandpa still train him," Rie added, punching Takumi's legs out from under him. Far from falling into a heap, as David would have, he turned his fall into an attack. David looked between them as they turned into a tornado of blows before returning his attention to the elder Matsumotos.

"I know that, it's just hard sometimes," David said softly. "The smallest things, a tree or the weather make me think back to Arizona, and the strangest part is I feel more at home here than I did there... and that scares me, and makes me a little sad. Every time I talk to my sister, there is less to say. She has her life, and mine doesn't seem to be a part of hers anymore."

Grandpa and Masao shared a pained, sympathetic glance with each other before returning their gazes to David. The silence was broken only by the light scraping of the wind against the shoji paper doors and insects buzzing in the afternoon heat. Rie pinned Takumi in a complicated hold.

"David, there is another sacrifice, one that among all the Jitsugen Samurai will affect you the most. You cannot leave Japan. The Kami that saved you is part of Japan," Grandpa said carefully. "While it would not be as problematic say, in the rest of Asia or the Americas, Japan is a series of islands. You must return to a Japanese island within twelve hours of departing, or your Kami, and thus you, will die. From what I've read, you will probably find it very hard to actually leave in the first place. If you do, you must return before the cycle ends."

David tried to process Grandpa's words. He was far past disbelieving, yet they never revealed the whole picture. As hard as he tried, he could not wrap his mind around the idea that he could never return. It was as if Masao had taken his sword and stabbed him right in his gut, letting him bleed out slowly. Panic rose within him. He wanted to run, to scream, to rage, and cry.

David ran. He flew through the forest, tears blinding his view as thoughts of betrayal, lies, and anger raced alongside him. He followed no path, when he met the gray stones of the outer wall he scrambled up and over, scraping himself but ignoring the pain. The forest stretched out before him no matter how hard he ran. He did not stop until his muscles rebelled against the abuse and gave out on him.

It was nearly evening when his body finally began to recover. Looking around David found he was near the stand of trees where he had hit his head during their Golden Week trip. With a sigh, he sat up and tested his limbs. His legs still stiff, he pulled himself over to the stump and fell into a dark brood. Rie found him there, just before sunset. David sat as still as if he were a new sapling from the old, his head in his hands.

"Now you know," she whispered coming up behind him.

"Now I know what?" His anger, usually held so deep within, flared.

"You once asked me what it's like, to be a Matsumoto." She spoke quietly, sadly, yet her steps were graceful as she placed each foot closer to him. "Now you know."

"Do you know what they mean by *Jitsugen*, David?" she asked, her feet moving without sound. "I know you know it means *true,* but it's more than that. You will hold lives in your hands. Can you sacrifice everything you have for those lives? It's a lot to ask, but still less than what the Kami that saved your life did."

"What of my family? I have a sister and a father that expect me to come home in less than a year. I'm an exchange student. What happens after this year?" David asked, avoiding her eyes.

"I believe it is an American expression to 'cross that bridge when you get to it,' no?" she said, smiling tentatively.

David would have cried, except all his tears had already been shed. 'So I can't go back? That doesn't mean I can't still talk to them. They could visit *me,*' he thought. 'Arizona is just a place, they are still my home.' David leaned back, his head resting against the tree. 'I fit in better than I did back in the States, at least now that I understand Japanese. Is a life of service too high a price to pay for my life?'

While he pondered, a shadow of a voice inserted itself in his mind and said, *'Japan is your home now, be calm, and do not worry.'*

The voice was familiar, as if from some long forgotten dream, but the words faded as he became aware of Rie sitting tentatively next to him. David felt his concerns blanketed by a warm wash of relief and reassurance, as well as other emotions that were harder to pin down. Although unable to explain why, he no longer feared the future.

"I know it's unfair." As she spoke, she stared off into the trees. "Even if you don't learn from Grandpa and my parents, if you got up and never returned to the Estate, if it was possible for you to return home, it's too late. Evil would seek you out. I don't know how they will deal with your family or the exchange program, but you need the skills they can give you. You aren't alone. Takumi and I have been training all our lives, for you, though we didn't know it."

'See? You are not as alone as you think.' The voice slid through his mind like a whisper, barely brushing David's conscious-

ness. David shook his head, uncertain if he had even truly heard anything.

"I must help you bear your burden," Rie said, her voice barely audible as night fell. Suddenly standing, she seemed more her old self. "Come on, come back with me." Rie picked David up off the stump with uncanny strength and grace. David felt like he should be embarrassed being picked up by a girl, yet he could not help but feel only gratitude.

"So who won," he asked noticing a few new bruises on her arm.

"I did, of course," Rie said smiling. "That's why I got to come find you."

In the dojo, David found the elder Matsumotos waiting for him. After a few words with Rie, Grandpa turned to David.

"I am truly sorry, David, but it is critical you accept the difficult with the good. From now on we will practice summoning the honshitsu so that you will be able to hold it long enough to forge a *Seikaku*. You must accept who you are, and know that within you lies great power, but also great evil if you choose." His voice sharpened as he stared at David. "Japan is at a crossroads. Evil is coming, and you must be ready. I ask again, David, do you accept the path of the Jitsugen Samurai?"

Although he could not explain why, David was at peace. While he still felt no closer to being a Jitsugen Samurai than he had on his first day in Japan, neither could he dispute the changes that had begun to affect his body and mind. He had a chance to be more than he was.

'Why not take it? What kind of person would I be if I ran away scared? All my life I've been afraid I might fail. Isn't this worth the effort? Don't the Matsumotos deserve as much from me as they give themselves? What would Jess say if I ran away?'

"I won't do this blindly," he said. His acceptance gave him a new confidence. "What am I? What do the Kami have to do with me? Why will I be responsible for others' lives?"

Masao stepped out of the deep shadows within the dojo. "Let's go for a walk."

Together with Grandpa and Masao, David walked through the garden towards the torii gate. The two older men were silent until they passed beneath. In the darkness, it was like a gray shadow above them.

"When the metal pierced your heart, you died," Masao said as he walked. Without giving David time to think, he continued, "Combined with the Shinto summoning chants, your sacrifice pulled a part of the Golden Tiger Kami into you. Just as Ninigi pulled part of Amaterasu into him. In a sense, a new Kami was created. It kept your essence from departing as would normally happen when one of us dies."

"So I'm a ghost then?" David asked, trying to understand. Despite talking about his death, he was somehow comfortable with the idea.

'Better to be alive as something else, than all together dead,' he thought.

"No, you still have a body, don't you? The new Kami did not just join with you. It joined itself to you *and* the honshitsu."

"So then all my improvements, with running and badminton, it's all because a ghost is in me?" He was suddenly worried that all his hard work had been for nothing.

"No! A Kami is not a ghost. A ghost is a human spirit that has left its body. There are both good and bad. A Kami is something more. Our oldest records say they were the souls of the planets and suns, vast beings."

As he spoke, David remembered that Masao and Grandpa were not just swordsmiths and kendo masters, but Shinto priests as well.

'I still can't believe that Masao of all people actually has a bit of a soft side,' he thought.

"The ancient Kami separated, creating new Kami. In the process, they diminished. The strongest of the new Kami were Water, Wind, Fire, and Earth. They multiplied and spread throughout the world. The Greeks called them Titans. But like the ones before them, they weakened with each separation. Eventually they lost many of their powers, with only a few retaining any influence over their brethren."

At the clearing, the elder Matsumotos turned, walking away from the shrine into the forest. David followed, curious. After a short walk, they came to a bulbous rock wall with myriad protrusions, caves, and crevices. Before one, Grandpa touched a stone and a wall moved aside, revealing a decrepit wooden shrine. Grandpa bowed then clapped twice and bowed again. Then Masao reached reverently forward and opened two large wooden doors. Within, David saw four metal sculptures that seemed to be made of different metals. Each was exotic yet exquisitely detailed. The swirls of color running through them seemed to shift, just as his honshitsu had glittered in the Dojo.

"Each is a depiction of one of the *Elemental Kami.* As they diminished from separating, they became dependent on other means to survive," Masao whispered. "Water and Wind found a way to grow, but always in balance. Earth was more conservative and retained more power, while Fire became jealous and in its haste became so diminished that now it relies on both Wind and Earth."

Without warning, David summoned his honshitsu. Unlike before, the honshitsu did not fall. Instead, it hung in the air glowing, as if basking in the presence of the statues. In return, the statues gleamed brighter in the starlight. David almost thought he saw the Earth statue smile. Through it all, Masao continued talking.

"It is our good luck that the Earth Elemental was careful. It separated slowly and carefully so that when it eventually created the first *Zodiac Kami* it was still potent. Twelve animals so powerful that cultures around the world still speak of them. The Zodiac Kami were able to create the dumb animals with only a minimal cost on their part. Relying on procreation, the animals flourished with the Kami to guide them. After being created many of the new animals found new homes with the Wind, Water, and even Fire Kami."

Finally, with a last flash of light, David's honshitsu disappeared.

"Over the millennia the animals changed, and while they contained only the barest spark of the original Kami they came from, they never diminished or grew in power." Grandpa clapped his hands and bowed to the statues before closing the shrine. Together the elders guided David back towards the Estate.

"When you died sacrificing yourself for another you proved yourself. Even though Grandpa was never in danger, even though the Kami had been going for the shrine and metal, you proved yourself a worthy protector for the newborn Kami because of your intentions and your actions. The new Kami chose you. And while the old Kami diminished, the new may grow to be even stronger than his predecessor. In return, you will become stronger, smarter, and essentially one with the new Kami as it matures. You will live longer, and when you die, the Kami will remain and continue to protect Japan."

"And you know all this because your family has been teaching Jitsugen Samurai since the first Emperor?" David asked dubiously as they passed beneath the torii gate. "If the Kami will make me stronger has all my work been for nothing?"

Laughing Masao gestured to the garden.

"Do you think this garden became like it is through magic or destiny? It took hard work, skill, and thought. Your Kami, whatever it is, will make you stronger, but not for a while yet. Your recent improvements are all within your normal ability and are due to your hard work and our training. When you come into your own as a Jitsugen Samurai you will be far more than you are now. It will require as much a sacrifice on your part, as it did for the Tiger Kami. Never forget. A god has entrusted part of itself to your care."

David noticed the twins watching him and the elders from the doorway of the dojo. As they stood beneath an elegant pine tree, the moon began to fade behind the tree line.

"You need time to think this all over, but remember: Secrecy is critical to protecting you, this family, and your Kami. You must promise not only to tell no one, but to be more careful. Now that you can summon the honshitsu, that does not mean you should."

Masao and Grandpa left David to think in the garden. Takumi and Rie both joined him, watching as complete darkness enveloped the Estate.

"I never really thought an actual Jitsugen Samurai would pop out of the stories and into real life," Rie sighed. Above the stars appeared, radiant in the sky.

"Who won this round?" David asked, noticing both were even more scuffed up than before.

"Mom," Takumi said. "She got annoyed and chucked a tray at us."

"I have a feeling I'm not going to have much time to read anymore," David said wistfully. He was just able to catch Rie's eyes flick to the forest as a wry grin spread over her lips.

David went to sleep that night trying to grasp everything Masao had told him. He could feel the metal's essence now that he knew it was there, slowly burning in his chest. If he wanted to, he knew he could probably call it back. Exhausted, David closed his eyes, willing himself to sleep. Oddly, he felt himself start to drift off almost immediately, a happy change from the weeks of nightmares and sleepless nights. As his mind relaxed, his consciousness drifted away.

'*At last. We begin.*'

十二

BEACH BIRDS

May,

You would have been frustrated too. Finally understanding the reason for your existence, only to be trapped in an invisible cage. Not a bad motivation to break free. And as with so many things, a little motivation…

As the clock near his bed counted towards four, a lone mouse ran along the farthest corner of David's room. In an instant, David was out from under his sheets, his ears twitching along after the sounds of scampering feet. His body tensed, neck snapping to take in the slightest sound. David flew off his bed just as Takumi entered.

"This is a nice surprise. It usually takes me at least ten minutes to get you up," Takumi said. David's head swung around to look at his host brother. Then the alarm sounded. Shaking his head, David stood and turned it off. Reaching up for a pull chain, Takumi turned on the light.

"What's in your hand?" Takumi asked, noticing the squirming gray fluff. David looked down at his hand then yelled and dropped the mouse. Jumping back, he crashed into his closet. With a shrug, Takumi left David to get ready for their run. "Hurry up or you'll be late."

Although jittery from waking up with a mouse in his hand, David made it to where the twins were waiting on time. Even though there was no school, they still practiced early on the weekends. Since the incident at the police station, Grandpa also had David practice summoning the metal every evening. Since it was Saturday, after badminton practice and lunch, they went back to the Estate so that David could have even more training.

The practices taxed his concentration to his limits. Whenever there was an external stimulus, like being attacked, David could quickly summon the metal. Unfortunately, he still had trouble calling it into existence when left alone. Holding the honshitsu required colossal amounts of endurance, and he was still having problems holding it for more than a few minutes, even after a week of training. Still, he enjoyed the work. Every time David summoned the metal, it seemed different, reflecting light in new and interesting ways. Luckily Grandpa was there to help him. He was a steady, if demanding teacher who allowed nothing but David's best.

Even with his tough schedule, David was able to find a few hours of freedom. He used one of them to find Rie. After his run-ins with Natsuki, and his acceptance of a future as a Jitsu-gen Samurai, David knew he had to integrate into Japanese society far more than he had. Natsuki made it all too clear he still had far to go, and that bowing was one of the most obvious skills he needed to master to clear the barriers between his past life and his new home.

"I'm glad you finally asked someone about this, but why are we meeting in the forest?" Rie asked. She shifted and stood a bit away from him.

"Don't laugh. I didn't know who else to ask. So what do I have to do?" David said.

Standing under the shade of a large tree, David learned the difference between a slight head nod and a low formal bow, about how low to bow in different circumstances and to different people.

"Bow from your lower back, keep your spine straight, no not like that," she said, laughing despite an obvious attempt to stay detached. Finally, she gave up, placed her hand on his back, and then pushed him over. Once he bent from his lower back, instead of just curving his spine, she moved on to the more subtle differences. She even showed him the difference in bowing between girls and boys, pointing out how he should keep his hands to his sides, rather than folding them in front, as she did. They ended with Rie giving him different scenarios. He grew suddenly self-conscious as he continued to bow, her almond eyes never leaving his.

"Well it looks like you have the basics down. I think if you remember those you won't insult anyone else," she said, smiling at him after his last bow. "You know you're actually a pretty quick study. I've been bowing my whole life, and you have got it almost as good as me."

Relieved, David promised to help her with anything she needed in repayment. Together, they waded through the thick trees towards the main house and dojo for their next practice.

In addition to working with Rie, David decided to find out more about what it meant to be a Jitsugen Samurai. The Matsumotos refused to tell him anything else, so he often practiced summoning the honshitsu in front of the mirror in his room, despite exhausting practices with it every day. Other times, he would walk through the forest, trying to find other new connections like the one where the honshitsu resided. He was convinced there was more within him than the Matsumotos would tell him. He abruptly stopped when one time he caught his image in the calm waters of the brook. He seemed to shift for the barest moment and something dangerous flickered in his eyes. From then on, David avoided the forest and the few mirrors in the house as much as possible.

As May turned to June, the weather changed from warm spring to hot and muggy summer. David got an immediate response to his attempts at bowing. Classmates seemed more relaxed, but the best change was from Mizuki and her friends. With no ammunition to use against him, the comments from the Natsuki's group died off dramatically.

David's week got even better when Rie surprised him outside the gym after practice.

"Guess what," she said.

"Umm, you were late for practice?" David said. Rie gave him an exasperated frown, and then punched him in the arm.

"I had a student council meeting," she said. "We're having a class barbeque at the beach this weekend! I'm going to have to get a new swimsuit." Her eyes widened and then she was suddenly gone, leaving David to wait for Takumi alone.

'She's getting strange,' David thought. 'It's like every time she treats me like... like a friend, she suddenly disappears.'

A few days later, David found himself sitting next to Takumi and Rie in the back of the Matsumotos' car, riding along a sea road with Yukiko at the wheel.

"I hope that the three of you did not forget anything. I will not be back until later tonight," Yukiko said as she turned into the beach's parking lot.

"We'll be great! All of Class 2B will be there to kick off the summer," Takumi said, even more excited by the party than David.

"It was so nice of the Ashikawas to plan everything and stay to help with the food." Yukiko's casual remark seemed to suck the excitement out of the air as Rie stiffened.

"They didn't say anything about that at the meeting," Rie moaned. Takumi suddenly gave all his attention to the grills, awnings, and the beach outside the window. Seeing his reaction, Rie nearly jumped across David to get to Takumi. "You knew!" Luckily, the car pulled to a stop behind a patio.

Waving goodbye Yukiko drove off to do shopping in nearby Himeji. The entire 2B class seemed to be present, minus Chul Moo. It took David a few minutes to figure out whom the group of girls looking longingly at the parking lot were waiting for. When they saw it was David and the twins, the group turned back towards the beach. Other groups of his classmates were already playing volleyball, swimming, and lounging under the awnings.

Takumi introduced David to the Ashikawas, Natsuki's parents and the Matsumotos' neighbors. Although not overly thrilled to meet the people who had raised his most outspoken critic, David did his best to bow as appropriately as Rie had taught him.

"Oh it's so nice to see you Rie!" Mrs. Ashikawa called to Rie as she tried to move quietly away. "You should come to the house, we miss seeing you. You used to be over all the time."

Forcing a smile in return, Rie gave a noncommittal reply and excuse before hurrying away towards some of her friends. Takumi continued to chat with Mr. Ashikawa, so David wandered away after a few forced smiles of his own. As he passed the volleyball net, he was pulled into a game by a short-sided team despite his weak attempts to protest.

After his fifth miss in a row, David gladly gave up his position to Daiki, and headed back to the awnings where Rie was sitting. Shou intercepted him half way there.

"Hey, a bunch of people are gonna go swimming. Go get ready!" Shou continued running from group to group, encouraging everyone to head over to the water. He ended with Natsuki and her friends, who were lying out on towels a bit away from everyone else.

David headed to the awnings to drop off his shirt and sandals while people began heading to the water. Naoto and Kenta were already horsing around in the water, throwing the soccer ball and trying to catch it before it hit the water.

"Hey Misaki, Ayaka, let's go for a swim. How about you Miu?" Rie asked, turning to the girls next to her.

"No thanks, I'll go help start the food. I *am* in the cooking club." Mie pointed to her apron and lack of swimsuit as she got up to help the Ashikawas. Ayaka and Misaki got up to follow Rie to the water.

"Hey David! Want to go swimming with us?" asked Misaki noticing David nearby.

"Sure! I'm from the desert after all, I can't pass up water." David was surprised by Misaki's invitation, he rarely had a chance to speak to Rie's other friends.

"Wow, really?" Misaki asked, her eyes wide.

"No, it was just a joke, I like the beach though," he said hurriedly after seeing her confused reaction. Sarcasm and other American jokes still did not translate well for him.

"Oh I thought it was some kind of strange rule, you have to take water when offered or something," Misaki said with a laugh.

As the four walked towards the water, Natsuki and a group of her friends talking in loud voices closely followed them. David walked to the waterline, but froze when he reached it. Unable to make his body step into the water, he felt an unnatural, and for him a first, fear of the ocean. He felt the depths and mysteries of it swell out before him and somehow knew the ocean was something just completely not a part of *him*. David's body tensed, his eyes glazed orange. Rie stopped. The salty blue water was up to her knees.

"Are you alright?" she asked.

From off to the side Natsuki gave a raucous laugh.

"Oh look! David's afraid of the water," Natsuki said loudly enough for everyone to hear.

David blushed red and tried to make himself get into the water. Unable to control the feeling of fear, and seeing Rie turn to face down Natsuki in his defense, David turned and walked swiftly down the beach before even more people were dragged into it.

David just caught Rie ask, "Should I tell everyone what *you're* afraid of Natsuki?" before they were out of range.

Confused, David wandered towards a patch of rocks down the beach. Sitting alone and wondering what had happened, he watched the groups swim and play in the shallow waves. His attention waning, David's thoughts drifted back over the last few months.

Although he felt stronger everyday as he continued running and training, he was still surprised by the random changes affecting his life. Although he could speak Japanese, he never knew when a bit of culture shock might hit him. Worse of all, his family grew ever more removed from his world.

His conversations with Jess especially were growing shorter since most things of importance in his life revolved around what was happening at the Estate. Masao insisted he keep his training secret. David constantly had to catch himself so as not to tell her about every success he made in summoning the metal, and his sister was not interested in badminton since she had never played. Instead, David relied on the twins. Takumi seemed determined to help him be more social, while Rie was just always there. He still harbored a secret fear that they would grow sick of his company.

Aside from changes in his relationship with his family, the effects of the Kami were beginning to change him. The danger of running into barriers, like the inexplicable inability to get in the water, seemed to hang over him like a shadow.

'There's still so much I don't understand about being a Jitsugen Samurai,' he thought. 'I'm still scared of my reflection. Is this part of it? Being afraid of the ocean, of water? Can I never go swimming again?'

David knew from the way the Matsumotos had spoken that more sacrifices would be coming, and possibly soon. As he thought about it, he tried to remember back when he had wanted to swim. When he thought about the ocean, even now when he looked out across the waves he felt no hint of the fear or aversion that had been so strong only minutes before.

David sat as still as the rocks around him. Lost, he searched his own mind for answers. As he sat, seagulls began to land around him on the rocks and sand. They squawked and jostled each other. Suddenly lunging, David dived after the birds nearest him, his eyes a bright orange glow in the early summer sun. Too slow to actually catch the wary birds, he leapt after them again and again. They easily fluttered outside of his reach, squawking at him angrily if he got too close.

Coming up from behind him, Rie lightly touched David on the shoulder as he squatted on the sand, intently watching the birds. At her touch, David spun and stood at the same time—his surprised reaction a combination of attack and defense he had practiced with Grandpa. David suddenly had Rie on the ground, her arm locked in his. David shook his head and released her as his eyes changed back to their normal blue. He blinked.

"What's up?" he asked curiously. Rie stared at him for a second, then took a deep breath as if readying for a sparring match against Grandpa.

"You know," she said slowly. "You never said anything about my new swimsuit."

Surprised, David tried to think of something to say, but before he could, Rie lifted her hand. Embarrassed, but not completely sure why, David pulled her up.

"Why were you on the ground?" he asked.

"I slipped. Come on! Time for food," she said as she trotted off towards the patio, David followed.

After they enjoyed plates of fried noodles and drinks, everyone lined up in front of a watermelon. Using a blindfold and a stick, Shiori, a classmate originally from Okinawa, showed everyone the art of watermelon smashing by missing beautifully and sending up a shower of sand. As each 2B student attempted to open up the watermelon, the rest shouted, attempting to misdirect the blindfolded student.

David smiled, reminded of the piñatas popular during Arizona birthdays. His face clouded a little then, as he remembered he would never go home.

'I've made my choice,' he thought and fixed a smile to his face. As Takumi stepped up to take his turn, a group of boys quickly stopped him from putting on the blindfold.

"No way!" Kenta said. David recognized the burly boy from the student council.

"Yeah, you and Rie go last. Otherwise none of us will have a chance," Tsubasa added. Only half joking, the wiry boy pointed to the back of the line.

Laughing, the rest of the class joined in and pushed the twins to the back. Since their point was quite valid, the twins merely smiled and let their classmates maneuver them. Either one of the Matsumotos would have easily been able to crack open the watermelon due to their training.

About halfway through the class Kenta pulled David to the front of the line. Known for clumsiness, he was sure they expected an entertaining show. Kenta blindfolded him, spun him around, and then handed him the stick. Well-schooled in the ways of the piñata, however, David stopped and listened to the shouts around him in order to orientate himself. He then took a few steps forward and brought his stick down on the melon.

Cracking it perfectly in two, David was greeted with cheers and slaps on his back. Those who had yet to go smiled ruefully, playfully punching Tsubasa and Kenta. After David got the first and largest piece of watermelon, his classmates divided up the rest and set out to enjoy the quickening dusk before lighting off fireworks and talking the rest of the evening away.

'I bet I'm the first Jitsugen Samurai with even a little international experience,' he thought thinking back on the watermelon. 'Maybe I really can do this.' He smiled as flames spouted around him from a hundred different rockets and sparklers.

十二

AWAKENING

June,

The moments of clarity were like the first glimpse of prey, yet they lacked something critical. The visions were little more than a teasing temptation, like visiting a zoo and suddenly realizing you're the one behind the bars...

In America, David would have been well into summer vacation. In Japan, however, he was displeased to learn that summer break was much shorter and that the first of three semesters lasted until the middle of July. So it was the Monday after the beach party, with plenty of school to look forward to, that David was suddenly woken up by the strange voice in his head.

'Wake up! Go hunt.'

Grumbling, David sat up and looked around for the source of the voice. Rie poked her head into the room, and, seeing David, smiled. He eyed her warily.

"Finally getting used to the early mornings, right? Let's go!" Rie's energy was contagious. Suddenly wide-awake, David got himself ready as soon as she retreated from his room.

The morning's practice was the best yet. He kept up with the twin's steady pace for a good portion of the five kilometer run, falling back only in the last two kilometers. He started practice already tired and sweating, but at least no longer splayed out on the floor unable to move. After the usual empty-handed basics, David took up his wooden sword and joined the twins in sword basics. Its weight had been hard on him at first, but as his arms adjusted, even that was becoming comfortable in his hands. Rounding out the session were brief sparing matches. The twins were still so beyond his level that he practiced choreographed fights called *kata* when they sparred.

David was especially glad for his ability to heal quickly. Even with the handmade set of armor that Grandpa gave him, David still received so many bruises from the twins that people at school would surely become concerned if he did not heal before classes began. Like the rest of the Matsumotos, David's new armor was in the style of the old samurai, but was made with modern technology and materials. The way Grandpa smiled when he received it made David wonder if there was more to the armor than met his eyes. It was completely black and un-adorned, unlike the twins', which seemed to have been painted by kindergarteners.

'I don't know about the skirt… Couldn't they update that design at least?' David had wondered. Takumi had shaken his head just enough to warn David not to comment aloud.

After practice, everyone changed and got ready for the school day. David joined Rie and Takumi in the main room for breakfast. The twins, already in their school uniforms, ate a traditional Japanese breakfast. Entering from the kitchen, Yukiko carried tea for the twins.

"Dad and Grandpa are still working and will eat later. Good Morning David, ready for breakfast?" Yukiko asked.

"Definitely, I'm starving. I'd really like some meat if you have it," David said with an air of distraction. Yukiko and the twins stared at him, but he pulled at a loose string on his uniform pants and didn't notice.

"Of course. Have a seat," Yukiko said, uncertainty in her voice. "Anything in particular? I have some steaks thawing I could get."

"That would be great! Thanks! Oh, rare please," David said, still missing the others' stares. Takumi and Rie glanced at each other as David sat down and Yukiko left.

"What's with the breakfast of just meat?" Rie asked quietly. David started to answer, and then stopped, confused.

"I don't know." David lapsed back into silence as he waited for Yukiko, trying to figure out why he had such a craving for meat.

'I normally just eat whatever the twins are having. How strange.'

Yukiko returned with a plate of steak cooked well, the way he usually liked it. After David gave his thanks, he took a ravenous bite and nearly choked. Grimacing he swallowed convulsively.

"David! Are you alright?" Yukiko gasped.

"Yeah! I was just surprised, I guess. It's pretty well done," he replied. Catching himself, he continued, "Uh no, I mean it's fine!"

He tried to reassure Yukiko that he did not need anything else, and she retreated to the kitchen while the twins finished their meals. David wolfed down the rest of the steak, licking his lips while Takumi watched him over the rim of his soup bowl.

"Must be a gaijin thing," Rie muttered with a grin. "We better go, or we'll be late." Rie gave David a final sidelong glance before getting up.

As David and the twins walked, he was so preoccupied that he missed Rie and Takumi whispering all the way to school. David's first three periods passed in a daze. It was not until fourth period, when Fukiko, the English teacher was up at the front of the classroom talking about subject changes and "be" verbs that David could let his mind wander free. Along with David, many of his classmates were dozing or staring out the window. Only a few hard chargers actually took notes, or at least worked on their homework.

'At least this is one class I won't have to worry about passing,' David thought.

'Without me you would fail every test. Or do you think you would know the Japanese meaning for all your English words on your own?' Unlike the few times he had heard it before, the voice in David's head was distinct, the tone mocking.

'I so don't need my subconscious giving me a hard time.'

Fukiko looked around the room at the lolling heads and vacant eyes. Turning, she began to write assignments and page numbers on the board.

'Like I am your subconscious… give me some credit.' The voice spoke once more before Mizuki's call to attention jerked David out of his reverie.

Standing with the rest of his classmates, David tried to catch Takumi alone as they walked to lunch, but was unable to get him away from Naoto and Shou. Getting in line for lunch, Rie and her friends Ayaka and Misaki followed close behind. Chul Soon waved to him from a seat in the lunchroom, having already gone through the line. David put the last lesson's strangeness up to hunger as his stomach rumbled.

"Hey David, how are classes going? Can you help us out with the English homework again? Fukiko-sensei gave us a lot!" Naoto grinned hopefully from the front of the group. Just behind, Shou glanced over hopefully.

"Classes are good, though I think just about everyone was out in English today. Takumi can get you a copy after I finish, right?" David said. He was happy he could finally use better Japanese. Most people figured he just had an inclination for languages, though David still made mistakes on purpose to throw off any suspicion it was far more.

"Yeah, I can. English is easy now that you're here. I sleep in class and still get the homework right." Naoto laughed again, stretching and yawning widely.

"It's bad enough you copy David's English, but it's even worse that you copy his Japanese... but then so do I." Rie's sudden input elicited a string of giggles from the girls behind her.

"Hey give the guy a break, do your own homework this week." Takumi's friends eyed him as if he had just stabbed them. Takumi on the other hand just eyed the *bentos*, Japanese boxed lunches. "Looks like today there is curry or stuffed fish."

"I think I'll just go with the curry today, I still haven't gotten used to eating the entire fish," David said, trying not to think about the previous period. He waited while Naoto and Shou both got their lunches then reached for the food. His hand froze. Just as he had stopped at the ocean, his hand seemed to ignore his will. His eyes furrowed in concentration as he fought to make his hand take the curry rice.

"Hurry up, I'm hungry," a third year shouted from further back in the line. It was one of Koji's friends. One of the students that had been there the day David was pushed around.

David's mind blanked in anger as his hand jerked to the fish. With fish bento in hand, he headed for their usual lunch spot. Takumi caught up with him as he passed the first tables.

"What was that about? I thought you still don't like eating the fish heads?" Takumi asked, confused.

"I don't. I tried to take the curry but I couldn't make my hand do it. It was like someone else was controlling my body." David's eyes unfocused and he nearly dropped his bento in surprise as the voice wormed its way into his mind again.

'What can I say? The fish looks so much better than that brown mush.'

"What's wrong? Your eyes keep glassing over," Takumi whispered while supporting David's arm. Takumi helped David over to their table, where they sat with Chul Soon and their other friends. Everyone was oblivious to David and Takumi's hushed conversation as the latest gossip about their favorite new pop idols and baseball teams were discussed with equal interest.

"I think I just need some time to get my head together. I swear I almost think I'm hallucinating," David whispered.

"After lunch let's skip badminton and take a walk around the school," Takumi said, casually eying the lunchroom. "I'll show you some places you haven't seen yet. That will give you a chance to clear your head."

Takumi spoke calmly. With a nod and grunt, David began eating, ferociously attacking the small stuffed fishes and accompanying rice and vegetables, completely ignoring the conversations around him. For the first time he ate the fishes as they were intended to be eaten: head, bones, and all.

After lunch, Takumi dragged David off, making excuses to their friends for missing the free period games. Walking along, Takumi allowed David to zone out again as he kept up a one-sided conversation for the sake of any passersby.

'*I'm surprised you have yet to figure it out. Based on what the Matsumotos have said, you have had plenty of clues.*' The voice was clear and distinct in his mind, as if it had been waiting for the perfect moment.

'Why won't you leave me alone? What are you anyway? I must have knocked something loose when I ran into the shrine. Japan is driving me crazy.'

'*That was weeks ago. Do you not find it strange that you think in Japanese now?*'

'I'm a quick learner. I've been here three months, of course I think in Japanese.'

'*Really, you should not lie to yourself. Maybe if you learned to enjoy some of your more... animalistic instincts, you could be more flexible. You spend all your time thinking things out, why not just react?*'

Takumi guided David through the halls and buildings, keeping him out of the way of other students with a light touch. Moving away from the school buildings, they walked towards the Gym.

'So you're a split personality? You made me take the fish today, and the thing with the mouse, the ocean, and steak?'

'Well it is boring just watching you all the time. And no, you are not crazy. Do you really think Kami just sit back and let the humans have all the fun?'

'Get out of my head! Leave me alone. I'm just a normal kid. I'm just a normal kid. I'm just a normal kid.'

'Repeating yourself will not help. You have never been normal. Besides, normal is overrated.'

David and Takumi entered the gym. Students were everywhere, playing badminton and basketball, sitting in groups talking, or otherwise occupying their time. Takumi waved to a group of friends as they walked. Chul Moo lurked in a corner of the gym. As usual, a group of girls spied on him.

'Hey, it is not all bad, right? With me around you can speak Japanese. And even though you are not paying attention, and I am only a few months old, I can already keep you from running into things.'

David veered into a wall. Bouncing off, he shook his head trying to regain his balance. Takumi grabbed David and pulled him out a side door.

'See? We are going to get along very well.'

'Very funny,' David thought with a scowl. Then as he thought about it, he chuckled. It *was* funny. 'Where did you come from? Why me?'

'You helped create me. When you sacrificed yourself, I was created, and at the same time, I saved you. You would have died if I had not possessed you when I did. We are mortally linked. A new Kami and a dead human, two minds that will learn and grow together. I am the source of your power as a Jitsugen Samurai. You are the reason for my existence, and it is a good thing too, because there is definitely a need for us. Now then, let us go find something to hunt.'

David and Takumi stopped before a room where a few students were practicing a martial art David was not familiar with.

'I'm not going to go chasing mice just because you tell me to.'

'Oh no?'

David fell into a crouch, freezing as his will battled the Kami's.

'No way! People already think I'm strange. I won't.'

"Hey! That's pretty good. I guess practice is starting to rub off on you," Takumi said, speaking to David directly for the first time since they began their walk. Takumi pulled him up from his crouch. David's movement had nearly matched one of the students practicing.

"Sorry I've been a bit distracted," David said. Shaking his head, he stood.

"Oh I know. Figured I'd give you two a chance to talk. Grandpa said this might happen soon. He also told me not to interfere unless he, or she I guess, was about to give you away." Takumi spoke carefully, bracing for the avalanche he knew would come anyway.

"You knew! I thought I was going crazy!" David's suddenly loud voice caught the attention of the martial arts students. Waving his apology, Takumi guided David outside, into the secluded area behind the gym.

"Dad said it would be better if your Kami made the introductions, rather than one of us trying to explain things," Takumi said apologetically.

"Right, well it would have been nice to have a warning, you know, something like 'Oh he might speak to you and make you chase after mice,'" David fumed.

"They didn't tell me until a few days ago! They only told Rie and I in case something like this happened at school. Anyway, what's it like? I know your Kami is just awakening, but I'm dying to know."

"Awakening?" David asked, once again confused. They continued walking alongside the school's soccer field, where a group of first years was playing.

"Well your Kami is part of the one you saved Grandpa from, but it's personality, powers, form, will all be unique. They'll also be infantile, but with some kind of deep wisdom or something," Takumi answered.

David's eyes flashed to a bright orange.

"Who is calling who infantile? You will not even ask Natsuki out." Takumi jumped back in shock, his body reacting to the change in David's eyes, voice, and manner by falling into a familiar Matsumoto fighting stance. Takumi had never said anything to David about Natsuki, but by his expression, David knew the Kami had been spot on. David shuddered and coughed, clawing at his throat. His eyes returned to their normal blue again as he spotted Rie coming up behind Takumi.

"That. Was. Strange," David said, coughing again. "The voice came out of me!" After the voice remained silent and David recovered, he continued, "I don't know if I would call an obsession with rare meat, mice, and string deep wisdom. Before today, he's only said a few words, and only while I was falling asleep. I thought he was my conscience or something. The whole body control thing is really disturbing, though it seems I can stop him if I concentrate."

David smiled to Rie. His host brother eyed him as if unsure who was in control of David's body.

"What's his name?" she asked.

Takumi jumped hearing Rie voice from right behind him. His eyes wide in shock he looked quickly between David and Rie, as if trying to guess how much she had heard.

"What's with you?" Rie asked, with a questioning look at Takumi.

"Sorry, David's Kami surprised me, it decided to say hello," Takumi replied sourly.

"Oh well, when I saw David earlier I figured it was the awakening and slipped away as soon as I could," she said brightly.

"I don't know what his name is. I'll check," David said frowning uncertainly. His eyes unfocused as he searched his mind for the Kami. As he concentrated, the nearby soccer players started to leave the field, heading to change before class.

'Hey, what's your name?' David thought. 'Hello? Oh so *now* you shut up?'

"He isn't answering," David said, unable to find the Kami within him. Rie simply stared back at him.

"Grandpa said that might happen," she said finally. "We better go." Rie started walking away from the gym. "It takes a lot for the Kami to mold itself to a human's mind at first. Though apparently as time goes by it will get easier, especially after you change." David stopped abruptly as the twins continued walking. A bell tolled the end of free period.

"What change? Haven't I already changed enough? Half my soul is locked in a piece of metal!" David raged, angry at once again getting only part of the story.

"Later! We will be late for Japanese!" Rie called over her shoulder. Seeing David behind them, she ran back and grabbed his hand. After the slightest pause, her hand tightened in his and she pulled him towards their class.

十四

OF DOGS AND CATS

June,

The first time was a challenge. I had been working up to it, but it was still far more exhausting than I anticipated. Finally, a chance to talk with David...

The trio made it back to class just before the bell rang. Natsuki, Kaeda, and Yuka, were talking by the entrance and eyed them with evil smiles as they entered.

"Oh look, it's Rie and her new boyfriend David. I knew her standards were low, but I thought she had *some* self-respect," Natsuki said. David felt his cheeks go immediately red.

'Rie and *me*?' he thought.

"And living in the same house too!" added Kaeda quickly.

"Scandalous," added Yuka enjoying the innuendo. David was so stunned he barely registered Takumi lock his hand around Rie's arm. The movement, however, brought his attention back to his host sister. She looked more dangerous and angry than anyone he had ever seen before.

"My, my, Natsuki," Chul Moo's voice, so rarely used, rolled deeply from his throat. The girls jumped in surprise. "You must be jealous, everyone being so interested in Rie."

Chul Moo's smile deflated Rie while Natsuki's eyes went wide. Her mouth worked silently, but the door opened again and Nakashita, the Japanese language teacher, came in.

"Alright everyone, take your seats so we can get started," Nakashita said, completely missing the awkward atmosphere.

The rest of the class was filled with whispering about David, Rie, Natsuki, and Chul Moo. Unbothered by the Kami, David had no escape from the stares and buried himself in his Japanese book. It only got worse as the day progressed.

'I've never thought of *anyone* like that,' David thought. 'Now I know how Takumi felt, well, I guess he does like Natsuki. Rie though…'

With the idea planted in their heads, the school was soon awash in rumors about Rie and David, plus the mysterious Chul Moo, who the students were always willing to discuss. By practice time, David was left out of the gossip as they focused on Chul Moo and Rie. The question of whether they were living together and dating was dropped in lieu of the popular interest in the unknown quantity of the *other* student in 2B.

Although glad to be left out of the gossip, David found the idea that Chul Moo and Rie could be together even more confusing. Chul Soon seemed to sympathize with David as they met in the boy's locker room after practice.

"My brother just shouldn't speak. People always tend to take his words the wrong way," Chul Soon said with mock dejection. "Now that he's the talk of the school he's just going to be that much more sullen."

"Maybe," replied David softly. Chul Soon talking about his brother made David think back to Jess and the latest email she had sent. They were becoming fewer and fewer. Her orbit was drifting away from him and he missed the connection. David said as much to Chul Soon. Just as he could not talk with his sister about being a Jitsugen Samurai, neither could he talk to

Chul Soon, yet something about him made David want to confide in him, at least a little.

"Rie has been so helpful lately. She reminds me of my sister a lot, but in a different way. I mean I guess she's my host-sister, but then, I'm not sure it's the same," David said.

With a smile and a wink, Chul Soon tried to console him. He was obviously interested in what David could not tell his sister that was dividing them, but had the tact not to intrude.

"Rie and Jessica are both obviously very important to you. You should hold on to both of them, no matter the cost." Chul Moo let his words drift away with a friendly smile. Leaving David with his own thoughts, Chul Soon got up to go find his brother.

After badminton practice, David met Takumi to walk home. Rie had a student council meeting, so they left before her. David knew he could not talk to Takumi about Rie, and was sure he would not appreciate hearing about Jessica again. Besides, he had far more pressing concerns that Takumi could help him with.

"Ok, so first, what is Natsuki's problem, and second, what else have you neglected to tell me about my new house guest?" David spoke as soon as they were out of earshot of anyone near them. Laughing, Takumi checked around again, the closest person being Chul Soon walking off in a completely different direction.

"That's rich coming from you, Mr. Exchange Student. I told you what happened in elementary. You like Rie. I mean she's your friend," he quickly amended, "so Natsuki doesn't like you. Plus, she thinks you don't have to work for anything, which really annoys her. Any chance to get a few points, she'll take, but I think she's still the old Natsu inside," Takumi said. "Hey I need to stop in the bank real quick, mind waiting a second?" Takumi turned just after the grocery store.

"Uh sure," David said, already distracted by his own thoughts on the day's events. Waiting in front of the bank,

David's eyes wandered around the old buildings. Across the street, where darkness gathered in the space between two buildings, a glint caught his eye.

Deep in the shadows, two large yellow eyes glowed, staring at David. As he shaded his eyes to see better, the shadows deepened and moved. A dog slowly stepped forward. Larger than any David had seen before, it was a super-sized, black haired wolf with interesting patterns of white fur around its snout and ears. David relaxed, taking it for a stray. Then the wolf changed in an instant. No longer was it a cute stray, its hackles raised, teeth bared, it turned into a vicious and horrifying version of its previous appearance.

Pushing back against a wall, David felt the fear rise within him, the same fear he had felt during the day on the beach and during Jahangir's attack. He stared back into the intelligent yellow eyes, unable to look away. He knew what it was; he had seen them in Grandpa's visions. The ōkami seemed to smile. The look of confidence a hunter might have right before making an easy kill. Then it sprang.

David dropped his bag and took off down the road. While two months of training had helped him improve, he was no sprinter. Still, with the ōkami hot on his heels, panic surged through him. Quickly tiring, he ran without paying any thought to his direction.

'*Run! It is going to get us!*' David's Kami was suddenly awake and powerful in his mind, as if fed by his adrenaline.

'I'm so not a runner.' David fought desperately, willing his legs to move faster.

'*It is almost here David, run! RUN!*'

Before the ōkami could reach him, David's body convulsed. A strange sensation, as if he was suddenly in a giant wind tunnel, ran through him. His perspective shifted. Unable to feel his own body, David panicked, screwing his eyes shut.

"*Hey! Stop that. I cannot see!*"

The Kami's voice growled aloud, echoing hugely in his suddenly sensitive ears. Opening his eyes, David found he was far, far too close to the ground. He was weaving in and out of overly large trees and bushes, cutting front yards and skittering along property walls. Orange furred paws flitted into his view then disappeared just as quickly. The sense of déjà vu was overpowering. All the strange dreams since the mountain trip came back in full force and clarity.

His tail flicked against a bush.

'I have a tail,' he thought, dumbfounded even as his new body moved of its own accord. It was as if he was in an immersion tank, all his senses cut off with only vague inputs making it through.

The ōkami, nearly on top of its prey, slid to a stop when David, in a nearly instantaneous transformation changed into a small orange fluffy ball, which sprouted legs and took off. Stopping only briefly at David's clothes, the ōkami sniffed deeply then growled. It sprang after the racing orange puffball even faster than before.

David and the Kami turned a corner trying to lose the ōkami. Though not in control, as he reached for his various senses they exploded into his mind, forcing him to draw back from the raw power of the animal body. It was strange and even painful to open himself to the sensations of the ground under his *paws* or the brightness of the early evening in his new eyes, yet it was even more horrible to be without any sense. Whenever he pulled back, he was left with such a profound sense of isolation he immediately reached back for some input. How strange and comforting even the barest sound or touch was when you were cut off from them. Aside from his new connections to physical senses, David also felt the Kami's surprise along with his own emotions as they suddenly passed under a pair of legs. Even more surprising was the sudden jolt as two hands lifted him high into the air.

Their shock deepened when Natsuki's face suddenly came into focus in such detail that he could count every pore on her face.

'Ewww!' was all David could think before he was enveloped by her arms. He caught a brief glimpse of Hidemi walking next to her.

"Aww aren't you cute." Natsuki's voice boomed through him as he squirmed in her arms.

The ōkami came to a sudden stop after flying around the corner. Its big head rolled as it took in the scene. David spotted it from between Natsuki's arms. The ōkami growled but did not attack.

"Oh so *you're* why he's running," Natsuki said angrily as she turned on the wolf. Taking her bag, Natsuki swung at the ōkami. After missing once, she hit it on the nose. Yelping, the wolf backed away. Turning its massive head between the two girls, it growled once last time before it turned and fled.

"You poor thing, you must be scared," Natsuki said as she nearly suffocated David's Kami in her arms.

"Savior to cats everywhere. A true animal lover," Hidemi said with a theatrical air. She smiled ruefully at Natsuki. "Though judging from that dog, you don't love *all* animals."

Takumi barreled around the corner carrying David's clothes and bag. Smashing into Hidemi, they both went flying. At the same instant, Natsuki froze then fell, David in the Kami's form, still in her arms.

Helping Hidemi up, Takumi bowed profusely as he apologized before turning to Natsuki who suddenly began giggling uncontrollably. On the ground, she squirmed as the Kami brushed against her neck.

"Natsu are you alright?" asked Hidemi, confused as to why Natsuki was rolling around on the ground.

"Yeah, I'm amazing, I dunno, I felt this... wow, it was so powerful that I fell down, and then it started purring and tickling me." Natsuki finally managed to sit up with the puff-ball still in her arms.

"Oh good, you found my uh..." Takumi bent closer, looking at the ball of fur nestling in Natsuki's arms, "cat."

"Ta-kun?" breathed Natsuki. "What are you doing with all that stuff in your arms? I figured you'd be babysitting the new badminton star."

"Actually I had to pick up something from the bank so uh, David isn't here," Takumi said his hand reaching for his hair. He was just able to turn the embarrassed gesture into a flick of his hair. "He forgot his stuff so I have it."

"I guess he's not into wearing clothes." Hidemi brushed the dirt from her clothes, eyeing Takumi with more than a little disbelief.

"So this is yours? What's its name?" Natsuki asked, all her attention on the cute orange fur ball in her arms.

"It doesn't have one yet actually," Takumi said, his mind running in high gear.

"That's horrible. Seeing as I saved it, I think I'll call him Kou," Natsuki said with her usual authoritative tone. Kou purred loudly in her arms. "See? He likes it."

"Well it's been a while." Takumi spoke desperately. Luckily, she was distracted by Kou and did not notice. "Why don't I walk you home? That is if you don't mind Hidemi?"

Takumi looked pointedly at his classmate. Catching the point, she sighed and ran off around the corner. Natsuki eyed Takumi suspiciously.

"What did you do that for?" Natsuki asked, scowling.

"I uh, *really* need to talk to you. You mind coming over for tea?" David just caught the look on Takumi's face before being overcome by the animalistic senses. Takumi was on the edge, as if he had never before been so unsure of what to do.

"Is *she* going to be there?" Natsuki's asked petulantly.

"No, of course not, Rie is with David at, uh, school," Takumi answered, stealing a glance at Kou while Natsuki was distracted. Takumi's face betrayed a storm of emotions: fear, concern, and even disappointment.

Picking up the bags and clothes, Takumi walked the rest of the way to the Matsumoto Estate with Natsuki in silence, Kou purring along the way.

十五
PARTNERSHIPS

June,

The first time we changed was as surprising to me as it had been for David. I finally felt real. I had a body, and was more than just a voice in the back of a thirteen-year-old human's head. Unfortunately, David got a bit lost in my new senses. Luckily, it did not take him as long as I to find his way back from the depths…

Takumi looked anxious, sitting quietly at the low table in the main room, stealing glances at Kou as he lay in Natsuki's arms. Natsuki knelt poised and relaxed, a strong contrast to her usual confrontational and outspoken manner. Waiting for Takumi to explain why she was kneeling there in his house without a word from him, she seemed like the perfect representation of a Japanese lady.

"You know, the more I look at Kou, the less he looks like a cat. But what in the world would you be doing with a tiger in Japan?" Natsuki asked looking up at her childhood friend. She stared for a few seconds, obviously expecting a response. When none was forthcoming, she lost the easy grace and refined manners that she used at home. Her calm demeanor fell away like a discarded scarf, her whole body tensed as she regained the intensity that she often displayed at school. Her graceful kneel turned into more the rigid *seiza* position students used at school when they got in trouble. "You invited me, but if you aren't gonna talk I might as well go home."

Natsuki stood, Kou still in her arms. Takumi jerked upright as if to stop her, but then looked past her and sat. Grandpa and Masao entered from the rear doors of the room, looking imposing in the soft evening light.

"I have already talked to your father and he has agreed to let you stay for dinner,' Masao said. His voice was kind but with an edge that left no room for argument. "He actually seemed rather pleased."

"Please have a seat," Grandpa added with his most heartwarming voice.

Takumi ran out of the room to get tea for everyone, far more relaxed than he had been only minutes before. Once everyone was seated again, Masao addressed Natsuki.

"Takumi said on the phone that you named him? What is he called?" Masao asked softly with a warm comforting smile.

"I called him Kou, he seems to like it," Natsuki said respectfully, her façade back in place for the elder Matsumoto.

"Takumi told me you saved him from a dog. Thank you. I am worried about him, however, since we just got him. Would you mind telling me what happened?"

"I was walking home when this orange blur flew under me," she began.

"Yes, I seem to remember you have an affinity for animals," Grandpa said with a smile, as if reliving a memory. Natsuki blinked.

"I picked him up then saw a big dog chasing him. It was a vicious looking thing," she said. "Luckily, it stopped and growled so I beat it off with my bag. Then there was this crazy feeling, I fell and suddenly Takumi was standing over me while Kou tickled me. Takumi said it didn't have a name so I called him Kou and here we are."

Moving in her arms, one of Kou's paws slipped out of her arms. Grandpa raised a lone eyebrow. Kou's paws were far too large for a regular house cat.

"You were right, Takumi. It is a good thing you brought her," Grandpa said softly from one end of the table.

As Natsuki looked confusedly between Grandpa and Takumi, a scrape of wood on wood announced someone at the front door.

"*Tadaima!*" Rie called, entering with the usual Japanese phrase for "I'm home." Seeing Natsuki shocked her dumb. Through Kou, David was just able to see Rie's quick glance take in the situation. With the tiger's senses, he could almost feel her shock, anger, even pain. "What's she doing here?"

When none of the Matsumoto men responded immediately, Rie spun and ran back out into the night. Takumi rose to follow but a short command from Masao kept him in place.

"Let her go. She knows her duty. That much has not changed, even if things are much more complicated," Grandpa said, steel in his voice.

"Sorry, but what's going on?" Natsuki asked.

"Rie!" David shouted. Natsuki looked around in surprise for David as she tried to contain Kou. He was squirming frantically in her arms. Looking down, Natsuki saw not a cat's eyes, but instead the deep blue of David's.

"Takumi! Quickly, a blanket," Grandpa shouted.

Takumi was off in a flash and back with a blanket from a nearby cabinet. Grabbing Kou from Natsuki, Takumi covered him with the blanket just as Kou transformed back into David.

Taking a long look at David in his blanket, Natsuki let loose a blood-curdling scream. Before she could bolt, Grandpa agilely blocked her exit. Takumi attempted to calm her. Struggling to stand, David saw the fear in every aspect of Natsuki's stance. After a brief pause, his eyes turned orange and he transformed back into Kou.

Running under the table, Kou leaped into Natsuki's arms. Immediately, she calmed down and sat, though she still looked horrified. Kou, standing up in her arms, looked into Natsuki's eyes.

"Do not worry. The elders will explain everything. This is new to David and I as well," Kou said. His voice was completely different from David's and surprisingly deep for having come from such a small body.

Natsuki looked like she wanted nothing more than to flee. Restrained by Kou's presence, however, she simply nodded dumbly. Grandpa sat, soon followed by Masao and Takumi. Takumi eyed Kou warily, as if he expected him to transform again.

"Let me tell you a story," Grandpa said, beginning to tell Natsuki the same story he had told David just over two months before. As he talked, David and Kou had time to have words of their own.

'I told you it would not be all bad. See? Our first time as a tiger and we are already making new friends.'

'I don't know about you, but Natsuki is *not* my friend... Eww, is that her? Ugh! It's like she bathed in perfume.'

Kou shuddered in Natsuki's arms, but the humans ignored him.

'We have new senses you are not used to. I'm sure you would not smell much better.'

'So what then? You're, I'm a tiger? It's hard to concentrate. If I try to see, smell, or use my senses they're too strong. It blocks everything else out. For a while, before you fell asleep, I couldn't even find myself. I was just lost, then you woke up, and Rie brought me back.'

'We are a tiger. From now on, I am you and you are me. If we need to be a tiger, we are. If we need to be a human, we become your old form. Right now our personalities, our perspectives are very different, so things will be a bit awkward, but eventually we should both be able to guide either form. It will take us time to learn how to see well with such alien eyes.'

"The main point is that David is now possessed by a Kami, apparently a Tiger Kami," Masao said finishing the story that Grandpa started, his eyes locking onto Natsuki. She looked down at Kou, his overly large orange eyes too cute to resist.

"Let's have some dinner. Kou, I think you should change back into David for now," Masao said with the full authority of generations of Matsumotos. Kou looked between Natsuki and Masao, as David and Kou tried to decide if she could handle his absence.

"Very well, I will be in our room, though I am not sure how long it will take to switch back. We have only done it the one time." Kou jumped out of Natsuki's lap. Running away awkwardly on his new legs, he headed for David's room.

Kou looked everywhere. Trotting under the bed and around the corners... he sniffed and saw the room through new eyes and senses. The colors were slightly off, and despite the fact he could not turn on the light, it was still easy for him to find his way around.

"I was right. You don't smell good," Kou said.

'Ok, let's do this,' David thought, eager to get his normal body back.

"Well, last time you wanted to take control. Your will was greater than mine, so if you want to change back, and I do not fight you, you probably will," Kou replied.

Kou closed his eyes and retreated into himself, attempting to leave control to David. Unfortunately, it was not as easy to let go of his new body. David mentally closed his own eyes and concentrated on being himself, but the image of his furry paws kept butting in. He fought to pull his thoughts away from the new smells, sounds, and feelings that came in rushing torrents, trying to remember the old David. When he opened his eyes, he could barely see in the dark.

'Something isn't right.'

David could feel his legs and body. He reached up to touch his face and felt fur on his cheek. His arms were still covered with fur, and one hand was still a tiger paw. His tail twitched under him.

'Let's try together. Use this memory, when you were looking in the stream and saw me through your eyes.'

With Kou's help, David imagined himself as he was in the memory. When they opened their eyes a few seconds later, David was his old self.

"I'm surprised it doesn't hurt, except for the initial jolt I can't really feel it at all." David stopped, laughing at the casual way he spoke about transforming into a tiger to the Kami possessing him while he dressed. "I was pretty scary there for a second."

'Why would you? It is just another part of you, as I am a part of you. As with everything, I am sure we will get better with practice.'

Back in the main room, Takumi was just bringing out the last dish for dinner when David entered. Apparently, Yukiko was out for the evening, but had left dinner.

"So why exactly do I care about all of this?" Natsuki asked. "As far as I'm concerned David can take his special new powers back to America." Her temper had not subsided in the few minutes David had been away.

"Although I hate to agree with you, that's exactly what I thought at first," David said, stepping around the table to sit. "About a month after I arrived in Japan, I was killed and possessed, then the next thing I know I'm being attacked and summoning lumps of metal. And of course, now I can turn into a *tiger*. Don't get me wrong, Kou seems great but I didn't ask for any of this." David glared angrily at Natsuki, who in turn bristled.

"Let's eat," Masao interrupted, breaking stony silence. After a few bites, David turned to Takumi.

"I don't know why you had to invite her. I agree with Rie, she's horrible," said David.

"That's it. I'm going home."

Masao restrained her with a look.

'Be nice to her. I like her. She did save us,' Kou thought.

"She saved you! Not us." Realizing he replied to Kou aloud, David looked around at the Matsumotos with an embarrassed grin. Looking up from his soup, Masao sighed and slowly put the bowl down.

"Unfortunately, it is not that simple," Masao said soberly. "Natsuki what you described earlier was a bonding. With David and Kou being so young I do not know the extent of the bond, but you are now more a part of this than anyone but David."

"Why's that?" asked David hotly, eliciting an elbow from Takumi for his tone. David bowed slightly as way of an apology. Masao ignored the outburst.

"The Jitsugen Samurai were not loners. The Kami would choose a Partner, usually someone of the opposite gender, someone who they felt an obligation towards," Masao said with a look that David was afraid implied Natsuki was his new Partner. "The Partner gains some of the physical benefits of the Jitsugen Samurai and is the only other person that can wield the Seikaku."

Looking to his father to continue, Masao went back to his soup.

"Due to the bond, Natsuki will begin to grow stronger as you do David." Grandpa smiled. "In addition, whenever you are in your animal form, Natsuki will be drawn to you, wherever you are. Natsuki, you can try to ignore this, but the pull will be very strong. I am afraid you are both in this together."

David, while trying to process what Grandpa and Masao were saying, caught Takumi's wide grin. He was surprised that Takumi would be happy to have Natsuki as Kou's Partner, whatever that entailed. Looking closer, David saw the smile did not quite meet his eyes. Frowning David looked back at Natsuki who was just as horror struck as he was.

"I guess this means you'll be coming back to train with us," Takumi said with a strained, overly enthusiastic voice.

"What about Rie? Can't she be my Partner? She already knows how to fight, and then I wouldn't be stuck with the princess," David said quickly, trying to find some way out of having to be Natsuki's Partner. Natsuki, spit out the soup she had just drunk. David's eyes flashed orange.

"I could not help it. She saved me. I had to return the favor, and I felt a connection with her," Kou said. David's mouth twitched in an involuntary smile caused by Kou as his eyes unfocused and Kou continued the conversation within the privacy of their mind.

'Besides, she is cute, if lacking some of the more feline charms, right? I am sure you will get along… err, eventually.'

It took the rest of dinner and well after for Masao and Grandpa to convince Natsuki and David the choice had already been made. While Natsuki could try to avoid the situation, the pull would be too strong for her to resist.

"It seems like I don't have much choice. I'll be here for training. But I don't talk to David. As far as I'm concerned he doesn't exist, just Kou," Natsuki said, finally giving in to the elder Matsumotos.

十六
PUNISHING PRACTICES

June,

The first days were the hardest for us. We shared bodies, yes, but our thoughts were different. David and I spent hours talking in the confines of our shared minds. Sometimes it was a struggle, and sometimes a fight, but the hardest part was not over thinking…

After the next morning's run, David entered the dojo to find Masao, Takumi, and Natsuki talking in a corner. Rie apparently had not come back or at least was not going to show up to practice while Natsuki was around.

"Good, you are not too late. From now on, Natsuki will be joining you in the mornings. Start basics then spar," Masao said.

David walked over to stand in his usual place next to Takumi. Natsuki quickly blocked his way, shoving him back toward the other side of the dojo.

"Now that I'm here you're at the end. You'll address me as *sempai*," Natsuki said.

'She wants me to use same suffix as older classmates? Like *she's* my superior,' he thought.

"Why not Princess Natsuki instead?" David asked. Natsuki's eyes flashed as she dropped into the familiar Matsumoto fighting stance.

"That's enough. Begin!" Masao called, visibly annoyed at their posturing.

The students worked through the Matsumoto basics. Takumi as always, was perfect. Natsuki, rusty from over a year of not practicing, was slow and made mistakes. David caught her constantly watching Takumi. Over a month and a half of training had helped David memorize the basics to the point he was smoother, though his form was imperfect. As with every practice, they worked through empty hand blocks, kicks, punches, and sword basics. After a quick break, the students donned their sparing gear. They replaced their wooden practice swords with the lighter bamboo swords, and then lined up at the back of the Dojo.

"David, you may have noticed that the others have different colors on their armor. It is to help with camouflage and to give them a personal character. Even Natsuki has hers. Since we now know what animal Kou is, we will paint your armor as well. Normally you would do this, but for a Jitsugen Samurai, there is a different process.

"More on that later, now let us see how Takumi and Natsuki do together. It has been awhile after all," Masao said seriously. David thought he could see a rare smile twitch at the corners of his mouth.

David moved aside while Natsuki and Takumi faced each other. At Masao's command, the pair bowed, Takumi lower than Natsuki. Thanks to Rie's lesson, he knew it was probably an attempt to flatter Natsuki. David was glad he had a mask to hide his disgust. A second command brought them to ready stances while a final command set off an explosion of bamboo.

David was stunned as the two connected repeatedly. The strikes and parries seemed a graceful dance. The quick-footed pair revolved around each other, seeking openings. The battle was evenly matched, two skilled opponents equally aware of the other's skill and ability. Nothing Natsuki had ever done in his presence had hinted at this kind of potential.

"STOP!" Masao called. Natsuki and Takumi halted mid-swing at Masao's command, then lowered the swords, stepped away, and bowed before removing their helmets. "That is enough. Natsuki, you have been away too long. Takumi would have beaten you on the second move if he had not been holding back."

Blushing, Takumi quickly turned away from Natsuki, who looked as if Masao had just slapped her.

"David, let us see how you do," Masao said. "Natsuki, remember he is new. For you, *control*, is essential, if you hurt David, you hurt Kou."

Natsuki's face hardened in determination before she replaced her helmet. As with the previous match, David and Natsuki followed Masao's commands, though their greeting bows were disrespectful, barely discernible spasms. At the command to attack, David raised his sword to block Natsuki's attack. Instead of continuing, she slid under his block, elbowing his gut and knocked him to the ground,

David rose gingerly. They bowed and attacked again. Natsuki feinted then moved in from above in a classic kendo strike. David, missed the block and took the impact full on the head, falling to his knees from the force of the blow. Getting back up, David attacked repeatedly. Each time Natsuki quickly beat him. Though he became slow and sluggish, David refused to give in. Masao sat quietly on the sidelines watching the pair but not intervening.

Finally, knocking David down for the tenth time, Natsuki took off her helmet, and bent close, her face full of contempt. "I can't believe Koji-sempai even bothered to beat you up. You're pathetic."

Filled with frustration, David pulled off his own helmet.

"At least I'm not constantly sucking up to a bunch of superficial jerks," David said hotly.

"You know Koji-sempai might just be right. You really aren't worth the effort," she replied.

"I bet Chul Moo loved your great badminton skills," David said in a whisper. He attacked as her eyes widened in rage. Natsuki's bamboo sword was up in an automatic guard in an instant. With his attack knocked aside, David's unprotected skull smashed into the unforgiving wood of Natsuki's sword.

'*A fallen leaf on the ground will be eaten by insects and decay, but a leaf rising on the wind can become a tempest,*' Kou thought as David regained consciousness. He groaned. '*That means get up.*'

Opening his eyes, David saw the dojo ceiling above, with the bright morning light streaming in. Slowly he got up, feeling his head he found his hair matted with dried blood, though the injury had already mostly healed. The only other person in the room was Natsuki, kneeling a bit away from him in the uncomfortable seiza position.

"Just because you contain a god, doesn't mean I won't still kick your butt. You better improve quickly or I'm going to become an expert at seiza, not kendo," Natsuki said, her voice strained but tightly controlled.

A loud growling laugh from Kou burst out of David as he struggled to stand. Natsuki jumped up and ran out of the room.

'Well that went well.'

'*Next time try to avoid getting hit on the head. It hurts. You'd better hurry or you'll be late for school.*'

Suddenly enthusiastic, David jumped up, swaying from the sudden rush of blood and the swelling knot on his head, which began to heal almost as soon as he felt it.

'You're right. Maybe Rie will be there and I'll be able to clear up this whole Natsuki thing.'

When David got to school, he was pleased to see that Rie had indeed gone on ahead. Unfortunately, she was off in the corner talking to Chul Moo so he did not have a chance to talk to her. Following Takumi as he went to his seat, David leaned in, taking the advantage of how late Moriyama-sensei was.

"Hey, since when have Rie and Chul Moo been friends?" he asked.

"I've seen them talk before, but I guess doing it so publicly is her revenge or something," Takumi answered.

Rie had changed seats, preferring the empty seat next to Chul Moo, rather than her usual spot. David's attempts to get her attention were cut off when Moriyama entered and started talking about the day's schedule and classes.

David was unable to get Rie alone until after school. Before badminton practice, he caught her coming out of the girls' locker room. As he sidled up to talk to her, Rie turned on him.

"I have to go. You should go hangout with your new play-mate Natsuki," Rie said, unusually harsh. Chul Moo stood in the shadowed corners of the gym staring intently at the pair while they talked.

"It's not my fault! Really!" whispered David hurriedly before Rie could walk off. "Kou went off and did the bonding on his own. You know I don't know how this stuff works. I hate her anyway."

"Whatever. I'll still play badminton with you and help, I mean we are still friends, but I can't be around her," Rie said with sad eyes. Leaving David alone, she walked off towards the other girls on the team.

'I don't get it. Natsuki is much nicer. Why are you so worried about Rie?'

Shaking his head, David walked over to where the boys were warming up, mentally replying to Kou along the way.

'Just help me win. I definitely don't need to lose anything else today.'

Reaching the group David fell into the rhythm of stretches by habit, ignoring the other boys around him.

'I'm still too clumsy with your body. You'll have to do that on your own. At least you're not as flabby as you used to be.'

'Thanks, you can just keep out of my memories.'

"Don't worry, she will come around. She's giving me the silent treatment too, though I wish she'd stay away from Chul Moo. The rumors are already bad enough," Takumi said from beside him.

'Look who's talking. All you can do is cute people to death,' David thought, still focusing on Kou instead of Takumi. Takumi leaned closer to David, jabbing him in the ribs with an elbow to get his attention.

"You really need to work on the 'paying attention to the real world' thing while talking to Kou. I've been talking to you for the last five minutes. Did you hear anything I said?" he asked, realizing David had been zoning out.

David's only reply was a "Huh?" before Tsukasa stepped in and began handing out assignments. Luckily, he paired David and Takumi together.

"Sorry, it's just so hard to concentrate on everything around me when I'm talking to him," David said, taking the opportunity to apologize as they walked to their court. "So who are we playing against?"

"You know, now that you've told me that, Grandpa is going to make you practice concentrating on multiple things during your evening practices. We are playing Natsuki and Mizuki," Takumi said with a grin. Groaning at both the pairing and the extra work he just loaded on himself, David took his spot on the right side of the court, waiting for Natsuki and Mizuki to show.

"Let's just hit them all to David, we're sure to win then," Mizuki said, more than willing to start their usual mental assault in her groups' usual overly-loud-listen-to-me voice.

"Maybe," said an uncharacteristically subdued Natsuki. Her lack luster reply surprised David as much as Mizuki, who looked almost affronted.

Despite several misses by David, Takumi was more than a match for both the girls at badminton, leaving the score relatively balanced. With Natsuki's team ahead on the last point, Mizuki lobbed a high shot towards David's side, a shot he missed several times already. His eyes turning orange, David leapt back, then vertically up, for him an astonishing move that placed the shuttle in a perfect smash position. The power from weeks of the Matsumotos' training matched with the perfect positioning of the hit sent the shuttle hurtling back towards the other side.

Natsuki, caught off guard by the change in David, froze. The shuttle sailed past her head, hitting Mizuki full in the face.

"Ouch! Natsuki! Jeeze, pay attention, you just let them tie!" Mizuki yelled. Despite the laugh that he could not help but let out, David thought the class representative was a bit overly annoyed for just a single miss.

With Takumi serving and both of the girls off balance, he quickly scored the last two points needed to end the game in their favor. Yelling at each other, Mizuki and Natsuki stalked off towards Tsukasa to tell him the score, but not before Natsuki turned and gave David an angry glare.

"*I think she is mad at us,*" Kou said aloud.

"Yeah, I think so." Takumi watched as Natsuki walked away. Turning, he saw David's orange eyes staring after Natsuki. "Hey. Not at school! I guess you mean you and Kou. Don't worry. Natsuki patented that glare when we were kids."

"Who's worried?" David asked, asserting control once again. His eyes their usual blue, David smiled. With a laugh, he walked over to Tsukasa to find out about their next game.

Back at the Estate, David learned that in deference to Natsuki, Rie would no longer train with him in the mornings. Instead, she would practice with Grandpa. Although David tried to talk to Rie at school and the Estate, she constantly found ways to be where he was not, no matter where he looked. Eventually, he stopped trying.

Even though they did not spar, David's practices with Natsuki resulted in a slew of new bruises, which fortunately healed before he got to class. David's evenings were filled working with Grandpa to merge his and Kou's understanding of their two forms. He was relieved that it was just as difficult for Kou to adapt to his human form as it was for him to get used to being a tiger. Unfortunately, Grandpa had plenty of exhausting exercises ready for them each night. Changing into Kou turned out to be no easier than summoning the Seikaku. It took so much concentration that both David and Kou ended up with a few mixed parts most times they changed.

"It should be natural," Grandpa said. "Work together, don't think about changing, just do it."

Kou growled in frustration, but together they redoubled their efforts. All the while Natsuki and Takumi looked on in amusement as they struggled through Grandpa's exercises.

"Funny is it?" Grandpa said with an evil gleam in his eye that immediately made Takumi frown. "I've got plans for you two."

十七
RIFTS

June,

*We soon learned that we did not have to put all our thoughts
into words. We simply understood each other. It helped that
I had been able to listen in on his dreams. Unfortunately, my
more animal tendencies often got in the way, and some things
were still foreign to both of us...*

Even as the summer days grew longer, it seemed Tsukasa-sensei had ever more for them to do at badminton practice. When David and Takumi left the gym to head home after another grueling practice, it was already darkening. As usual, Rie disappeared with Chul Moo before the boys had finished changing. Left alone, David and Takumi took to the deserted farm roads through Nakano town.

"You really should give Natsuki a chance. She's not all that bad once you get to know her," Takumi said as they walked. Natsuki and her friends had a new tactic. Whenever David was around, they made a point of chatting happily with Takumi, while completely ignoring David. Even Shou and Naoto had commented on the palpable tension between them. "With Natsuki back on the Estate, I'd prefer not to have to play peacemaker every day."

"Hey it's not my fault. She's the one who's always yelling at me," David replied. His first memories of Natsuki had yet to fade. As far as David was concerned, Natsuki could just stay with her pack of friends.

"*I think Takumi is right. She is a hunt mate, it is never good to have someone so close, be so angry,*" Kou added.

'You're not helping,' David thought, letting his annoyance at both Takumi and Kou for bugging him about Natsuki wash through him.

"I hear Kaeda has been egging on Koji," David said. "Like Natsuki didn't put her up to it. I should show him what a chunk of metal through his foot feels like."

"I'm pretty sure Kaeda would be happy to see you get beat up again without any encouragement," Takumi said carefully. "Koji-sempai and his goons are a problem, but you know we can't reveal what you've learned. If you suddenly beat him up then you'll blow your cover. Let Rie and I think of some way to deal with them."

David gave his host brother a long stare, and then dived into a row of high plants. After a few minutes of struggling about the sugarcanes, the cute puffy haired Kou came prancing out of the tall stalks.

"*Do you mind grabbing David's clothes? We might need them later.*" Kou looked up at Takumi, batting his big tiger-eyes.

"Hey you shouldn't be running around as a tiger! Someone might see!" Takumi said, quickly checking to ensure no one was nearby.

"*We need to practice. Besides, I am tired of walking around on two legs all the time. It is dark and we will be to the trees soon anyway,*" Kou said using his head in place of arms to gesture to the lonely sugarcane fields to either side. Not a soul was in sight along the deserted dusty road.

When they got to the main road, Takumi quickly dashed across. Feeding on David's sense of humor, Kou pranced slowly across. Takumi scowled down at him as they entered the trees.

Kou gave Takumi a glimpse of his fangs and a snarl in return, and then took to the tree branches to head home.

Kou heard Natsuki coming long before Takumi. Lacking Kou's animalistic senses, Takumi fell into his fighting stance minutes after Kou had first heard her approach. Suddenly dropping into a protective stance, Takumi circled looking for the intruder.

"Oh stop," Natsuki said as she stepped from a stand of trees. "Like you'd be able to stop me if I wanted to get to you. "This is *really* unfair. After this week there's no *way* I should have anything to do with the possessed gaijin. But no. He transforms and poof, here I am."

Kou jumped out of a nearby tree to land in front of Natsuki. Still all kitten, his overly large eyes peered at Natsuki past his short multi-hued fur. Kou's short ears and snout made him look all the cuter given his big paws.

"Well we have to practice sometime, correct? Plus is it not more convenient to feel the pull when we should be heading for evening training anyway, rather than say, in the middle of a bath?" As if to accentuate his point, Kou licked his paw and started brushing it through the puff of fur on the top of his head. All the while his tail flicked excitedly behind him. When this did not get Natsuki to change her reaction, Kou sat back on his hind legs, giving an unmistakable smile and batting his eyes again. It was such a human gesture from an animal that both Natsuki and Takumi burst out laughing.

"Ugh! I can't even stay mad at you. Why can't you just stay a tiger all the time," Natsuki asked, ignoring the fact that David was still inside, listening to every word.

"Whether you like it or not, we are one," Kou said.

"Well at least Rie won't be bothering us. She can have Chul Moo," Natsuki said. David thought he heard a hint of disappointment in her voice.

'I wonder if it's for Rie or Chul Moo,' David thought.

As the Estate came into view, David sank back into his own mind, letting Kou take over. Reveling in the freedom, Kou climbed a tree and jumped from branch to branch while Takumi and Natsuki talked softly below him.

Once on the Estate, Natsuki headed for the Matsumoto workshop, while Takumi and Kou headed to their rooms to drop off their bags before evening practice. In his room, David struggled back into their human form and donned some clothes before following after Natsuki. The workshop was the third building on the perimeter of the central Japanese garden. Lower than the dojo, its air of antiquity contrasted sharply with the more elegant main house and stylized dojo.

In the dim glow cast by a small fire in the corner, David and Natsuki stood apart. Grandpa, Masao, Yukiko, and Takumi surrounded them along the perimeter. More than anywhere else on the estate, the Matsumoto's blend of modern technology and ancient traditions showed most clearly in that single space.

Takumi watched from near the coals, merely an observer. As one of the heirs to the Matsumoto legacy, it was his responsibility to prepare himself to teach his own children so that future Jitsugen Samurai would also have mentors.

"You two will have to overcome this animosity if you are going to work together. Look, you stand apart as if you might infect one another," Grandpa said, beginning the evening's training by commenting on David and Natsuki's positions in the building.

Looking to the other simultaneously, both David and Natsuki turned quickly away again, crossing their arms. From the corner, Takumi let out a loud laugh.

"See? You two are more alike than you think," Takumi said, suddenly frowning at his own words.

"And *you* are not helping. Just sit there and pay attention. This is important, all the more so since your sister is not here,"

Masao said, staring down Takumi. Finally looking away, Takumi bowed his head and remained quiet. After ensuring Masao was done with Takumi, Grandpa turned to David and Natsuki.

"Now… Try again. You are better at holding the honshitsu, which means we can start forging soon. Unfortunately, you still do not seem able to transform and hold the metal so that Natsuki can take it. If she is going to fight alongside you, you are going to have to trust her," he said firmly, trying to coax the two past their animosity.

"How can I trust her? She's been nothing but horrible to me since I got here. It's not my fault I make her look bad at badminton," David said, frustrated at having to work with Natsuki. He had never understood why she had treated him so meanly when he first arrived. He had yet to forgive her.

"Oh you are *so* conceited. It's all about you, isn't it?" Natsuki said. Her reply had enough venom to make Grandpa raise his eyebrows.

The elder Matsumotos stood waiting expectantly, but did not interfere in the exchange. After a few seconds, in which both David and Natsuki traded devastating stares, David turned away.

"Fine. Here we go." David closed his eyes, and his hands rose from his sides. The metal appeared in front of him, like a star appearing in the darkest night sky. David deftly caught it, smiling. His evening training with Grandpa had given him the ability to summon the metal at will, without having to rely on someone surprising him. It still took massive amounts of concentration to hold it, but at least he was improving.

"Good," Grandpa said. "Now keep your focus on the metal while Kou transforms. It is the opposite of the work we have been doing lately, getting you and Kou to work together more seamlessly. Instead of both of you trying to do the same things together, here you must separate your actions. David you will concentrate on the metal and nothing else, leave your body to Kou."

"Remember, act. Do not over think things or you will make a mistake," Masao added.

"Natsuki, you must be ready to take up the metal if it stays during the transformation. Move closer," Grandpa said with his usual good humor, completely ignoring the social war going on between the two teenagers.

With reluctant steps, Natsuki moved slightly closer to David. Taking slow deep breaths, David readied himself. Retreating into his own mind, he concentrated on the metal to the exclusion of all else. His eyes changed to orange as Kou took over his body. Kou gave a slight nod before David disappeared, his clothes in a heap around him. David fought the slew of new senses. He was slowly getting used to the alien input, but he had to fight to keep his attention on the metal. It hung in the air for a split second before it fell to the ground, and disappeared.

"What was that? I actually did it this time and the princess is daydreaming!" David shouted. Kou's eyes turned blue as Kou's face attempted to match David's outrage. Takumi stifled a laugh that prompted another glare from his father. Kou had David's ears stuck on top of his head.

David and Natsuki's voices overlapped into a loud squabble as an adolescent tiger and teenage girl faced off yelling at each other. David used Kou's body to jump awkwardly up onto an anvil, bringing him eye to eye with Natsuki. Tackling Kou and wrapping him in a blanket, Takumi had them outside before David could exert full control and transform. Once outside, David walked behind the forge to sulk until Takumi could bring his clothes.

"You missed the metal a lot before you could finally catch it regularly," Takumi said while tossing David his clothes

"She gets me for every mistake. It's nice to get a shot in occasionally," David said, as he struggled with his pants. It took him a second to realize his foot was still a paw.

"You don't know her like I do. None of this is easy. Try and cut her some slack… She hasn't had the easiest life," Takumi said hesitantly.

'Does he really like Natsuki?' David thought.

'*Why else would he be afraid of her spending time with us?*' David shuddered, unwilling to continue the conversation.

"Fine, I'll go back and we can try it again," David said.

"She's gone. I doubt she will show tomorrow morning either."

"*So much for apologizing,*" Kou growled.

"Let her cool off. She'll be back. Anyway, Grandpa and Dad are waiting for you with some exercises." Takumi smiled. David suspected he was happy that at least *he* did not have to do the exercises. David got up and followed Takumi back around to the front of the workshop.

十八
SECRETS AND SUCCESS

June,

Natsuki was the greatest point of contention between us, really the only point. Kitten that I was I could not bring myself to dislike her. There was something good about her in there somewhere, even if she refused to show it. And with the constant itch, that feeling something was coming, I knew we would need all the allies we could get...

Just as he was losing his connection to Jessica, David saw less and less of Rie as the days went by. She refused to leave her room when Natsuki was on the Estate. At school, Chul Moo constantly accompanied her, to the point that most people had decided they were dating. Chul Moo's angry scowls, always ready for him, were so disturbing that David avoided them both.

The situation was most apparent when they worked in the school gardens. Their science teacher, Mrs. Minaku, seemed to take perverse pleasure in placing David in the most uncomfortable groups. Whenever they were working in the gardens, he was put with Rie, Chul Moo, Mizuki, and Tsubasa. While he did not mind Tsubasa, Chul Moo spent the entire time staring at David as if trying to decide whether to eat him or simply kill him. David got the impression that he restrained himself only because Rie was there and that he would be too foul a meal.

Tsubasa spent the whole time talking about ways to make their job easier, to the point he did little real work. As class representative, Mizuki just straight refused to get her hands dirty. That left most of the actual work to him. Luckily, his father's experiments had taught him quite a bit about gardening.

After one particularly long day of weeding, David sought out Takumi in his room. He knocked lightly on the sliding door that separated Takumi's room from the rest of the house.

"Hey David, what's up?" Takumi asked, his voice barely muffled by the thick sliding doors. Entering, David gazed around the room, trying to take in all the details in one glance. Grandpa had assigned the observational practice after noticing David tended to concentrate on details instead of the whole picture. Despite his attempt, he only registered Takumi's desk in the corner and an empty sword stand in the *tokonoma,* the alcove in most Japanese rooms set aside for an artistic scroll or shrine.

'*You missed the spider web in the corner, the closet, and some kind of marking in the post,*' Kou thought smugly within David's head.

"I was wondering about Rie. I've tried to talk to her a few times, but she's always locked away in her room, and at school Chul Moo is always around," David said, brushing aside Kou's thoughts. Takumi took the opportunity to unfold his legs and turn to David.

"Really? She's the same as always. Rie's not training with us anymore because she is practicing with Grandpa. I think she has also been in the workshop a lot lately. As for school, if I had to guess, I'd say she's trying to break Chul Moo out of his isolation. He's always been a drag on our class's reputation. I bet the student council asked her to do something about him. I saw her head out to the mountains last weekend too. It's a great way to let off steam."

Surprised, David left to talk things out with Kou. Running through the Matsumoto forest at night in their animal form was quickly becoming their favorite activity. The elders were fine with Kou being active at night, but only as long as they knew when he left and came back. It gave David and Kou a unique chance to learn more about each other.

David's adjustment to the training schedule finally gave him a reprieve from the constant pain and soreness that had been his companion for weeks. Their time spent as Kou revived David, as if his physical body was resting while he was a tiger. Kou too, was full of energy every time he emerged. The longer they stayed in one form, the more rested they felt once changed back. Dodging around trees in the thick forest David pulled himself away from the immersive tiger sensations in order to talk to Kou.

'Even though you chose Natsuki, Rie helped me so much when I first got here,' he thought.

Simply thinking about his first few days in Japan allowed Kou to understand his point. The memories rushed through them, full with his emotions, even as Kou clawed by the Estate's trees.

The times Rie helped him, such as with his shoes and his first meal, played for Kou with perfect clarity. He showed Kou how Rie was the one who had taught him how to hold his soup and rice, so as not to appear completely uncivilized. Their first day at school, she introduced him to students, including all her friends. Without her, he never would have been asked to join the badminton team. The memories and more flooded through his mind as Kou took to the tree branches.

'It just seems like maybe I've lost something. Rie is never around anymore, and without her or Jessica... Anyway, training just isn't as fun without her there. I mean anyone could tell you I hate...'

Kou came to a jarring stop on a large tree branch. Cocking his head, he lifted an eyebrow. It was a gesture he had picked up from David, and he used it emphasize the question in his own mind.

'OK, well we don't *like* each other. Anyway will you help me figure this out?'

Satisfied with David's retraction, Kou continued bounding from tree to tree, his tail stretching out behind him.

That's not really something that was included in, how did Takumi put it? My ancient wisdom. We better get going before we wake Natsuki up.'

Kou ran along the next branch, and then digging in with his claws, ran down the trunk. Turning towards the main house, David let Kou run on. He was left with too many unanswered questions to focus on dodging bushes and trees.

Over the next few weeks, David continued his morning practices, strengthening his body and expanding his knowledge of the Matsumotos' kendo. Natsuki returned after a brief period of pouting. Kou promised they would keep their night runs short and late enough that Natsuki would be able to sleep. While she was asleep, she was able to resist the pull, though she was still plagued by strange dreams that would wake her if David stayed as a tiger for too long. It was an imperfect compromise, but in return, Natsuki promised she would try not to provoke David anymore.

David was forced, albeit reluctantly, to admit that he really did no longer hate Natsuki. After her agreement not to provoke him, she became almost civilized. It was so surprising that it took David a few days to learn how to speak to her without confrontation.

David and Kou spent their mornings training in the dojo, the hot summer days at school, evenings training their mind, and nights running through the forest. Life was far from perfect. He still had much to learn about Japan's social niceties, and Koji was still a constant source of both fear and annoyance.

To make matters worse, while the Matsumoto elders were fine with Kou running through the Matsumoto forests during the evening, they locked the house down at night, meaning they had to get permission first, before they could leave. Kou and David had decided that they would like at least some time to themselves, a few hours where the Matsumoto would not be able to keep an eye on them.

It took David a week to learn how to sneak out of the main house. Grandpa, Masao, and Yukiko were all on alert late into the night, making his first few attempts a disaster. David passed the first few botched escapes off as a combination of sleepwalking, Kou taking control, and nighttime hunger. David was unable to escape the Matsumotos' watchful eyes until he found a loose floorboard under the tatami mats in his room. Pulling up the tatami, he was able to crawl out under the house.

His freedom secured, David and Kou delighted in exploring the extent of the Matsumoto Estate late into the morning. The longer they stayed in tiger form, the more David enjoyed it. After what seemed like ages to Kou, David gave in and let Kou hunt. Though it was disgusting at first, immersed in the tiger he could not help but feel the excitement as they crept among the trees and undergrowth. It was quite by accident that they found if Kou ate, David would be full and vice versa.

'Good to know we will not starve if we get stuck in one form or another for too long.'

'Still, do you *always* have to play with your food?'

'I'm a kitten, get over it.'

'If I have to deal with rat tails the least you could do is help me with Rie.'

'Why not just go talk to her. Takumi said she's been in the workshop a lot lately, didn't he?'

David had to wait until later in the week to visit Rie. He finally found her bent over a box in a corner of the workshop. Since she did not seem to notice him, David decided to try some of the techniques for being stealthy she had taught him in the forest.

As his finger reached out to tap her shoulder, Rie spun. David suddenly had a long metal poker at his neck.

"What," she said, her lips tight in annoyance. David frowned. He had hoped she'd appreciate the joke.

"Well I thought I'd come see what you're working on. We don't get to talk much anymore."

Rie frowned, and then just as suddenly as it had appeared, the frown was gone and Rie's face seemed to radiate like the sun appearing over the dusty desert mountains.

"You know, you're right. Can you keep a secret?" she asked.

By the end of the next Friday's lessons David just wanted the night to come so he could finally meet with Rie and find out what she was working on. As David stood in the gym, mind on the Matsumoto workshop, he completely missed the conversations and stares directed at him.

The last month of training had left him nearly as thin and toned as Takumi. He had also grown. David was taller than any of his classmates. He had the legs of a runner and arms of a swordsman. The changes had been so gradual that he had not noticed, but he was as fit as any of the boys in his class. He would have passed for one if not for the blond hair, cut in a popular Japanese style, and his blue eyes. His hair was the envy of most of the boys while the girls secretly hated him for having such a light skin tone without having to use whitener.

Aside from the physical changes, David's Japanese ability and helpful attitude toward his classmates was quickly changing his social life. Chul Soon, who was fast becoming a close friend, was so outgoing that he continuously brought new people to meet David.

David's relaxed attitude, borne from the Matsumotos' training, his success in class, and more recently in sports gave David a confident air that drew people to him. His unassuming speech, and obvious struggle to adapt to Japanese customs, kept them there. When he made mistakes, most people overlooked them because of his vast improvement, and his willingness to learn. Only Koji and Natsuki's friends still gave him a hard time.

'You know, I've noticed Koji hasn't been laughing at me lately,' David thought. 'Every time he spotted me he'd been sure to point me out and laugh, and his friends would follow along. Now he just glares like he wants another go… and his friends almost seem like they're trying to distract him.'

'*You need to be careful,*' Kou replied internally as David maintained a conversation with a group of boys, a hard-earned skill from his evening training with Grandpa. '*He is a dangerous one. A predator who hunts for fun, not survival. All the same, he is only a boy. We cannot reveal what we know, no matter the provocation.*'

'Says the god tiger who tries to get me to go running after every small animal he sees.'

'*Looks like Natsuki and her friends are fighting. She is definitely standing apart from them.*'

'What are you talking about? They're right there together. Hey, don't change the subject.'

'*Sure they are in their regular group but look how Mizuki and Kaeda are whispering together, with Natsuki off to the side just a little. It is as if she is the injured animal that is left to creatures like us. In Japan, it is never good to be outside the group.*'

'So what? They finally figured out she's no fun to be around?'

'*Oh you know that is not true. You two have been almost cordial lately.*'

'Hmm I doubt that. Anyway,'

'*Tsukasa is coming.*'

'We better get rid of these guys.'

"Yeah you're right that game is great, oh looks like Tsukasa-sensei is here, talk to you later," David said aloud, disengaging himself from the other boys. Tsukasa called the team to attention, waiting while they gathered around him.

"OK you all know about the summer badminton competition coming up that we have been practicing for, right?" asked Tsukasa. "This time there will be both mixed and regular doubles teams, as well as singles. The regular doubles will stay the same. If you're not on one of the competition teams come talk to me and find out who your partner is. From now on you will practice with your competition partner."

With a babble of conversation, the students filed away to find their partners or get new assignments. David weaved his way through the crowd easily, he was amazed at how training could make moving so much easier.

"David, you are still pretty new so you will be in a mixed pair team, rather than singles," Tsukasa said while checking his list. "Natsuki, you've been slipping lately so I'm putting you two together. You should balance each other out nicely. You did well together last time."

Instead of her usual indignation, Natsuki slumped in defeat. David was just able to catch a mysterious look pass between Mizuki and Kaeda before they turned and walked away, leaving Natsuki alone.

'Great! Now we get to practice with Natsuki here and at home!' Kou thought. David did not bother with a reply. Kou knew how he felt.

"As if it things weren't bad enough already. My friends are already getting upset with me for 'spending every waking moment at Takumi's with that gaijin.' Now I have to deal with you here?" Natsuki said as they walked toward a court, a bit of her fire returning in David's presence.

"It's not like it was *my* idea, though Kou seems pleased," David whispered, trying not to provoke her at school.

"Of course he would be!" replied Natsuki harshly. "We better win this thing or I'm going to take that chunk of metal you've been practicing with and bash one of you over the head with it. Be it Kou or David!"

David and Natsuki began warming up with two other mixed-team students. Frustrated, Natsuki hit the shuttle with so much force that the strings on her racket broke.

"Will nothing go right?" As she ran off the court to get a spare racket, David almost thought he heard her muffle a sob.

By the end of practice, even David was starting to feel bad for her. Natsuki seemed depressed and when she left, it was without her usual escort of Mizuki and Kaeda. Despite his plans to help Rie later that evening, David decided to follow her home.

'After all, we are essentially neighbors,' he thought.

十九

GHOST IN THE SYSTEM

July,

Even with the persistent feeling of danger, that which had prompted... us to follow the Matsumoto summons, I never realized how close the danger was, and how unprepared we would be...

Although Natsuki lived just past the Matsumoto Estate, she always walked home with Mizuki and Kaeda. Since they lived in the same direction, but in a different part of Nakano Town, Natsuki always took a roundabout way home. David kept his distance as he surreptitiously followed her down the unfamiliar route.

"Stupid Tsukasa, making me work with *him*," Natsuki muttered, alone on the dusty road. "Oh, look at me, I'm so cute, I don't have to work for anything. Jeeze, why isn't Takumi the Jitsugen Samurai? And *what* is with Mizuki and Kaeda thinking we are dating, ugh! Like that would ever happen."

If she had known David was in the shadows behind her, she no doubt would have turned as red as he did hearing her mutterings. He almost turned aside, but doing so would have made his route even longer. As the road straightened, David had to slow to keep from giving himself away, letting Natsuki almost fade out of view and hearing.

Halfway home, she must have realized she was taking the long way. David caught her stop and look around. She was in an odd part of town, where a park and an old section of forest cut into developed buildings and farms. He backed off as her gaze swept towards him.

After waiting a few minutes, David crept around the tree he had hidden behind, and then followed the road as it curved around the forest. David was surprised when he could not see Natsuki ahead on the relatively straight road that followed along after the curve. It took him a few minutes and some advice from Kou to find Natsuki's tracks off the road.

By the time David caught sight of her again, she was far along an old forgotten path. The forest was close and dim, only her white uniform shirt kept her in view in the darkness. David quietly cursed as Natsuki easily navigated among the ancient roots, hanging limbs and bits of old crumbling ruins, while he stumbled along.

'I can't believe I'm stuck inside such a completely ungraceful being,' Kou complained. 'Let me take over before you scare everything away.'

David ignored Kou, passing the edge of a particularly large mass of old stones. Farther in, Natsuki shivered and wrapped her arms around herself. David frowned. The close humid air beneath the forest canopy was warm, yet Natsuki looked as if she had just walked into a cold, frosty winter morning. David dashed behind a group of high ferns as she checked the area again.

Off the path, the ruins suddenly formed into a recognizable pattern. Natsuki had walked right into the foundations of an ancient castle. Long forgotten, the forest had completely reclaimed the old burnt out battlements. The hills on each side of her were all that remained of a massive gate, now covered in dirt and plant growth. Shivering again, she continued forward more quickly, as if eager to escape the cold and dark towering trees around her. David followed.

Before Natsuki could find her way out of the moss-covered gully of crumbling rock she stopped again. This time she huddled down into a crouch. She wrapped her arms around her bare legs and shivering so badly that David could easily see her shake from outside the castle. Ahead, a young girl with wild hair and old tattered clothing seeped out of a nearby stone. The apparition glowed dimly in the deepening night, her face vicious with curving lips and straight eyes. The *obake* raised one of its hands, revealing long waving fingers. The tendrils moved as if they were fluttering on a breeze.

Natsuki froze in the chill windless night. David's walk turned into a run. He knew the thing in front of Natsuki was an obake, a soul separated from its human body, but one that had not passed on. The thing was straight out of the Japanese legends he had found in the school library.

The obake smiled, making its feral visage that much more horrifying. Its arms outstretched, elongated fingers groped in the night, searching out Natsuki. Closing on her, the obake swelled with the anticipation of a kill and the nourishment her soul would provide. Natsuki's knees buckled as the oppressive weight of the obake's will crushed her to the ground.

The obake's advancing figure was nearly indistinguishable from the air around it, yet David could see a savage hunger on its translucent face. Natsuki simply curled into as small a ball as she could as the obake held her in a stare of unbending will.

David was still too far away. The obake was so close to Natsuki that the very air around her seemed to freeze in place. Frost littered the ground as the very air was turned to fog.

'Let's go,' David thought. Kou caught his meaning immediately. David thought 'tiger,' but was out of synch with Kou. David convulsed but did not transform. Trying to settle his racing heart, David tried again. The obake's ghastly hands reached Natsuki and stroked her, passing through her skull with each sweep. The horror of it rocked through him like a sympathetic wave.

Kou's claws sank into the air, yet they did not fall onto Natsuki. Instead, they were suddenly flung about as the obake screamed with a sound that threatened to sever their very soul. Kou, grown to the size of a small dog and full of muscle, struggled to pin the obake as it staggered away from Natsuki. Despite the obake's lack of substance, as a Kami, Kou was still able to knock it around with his large paws. The obake's translucent lips snarled, and she threw him off.

With the obake distracted, Natsuki was released from its deadly hold. Moaning from the nightmarish images that had flitted through her mind while dominated by the spirit, Natsuki heaved, her body reacting to the mental abuse.

"*Natsuki, are you all right?*" Kou called to Natsuki while struggling with the obake. Seeing the fear in her eyes, like a mouse about to bolt, he spoke quickly. "*Do not leave. I am going to need your help. This is an obake. Do you remember what Yukiko said about them?*" Natsuki heaved again. Shuddering, she rolled away from the steaming puddle.

Kou and the obake grappled amongst the high ferns, sending crickets and small animals running from the disturbance. They fought against the obake's powerful attacks. Using speed and agility to combat the apparition's vicious attempts to free itself, Kou became a blur of orange and black fur. Natsuki, her stomach finally empty, stood slowly.

"You have to wield the honshitsu!" David called to Natsuki as Kou concentrated on the obake. She looked as if all she wanted was to flee. "We can't do it alone. I can only keep it occupied."

Steeling herself, Natsuki took a tentative step towards the fight, then with more confidence moved forward quickly. Kou swung at the obake. Connecting with its head, it sickeningly doubled over the wrong way.

"Here! Here! I'm here!" Natsuki waved her arms at the obake, throwing a fearful look at Kou as he disappeared behind a tree. The obake righted itself with a jerk, and immediately tried to attack Natsuki. From behind the tree, David sent his metal shard, the honshitsu, flying. Following close behind the metal, David changed back into Kou as they emerged from behind the tree. Aside from their first time, it was the smoothest transformation they had yet managed. Natsuki caught the metal just as the obake closed to attack her. Seeing the honshitsu, the obake stopped just short, confusion then fear rippling across its distorted features as Kou tackled it.

"Now! Natsuki, do it now!" David said, his muffled voice struggling to make its way out of Kou's mouth. The little tiger had its fangs sunk securely into the obake's neck, yet David still managed to spur her into action. Natsuki raised the heavy metal shard over her head. Kou swung aside, keeping his jaws locked on the neck while Natsuki brought a sharp point of the honshitsu down into the center of the obake.

Shock crossed the obake's deadened eyes as they rolled down to take in the metal protruding out of it. Then, with a suddenly contented expression, the cold night air faded even as the obake disappeared. Kou's whiskers twitched as a ripple ran through his fur to the tip of his tail.

Natsuki collapsed. Kou, drawn by her distress, brushed up against her as she shook with an adrenaline release. When she had settled a bit, Kou turned and ran back into the forest. A few seconds later, David emerged buttoning his uniform shirt. Natsuki sat curled into a little ball, sobbing and alone in the dirt.

"Natsuki-san?" David asked, gingerly stepping around her lunch. With no response, David frowned. Unsure of what to do he knelt next to her.

'Try to comfort her. It must have been very traumatic. Yukiko said obake can call all kinds of images to their victims' minds before they kill them,' Kou said in his mind. *'We felt only the barest edge of what she experienced.'*

David hesitantly stretched his hand out to pat her shoulder, but Natsuki looked up, her eyes red.

"You were following me? I didn't feel Kou," Natsuki said, her face inscrutable.

"Umm, Kou was worried about you, and uh, I needed to practice tracking so..." David waved his arms vaguely, trying to come up with a decent excuse.

"It is a good thing we did too. Without you, all we would have been able to do is beat it up a bit, maybe scare it off. And if the obake had you on its own, well, they might find your body... eventually," Kou said. David reached forward, helping Natsuki up off the ground.

"My sword skills probably aren't good enough on their own, especially wielding a big chunk of metal. Plus I might have been just as vulnerable to the obake's aura as you." David was confused by Natsuki's expression and uncharacteristic silence. Just as he was beginning to fear she had been injured, she breathed deeply, steeling herself.

"I guess I'll just have to kick your butt harder in training then," she said. "That way I won't have to do your dirty work." Natsuki's sudden bravado never made it to her eyes. Kou caught the fear and subsequent relief that raged within her. She abruptly turned away. Kou kept his observations to himself, letting David stay confused for Natsuki's sake.

"You're welcome, PRINCESS!" David shouted, annoyed she refused to thank him, even after saving her life. Natsuki jerked to a stop.

"S-Stop calling me princess!" she stuttered. Without looking back, Natsuki left David in the ruin's shadows.

When David got home, his plans to help Rie were put on hold while he explained what happened to Masao and Grandpa. He met them in the dojo and they both insisted he tell them everything in detail after finding Takumi to listen in.

"So you have dispatched your first obake, excellent. Just remember, not all of them are evil. The one that attacked you was probably an evil spirit, but others may be more helpful. I think the time has come for our Jitsugen Samurai to have a Seikaku," Grandpa said. Although usually leaving most daily decisions to Masao, Grandpa's suggestions still carried the weight of command.

"Yes. David, you are now strong enough to hold the metal long enough for us to shape it. Although Natsuki is your Partner, she may not always be there, and if you meet another evil obake, you will not be able to dispatch it with Kou alone. You are probably tired. Get a good night sleep, and tomorrow, we will begin forging your Seikaku. It will be a difficult and long process. Prepare yourself."

'I guess we'll have to ditch Rie,' David thought as they headed to bed.

'It cannot be helped. She did say it was just for her to practice after all. There is always next weekend.'

ニ十

TRUE SWORD

July,

David and I were both looking forward to forging a Seikaku. After the incident with the obake, neither of us was comfortable being so unprepared for the dangers ahead. David was especially eager for a way to protect himself that did not rely on Natsuki...

The next morning David woke on his own with the early Saturday sun shining through the small window in his room. Surprised, David dressed and went in search of the Matsumotos. He found them sitting around the breakfast table drinking tea. Rie eyed him darkly.

"Oh good, we were just about to have breakfast," Yukiko said as she rose and headed for the kitchen. David smiled widely, grateful for the breakfasts Yukiko made every morning. He was also happy that since he began letting Kou hunt, his other half no longer influenced his food choices while human, though he could not always escape Kou's disparaging comments. Looking around the table, David's gaze eventually fell back on Rie.

She looked as she had for the last few weeks, more subdued and calm than she had been, less interested in her old competitions with Takumi. David realized she had become almost quiet, fading into the background of everyone's notice. When she caught him looking at her, however, her eyes blazed. He had let her down. She had been depending on him and he had not showed. He hoped she would give him a chance to explain himself, but knew it would be tricky since he had been with Natsuki.

"David, how do you feel? Are you ready? Everything is prepared for after breakfast," Grandpa said, his sudden and causal questions, pulled David away from his musings about Rie.

"Grandpa is a bit excited," Masao said. "He, we have waited our whole lives for this day. We are both expert sword makers, but today… Today is special." Even Masao was unable to subdue his excitement. Always the serious one, David caught a glimpse of a much different man.

Yukiko returned with a light breakfast for everyone. They ate and talked easily, though Rie seemed uninterested in the conversation. By unspoken agreement, no one lingered after they finished. Yukiko hurried to clear the plates, while the rest of the Matsumotos and David headed for the workshop.

"David, Kou, the time has come to finally forge your Seikaku. Although Natsuki is your Partner, this secret is not for her. Takumi and Rie are here as observers. They have not yet completed their own swords, so they will not help in the process," Grandpa said once everyone was settled.

"Takumi, Rie, learn from today so that you may teach your children," Masao added gravely. "This is a singular event for the Matsumotos. It may turn out to be the highlight of our lives. It may also help inspire you when you make your own sword."

Grandpa gestured David over to the smelter, a fixture in the building made of clay and brick designed to draw impurities out of metal.

"Unlike regular metal that must be treated, the honshitsu is pure. We will still need to temper it to varying strengths but this process at least we can skip. No one but your Partner will be able to hold the honshitsu in their hands, however, using our tools we will still be able to manipulate it if you keep it summoned. We will also have to split the metal honshitsu into different parts before folding them back together. This is where your multitasking training will come in hand. You will have to focus on each piece separately to keep them there," Grandpa said as he peered at David, his gaze searching.

"David, Kou, are you ready? We will work as fast as possible, but making a sword cannot be rushed. You must keep the metal summoned throughout the entire process. If either of you fail, we must start over." Masao stepped close to David, appraising him with his deeply intelligent eyes.

"I'm ready," said David, suddenly confident.

"We are ready."

Closing his eyes, his arms raising away from his sides, David summoned the honshitsu. He caught it lightly as it appeared before him. He had struggled for weeks, working to keep the metal whole as Grandpa tried to distract him. Finally, he felt the metal as an extension of himself. Keeping it sustained was no more taxing than holding up his arm.

Grandpa stepped forward as David opened his eyes. Gesturing, he showed David where to place the honshitsu, and then where he could sit so as not to interfere with the two elder Matsumotos.

"Remember, focus on the metal, but also watch what we do. Your intentions will be just as influential as our skills," Grandpa said, reiterating previous discussions during their evening training sessions.

Long hours passed as Masao and Grandpa moved together seamlessly, nearly reading each other's minds as they coaxed the shining metal into a deadly tool. The twins stood off to the side, watching intently. Since they were limited by David's endurance, the two master smiths worked exceedingly fast. Occasionally they called for Takumi to tend the fires and bring ingredients. He kept them burning so hot David could easily feel the heat from where he sat.

David concentrated, his brow dripping, willing the metal to become a sword. Sure enough when the time came to separate the metal by strength, the task became far more difficult. Instead of lifting an arm, it was like balancing on one foot with both arms out in front. The task was not overly difficult in itself, but when held over such a long period it was taxing.

The Matsumoto smiths divided the pieces and then worked them separately before folding them back together to give the sword both strength and flexibility. As they worked, Takumi was tasked with explaining things to David so he would understand, and be able match his intentions to the Matsumotos' actions.

David lost track of the time as heat and fumes and sound flooded through the small low building. His whole world became the blade slowly emerging at the behest of the Matsumotos. Finally, a loud hiss of steam brought him back to the workshop. The Matsumotos stood over a brine bucket as Grandpa removed the finished blade.

David was somewhat surprised to see not the shining new blade of his imagination, but a long hunk of clay. Seeing his expression, Takumi quietly explained.

"The clay allowed the blade to cool at different speeds, leaving the edge stiff and the back more flexible."

"Yes, we are lucky it did not break," Masao said with a dry gasp.

Wearily, Grandpa placed the blade on the anvil, and then knocked the clay off with a small hammer.

"It is finished," Grandpa sighed. "We will still need to polish and grip it of course, but the blade is complete. The first Seikaku in more than a hundred years. David, pick up your destiny."

As Masao and Grandpa backed away, expectation etched in every line of their faces, David moved towards the anvil.

The sword was much longer than David's practice sword and curved slightly on the backside. One end came to an abrupt point, while the other tapered to where a handle would be fixed. Fresh out of the brine and clay it was covered in a crusty black coating like asphalt.

The sword called to David sitting there alone on the anvil. Where the coating cracked, David could just see the glint of metal, reminiscent of the crystalline layers of the metal from which the sword had come. Reaching out, David drew a finger along the blade, dragging off flecks of black.

From where David's finger touched, color erupted along the blade. A rippling textured wood replaced the steel that had been on the anvil a moment before. Jumping back in surprise, David looked to the Matsumotos for answers. He saw their attention remained fixed on the anvil, and his attention was drawn quickly back to the Seikaku.

It had a fine grain and deep color, but otherwise looked exactly like the wooden practice sword he had been using for weeks, though the craftsmanship and quality of the wood easily surpassed what he had created.

"What did I do?" David asked breathlessly.

Drawn in by the hypnotic lines of grain in the sword, David's hand reached forward again. This time picking up the wooden sword, he found it fit his hands perfectly, grooved to match every crease and bump of his hands. As David and the Matsumotos watched, the sword reverted to its unfinished form. This time clean, the bare metal flickered in the firelight. As David looked closer, he saw the faint outlines of wood grain embedded in the metal.

"A Seikaku follows the elemental type of the Jitsugen Samurai's Kami. Kou is a tiger, of the earth. I expected his sword to be either wood or stone," Grandpa whispered, his voice full of reverence. The sword seemed to fill the dark smoky room as he gestured along the length of the blade, careful not to touch it. "The Seikaku has two forms… The first is this. The second is its elemental form."

"What good is a wooden sword though? And how do I make it reappear?" David asked, rubbing his hands along the length of the smooth steel. His hand slipped, sliding across the edge, yet it did not cut him.

"The sword will react to your intentions and need, just as the honshitsu appeared when you needed it," Grandpa said. "In either form it is more than it appears, though once finished it will look fine indeed."

"You need not worry that your new blade is toothless. Go ahead," said Masao, placing a steel bar between the anvil and a table. "Cut it."

David stepped into a fighting stance, holding the sword as he had practiced for weeks. He looked back at Masao uncertainly, sure he was about to jar his arm the same way so many had with the watermelon at the beach. After a nod from both Masao and Grandpa, David swung through the heavy metal bar. Although it seemed unchanged, seconds later, the iron fell clean in two.

"Takumi. Go get the *Book of Swords*," Masao said quietly to his son. Takumi ran off to find the book, while David continued to examine the sword in his hands. Throughout it all, Rie hung back, staying in the shadows.

'You've been pretty quiet this whole time. What do you think?' David asked Kou.

'*Now you have claws too. Maybe next time a mongrel dog shows up I will not have to save us.*'

'I thought it was Natsuki who saved us, not you.'

'*Glad you finally admitted that.*'

"Each Seikaku is as unique as the Kami and Samurai," Masao said, pulling David's attention away from his conversation with Kou. "Each has had its own characteristics, though they tend to follow patterns, which we have recorded over the centuries in the *Book of Swords*."

Running back in, Takumi carried a large modern volume under his arm. Grandpa gestured to a table and together they circled around to examine the tome. Finally letting go the part of his consciousness that had kept the Seikaku summoned, David let it fade back into him.

Sitting, Masao took the book from Takumi. Opening it revealed a collection of ancient to merely old writings describing the Seikakus the Matsumotos had made. The entries included sketches, descriptions, and bits of stories referring to them. While Masao and Grandpa poured over the book, Takumi turned to David.

"That was the most amazing smith work I've ever seen, and I've been watching those two all my life. They've been holding back, and their swords are the *best* in Japan," Takumi said, awe unmistakable in his voice. "I've never seen them move so fast."

David glanced over to the book as the older pair flipped through. From the beginning, it showed vastly different pages, copies and preserved originals of barely legible writing and depictions of swords wildly different from the famous katana. Seeing David's interest Takumi filled him in.

"The first swords in Japan were double edged straight swords," he said. "That would have been the kind that the *Kojiki* says Ninigi used, you know, the Grass Cutter. Over the centuries my family has included every new technique and advancement into the creation of the Seikakus." Takumi spoke proudly of his heritage. Every Japanese sword was a testament to the progress of his ancestors.

"According to this, you do indeed have a *wood* sword," Grandpa said. "A Seikaku will cut most things without dulling, however, if you change it to the *wood* form and if you strike wood, instead of cutting it, you will be able to *affect* it. By affect I mean make it grow, die, explode, things like that. It will follow your will, within limits." Grandpa looked up from the book to watch David's reaction. A smile played across his face as David processed his words.

"The elemental form, for example the *wood* form, will also damage spirits without damaging anything living. Be warned. If you hit a person with the elemental form of the Seikaku it may kill them, banishing their spirit, but leaving their body intact," Masao said gravely, causing David to start, shocked by the deadly power he held within him. "Yes. Like most tools, the Seikaku is dangerous, however, unlike most tools, the sword responds to your *intent*. You must still be careful. This book talks of many accidents before the Matsumotos and the Jitsugen Samurai discovered the Seikaku's powers."

"So you're telling me the Seikaku in metal form will cut just about anything a normal sword will, and then some, and the elemental form will cut spirits and control wood?" asked David, trying to wrap his head around what a Seikaku really was.

"Succinctly put," Grandpa said. "It will allow you to take care of any more obake you come across, as well as... other things. That being said, you will need to practice with the Seikaku, but must avoid injury."

A sudden yawn from Takumi made David realize he had no idea what time it was. Looking at his watch, he was shocked to find it was four in the morning on the fifth of July, Sunday.

"Wow, I didn't realize how late it was," David said, suddenly exhausted.

"Yes, it is time for some food and bed. None of us have eaten or rested since early yesterday morning. We will continue this evening." Masao stood, swaying slightly with fatigue, it was the first time David had ever seen him so much as yawn.

二十一

SWORD PRACTICE

July,

Though I tried not to let it show too much, I was excited by the Seikaku. Despite the freedom and thrill we felt as a tiger, it even made me want to spend more time as a human…

After a nap that felt all too brief, David stood alone in the dojo, the light from the afternoon sun fading over the western trees.

'Do we really need to antagonize her? Today was supposed to be her day off. We could just call her.'

"Masao will be here soon so that he can explain the Seikaku to Natsuki. Why waste such a good opportunity to mess with her a bit?" David asked, closing his eyes.

"*As you wish,*" muttered Kou as David transformed. Perhaps because of their difference in opinions, it took longer than usual to complete the transition. Kou gave a growling laugh as David imagined what her reaction might be when she showed. The young tiger dragged David's clothes over to an out of the way corner.

'Like you don't want to show off a bit, I know you like the Seikaku,' David thought.

'You know, your clothes do not taste very good, you could have done this before we changed.'

'Bet you wish you had opposable thumbs. It's not my fault you forgot to remind me.'

'I'm going to start making you carry around my fur in your mouth.'

'It's already all over my bed. A bit extra in my mouth won't matter. You know, for being a spirit you sure can be messy.'

'It would be horrible if my teeth were to slip and make a hole in an embarrassing spot…'

'You wouldn't…'

After disposing the clothes, Kou trotted back into the center of the room to wait. Lying down with his legs splayed and forepaws tucked beneath him, Kou watched as the bugs flew above the garden outside. He refused to answer David, instead letting a wave of snide satisfaction roll through their minds at David's embarrassment. Only a few minutes later his keen ears picked up Masao coming in from the main house. When he entered, Kou tilted his head. His animalistic pride kept him from getting up and bowing.

"I see Natsuki is on her way… and that you are giving her a hard time again," Masao said, deadpan.

Kou's eyes flickered blue as he grinned, a feat for David since he had to use a tiger's mouth. Kou twitched, his ears pointing towards the entrance as he picked up Takumi's voice. His host brother entered the dojo holding a phone away from his ear. It did not take Kou's advanced hearing to pick up Natsuki's yelling voice.

"Yeah, Natsuki is *not* amused, but she's on her way. Apparently this time you really did catch her in the bath," Takumi said after cutting off the call. Kou let loose a growling laugh that was surprisingly shared by Masao.

Walking in shortly after, Natsuki looked as if she had spent hours getting ready, despite her damp hair. After making quick eye contact with her, Kou turned and trotted back toward David's clothes. They returned to the room as David, clothed in his practice gi.

"What's the big idea?" Natsuki yelled after seeing David re-emerge.

David stopped, closed his eyes, and summoned the newly finished Seikaku. His arms moving with blinding speed, David caught the sword's grip before it could move.

Grandpa had finished polishing and gripping the sword just before. With David watching, and careful not to touch the sword, Grandpa had performed a complicated ritual in order to bind the grip and guard to the Seikaku. David was surprised that the wood form was unaffected, and the sword maintained the additions even after being summoned and released repeatedly. Although he had asked about it, Grandpa had refused to explain the process.

"You are not a smith so it would mean little to you," he had said with a tired look. Seeing David's disappointment, he smiled a little. "I *will* take the time to explain more about the rituals, however, I am tired. It will have to wait."

'Why's it so long,' Natsuki asked, shaking David from thoughts of the ritual.

"It is meant to be grown into," Masao said simply.

"Just how big is he going to get?" she asked with wide eyes.

"Oh well, let's just say most Japanese clothing stores will probably not carry his size," Masao said.

'I already have to get my clothes in the men's section,' David thought as Natsuki's anger melted away. All her focus was on the Seikaku.

"Natsuki-chan's knowledge of swords is far more intimate than the average junior high school girl, I believe," Yukiko said entering with a customary bow and smile. "I am sure she can appreciate the artistry and skill put into the blade."

"Yep, thought you'd like to try it out, now that it's finished. Not to mention Masao-sensei needs to explain some things about it," David said.

Masao explained the dangers and powers of the Seikaku to Natsuki. In addition to what he had told David and Takumi earlier, Masao added a few words applicable to the Jitsugen Samurai's Partner.

"When using the Seikaku, you will not be able to change its forms. The sword will respond only to David's intentions. Thus, you must work closely together so that if you strike, David's intention will make the sword also cut, otherwise it will be little more than a club." Masao gestured to David. Taking his cue, David demonstrated the change between the two forms for Natsuki. While Natsuki took in the elemental form, Masao once again emphasized the dangers.

"Now that Natsuki knows to be careful, we should try having her hold it. You successfully transferred the honshitsu. The Seikaku should actually be easier as it has a more basic and familiar structure for you to focus on," Masao said.

David and Natsuki readied themselves. Takumi backed away, moving to sit on the top of a sword rack to get a clear view. After Natsuki nodded her readiness, David tossed the Seikaku to her, hilt first.

'He's right, it's even easier to keep summoned than the shards were. It's like a perfect copy of the sword is in my mind whenever I want it.'

'It is perfect because I have an indelible memory. Anything I see once I can recall for you, though the definition is better with my eyes than with yours.'

Catching it expertly, Natsuki swung it through a complicated series of moves designed to get the feel of its weight and balance.

"Be careful, it is a bit longer than you are used to. Ok, good, you have it... David, change into Kou. It will be easier for you to concentrate on just the sword that way. You can let Kou take care of your body. Natsuki, go through the Tiger kata, and be careful!" Masao eyed Natsuki warily as he backed away.

As Natsuki began the complicated series of poses comprising the Tiger kata, David changed into Kou. Once again, Kou gathered up David's clothes and began dragging them.

Takumi quickly jumped down and moved them into the corner for him. Kou gave him a fearsome grin. Walking back, Kou laid down, making it easier for David to concentrate. Kou's deep orange eyes followed Natsuki's movements as his tail moved languidly over the floor, it's white furred tip occasionally roaming above them.

Halfway through the kata Natsuki's face furrowed in sudden surprise and pain as the Seikaku flew out of her grip midswing. Kou was instantly on all four paws, claws out, fur and hackles raised and growling. Before it could hit anyone or anything, David recalled the sword. The Seikaku disappeared. Takumi dashed over from the corner as both Masao and Kou moved towards Natsuki.

"It burned me!" Natsuki, looked down at her hands, surprise in every feature of her face.

"Try again, I need to be sure," Masao said staring gravely at her, refusing to reveal even a hint of his thoughts.

"*Of what?*" David and Kou's voices blended as they came out of Kou's throat. Masao stood silently unwilling to answer either the spoken question or Natsuki's look. Takumi peered anxiously between Masao and Natsuki.

'This is pushing the whole master student thing a little far. What if it hurts Natsuki again?' David thought.

'*Was that concern? For Natsuki? You know Masao will not explain anything until he is good and ready.*'

Outwardly, Kou merely rolled his shoulders, and then gathered David's clothes in his jaws and left the dojo again. David came back with only his trousers on.

Walking up to Natsuki, David summoned the Seikaku, flipping it to hand it to Natsuki hilt first. She reached out gingerly, took the sword, and then sighed as it acted normally. David transformed again, Kou backing off a pace where he sat and began licking the fur around his paws. Natsuki merely held the sword. After about the same amount of time passed, she shouted and dropped the sword again.

"It seems your bond is not strong enough to maintain the Seikaku for longer than about a minute. That would happen immediately if anyone but a bonded partner tried to touch a Seikaku." As he spoke, a tired edge crept into Masao's voice as his eyes narrowed in concentration. Kou stopped cleaning himself and came over to where Masao and Natsuki were standing.

"Natsuki and I are like miso and bread, they kind of work, but not as well as miso and rice," David said. Kou's eyes were completely blue.

"*I have been more and more influenced by David's view of Natsuki. David no longer hates her, but neither am I the love struck kitten,*" added Kou, his eyes changing back to their usual orange as he took over the conversation. As Natsuki flushed, Kou attempted to take the sting out his words by brushing up against her leg. Natsuki tried to conceal the emotions playing across her face, but Kou caught her eyes flick between him and Takumi.

"It seems David and Kou's experiences are drawing them closer together," Masao said. "You will still need to practice together Kou, Natsuki... But it seems Natsuki will have to start carrying her own sword."

"Maybe Takumi can help with that," Grandpa said, walking into the dojo. A slightly amused crease around his eyes that Kou's advanced vision barely caught. Takumi was suddenly eager, and with a huge smile on his face, literally jumped at the chance.

"I could make you a concealed sword so you can carry it without getting in trouble," Takumi said immediately after landing from the sword stand. "That is, once I finish my own first sword and Dad thinks it's good enough." Takumi eyed the floor. The trial of making his first sword alone was something he had been working toward his whole life. It was not something Masao would allow lightly.

"You are ready to make your own sword," Masao said. "Next weekend I think will be the perfect time for you to begin. If your first sword is good enough, you can make

Natsuki's as well." Kou's ears picked up the pride in Masao's voice, despite his calm appearance and iron control.

"*So where does this leave us?*" asked Kou, his voice bringing them back to the issue of Natsuki, David, and Kou as Partners.

"It means that you are still Partners, but I have no idea how the weakened bond will affect Natsuki or her powers. I have read of things like this in the past, but they are rare, and as I said, you and David are much younger than normal. For now, we will practice as usual. Takumi will make his swords, and hopefully, David will not be called upon to fight anytime too soon." Masao took his leave with Grandpa.

Later that evening as Kou was sneaking out to run through the forest a shadow caught his attention. Following it, Kou was led down a path towards Yukiko's vegetable garden. Rie stood waiting for him in the moonlight.

"So Grandpa finished your Seikaku then?" she said.

"*Yes, it is a shame you were not there to see it,*" Kou replied. David was too embarrassed to speak.

"I can't believe you let me down," Rie said, stepping out of a shadow. Her face seemed so sad to Kou, he knew that being able to see every crease and flicker of muscle would be a curse to David. "You said you wanted to help me. Without the metal, I won't be able to practice. And now Takumi will be hogging the workshop so he can make his own swords first."

"I'm really sorry!" Kou stood up on his hind legs, clasping his paws together to beg, Japanese style. Although they were in tiger form, Kou let David control their body to talk with Rie. "With the ghost and everything there wasn't much I could do."

Rie frowned and eyed him quietly for a moment, and then her expression changed as if someone had re-set her to the kind and soft-featured Rie. Stepping forward, Rie smiled. "Well. Maybe there is one way you could make it up…"

＝十＝

ALLIANCE

July,

With Natsuki unable to use the Seikaku, it meant we would be more reliant on our own skills than our predecessors were. On top of that, it was difficult for me to understand how pre-occupied he was with helping Rie. In the forests, we take what we want. We do not give back...

Rie's request turned out to be two-fold. Originally, she had wanted David to sneak an order of steel to the Estate so she could practice without the elders knowing. Her reaction to Takumi getting to make his swords first, made it clear to David that her request was all about their sibling rivalry. With her plans thwarted by David's run in with the obake, she asked him to deliver her supply to her friend Misaki for safekeeping. Though he thought the cloak and dagger stuff was rather funny, David found it trickier than he had expected. Ditching Takumi was no easy task, and with training and school, he had to do it little by little. Nevertheless, he finished the task, only to have the more difficult second half of her request. David pondered his new problems during his morning run.

'Well, at least I finally got the metal to Misaki's. Maybe Rie will forget she asked me the other part,' he thought hopefully, careful to keep his footing on a patch of slick leaves.

'I doubt it. You promised to help her. I'm starting to see why she and Natsuki used to be friends.'

In addition to his courier tasks, Rie had asked him to try to help Chul Moo make friends. Although Chul Moo was antisocial, the boys ignored him and the girls tended to stare from a distance. He had only ever heard Rie actually talk to him.

'I have no idea how we are going to break through all of that and make Chul Moo some friends. I have a feeling I'm going to be running into a lot of blank stares and laughs.'

"Your classmates are conditioned to keep problems within the group. Some of them keep things so close they do not consciously recognize there is a problem," Kou said as David splashed through a puddle. *"They ignore Chul Moo so that other classes don't take note."*

'Is that why Chul Moo has been left to his own devices for so long? How am I supposed to get past that?'

'Especially since she swore you to secrecy. Takumi cannot help you. Even though he knows why Rie is spending so much time with him.'

'Maybe I can get him to join in one of the games the others are always playing... Chess or even the stamp on people's foot game or something. Hell, even rock, paper, scissors, would be more participation than usual.'

After his run, Takumi and Natsuki joined David for morning practice. The months of training were paying off. David had the toned muscles, strength, and endurance the others had always taken for granted. Unfortunately, their years of training lent Takumi and Natsuki a grace and fluidity he had yet to match. When they sparred David was able to keep up, but he always lost. His two competitors knew techniques he did not, and tended to keep more than a few tricks ready if he caught them off guard.

At school there was the palpable tension caused by the anticipation of a month off and the hectic worry of semester finals. It was refreshing for David to see everyone running around fretting about end of semester tests. While many things were different in Japan, at least there seemed to be a few universal constants. David felt sure he would do well. While his memory had always been suspect, Kou had no such problems. Anything they learned anew, Kou was able to recall for them at will, provided David could keep his attention from wandering. While his other half had bridled at being relegated to the role of reference, David had cajoled and even made several promises to ensure Kou's help.

Despite the tests, Takumi spent all his free time getting ready for the weekend. He gathered and triple checked all his equipment and supplies in order to forge his first sword. In the past, Takumi had helped in the completion and creation of some of the Matsumotos' best works. This time around, he had to use all his own tools, and finish the sword with no help. It was not an easy prospect, even for a master smith. When David caught up with him running from the dojo, Takumi barely slowed.

"I have to complete everything, from the first ritual before the family shrine, to the smallest trim on the scabbard," he said. "The only thing I have going for me is that I can buy the metal from a dealer. That and I always keep an ample supply of all the types of coals for Dad and Grandpa."

Since Takumi had only from Saturday morning until Monday when school started again to finish, Takumi was frantic in his preparations. Their classmates started comparing Takumi to David when he zoned out. Luckily, none of them knew that David was talking to a god, and Takumi planning a sword.

David's dilemma, however, was not ensuring he had a good supply of clay or wood chips. Instead, he had to figure out what to do with Chul Moo. To make matters worse, in the aftermath of Natsuki and the Seikaku, he had agreed not to change into Kou at night for the duration of the week so that she could get enough sleep to study for the tests.

With only half the tests over, David joined the Matsumotos at the shrine Saturday morning for Takumi's summoning ceremony. Although David saw no Kami appear, Kou seemed to churn with him as Takumi chanted.

'The words call to me, they make me want to run.'

'It's like we've never wanted anything as much as we want to go,' thought David, feeling the pull through Kou.

Unable to control themselves any longer, David transformed almost instantly into Kou. Running forward, they touched their nose to both pieces of metal then Kou sat waving his tail throughout the rest of the ceremony. Natsuki arrived towards the end, interested and surprised by the ceremony. At her approach, Kou caught Rie stiffen. Quietly, she moved away from the rest of the Matsumotos.

"I figured you'd come with Kou running around. Sorry, I didn't expect David to change, but it's just as well, you have practice, and I have a sword to make. We just finished the first part," Takumi said smiling broadly.

As Natsuki walked up to Takumi, Kou stumbled around underfoot. Still energized and a bit befuddled by the ceremony, both Kou and David were nearly lost within Kou's muddled animal instincts. Natsuki stopped, seeing Takumi for the first time in the traditional garb of the Matsumoto priests. As Natsuki stared at Takumi, Rie stalked off towards the main house.

"You look…" Natsuki stopped short, mumbling, she was not given the time to search for the right words as Masao took Takumi off to begin his sword. Grandpa came and attempted to pull David and Kou out of their stupor so they could start their weekend training.

"There is no use practicing today," Grandpa said. "Both of your heads are in the clouds. Take the rest of the day off so I can go watch Takumi work." Kou barely caught him murmur "addled" and "waste *my* time" before Grandpa stomped down the path.

'I think he just wanted an excuse to go watch Takumi,' David thought, finally pulling himself out of the weird visions he and Kou had been sharing.

'*Maybe we should peak in too.*'

'I wonder where Rie is…'

David struggled against the images roiling within Kou's mind, threatening to suck them back into their stupor. They reminded him of the nightmares that had plagued him after their Golden Week training. Dreams he now knew were old memories from the *Golden Tiger*. While he had not remembered them after dreaming, he often saw glimpses from Kou. Together they had made the connection.

As Takumi toiled away in the workshop, Natsuki spent the rest of the day running around the main house chatting with Yukiko. The only female besides Rie who knew the Matsumotos' secret, Yukiko was Natsuki's confidant on the Estate. With Rie constantly off training, Yukiko drew Natsuki in with the promise of a ready ear and good advice. David spent most of the morning watching Takumi work before leaving to finish his homework for the week and study for the remaining tests so he would be free in the evenings.

Even in their room, Kou insisted they stay aware of their surrounds, yet David ignored Natsuki when she stopped after Yukiko passed his door. He was intent on finishing so he could spend the rest of the weekend trying to get back on Rie's good side. Natsuki's mouth tightened around the edges, her eyebrows constricting as she looked up at the ceiling. Finally, just when he was about to give in, she cautiously entered his room.

"So I was hoping you might be willing to help me with a few questions before the English test," Natsuki said without preamble. Sighing, David looked up from his math homework.

'*Go on, you know it will be easier to just answer her questions. It probably was not easy for her to ask you for help,*' thought Kou as David hesitated.

"What do you want to know?" David leaned back, inviting Natsuki to sit at the end of his bed and ask her questions.

That night, David wandered the Matsumoto Forest. Having had an almost normal conversation with Natsuki had unnerved him. It was just too strange having her come to him for help. Her presence in the house did have one upside for him though. David was hopeful that Rie might want to escape after having hidden in her room all day. While sitting in his favorite tree, the sun finally faded, shrouding the Estate in darkness. David had heard Natsuki leave the Estate, yet had not caught a glimpse of Rie.

'We have been sitting up in this tree for hours, she is not coming, and if she is, we will not see her with your poor eyes. Let us go have some fun, or at least practice if we are going to stay up all night. Natsuki should be asleep soon.'

'Oh I get it. You just want her to dream about you all night so she'll want to come straight here in the morning.' David filled his thoughts with as much repulsion as he could muster, yet he could not hide his amusement from Kou.

'What can I say? I am a ladies' man... ladies' cat... tiger... whatever.'

'And I thought Naoto was bad.' Sometimes Kou's personality was oddly similar to some of the other students at Nakano Junior High. Other times, he was so archaic that David could barely glean any meaning from his words. Together they listened to Takumi's hammer blows ring through the forest. Finally, it was dark enough that they were sure Natsuki was asleep.

'I want to try something,' David thought. Without giving time for Kou to react, David dropped off the high tree branch. With a satisfied growl, Kou took over and they transformed in midair. Kou caught David's clothes in his teeth, and then ran north through the forest.

'That was our best yet! You know, we really have to figure out what to do with the clothes once I transform.'

"*You are telling me! These taste disgusting.*" Kou's shout was muffled by David's shirt.

'Natsuki isn't going to be happy is she?'

'*Well. We did promise to stay in for the week so she could study. We did not, however, say anything about the weekend.*' While Kou still liked Natsuki, and David was slowly coming around, neither of them enjoyed the limits her Partnership placed on their freedom to change between tiger and human. As Kou and David slowly adjusted to their new reality, they enjoyed the sharing of each other's experiences more and more.

After ditching the clothes near the wall of the Estate, Kou started truly running. Leaping and extending his claws he barely touched a large tree before jumping to the next, blazing through the Matsumoto forest, tree trunk to tree trunk. Once on the other side of the Estate, Kou dropped to the ground, his long white whiskers twitching in delight.

'*OK, now you take over.*' Kou's eyes changed to blue as David exerted control over Kou's body, merging himself into the feline senses, but also remaining careful so he would not transform or get lost in the intensity of the sensations. Still shocked by the flood of information, even after feeling the heightened senses filtered through Kou's perspective for so many weeks, David laughed and twitched his tail.

'I still can't get used to having a tail! There's so much it does for you.'

Running forward David lunged onto the nearest tree and followed Kou's path back along the Estate. Unlike the first trip, where Kou had an easy grace, David lumbered from tree to tree. Digging in with Kou's claws, he landed on each tree before going to the next. As David ran, he attempted to fine-tune his control. Focused as he was on his task, the sudden voice that wavered through the forest caught him by surprise. He missed his tree completely.

"Kou is far better at that you know," the voice said, echoing from around the forest.

As used to hearing voices as David was, he was still un-nerved. This one had a quality he had heard before but could not place. David let Kou take over as they dropped into the large ferns that covered the forest floor. Kou began to stalk through the underbrush, his senses working to take in as much information as possible. Both David and Kou concentrated, analyzing what Kou's body was telling them, attempting to find the voice's source.

"Don't worry. I am not here to hurt you. In fact I have a favor to ask… and information as payment." The voice grew more distinct, obviously male.

They transformed quickly, summoning the Seikaku and falling into a protective stance as David remembered where he had heard such a similar voice before. Turning slowly in his own body, David retained a bit more of the feline grace he had learned from Kou and his long training with the Matsumotos. His ears twitched at the forest's night sounds.

"Talk quickly then," replied David, still searching. Walking through the high ferns, he used his feet to check around him, while he used his eyes to peer into the forested depths.

"Not completely unskilled after all. You're learning quickly. I'm a ghost." The voice was closer, the echo less intense. David crouched, ready for an attack. "Yes, that's why I haven't shown myself yet. I don't have any desire to acquaint myself with that new sword of yours… First, my payment. A warning. There is a pack of ōkami living in the valley, and they are planning something. I used to be a Matsumoto, and may also have other knowledge that might be useful to you."

"*And the favor for which you pay?*" Kou asked, David's eyes turning orange.

"Ah yes, well it's gotten rather boring floating around woods all the time. I'd like to go haunt, for lack of a better word, the Estate. I promise I won't attack anyone, I just want to be back home, without of course you banishing me. How about it?" The voice was surprisingly sincere. David thought he could almost feel the pain and loneliness in his words. Still stalking through the forest ferns, David spoke privately to Kou.

'Well? What do you think? We will have to tell Masao of course, but if there really is a pack of ōkami running around, then it might be worth... the risk. *We can always take care of him if he gets out of line. I would say get the information and then have Grandpa confirm his identity. Masao did say not all are bad.*'

"If you're really a Matsumoto why didn't you come before now?" David asked aloud.

"Because I wasn't aware of them, or you, until recently. You'll hear the news soon, one of your classmates has disappeared." The voice spoke simply, almost a whisper.

Stopping, David dropped his head, his Seikaku coming down with it. Suddenly, he flipped the sword behind him changing it into its elemental form at the same time. The surprise at having it actually work almost caused him to drop it, but Kou was there to help. David thrust the Seikaku's point behind him into the tree. In response to his will and the Seikaku's power, the tree opened revealing the misty outline of a young man, strikingly similar to Takumi.

"Tell me what you know. I'll leave your fate to the Matsumotos." David turned to face the obake hidden within the tree. The Takumi lookalike's misty features gulped. The tip of the Seikaku was inches from his face.

二十三

LOST AND BROKEN

July,

> *Ryohei proved a valuable addition to the Estate. While a bit eccentric, apparently so was I. He kept to himself, except to occasionally follow us in the forests. After his arrival, it was hard to imagine the Estate without him…*

David strode through the Estate with Ryohei the obake while the peal of Takumi's hammer rang through the trees. Luckily, he had been able to struggle back into some clothes before leaving the forest proper. Ryohei ignored David's sword and stared in awe at the buildings around him, drinking in the comforting similarities, and examining the changes.

Despite the late hour, David found and roused Grandpa at the retirement cottage. When the twins had been born, Grandpa had moved to a small building near the gate so that Masao could raise his children without a third generation living directly with them. Despite his symbolic separation, however, Grandpa was still master of the Estate.

After hearing Ryohei's story, Grandpa left to gather the *Matsumoto Family Histories.* He quickly found that Ryohei Matsumoto had died during an accident when forging his first sword. Convinced of the obake's identity after a lengthy questioning, Grandpa agreed to let him stay, provided he helped where he could and did not try to feed off anyone on the Estate. In return, the ghost of Ryohei was able to be a part of the Matsumotos again. Since Ryohei had already told David all he knew about the pack of ōkami, David let his Seikaku fade away. Ryohei decided to haunt the Matsumoto Garden. It too was his favorite place on the Estate.

"It is troubling that there is a whole ōkami pack," Grandpa said as soon as Ryohei was gone. "I will check into Ryohei's information on Misaki immediately." Frowning, Grandpa wandered out to the kitchen for tea. David followed him towards the main house. Instead, of entering, he headed for Rie's room. When he knocked on her door, he was surprised at the immediate response. She was already awake.

"Rie, I have some bad news," he started. She simply stared back stonily. "I just found out that Misaki has disappeared. You know it's strange, but when I delivered the last package of metal, there was just a note on her door telling me to leave it. Do you think she's been gone since then?"

Her eyes unfocused as if she was trying to gaze through him. For the briefest moment, David thought he saw her brown eyes glisten with a tear. Then just as suddenly, her door slid shut between them. David tried to get a response but was left with the sounds of her scraping around the room.

'I hope she's alright. *We should keep an eye on her, just in case she* tries to go find Misaki *on her own.*' David and Kou's thoughts were so coordinated that they blended. David turned and headed to his room so that he could sneak out. Although he knew Masao was with Takumi, he could not be sure that Yukiko or Grandpa would not be keeping an eye on the doors.

In the deep of early morning, David snuck out of the main house via his improvised trap door. Turning into Kou in order to maximize their stealth, Kou grabbed David's bare clothes, and like a shadow, ran through the Estate. His paws kept time with the pounding of Takumi's hammer. Kon climbed a tree near the main house, and then transformed to keep from waking Natsuki.

'It's amazing what a ghost showing up can do.'

'Yes, and it should be interesting having him around. I assume you will want to play a prank on Natsuki?'

David's laugh came out as half a growl.

'I don't know, she seemed pretty freaked out the last time,' David thought, letting the incident in the ruins play through his mind.

'You should have asked Rie about the strange note right after you got it... or investigated more.'

'Rie's the one who wanted me to keep it secret. I figured the note was there because Misaki had better things to do than wait around for me to show up.' As the time passed, they listened to the familiar sounds of night on the Estate. David yawned at the monotony, and decided to find out more about Kou. 'So tell me more about Kami... What are you exactly?'

'We are as in the dark about our origins as humans. Thanks to the Matsumotos we know some of our history, and my own memories as part of my... father... answers some more of what you are asking.'

'But don't the Japanese worship Kami? Are you gods?'

'It depends on how you define a god. We are spirits that have the ability to affect the physical world. We guide and care for our charges. The water Kami stay in the water, fire in fire, air in air, and earth on land.'

'What about you? Why are you with me?'

'My predecessor, the Golden Tiger, was the original Zodiac Tiger. The Matsumotos do not even know that, by the way. He and the other zodiacs...'

'Wait, I thought there were only twelve zodiac animals total.'

'You humans always mix things up. The others were conveniently forgotten so they could fit your calendar. Anyway, the zodiacs were the first animal Kami, diminished from their Elemental Kami ancestors but still strong. Most of the original zodiacs diminished as they procreated until their offspring became just dumb

animals, with only the slightest spark of life in them. The animals could no longer split themselves, but flourished by finding mates. Afraid of falling to the level of the animals, a few of the zodiacs split rarely, until they found that if they entered a human they could incubate their offspring until the new Kami emerged more powerful than before.'

'Then why aren't there more Kami running around?'

'Why else? Evil. Whether the humans corrupted the Kami, or the Kami corrupted the humans is not known. What is known is that the corruption occurred and resulted in the evil things that roam the land today. Ōkami, oni, yūrei, and the many monsters you read about are due to corrupted Kami. The Kami swore never to possess another human… That is until part of Amaterasu's predecessor, a powerful Kami, was accidentally pulled into Ninigi during the Matsumoto ceremony. Ninigi's sacrifice proved he had no corruption, making it safe for the Kami to grow again. Since then only the Matsumotos know how many human-Kami joinings there have been.'

'Why me though? I mean, I get that there can cannot really be all that many people being killed at shrines, but still.'

'There are actually quite a few shrines in Japan, almost too many in fact. Since there are so many not all have regular Kami visitors, but there are enough that there is a good chance someone, somewhere will end up dying near one. The circumstances and person dying matter though. The Zodiac Tiger was there because he was listening for the Matsumotos' call. The Kami feel a responsibility for the world. We swore to fight the evil that was unwittingly unleashed into it, but we can only do so much alone. Together with a human, we are far stronger than either half. Evil has returned, so when you sacrificed yourself, the Zodiac Tiger gave part of himself to create me… us. Evil has been growing in the world, and now it is back in Japan. We must fight it, we will be strong.'

'What about humans? Aren't we descended from apes? I mean how does that fit into your story?'

'It is not a story. Humans involved a disturbing piece of our history… but it will have to wait. Rie is coming.'

David suddenly saw a shadow slide out from beneath the main house. Still early enough not to wake Natsuki, he changed into Kou. They watched as Rie ran swiftly through the shadows. Dropping carefully to the ground, Kou made it to the wall just in time to see Rie slide through the stream and under the wall.

She moved through the darkness purposefully, not even taking the time to watch for pursuers. Neither David nor Kou were sucked into underestimating her. David clearly remembered their time in the mountains, and knew if he tried to track her without Kou, she would know he was there far before he got close enough to see her.

Kou waited until Rie was well past the wall before going under himself. The forest was pitch-black. No moon shone through the trees and the stars were hidden by thick clouds overhead. The only light came from the slight glow of Nakano Town.

'It is a good thing we do not have to rely on your sight or we would be as blind as... well, a human.'

Kou padded after Rie swiftly but more silently than the barely-existent wind. The stream curved through the forest heading to its mountain source. Rie continued walking along the water until she reached a curve, then stepping out she headed quickly into the hills. Kou continued to follow, giving her more lead as the trees thinned slightly.

Turning into a vale, Rie suddenly disappeared from view. Kou hurried forward coming around the corner seeing an open area behind a low hill, with the beginning of a tall mountain behind it. There was no trace of her.

Unlike the Seikaku, Takumi's sword required the full process to create. When David arrived at the dojo a bare hour after returning to the Estate, only Grandpa was there.

"Takumi is taking a break. He finished the first stage of the sword a couple hours ago. He will continue after he rests so as not to make any mistakes. Unlike a Seikaku, normal swords do not need to be finished in one sitting. I tried contacting Misaki's parents, but they were out. I called Yonamine and he confirmed she is missing, though they think she just ran away. She apparently left a note. Natsuki should be along shortly and then we can begin." Grandpa sat as usual behind a low table drinking tea, fresh from finishing his own morning practice while David had been running.

Natsuki arrived shortly after David. Late and sleepy looking, she tossed David an annoyed scowl.

"You were running around with Kou again last night weren't you? I barely slept with all the crazy dreams I was having." Natsuki yawned widely, trying to shake off her sleepiness. Grandpa raised a gray haired eyebrow at David.He answered with a guilty smile. Shrugging, Grandpa turned to the pair.

"Since Takumi will not be joining us this morning, I would like you two to finish up your basics and then spar," Grandpa said. He raised his hands to stop their simultaneous reactions. "I know. Your last time did not turn out so well. But you have only spared with Takumi since. I want to see how you two are really doing."

Without Takumi and Rie, Natsuki lead basics. David furiously kept pace, aggressively anticipating Natsuki's movements to the point he kept her moving faster and faster to outdo him. By the end they were both drenched in sweat, something neither had encountered for weeks.

Grandpa merely sat on the sidelines chuckling to himself as Natsuki and David fought, their wills striking with every step, punch, block, and kick. Trying to hide her fatigue, Natsuki turned briskly and walked to the back of the dojo to collect her practice sword. David simply stood lazily, smiling, pretending as if he had been waiting for hours.

"Well? What are you waiting for, go get your sword," Natsuki said with as much distain as she could muster. With a smile and a wink, David summoned his Seikaku. Instantly, he was ready for sword basics, his blade in hand.

Natsuki stood slightly dumbstruck as out of nowhere Grandpa let out the loudest, hardiest laugh David had ever heard. David was so surprised his concentration faltered and the Seikaku disappeared. Natsuki and David turned in unison to stare as Grandpa rocked forward, pounding the low table before him.

"That was hilarious, I was just about to tell you off for wasting time, and sure enough, pop... out comes the Seikaku," Grandpa said rocking with his laughter. "Of course you should practice basics with it. Ah the look on your face was priceless Natsuki-chan."

Turning to look at each other, both David and Natsuki burst out laughing at Grandpa in return. Once everyone had settled down, David re-summoned his Seikaku and they worked their way through sword basics at a normal pace.

Once they finished all their basics, they returned to the back rooms and donned their armor. David's was painted in the black, orange, and white stripes of a tiger. Grandpa had replaced his old mask so that even in human form he had the fierce visage of a growling tiger. As David and Natsuki squared off to spar, armed with the lighter bamboo swords, David's eyes glazed to orange.

"Try not to knock David down so much this time," Kou said, making David frown awkwardly. *"It hurts."*

"Sure, tell him not to fall down, then there won't be a problem." Natsuki smiled behind her helmet and mask as they squared for battle. Shaking his head, David attached his mask, securing it with ropes under his chin, then smiled, taking full control from Kou.

At Grandpa's signal, the pair came to attention, bowed, and readied themselves. Another signal unleashed twin attacks. Just a month before, Natsuki had easily knocked David down repeatedly. With the mid-July sunrise streaming through the open doors, David stood physically fit, with two and a half months intensive training, and the ability to multi-task, thanks to Kou and his evening lessons with Grandpa. None of it stopped Natsuki from getting in the first blow. Her years of training more than made up for the year she had spent flitting around with the class representative. Natsuki had worked just as hard as David, and was in better shape beforehand.

She caught him along the arm, raking down along his armor before David was able to deflect her sword away from his body. Unperturbed, Natsuki used the momentum from David's deflection to start another attack. Natsuki was, however, unprepared when he suddenly dropped and turned his sword, flipping in an imitation of the move he had used on the tree in which Ryohei had hidden. The tip of David's bamboo sword caught Natsuki right in the solar plexus, driving her breath out, despite the armor. David was up and away again before she could recover.

'*Attack.*'

'Not while she's down.'

Grandpa called a halt to check on Natsuki.

"Not very fair using that trick on her. You only thought of it because you saw me," Ryohei said, his shadowy voice echoing through the dojo as he glided out of the wall behind Natsuki. Turning, Natsuki's eyes went wide in shock and fright. Backing away and into David, Natsuki grabbed him, pulling him in front of her as a shield.

"It's a… g-ghost. Hurry David, kill it, kill it, kill it!" Natsuki said, her voice increasingly shrill.

"I guess that wasn't the best way to introduce myself," Ryohei said as he floated in front of them, his translucent hand scratching the back of his head in embarrassment. Due to her connection with David and Kou, Natsuki was fully capable of seeing him. David sighed, then transformed into Kou, brushing up against her until she calmed enough to listen to Grandpa.

"Do not worry Natsuki, this was Ryohei Matsumoto. He found David in the forest and we agreed to let him stay at the

Estate. He is not evil, not like the obake you met." Grandpa spoke soothingly, seeing the fear in her eyes.

"I think I'll just go back to the garden. I didn't know you met one of the others. Just thought I'd say hi," said Ryohei, gliding back out of the dojo.

'Well, you did want to play a trick on her…'

'That was your idea. I didn't want to scare the wits out of her in the middle of a sparring match!'

Natsuki eventually settled down, calmed by Kou and Grandpa's words. David looked around for his armor so that he could get re-dressed after changing back into his human form but could not find it anywhere. Only the gi he had worn beneath it remained on the floor.

"Go ahead, change back," Grandpa said impatiently.

Kou eyed Grandpa carefully, and then rolled his shoulders for a shrug. Before he transformed, David made him turn away from Natsuki, his paws awkwardly trying to cover himself. Relieved, David reappeared with his Tiger Armor firmly in place over his human body, minus the cloth barrier that had been between his skin and the armor. Natsuki still sat on the floor staring off into space.

"Your armor is special. I'll explain later," Grandpa said, gesturing pointedly at Natsuki.

'You are going to have to push her buttons to get her mind off Ryohei.'

'I doubt it is Ryohei she's thinking about. But hey, pushing Natsuki's buttons? That's easy.'

"Well I guess I won then, too bad, Natsuki," David said, putting on the best smile he could muster. Natsuki stared at him for a second before comprehension overcame her fear and she started to stand.

"No way you win. You only got me one time." Natsuki's voice rose as she spoke. Anger colored her cheeks as she watched David smirk.

'More. Use the princess bit.'

"Well I just figured the *princess* wanted a rest, you *have* been sitting for quite a while after all," David said, waving his hand and rolling his eyes to give the show a final touch. Natsuki slammed her helmet back onto her head and picked up her bamboo sword in one fluid motion. She advanced without even commenting of the fact that David still had his armor on.

'I hope you're satisfied,' David thought. Kou purred within, letting him know that he was.

"That's it, let's go," Natsuki said fiercely, the fiery gleam back in her eyes. With a wink to David that Natsuki completely missed, Grandpa called the beginning of another round.The ensuing battle was ferocious, with Natsuki venting her anger and embarrassment. In reply, David gave everything he had, and used every trick he had learned, both in practice and from watching Takumi and Natsuki spar. Neither of them was willing to give up as they rained heavy blows, attempting to find an opening. Their match pitted Natsuki's experience against David's unorthodox moves and Kou's help.

Finally, with a shout, Natsuki and David attacked at the same instant. The bamboo swords shattered as they met, the force of the blow breaking the bindings and sending pieces flying. The sudden lack of resistance sent Natsuki and David hurtling into each other, leaving them in a heap on the floor.

"I guess we call this a draw?" David was the first to extricate himself. Pulling himself off Natsuki, he sat back and looked at the bit of bamboo still clutched in his hand.

On the floor, Natsuki began laughing uncontrollably. She continued so long that David stood up, staring at her. Finally, Natsuki raised an arm for David to help her up. Jerking up, she rocked in close and in a whisper said only "Thanks," before pushing him down.

"That's for breaking my favorite sword. I'm going home before that obake shows up again. You can explain what you had to do with that later." Natsuki turned and walked out, dropping armor along the way.

"I guess it is time for you two to switch to wooden swords when sparing," Grandpa said soberly, watching Natsuki leave. With a laugh he turned, leaving for the main house.

"And I thought *you* were hard to understand," David said as he put away the gear.

'Females are an interesting species.'

二十四

BIRTHDAY PRESENTS

July,

Who knew all it would take was a fight to finally break the negativity between David and Natsuki? I should have gotten them to fight earlier, but even with the breakdown of their animosity, she still could not hold the Seikaku...

Takumi finished the blade of his first sword late Sunday night. His crow of triumph echoed through the Estate. He had withdrawn his blade from its final quenching and it had not cracked. With the hardest part done, and approved by the Matsumoto elders, Takumi was finally able to relax. For him that meant joining Natsuki and David for practice before school on Monday.

"You look like David during his first week of training," Natsuki said.

"Yeah, I'm tired, but I did it," he said, his eyes bright. "Now I can start building my own reputation as a smith. Now I can work towards becoming a master. I passed a test so much more important to me than the ones at school."

"Don't let Yukiko hear you say that," David said with a laugh.

Although neither Natsuki nor David brought up the previous day's incident, things had changed. Without Natsuki's usual verbal jibes, he had nothing to play off, so David was sure the quiet was why Takumi kept glancing between them. Takumi kept his peace until they were alone.

"Hey, so what was up with you and Natsuki today at practice?" he asked.

"I dunno. It was weird. I think it's because she ran into Ryohei yesterday. She's uncomfortable with ghosts," David said. For some reason he felt the need to explain more than usual. "I kind of distracted her after the attack and we ended up busting two of the bamboo swords.

"Really?" Takumi asked, staring off into a wall.

"Hey, have you seen Rie this morning?" David asked. He immediately wished he had not. Takumi's whole bearing shifted as his muscles tightened. David recognized it as *in control* Takumi.

"My sister," he spat, "Decided not to be present for the most important event in my life. We used to do everything together and now she's let the one other person…" His jaw locked as he stomped toward the kitchen.

'It's probably about as easy for him to talk about as it is for you to talk about your problems with Jessica.'

Yukiko was there waiting for them when they made it to the main room.

"Natsuki ran home," she said. "She forgot some of her homework. Hurry up and eat."

"So did Rie leave for school already?" David asked after settling into his rice.

For the rest of the meal Takumi stared broodingly into his bowls as he wolfed down his rice and soup.

"You know… I did not see her get up or go out, though when I was coming in from the kitchen I saw her out front of the Estate meeting that Chul Moo boy. She must have gotten ready and snuck out early." Yukiko frowned, as if trying to re-member something just forgotten. Unable to grasp the thought, she busied herself with clearing dishes instead.

'*I wonder if she even came back to the Estate yesterday.*'

'Who knows? At least she's still going to school.'

David finished breakfast well after Takumi had left the ta-ble. Giving his thanks, David said goodbye to Yukiko and went off to finish getting ready for school.

As in schools all around the world, the last week before summer vacation was essentially just for show. Even though there were a few tests, everyone, teachers included, was al-ready mentally on vacation. Summer homework was passed out and ignored, and conversations revolved around plans.

The news of Misaki's disappearance spread quickly through-out the school. The homeroom teachers gave long speeches about the need to help locate her, and the dangers of running away. After second period, most of his classmates were in the back of the class. As David switched out his books, a sudden fiery pain that nearly unleashed Kou, raced up his foot.

"You're out," Naoto said with a grin before he went to try to step on Tsubasa's foot. He only made it one-step before their wiry classmate caught him. David recognized the game. The last student without being stepped on won. The challenge was everyone was trying to step on each other's feet at the same time. His own concerns forgotten for a while, David joined in the next round.

A warm feeling of acceptance stayed with him throughout the rest of the morning. As each test was finished, Class 2B's excitement grew. David decided that instead of badminton he would check out a few books from the library. Reading would be a convenient and believable cover so he could sneak out at night to try to find out where Rie was going.

'I bet she's helping Misaki.'

'*Yes, we should hunt them down ourselves.*'

To get to the library, David went behind the lunchroom to a usually secluded walkway squeezed between various buildings. Still high on having the end of semester tests over, David turned the corner.

A young girl stood there, a first year from the look of her, short even for her age. Across from her, Koji stood alone, tall and threatening, but with a blank look in his eyes. David looked to the girl, she was nervous, one knee bent, the other straight. Her hands clasped tightly in front of her as she eyed the ground.

'What did he do to her?'

Then Koji saw him standing there and his whole body tensed. The girl turned, and seeing David shrunk against the wall. Koji took a step towards him, his eyes ablaze.

'*Now's your chance to show him you have grown some claws.*'

'I can't use what the Matsumotos taught me... I'll just make sure she's alright.'

"Are you OK?" David asked the girl. The question stopped Koji cold. Her eyes met David's and she shook her head just enough to tell him she was all right. "Oh, I'll just slide by you Koji-kun."

'*That's the suffix for equals and people below you!*' Kou yelled within as David attempted to get by Koji. Kou must have sensed the punch coming because David's head jerked out of the way just in time. Koji's hand slammed into the concrete, so close to his ear, David could hear the bones pop. Whirling, David turned to block a second blow. The girl was gone and Koji was balling up to cradle his broken hand. David ran.

Before school was even over, classmates from 2B were asking him about how he had broken Koji's hand. No matter how often he told people that he had not done it, they did not seem to believe him. It was as if they had completely forgotten Koji's stories about how the weakling gaijin had hurt himself at the beginning of the year. Somehow, they thought him completely capable of taking out Koji.

'Have I really changed that much?' he thought. Then another thought coursed through David's mind. 'I wonder if Koji could be one of the ōkami Ryohei told me about.'

"It's a possibility," Takumi said when David brought it up after school. "He's always been especially mean. If he is an ōkami then the pack has been here for years. I'll ask dad."

Later in the week, David learned that Koji had confessed his love to a first year. The rumor was she had rejected him and in his anger, Koji had attacked but David had beaten him.

'Koji must have thought you had overheard the confession, and your slip, using kun instead of san must have sent him over the edge. When he comes back to school, he will want your blood.'

'But if he was trying to seduce the girl… Isn't that one of the ways ōkami feed?'

The uncertainty stayed with them as they spent every night trying to track Rie without success. No matter where they followed her, she always disappeared. Even more frustratingly, she never took the same route, so that David lost an entire night trying to ambush her.

"You know, I don't think we are going to be able to figure out where Rie is going on our own." David was so frustrated he spoke aloud as Kou slinked along the trees outside the Matsumoto Estate.

'It is time to bring what we know to Grandpa. If anyone knows what to do, he does. She might be training, but if she is hiding Misaki, then Rie is not making good choices.'

'Well with an ōkami pack out there somewhere shouldn't she be more careful?'

'Especially if Koji is involved.'

Sliding under the wall, they changed back into their human form. David groped under a nearby tree for his clothes. Before he made it past the main house, Grandpa emerged from the shadows.

"Grandpa! What are you doing here? I was just coming to find you." David jogged closer, bowing to the elder Matsumoto.

"That obake of yours suggested I go outside," Grandpa said. "It is strange talking to someone you cannot see, but then we cannot all be a Jitsugen Samurai's Partner. Let's go to the dojo to talk. I doubt anyone else will be there, and we can get a little extra practice in since you are already up."

Wincing at the thought of no sleep, David followed Grandpa in the deep darkness of early morning to the dojo. Grandpa sat, looking at David with an appraising eye, and then said, "I suppose you're going to tell me why you've been sneaking out of the Estate every day this week?"

Standing respectfully, David outlined everything he knew about Rie. Kou jumped in to add his perspective and memories.

"We've spent all week trying to find out where she's been going," David said. "I think she's helping hide Misaki. If it wasn't for Chul Moo I might have been able to try and talk to her more, and because of Koji, it's been an… interesting week at school." David waited as the minutes passed without a response from Grandpa.

"Grandpa? Are you alright?" Kou asked aloud.

"What? Oh, right… I… I need time to figure this out. David, forget about practice today, go get some sleep, you look terrible. Let me worry about Rie." Grandpa's smile was betrayed by a twitch in his eye that Kou interpreted as deep concern. Confused but knowing better than to ignore Grandpa, David stood to leave. Before he made it out of the dojo, Grandpa's words halted him.

"David, Kou, thank you for telling me all of this. I will take it from here. If you are right, well… never mind." Grandpa dismissed David with a wave. David looked back just once more. He comforted himself with the familiar image of Grandpa meditating, and then left to find his way back to the main house in the dark.

The rest of the weekend was frustratingly normal. David did not see Grandpa again, but the rest of the Matsumotos went about their routines as if nothing was amiss. Rie left a note with Masao and Yukiko telling them that she was spending the weekend training in the mountains and Takumi was already at work on Natsuki's sword. Yukiko glided around the house and out in the garden as usual, and Masao oversaw Takumi's work and their normal training. The only change in routine was the absence of Grandpa at their evening training practices. Masao took over those lessons, focusing on exploring the potentials of the wood form of David's Seikaku.

Several trees from the Matsumoto forest were sacrificed for his training as David made them explode. At first unable to control the destruction, he was soon able to make the trees attack a specific target without destroying the entire tree. Though Grandpa was a tough taskmaster, Masao was brutal. He gave David tasks and drills that made his mind feel as sore and beaten as he had felt during the first weeks of training.

Natsuki spent most of the lessons sitting in a new chair grown for her by David from one of the trees. Since she was unable to hold the Seikaku for more than a minute, most of her time was spent merely watching David work. A task she enjoyed far too much for David's taste. She even turned his princess jokes on him. Instead of getting angry at the flourishes in the chair that made it look more like a throne, she took to it immediately, giving David orders from her perch.

With school done, the month long summer break stretched out before them. For the Matsumotos, this, like Golden Week, was a time for training, sword making, and contemplation. David got up at the usual four in the morning Monday to run and train with Takumi and Natsuki. Their run turned into more of a race. David and Takumi ran the full five kilometers, all the while egging each other on to increase the pace. On the last leg, Natsuki joined them, having already completed most of her run around her own house. While David was fit enough to complete the run, he still had to fight past his own body's limitations. After the first kilometer, running became more difficult for him, and it was only by pure determination that he was able to push himself to work through the pain and soreness. It helped that since his possession he knew he could recover quickly after his ordeal was over.

The last stretch was through the trees of the Matsumoto Estate, a task that would have left David with a broken ankle just a few weeks before. Back in the dojo, Takumi excitedly pulled Natsuki towards the back room.

"Close your eyes." Takumi smiled mischievously. David stood off to the side. He had a pretty good idea what Takumi was up to, even though Takumi had not told him anything.

'I do not get the human fascination with closing your eyes in order to surprise someone. Why not just ambush them from some tall grass?'

'We depend on vision more than you do. Imagine if you were blind and deaf.'

After ensuring Natsuki's eyes were firmly closed, Takumi went into one of the back rooms. He returned holding a long object in a velvet bag.

"Hold out your hands," Takumi said, throwing a hesitant glance at David before turning his attention back on Natsuki. Natsuki complied, trying to hide a smile that twitched at the corner of her mouth. With a huge grin, he placed the bag in her hands.

"OK. You can open them," Takumi said, his voice was so awash in relief that even David caught the undertones.

'You still need to work on your observational skills. Look at the color in his face. And if we had my ears we could probably hear his heart beating twice as fast.'

Natsuki opened her eyes, peering down at the bag. Suddenly understanding what she held, her face betrayed every bit of the surprise she felt.

"It's a scepter for your throne, princess." David's deadpan joke was completely ignored by both Takumi and Natsuki as she stared at the bag in her hands, mouth agape.

"How, when? Is it…" Natsuki's words were lost in her own surprise as she examined the weight and form within the bag.

"Go ahead and open it," Takumi said beaming with pleasure at Natsuki's reaction. Natsuki un-cinched the bag, slowly pulling it back to reveal a thin, barely curving, unfinished blade.

"I just finished it this morning. Happy Birthday, Natsuki," Takumi said. Natsuki threw her arms around him, completely catching him off guard, and nearly impaling him with her new blade.

'So that's why he spent every ounce of free time this weekend in the forge… It's her birthday…'

"I'm sorry it's not finished yet. I just finalized my first sword last week and got permission to start yours. I can polish and finish the scabbard and handle this week. I think David can help with that," Takumi said as she finally let him go. He turned toward David with a hopeful, inquiring glance.

"Well normally we would be obligated to make things more difficult for Natsuki, but since it's her birthday, I guess we could make an exception," David said. His head shook and eyes turned orange as Kou asserted himself.

"*Speak for yourself,*" Kou said primly. "*What did you have in mind?*"

"Well I was hoping you two could use the Seikaku to help make a scabbard and handle so that Natsuki's sword would appear to be nothing more than just a wooden practice sword. I could do it, but it would probably take weeks and would not be as good as if you would do it." Takumi's tone begged while his eyes screamed you owe me one. With mock exasperation, David agreed to try. With both Natsuki and Takumi in great moods, they began morning practice.

二十五

MISSING

July,

We could not bring ourselves to be as happy and carefree as everyone else around us seemed. Rie's behavior and Grandpa's absence made us feel as if somehow we were the prey...

After Monday morning practice, Yukiko surprised Natsuki with a huge birthday breakfast. It took David a few minutes to realize why his host mother kept looking towards the mountains every time she came into the room.

'Rie must not be back from training. I guess she decided to stay longer since school is out.'

'Maybe. I wonder what Grandpa is going to do about her. He must be preparing something since he has not been at our evening practices.'

After breakfast, the trio met a few classmates for a game of soccer. Although summer break was in full swing, the small Nakano town left students without vacation plans little to do. While Takumi, David, and Natsuki were far busier than their friends were, their classmates were generally ignorant of the Matsumotos' other activities. In order to keep up appearances, they made a point of showing up around school. Enough students turned out for four full soccer teams. They played until lunch, at which point Natsuki started packing up her bags. Before leaving, she ran back to David.

"I don't care if the world is ending," Natsuki whispered. "No turning into Kou or I'll stab you with my new sword! I promised my dad half-a-day with no training. I won't be by tonight."

Natsuki smiled and with a wave, she ran off again, leaving David and Takumi together. Takumi stared after Natsuki.

"What was that all about," he asked. Turning, David realized how her whisper might look to him.

"Oh don't worry… She just threatened to stab me if we summoned her tonight. Dinner with the parents or something," David said lightly, trying to make it sound like more of a joke than Natsuki had.

'Definitely not someone to cross lightly. For all we've been through I don't think we've seen Natsuki's bad side yet.'

'I like the fact she has some claws of her own.'

Takumi laughed, pulling David out of his conversation with Kou. Gesturing, Takumi led the way to the local convenience store to grab lunch and hang out. They passed the time playing video games with Naoto and Tsubasa.

"I'm surprised the third years didn't clobber you in soccer today. I was sure that's why they picked you," Naoto said while Tsubasa and Takumi were playing. David tried to shut him up, but the damage was done. Takumi turned away from his game. "Koji-sempai wants to kill you when second semester starts."

Takumi's eyes widened just enough for David to catch, but then he turned back to his game, leaving Naoto to continue talking about what had happened. It was nearly six in the evening when Takumi pointedly suggested they head home.

"You better tell me everything," Takumi began. With a raised hand David stopped him, then told him exactly what had happened with Koji. With Takumi occupied with his sword making, David had hoped the incident wouldn't get back to the Estate.

"I wanted to make him pay, but I kept my promise, I didn't do anything. It's not my fault the girl went and blabbed to everyone," David said, annoyed at having to defend himself.

"Koji-sempai is going to try to make your life hell," Takumi said. "Now there's almost no way you'll avoid another fight with him before he graduates. He could be an ōkami you know. Dad said there have been disappearances in the surrounding towns over the last several years."

Annoyed that Takumi was less than appreciative about how he had dealt with the situation and the subsequent rumors, David decided to change the subject on him.

"So what's the deal between you and Natsuki?" asked David leaning in.

"It's complicated," replied Takumi shortly.

"Why not just tell her how you feel?" Kou asked aloud, still a rarity for him. Takumi sighed at Kou's sudden input.

"That's not how things are done in Japan. Besides, she's your Partner," Takumi said slowly, as if every word was being dragged out of him through some obscene torture.

"I dunno... it just seems wrong somehow. You two fit together so well. You stayed friends even with Rie's disapproval. While we get along now it's still like we are constantly at war. Look at today. Besides, who says you can't date a Jitsugen Samurai's Partner?" David was sick of dancing around the issue of Natsuki. He had no interest in her. He would not have even thought of her in that way if it was not for Takumi's obvious interest and Kou bringing his attention to it.

"If you'd read more of the Matsumoto histories, you'd know that dating a Partner doesn't usually end well for the suitor, one way or another. Anyway, I thought today went pretty well."

During one of the soccer games, David had tried to stop Natsuki from scoring. Instead of going around him, she had dropped, sliding under David while still controlling the ball. Once she was behind him, Natsuki had brought her hands together, first fingers out and jabbed him in his behind to the raucous laughter of both teams. The *kancho*, a favorite of elementary and junior high students in Japan, was one of those unique cultural differences David still had trouble getting used to. David had learned early on not bend over lest he get *kanchoed*. While everyone laughed, Natsuki had popped back up and scored.

"Don't worry about that. It just means she's warming up to you. She was a terror in elementary. She even got the teachers!" Takumi said while laughing. David's face remained red until they passed the Police Station. Its taped window, and the memory of Jahangir's attack, sobered him.

"Well it's too bad she hasn't outgrown it yet then. Why do you do that in Japan anyway?" David asked, completely forgetting about their earlier topic.

"It's funny isn't it?" Takumi stared into the distance.

"Not if you're the target." David's eyes darkened for just the slightest instant before lightening.

'*There really was not any of the meanness that you Americans attach to such actions. It was not an act to ostracize you, but more an affirmation of your belonging to the group.*' Kou's thoughts on the subject made David take a hard look at his reactions to Natsuki.

"It's like swirlies or that wet-finger-in-the-ear thing," Takumi said, missing David's inner conversation.

"I dunno, maybe your right," mumbled David, lost again in thought. David and Takumi turned onto the main road.

"*Have you talked to Rie lately?*" Kou asked, taking advantage of David's distraction.

"No I haven't. I wish you'd stop bringing her up. She's obviously happy with her new loner lifestyle," Takumi replied hotly. He was still mad she had ditched him during his most important rite of passage as a Matsumoto.

"I'm not so sure she's been alone," David said carefully, jerked out of his subconscious by Kou's mention of Rie.

"What, you mean Chul Soon? Yea they hang out together between classes and stuff, but that's just him, he's always been really outgoing. They've been friends since nearly his first day." Takumi shrugged, trying to end the conversation as quickly as possible.

"Chul Soon? No, I meant Chul Moo… he's always hanging around, stalker-like. And Misaki—" David was cut off as they turned off the main road to find Ryohei coming towards them.

"Masao-san sent me to find you. You better hurry, he seems really agitated," Ryohei said. His willowy voice reached them before a normal person's would have. David shared a brief glance with Takumi before changing into Kou. Masao would never send Ryohei outside the Estate for less than an emergency, yet even more disturbing was the thought of an agitated Masao. Kou was off in a flash of fur. Takumi and Ryohei came just behind, Takumi stuffing David's clothes into his bag.

Kou made it to the Estate first. Using the trees, he was able to cut a straight path to the entrance, rather than follow the winding road. If he had not been looking so serious, David would have been amused at Masao's lack of reaction when Kou dropped directly in front of him from the gate.

"*What is wrong?*" asked Kou bowing quickly.

"Grandpa is missing. Wait for Takumi and Ryohei, then come meet me in the dojo, I am going to get Yukiko." Masao turned and walked towards the house.

'*Grandpa is missing?*'

'That's strange; I thought he was still on the Estate. Maybe he tried to go find Rie when she didn't come back from her training this morning.'

Kou paced, the tension of the situation bringing out the animal in him. Before long Takumi came barreling through the gate, nearly slamming into Kou, who jumped nimbly aside.

"*We are all supposed to go to the dojo,*" Kou said bounding towards the main house. He entered the main house from the outside sliding doors, and then jumped into his room just long enough to transform and throw on a pair of shorts before going to the dojo. Takumi and Ryohei caught up with him just before he got to the entrance.

David was lean and well muscled from the months of training, taller and with bigger shoulders and arms than Takumi. He was beginning to look formidable, the tension running through him lending a ferocity David usually only associated with Kou on the hunt. Masao was waiting with Yukiko at the low table in the dojo.

"Grandpa is missing," Masao said without preamble. "I have not seen him around the Estate. All I had was a note saying he could not do your evening lessons on Friday and possibly Saturday. I began to be concerned when he did not show, as far as I know, Dad has never had to use his wiggle room." Masao shifted, looking from Yukiko to Takumi to David as he spoke. "Then today, Ryohei found me and told me he saw Grandpa leaving the Estate. Normally I would not worry, but he did not warn me in advance that he might be gone longer. Rie is gone as well. I thought she was just training as usual, but she did not return last night or this morning, as is the custom. At first I assumed they were training together, but Ryohei said that Rie left before Grandpa."

David sat, his eyes glazing orange.

"He has been gone three days?" Kou spoke for David, his mind still racing, trying to remember every detail of their last conversation.

"Yes. Apparently he left late Friday afternoon," Masao said, looking at David questioningly. Takumi also turned to David, the surprise on his face at Masao's words turning to confusion at Kou's.

'He must have tried to follow after Rie. Did something we said mean more to him than to us?'

"I think I know where he went, and at least part of why," David said, pulling on his shirt from Takumi's bag. The entire table looked to David as his head popped out again.

"Oh he went after Rie didn't he? You should have done something about her sooner," Yukiko said, glaring at Masao.

"I've been trying to track Rie. I don't know how long she's been sneaking out, but once I knew how she was leaving I tried to follow, or anticipate her, but no matter what I tried, she always followed the stream, then went into the mountains and disappeared."

Agitated, David stood and began to pace, his words blending with Kou's.

"We couldn't think of anything to do, *so we went to Grandpa* to see if he could help. *Three days ago*, we told Grandpa everything we knew about Rie since our… *transformation*. Something I said must have meant more to him than he let on. We didn't even realize *he was gone from the Estate*." David stopped pacing, realizing the entire family was staring at him. "What?"

"It's hard to follow you…" Yukiko said, blinking. "Your voice keeps changing between Kou and yourself." Although her soft features were full of confusion, Yukiko still maintained her usual tact.

"Yeah, you're creeping me out," Takumi added, much less concerned over David's feelings at the moment.

"So you are saying Rie has been leaving every night and going to the mountains?" Masao asked, ignoring the others.

"Yes, I think maybe she is helping Misaki, the girl who ran away," David said.

"I am not as familiar with that area as Grandpa is, but I cannot think of any reason for her to go there. You had better show us where you lost her, and see if we can't track Grandpa. Takumi, get your sword and armor. After all, there may still be ōkami around. I am sure Kou will want to do the initial tracking."

David nodded for Kou. Suddenly, the dojo's sliding door slammed open.

"One Night! I asked you not to transform for ONE NIGHT! Takumi! Where's that sword so I can stab him!" Natsuki stomped up the stairs into the dojo with an explosion of yelling and raw fury. She stopped short seeing Masao, Yukiko, and the boys sitting around the table, with Ryohei floating nearby.

"Good, you are here. Happy Birthday. Takumi, fill her in while you get her armor and a sword for her, I know you have not had a chance to finish hers yet. Everyone meet in the garden when you are ready."

Takumi steered Natsuki to the back of the dojo. They emerged seconds later with their armor. As Takumi whispered to her, they headed to the house to change and retrieve the swords. Yukiko got up to prepare traveling equipment, while David went and donned his own armor. Leaving the back room, he changed back into Kou.

"Do you really think we will need full battle gear?" Kou asked, surprised by the Matsumotos' sudden action.

"No, but it is better to be safe than sorry. I feel... that I have missed something important about all this." Masao waved his arms vaguely, searching. "I have something for you by the way."

Masao disappeared into the back of the dojo. A few minutes later he came out wearing the full armor he had worn with Grandpa during the Golden Week mountain outing. He was also carrying several large bundles wrapped in cloth. Opening them before Kou, Masao produced sections of armor.

"You may soon come up against an enemy with a sword, arrows, or a gun. As a Kami you have a great deal of protection against some things, but you should also have some extra protection from anything not of the spirit world," Masao said, crouching down to Kou's eye level. "You are still smaller than you will become, so Grandpa made these for you. They have the same qualities that allow David's armor to disappear with him. It will stay with you, no matter how many times you transform, unless you take it off. David has the Tiger Armor we gave him before, and now you have yours. There is another set for when you grow larger."

Masao took one of the largest bundles and withdrew a tangle of synthetic leather and metal plates. Unraveling it, he placed it on Kou's head. It fit him perfectly. Made of brown material and reinforced with black and orange metal plates it was designed to protect and enhance Kou's furry head, yet remain flexible. The armor was also adjustable, with straps so that it would adjust as he grew. Kou worked his jaw, flexing experimentally.

The helm gave Kou a fierce visage, masking the cute baby tiger beneath its hard lines. Masao then attached the rest of the light armor. As with the helm, it molded to Kou's lines, leaving his movement unrestricted.

"This will not stop everything of course. It is mostly just an extra layer of protection. You will need help with the bindings when you put it on or take it off." Masao spoke automatically. His mind was on the mission, Rie, and his father, rather than on Kou's armor.

"Thank you very much." Kou's eyes flashed blue as David spoke for them both. Kou looked in a nearby mirror, standing with his paws on the wall so he could get a better look.

"*Hey! I look good. Of course, my fur is better, but I like the helm.*" Kou gave a menacing growl, and then laughed.

"I am glad you like it," Masao said. "He out did himself working on this. I have to get my sword. Meet the others in the Garden and we will be off."

Masao left for the main house, the rustle of his armor audible only to Kou. With one last glance in the mirror, Kou disappeared into the shadows.

二十六
SACRIFICES

July,

The cloud was back, stronger than ever. It was that hanging feeling of something dark on the horizon, a growing danger to not only ourselves, but to others…

Ryohei hovered in his usual spot over the stone bridge above the pond. Natsuki and Takumi stood next to a shaped tree in full armor, their swords sheathed, heads hidden by helmets and their individual scowling face guards. Coming up silently on the pair Kou heard Takumi whispering to Natsuki.

"I'm really sorry we had to drag you into this, and on your birthday." Takumi's voice was surprisingly soft in the still night air, but even so, Kou heard him as well as if he shouted.

"It's Grandpa," Natsuki said with a sigh. "I would do anything for him. Just don't tell David that."

"*Good to know you are not too mad,*" Kou growled from behind Natsuki. Both teenagers jumped at hearing Kou's voice from so close behind them.

"I really am sorry though. I would not have transformed if I could avoid it," David added as Natsuki glowered down at Kou.

"Just be glad Takumi hasn't finished my sword yet or I might have accidentally found a way to prick you with it," Natsuki said dangerously. "Do you know how hard it is to sit through dinner with your summons pulling at me? My parents kept asking if I had to go to the bathroom. So embarrassing." Natsuki had her usual bluster, but David and Kou were learning to read her too well, easily recognizing it as a façade.

"We'll make it up to you. *Your sword will be the finest ever made short of a Seikaku.* Matsumoto blade, *Jitsugen Samurai sheath.*" Once again, David and Kou's words blended. Their thoughts so close together they forgot to distinguish themselves while talking. Moments later, Masao and Yukiko came out of the main house carrying a bag with supplies.

"Kou, please lead," Masao said, eying everyone present. "Natsuki and Takumi, take the flanks, I will follow behind. Stay alert, I do not expect any trouble but let's be ready in case there is. Yukiko, stay here in case either return. Use the disposable phone if you have to make any outside calls."

"Rie left the Estate through the hole in the wall where the stream flows through. She probably got the idea from David," Kou said, leading them to the opening. Kou eyed the soft ground, sniffing and extending his senses. *"It looks like both Grandpa and Rie have been there, but I have no idea when. Grandpa's marks are almost obviously clear, though he would not have been able to fit through."*

"Interesting… let's check the other side, Kou lead the way via the Estate's main entrance," Masao commanded. Dutifully, Kou led the group back around to the front of the Estate, past the retirement cottage and through the gates. As soon as they made it back to the stream, Kou was able to pick up Grandpa's trail again.

'*Grandpa obviously wanted us to be able to follow him if we needed to. He stayed out of the water. Look, even after a few days, he left us a clearer trail than a herd of elephants would have.*'

'And just how do you know what a trail made by a herd of elephants looks like? You've never left Japan.'

'But you watch TV.'

Kou continued along the bank, even he could barely hear the three humans following him. While the spot where Rie usually disappeared was not overly far from the Estate, Kou went slowly to ensure he missed nothing. As they neared the curve in the stream that would mark her departure, the wind suddenly shifted, blowing a coppery smell that was all too easy for the animal part of him to recognize.

"*I smell blood,*" Kou said, stopping even as he called to the others.

The ring of swords leaving their sheaths barely disturbed the darkening sky's stillness as Kou hurried forward again, followed closely by the three human shadows. Kou paused when he reached the place where Rie usually left the stream to head into the mountains. Circling the area, he studied the tracks and smells, relying on his instincts to interpret his senses.

"*This is where Rie would head towards the mountains, but the blood I smell is fresh and leads away from here. It is on the other side, and farther upstream.*" Kou's voice grew strained as he fought his instinct to hunt down the source of the blood.

"Follow the blood first," Masao said, closing in on Kou with Natsuki and Takumi. "We can worry about where Rie's been going later."

'Let's just hope the blood and her disappearances are completely unrelated.'

'*Right. Like that is even a possibility.*' Kou continued his search, stopping away from the stream in a patch of tall grass. "*Look here. There are some books that smell like Grandpa.*"

"Takumi, grab the books, Kou, lead on." Masao's whispered commands barely carried on the wind, yet his urgency was as clear as the mountain stream running by.

Takumi ran over to Kou, covered closely by Natsuki, who kept her eyes on the forest around them. As soon as Takumi had the spot marked, Kou turned and splashed through the stream to the other side.

'At least the stream isn't giving us any problems.'

'We have a complicated relationship with rivers and lakes, we depend on them. The sea, however...' Kou growled and let the thought fade as they reached the other shore.

Having recovered the books Takumi slid them inside his armor for safekeeping. The three humans quietly became shadows again, trailing swiftly behind Kou. The small tiger paced faster as the smell grew stronger, threatening to overwhelm them. Unfortunately, the breeze was just as strong as his sense of smell. It took them much longer than David had thought it would to find the source of the scent.

A change in the light alerted them to a clearing just ahead. Kou stopped to listen then trotted out into a small open clearing at the side of the main road. The familiar sounds of Nakano Town carried over the still night air.

Grandpa lay in a crumpled heap in the center of the clearing, battered and bloody. Kou checked the surrounding trees for any sign of ambush since there was nothing he could do to help the old man. Rushing past, Masao reached Grandpa first, bending down he checked his father.

With Natsuki and Takumi keeping guard, Kou trotted over to the elder Matsumoto. Grandpa had been tortured. His clothes were ragged and bloody, with numerous gashes along what had once been his proud arms and legs, all of which appeared broken. One stump, hand missing was pressed against his shirt, the whole of which was caked in dried blood.

"Dad, can you hear me? Dad?" Masao checked for a pulse. With no response, Masao leaned closer hissing something that even Kou's ears could not pick up.

"The SHRINE! – Ōkami – Rie!" Grandpa's eyes fluttered open, gasping for breath his words rattled out in a pained voice. As quickly as he had awoken, Grandpa passed out again. His shallow breathing came in ragged pulls. Masao whirled wildly on Takumi.

"The books! Quickly!" Masao demanded, grabbing the books from Takumi and turning on a light from his bag. From between the books, Takumi caught a piece of paper as it fell.

"It's a map of the mountains, with caves hand-marked," Takumi whispered, trying to avoid looking at Grandpa.

"Caves. Of course…" Masao said distantly as he looked up from one of the books. Masao suddenly shook himself back to the present. "Go back to the house. Head for the shrine. You must stop them no matter what. Even… Even if you have to kill *everyone* there, stop them. I will get word to Yukiko and take care of Grandpa. I would only slow you down now… Go!"

Masao's urgency, his total focus on the three despite his father lying at his feet dying brooked no hesitation. Kou, Natsuki, and Takumi, turned and ran.

"What was the book he found? What's at the shrine?" David asked. Takumi had to shout, although Kou was not yet running full out, he was still ahead of Takumi and Natsuki and gaining ground.

"It was the Matsumoto books on ōkami and the lands surrounding the Estate. The pack of ōkami must have Rie!"

'Koji!' David's thoughts screamed out in a sudden rage.

The three runners needed no more prompting, with a burst of speed they ran harder, using every technique they knew to get back to the Estate as fast as possible. As part of his evening training with Grandpa, David had learned about the various forms of evil that he might one day face. The ōkami were a horrible combination of human, animal, and corrupt spirit. Able to appear either attractive or vicious in either their human or animal form, the ōkami were dangerous on their own and murderous in a pack. With the ability to exert a powerful domination over a human caught unaware, the ōkami were extremely good at manipulating their prey. Ōkami fed off the souls of their dominated captives, much as evil obake were known to do. Unlike obake, however, they also fed off their preys' flesh.

The part that had Kou, Takumi, and Natsuki using every ounce of speed they had was that Grandpa had told them that packs of ōkami usually were driven by a yūrei. One of the most horrible, powerful, and deadly types of monster, yūrei were the dark shades that haunted the collective memory from ages past, and still manifested in the nightmares of today. Evil so pervasive humans could never quite forget it. Ōkami packs without a yūrei were often driven to create one from their greed and lust for power.

The yūrei were able to summon oni and control ōkami. In return, the ōkami would become far more powerful, drawing strength from the corrupt Kami within the yūrei. To create their abomination, the ōkami would need a person of strong body, whose will they would have been able to weaken over a long process of dominion. They would also need access to a true Shinto shrine, one where Kami would visit, one like at the Matsumoto Estate.

二十七

IN A CLEARING
AMONG TREES

July,

Even though I did not really know Rie very well, David's memories of her, few though they might be, were more than enough to make my fur stand on end...

Kou flew through the trees within the Estate like a silent wraith. He kept up his furious pace until he caught movement and slowed as he neared the shrine. His night vision caught Jahangir, the stranger from the police station, standing before the Matsumoto shrine wearing a dark cloak with hood pulled low over his face. His insistent chanting was reminiscent of Grandpa's summoning chant but had a more insistent tempo and far harsher quality.

Rie sat on the altar of the shrine, a place usually reserved for the steel of a new sword. She stared into space. Her usually bright features were veiled by a vacant smile and misty eyes. As Jahangir continued his chant, a young girl ran into the clearing from the direction of the house. Scrawny and ragged she was nonetheless beautiful.

"I heard the mother talk to the old one on a phone," the young ōkami called. "They're coming." Her message delivered, she turned and headed for the trees opposite Kou. Jah-angir's chant increased in volume and speed as he attacked his way through the rough words. Before the young ōkami could reach the trees though, Kou jumped into the clearing, his teeth bared.

As Kou hit the clearing, he froze in shock as he saw a giant fiery Kami descending on the shrine. It contained a blinding radiance that caused such debilitating waves of fear within David that Kou froze as surely as the ancient trees around him were deep rooted. David swallowed past the terror roiling through him, uncertainty locking him in place. Kou's fur stood on edge as he battled against David's indecision. The young girl ran towards them.

Entering the clearing with Natsuki, Takumi ran straight past the young ōkami. It was as if the trees, rocks, monsters, and his friends disappeared from Takumi's view. He rushed towards the shrine, ignoring everything else around him. Ta-kumi bowled past Jahangir, who stumbled, but continued chanting, focused on the ceremony.

'Should we attack as Kou or David,' David thought, the seconds flashing by. His uncertainty burned within as he felt a growing need to act. Kou roared within, wanting nothing more than to attack. David's eyes locked on a shape leaving the woods next to the shrine. His determination and strength returning, David opened himself to Kou's input but with Kou straining against him, it took precious seconds for them to merge. They changed, and despite retaining Kou's tail, sum-moned their Seikaku.

Before him, Natsuki was already engaged in combat with the young female ōkami as Takumi hit the stone steps. Natsu-ki's borrowed sword flashed against metal gauntlets with long wicked claws. Takumi's hand wrapped around Rie's arm, ready to pull her to safety. David wanted to scream.

Even as Kou and David moved towards their host brother, howling to him in their mixed voice to run, a large black furred ōkami with white markings around its snout and eyes sprang from beside the shrine. David saw every instant of horror as the ōkami's vicious fangs ripped into Takumi's neck.

The black haired ōkami's teeth and powerful jaws bit through Takumi's muscle and bones with a crunch audible throughout the clearing. His hand slid slowly down Rie's arm, Takumi's last strength left him in a vain attempt to hold onto his sister. With a jerk of the ōkami's head, his eyes blazed with shock and sorrow before fading completely, his hand falling away limply.

As the black haired ōkami attacked, another slightly larger grey furred ōkami sprang from the forest. Horrified by the scene before him, but otherwise alert for danger, David took the hit from the grey ōkami in the side, his armor protected him as the ōkami's claws tried to slash him. Rolling, David was able to right himself and face his opponent, Seikaku in hand, shaken, but still whole.

Cagey, the ōkami circled David, staying out of range of the sword. Though a brute animal, its familiar hate-filled eyes sent shivers down his spine. David checked on Natsuki with a quick glance. Her sword was locked in between the young female ōkami's gauntlets. Natsuki struggled, her strength against the ōkami's strength, something Grandpa had taught them to always avoid. Catching David looking away, the ōkami lunged, testing David's defenses.

Jahangir finished his chant in crescendo of vocal power. Before him, Rie's eyes flew open with a piercing scream. In the clearing, Natsuki flinched. Off balance, the female ōkami drove her to the ground, her gauntlets ripping Natsuki's sword from her hands. On the alter, Rie's eyes became deep black voids, her whole body twitching as if she was being burned alive. For one brief moment, David forgot the ōkami prowling before him as his entire being absorbed the pain and violation on Rie's face. Then it was over and she fell off the altar, rolling down the stairs to Jahangir's feet.

Howling, Jahangir scooped up Rie's lifeless body and ran into the forest. The black haired ōkami followed immediately, leaving Takumi's corpse behind. The grey ōkami snapped at David, then smiled.

"She is ours now." Chul Moo's voice, distorted by its new source, was nonetheless all too familiar. Before David could react, Chul Moo leapt away, sprinting after Jahangir.

The female ōkami, poised to strike a killing blow ignored the rest of her pack. Her eyes and body no longer seemed human, mouth open in a wild grin, she loomed over Natsuki.

As her gauntlet fell, David *moved*. Rushing forward the Seikaku gleamed as it sliced the ōkami's arms. Surprisingly, the heavy blow did not cut through. Instead, it merely opened large gashes, deflecting the deadly weapons enough to save Natsuki. The ōkami's outraged howl was sucked from the air as David used the momentum from the first strike to reverse the blade's direction. Changing the Seikaku to its elemental form, David thrust the wooden blade behind him into the center of the ōkami.

David froze, his gaze locked with the animal Chul Moo, standing among the trees at the edge of the forest. His shining black eyes inscrutable, David tried to find some meaning behind the stare, but even Kou was at a loss. Another howl from far away sounded, and Chul Moo was gone. Behind him, David's tail brushed something hard and he turned to take in the small wooden statue of an ōkami that stood in place of the young girl. The statue's wolven features were horribly lifelike in the hatred glaring from the eyes. Every grain of the wood seemed to scream the rage the ōkami had felt at losing its prey.

"You should keep the tail," Natsuki said as she took in David standing over her. Her smile faded as she searched the area. Finally, her eyes found Takumi's body.

Hours later in the main house, the rising sun was just beginning to illuminate the straw tatami mats. The shoji doors were open and a ragged Masao Matsumoto sat at the large low table in the main room. Haggard from the night's events, he still wore the same blood stained kimono that he had worn beneath his armor the night before. Across from him, David sat staring into the eyes of the statue standing between them on the table. Arrayed around the statue were scattered the books Kou had found in the forest near the stream and Takumi's sword.

"There was nothing we could do for him, the ōkami made sure of that. It is obvious now he was left to attract attention and lure us away from the shrine. If you had not tracked him down, someone would have found him by the road." Masao had recovered somewhat from the past night's events, though he was changed. David recognized more of Grandpa in him. Reaching forward he took the old, hand-marked map of the forest around the Matsumoto Estate.

"So the ōkami were there the whole time? Hiding in the caves, feeding off Rie?" asked David, Kou's anger feeding his own, burning within him. He had literally stood on top of some of the caves.

"Grandpa knew these mountains better than anyone," Masao said, sighing with fatigue. "He probably suspected one of them was the den based on what you said. After Grandpa... after Grandpa was taken care of, I searched the caves and found the remains of a den, and what I believe to be Misaki's remains. Yukiko placed a call. Someone will discover the body of a runaway mauled by an animal. When they identify her, they will assume it is the same animal that killed Grandpa. There will be searches, but they will not find anything. The ōkami's lair was cleared out before the ōkami attacked the Estate." Masao spoke with a deep resignation, his eyes staring into the statue's carved features.

"What kind of Jitsugen Samurai am I?" David asked, tears in his eyes. "Not only did I cause Grandpa's death, I couldn't even save Rie. How many days did I sit and talk with Chul Soon and do nothing. He was my *friend!* All those days trying to help Rie, when in reality I was helping the ōkami. And then worst of all, when it truly mattered I hesitated. I let fear control me. I should have been with Takumi."

"We have failed. One less ōkami does not even begin to repair the damage we have caused." Kou's orange hue and David's tears turned his eyes into great shining suns.

"Grandpa was responsible for his own actions. It is the *Matsumoto* who have failed. We missed the signs. I missed the signs of an ōkami's dominance in my own daughter. Misaki's death is on my shoulders. We are only lucky you did not succeed in breaking Chul Moo from his isolation. As for this ōkami, be glad you have a wood sword and not a stone. We will burn it to prevent it from ever being animated by another spirit."

Masao withdrew into silence. The sad brooding between the two was broken by a slow, pained groan from beneath the table. David pulled his gaze away from the statue's eyes as hand grabbing the table. Takumi lifted himself up into a sitting position, his eyes glazed.

"What happened?" Takumi asked, clean and dressed in fresh clothes. He looked around bewildered.

"You fell asleep again. I assume you still remember everything?" Masao asked as Takumi's eyes tried to focus on him. His eyes filled with tears.

"Yes, I remember. What are we going to do? We have to help Rie. What about Grandpa? Where's Natsuki? I can't believe we let Rie be dominated by ōkami all this time. We need to go. Let's go get her, right now." Takumi tried to stand, but staggered. He would have fallen over the table, but David was there, helping him back down.

"Natsuki went home. She had to sneak back in before her parents woke up… It was her birthday after all…" David spoke gently, unable to continue he sat again, eyes falling back into the wooden pits of the statue's eyes. Masao continued where David left off.

"Grandpa died about an hour ago. The ōkami made sure there was nothing we could do for him." Masao's voice gained strength as he spoke, his eyes tightening in anger and outrage. Takumi sagged, defeated. His sister and Grandpa torn away in the same night. "As for what is next, we will cremate Grandpa, burn this ōkami's statue, then track down the rest and do the same to them. Then, and only then will we be able to destroy the yūrei."

"What do you mean 'destroy' the yūrei?" Takumi asked suddenly shouting in a rage. "You mean kill Rie? It was our fault this happened to her. We can't just kill her!"

Masao waited for Takumi to calm himself before replying.

"We do not know how much Rie was in control of her actions. If she had any choice in the matter, if she chose any part of it, we may not be able to save her. What we **do** know, is that the ōkami found out about David… probably when he first changed. David that must have been Chul Soon that chased you that first time. From what you have said, the markings were the same. They have probably been hiding out since they found out you are a Jitsugen Samurai. With a yūrei, however, they will grow much stronger. They may not realize that they have also bound themselves. A yūrei will control them, not the other way around."

"It was *definitely* Chul Soon, he made sure I knew it was him," Takumi said.

"When you say destroy, are you saying we have to kill Rie?" Kou asked. David was surprised at how repulsed Kou was by the thought.

'You do not yet understand, but she has already made enough sacrifices. It is our turn to be there for her,' Kou thought, answering David's curiosity.

"I hope it does not come to that," Masao said, his voice breaking. "I just lost my father. One of your classmates has paid for our negligence. I do not want to lose a daughter too. There may be a way to exorcize the corrupted Kami within her, but I will need time to find out how."

David's sudden look outside alerted them to Ryohei's approach.

"I searched the entire mountain range. I couldn't find a trace of them anywhere, and the only other ghost wouldn't tell me anything. If they have a new den, it isn't around the Estate," Ryohei said as he drifted through the doors. His willowy voice filled the air within the main room, while his aura chilled the three mourners.

"Thanks Ryohei," David said with a shiver. "Ryohei agreed to double check the mountains after Masao-sensei and I checked them. We didn't find anything either."

"Huh, I can see him. Nice to finally see you Ryohei... you do look like me." Takumi stared into the obake's face as if looking into his own.

"I'd say you look like me." Ryohei smiled widely. "If I remember correctly from my own training, the yūrei won't be able to summon any oni for a while yet. The ōkami will begin to grow stronger immediately, but the yūrei will take a long time to learn the host's body and gain the knowledge necessary to summon an oni."

"So then we need to find Rie before she can unleash an oni?" asked David.

"Yes, that is the first task for us once the more pressing matters are taken care of... We also have to prepare for the Nakano Festival. We cannot cancel or postpone that since the festival is for the Kami that visit our shrine... there has never *not* been a festival since the shrine was built," Masao said, growing more calm and collected with every passing minute. As the list of things to do mounted, he became more his old self.

"Speaking of us... What does all this mean? Is Takumi a Jitsugen Samurai now?" David asked, confused that one of the most obvious questions had yet to be answered. Masao sighed, the pressures hardening him like carbon into a diamond.

"No. There was no metal. The Kami, while corrupted must have had at least some part of it that was still good. That part would have escaped into Takumi before it would possess an unwilling host. Only the corruption would seek to dominate. Without the metal though, there was nothing to bind them together. As you know, part of your soul is in the honshitsu, as is part of Kou. That is the bridge between you, and without it, Takumi will be far less.

"He did, however, die during a summoning ceremony at which a Kami was present, so the part of the Kami that was pulled apart became a new entity. That new entity saved Takumi's life. He is possessed, but not fully, and not by a mature Kami which is how the ancient monsters were created. He will be a shape shifter. As for the form and power of the Kami, and any other powers he may have, well, we will just have to wait and see."

Despite himself, Masao smiled, looking at his son with pride. Takumi unconsciously reached up, touching where Chul Soon had ripped at his neck. A jagged scar betrayed the savage injury that had caused his death just hours before.

"I don't think this scar is going to go away like your injuries did," Takumi sighed. "I guess I know how you felt. Even with years of stories and training, even after seeing you, it's always someone else that it happens to. It's always someone else's story. It is hard to believe a Kami lives within me... It seems there's a lot I can't believe... Grandpa is gone." Takumi looked to Masao, his eyes full of the essential bond between twins, the complete understanding the two had. "There's no way Rie would willingly be a party to what they did to Grandpa. We have to find her."

"We have already found where the ōkami had been staying in the mountains. Ryohei confirmed they are no longer nearby. If I am right, they will lay low, recover, and wait until the yūrei can use its powers. Yes, we should attack before the yūrei can summon an oni but we too must wait until we find them, and grow stronger ourselves." Masao stood. The echoing crash was the only warning David and Takumi had as Masao brought his fist down onto the ōkami statue.

The table below shattered while the statue remained unharmed. Masao took the statue and walked outside as blood flowed from his hand. That night a fire burned high into the trees before the Matsumoto shrine. Green flames swirled as the evil departed forever.

二十八

FAMILY FRIENDS IN KYOTO

July,

We were failures. Grandpa—Masato, we finally learned his first name—Misaki, and Rie all lost. David and I vowed to do whatever it took to right those mistakes. Masato had been like a cagy old tiger, tired with matted fur, a ruse, a lesson taught with sharp claws and a powerful swipe...

Grandpa's funeral was, like most major events, at the Matsumoto shrine. The estate was opened to the public, with mourners coming from all over Japan to pay their respects to the renowned sword maker as incense infused the clearing. Masato Matsumoto's death was attributed to an animal attack, which meant he quickly became just another statistic. The number of such attacks was, as many pundits mentioned, up 15% across Japan from a year earlier and 40% from two years earlier.

The guilt David felt was made all the worse by the attention Yukiko and the others showed him. David wanted to call Jessica, he knew his little sister would be the only one other than Kou that could completely understand him, yet due to the circumstances around Masato's death and Rie's disappearance, he could not think of a way to tell her his problems without giving away the Matsumotos' secrets.

David and Takumi attempted to distract themselves from their losses by finishing Natsuki's sword. Takumi made a rough handle and scabbard in the traditional manner so that David had something clear to focus on. Then over a few days and several tries, David finally succeeded in creating a sheath and handle to perfectly match Takumi's blade. Using the elemental form of the Seikaku, David coaxed the un-finished handle to grow around the blade so securely that it needed no other fittings. The scabbard matched and David devised a locking mechanism so that when finished, it did indeed appear to be nothing more than a practice sword.

That task complete, to the astonishment and joy of Natsuki, David continued his nightly searches with Kou. A few days after the funeral, Masao was waiting for David when he returned.

"Anything?" Masao asked from the shadows as David crept into the main house. Though he was secretly relieved not to have to crawl under the house anymore, his searches, direr than ever before, left David more worried with each night.

"Not a sniff, track, or sight of any of them," David said, disgusted. "It's like they disappeared into a black hole."

"I think they are probably smart enough not to leave anything for you to track. We will have to find some other way of locating them," Masao said calmly, his old manner completely recovered after the outburst with the ōkami's statue.

"*I assume that is not why you are up at three in the morning?*" Kou asked.

"No. I have spent the last few days going through every record we keep. I cannot find anything on destroying yūrei apart from killing them."

David stepped closer. Although calm, Masao's face betrayed days without sleep. He was close to the edge. Losing his father was bad, but David could tell he would be destroyed if he had to kill his own daughter, even to protect Japan.

"Is there anyone else we can ask, any other information?" David asked, trying to control his voice.

"Yes actually, and that is why I am up at… well now," Masao said. "We are all going to Kyoto tomorrow, today. We leave in a few hours. Some of the oldest Matsumoto records and other books are Imperial Treasures. We have to go to the old imperial palace to get permission to view the materials. I think I am going to have to introduce you to some people as well. I can explain it better later. Go pack. We will have to leave quickly and quietly… We do not want the ōkami to know we are gone. Natsuki-chan will have to come to practice as usual, just in case."

"How long will we be gone?" David asked, eliciting a growl from Kou for his tone. "I can't look for Rie if I'm not here."

"We will be there as long as it takes to find a way to save her. Even if you found her tonight, we could not help her. Go, it will be alright." Masao's smile told David he understood better than the young American did what was at stake.

The three Matsumotos and David waited for Natsuki to show for her normal practice. When she arrived, they told her all about their plans, asking her to watch over the Estate while they were gone.

Since his only experience was with trips within the United States, David assumed the traveling and all its preparations would take far longer than they did. It turned out that the ancient city of Kyoto was under two hours away from Himeji by train. Once the house was settled David and the Matsumotos drove through the mountains surrounding Nakano to Himeji Station. They were there before the first train of the morning to Kyoto.

"I have called ahead to the Imperial Palace," Masao said to the group before getting to the station. "There will be a car waiting for us at the station to take us directly to the palace. The Emperor is currently in Tokyo, however, we will need to make introductions to the Crown Prince Nakahito, and seek access to the records."

"By Crown Prince, do you mean the next Emperor of Japan?" David asked incredulously from the back seat of the

Matsumotos' car. Takumi, in his stoic mode, merely stared at David.

"Yes. The Matsumotos have maintained close, if discreet ties with the Imperial Family for hundreds of years. As Crown Prince, Nakahito will be aware of the true history of Japan. Even if we did not need his help, we would still have to inform him that a Jitsugen Samurai has awakened. He will need to know there is danger, and that both you and Takumi have been possessed. I was planning on waiting until you were older, better trained, but we need those books, which means explaining the situation. The Imperial Family may call upon you at any time once they know you exist." Masao eyed the pair in the back seat wearily as, with his usual disregard for traffic rules, he swerved into a parking spot before the station.

David spent the hour and forty-five minutes while on the train talking with Kou. Since the family was in a public place, they had to keep their conversations to the realm of their guise as tourists. While the family chatted, David brooded on his up-coming meeting. He had never even met the Mayor back home, let alone a prince or anyone famous. It also disturbed him that the prince might not just meet him, but expect something from him. After all, though far more than he had been, he still did not feel like he was a Jitsugen Samurai—defender of Japan.

As promised, a car was waiting for them at the station... if you could call a stretch limo with dark windows a car. David stared at the city as the limousine wove through the tight streets of Kyoto. The modern buildings were mixed with clas-sic architecture, buildings reminiscent of the Matsumoto Estate.

They entered the Imperial Palace grounds from a side en-trance, the beautiful buildings matched by stunning gardens, ponds, and tree lined paths. The family was quickly taken into an ancient yet well-maintained security office. After their iden-tities were checked, David's several times, they were asked to change into ceremonial robes for the occasion of meeting the Crown Prince.

It took David several tries and many suggestions from Kou to struggle into the voluminous garment. After ten minutes, a well-spoken valet came and showed David to the rest of the family, helping to fix his sagging belt along the way. Afterward, the family was back together and seated at a low table, where they were served green tea while they waited. A few minutes later, another valet came in and described the procedures and etiquette for the meeting. By the looks on the Matsumotos' faces, David was sure the information was for him.

After another hour of waiting, the Matsumotos and David were finally led from the security building to the main complex. They walked through corridors few foreigners had seen. Walls and sliding doors were covered in stunning murals depicting scenes from Japanese history. Finally, after much bowing and set phrases they were before a man sitting stiffly in an elegant chair.

The forty-nine year old Crown Prince was black haired and smiled warmly through the greetings. Dressed in a modernly cut suit, appearing as any diplomat might, his face remained in a pleasant mask through the lengthy words demanded by etiquette. Once the attendants were gone, however, his face fell as sadness creased his eyes.

"I am so very sorry about Masato-hanshi," the Prince said, his head hanging a little in sorrow. "You being here, and with a foreigner no less, tells me he did not die by an animal attack. I would have liked to attend the funeral. I am sorry circumstances kept me away. I remember my boyhood training fondly." The Crown Prince spoke in regular Japanese, a distinct change from the formal and ancient words used during the greetings. "Sorry about the clothes as well, but my security guards thought it best, good to keep up appearances you know. Now, I have an inkling why you are here. The Imperial House has been monitoring world events, and the news of late, when taken together is disturbing."

Standing upright, Masao spoke formally to the Crown Prince, despite the common speech used by the latter.

"We came to warn the Crown Prince that indeed, Evil has returned. Masato Matsumoto was killed by a pack of ōkami. What is more, we now know there is a yūrei as well. We bring good tidings as well. A new Jitsugen Samurai has awakened," Masao said bowing low.

Nakahito eyed the boys, gauging them with intelligent scrutiny. "Where is Rie? Why have you brought a foreigner?"

"Are *you* the Jitsugen Samurai?" asked Nakahito, suddenly switching to Oxford accented English and staring pointedly at David.

As Kou took control, David's eyes changed to orange. David bowed. *"Yes, we are David and Kou."*

"Really! A foreign Jitsugen Samurai, no wonder you came," Nakahito said. Sitting back, his carefully crafted demeanor broke as he laughed. Nakahito then turned back to Masao, leaning towards them in interest. "Tell me more."

"How did the Crown Prince know it was him?" Masao bowed again, a smile playing at the corners of his mouth.

"You brought him, and he watched me while I spoke, he understood the ancient phrases during the introductions," Nakahito said simply.

"You still remember your training well, very observant," Masao said with another bow. "David is not the only one who is changed. Takumi also has been possessed, though this happened only a week past. He will be a shape shifter. Rie... Rie was captured by the ōkami and turned into a yūrei. They lured us away from the Estate by torturing Masato, and then turned Rie before we could stop them. David has only been a Jitsugen Samurai for a few months, shortly after he arrived in Japan as an exchange student. We have come to humbly request access to the Imperial Treasures, so that we may find a way to destroy the yūrei without killing Rie."

Masao fell to the floor, the rest of the Matsumotos and David followed suit and bowed, nearly prostrating themselves when Masao gave his request.

"Please, stand," Nakahito said, betraying the agitation he had hidden so well by standing. "Masao, we have known each other all our lives, of course you can search the records. I hope that for all our sakes you find what you need. Where there is one ōkami there are more. David, Takumi, you need bow to no one but the Emperor, and then only as friends. I am well aware what you must have gone through. Now, unfortunately, I have pressing matters, but I want to hear everything. Masao, you know where to go, you have free reign anywhere in the grounds. David, Kou, Takumi, I will talk to you later, I hope. Until then, please enjoy this beautiful city. Masao, let your attendants know what you find, I will see you all again before you leave."

The Prince stood and left. They were soon met by new attendants and guards. Masao hurried away to do his research while Yukiko, David, and Takumi were taken on a tour of the grounds, before heading to a residence for the duration of their stay.

Masao did not join them again until dinner, which was brought to a room for the family to eat together. Masao looked tired, and although the food was lavish and beautifully displayed, he ate quickly, barely stopping to appreciate the artistry behind each of the small dishes.

"I wish the two of you could help me look, there are so many books to read through, and David has a better understanding of ancient Japanese than I do. Even though I am known around the palace, it has caused a bit of an uproar among the staff, me being given complete access. The two of you will have to pretend to be nothing more than my sons in front of anyone but the Emperor or Crown Prince."

Finishing, Masao left quickly to continue his search of the Imperial Treasures late into the evening hours. His parting remarks were to David.

"Do not forget, no changing into Kou…" Masao said. "We do not need Natsuki-chan getting drawn away from the Estate."

David, Takumi, and Yukiko did not see much of Masao Matsumoto over the next two days. Although he was obliged to return to their lodgings every night for at least a few hours' sleep, Masao was driven in his search for a way to save Rie. While the rest of the Matsumotos and David were given relatively free access to most of the Palace grounds they were constantly accompanied by attendants. David soon realized from the way they orientated themselves around him and Takumi that they were there as much for his protection as for general security of the grounds.

With nothing to do in the Palace and with the news the Prince had flown back to Tokyo to consult with the Emperor, David, Takumi, and Yukiko left the Palace to explore the historic sights of Kyoto. Once again dressed as tourists, the family and their guards were guided through the city by one of the House Attendants, disguised as a tour guide.

Their status and escort allowed the Matsumotos and David through all the major historic sites without having to wait for lines or ticket counters. This let them see many of the major sites in Kyoto far more quickly than usual. David was especially glad to play tourist since he was able to get souvenirs and pictures from many of the locations they visited for his sister and father. As soon as they saw their first temple David was sure he would have plenty of non-samurai material to talk about the next time they spoke.

When they returned after the second day of tours, it was to find Masao waiting for them, triumphant. Once they were alone in their room, Masao spoke quickly, excited and energetic despite days with minimal sleep.

"I found it!" Masao crowed. "I actually found it! There is a ritual we that will obliterate the Kami within Rie without killing her or dispelling her soul. It talks of needing the 'Emperor's Sword' referring to the Imperial Regalia, and using it to cut out the corrupt Kami from within the yūrei."

"Isn't the 'Emperor's Sword' a copy the Matsumotos made centuries ago? The first Seikaku would have dissolved when Ninigi died," Takumi said, confused and looking at his father as if maybe he needed more than sleep.

"Exactly, which means we need a Seikaku, not the Emperor's Sword." Masao smiled, showing them an ancient text. Everyone looked between David and the text, uncertain but hopeful.

"Great, then all we need to do is find her, you tell me what to do, and I'll cut the Kami right out of her," David said confidently.

"It is not quite that simple." Masao sat, the weight of his search finally getting to him. "We are going to have to capture her and bring her back to the shrine. Not an easy task. And it is not as simple as just stabbing her with the Seikaku. We will have to be very careful otherwise you will dispel whatever is left of Rie instead of killing the Kami inside her. I have made copies of the text explaining what we need to do. The Crown Prince needs to see us before we head back to track her down. Let's go."

The second meeting with the Crown Prince went without all the ceremony. They met in a small comfortable room away from the prying eyes of house staff.

"The Emperor, my father, sends his greetings to Yukiko, David, and Takumi," the Crown Prince said somewhat stiffly. David looked to Masao, but if his host father noted the greetings had not included him, he ignored it. "We are both overjoyed that you have found what you need, and realize you are all in a hurry to return to the hunt for Rie. If we can offer any assistance, please let us know, though of course we do not have the resources we once did. We must also keep these things secret from as many people as possible.

"David. You are the first Jitsugen Samurai in many years. You have a great responsibility and we may need to call on you in the coming years. Takumi, we charge you to continue the Matsumotos' tradition. Help the Jitsugen Samurai, help David, in any way you can. David, although the Imperial Family are little more than figureheads now, we do still have some influence.

"We know you have already made significant sacrifices for our country, and may make more. In accordance, you will never have to worry about school, money, or having a place to live. It has been a long time since there has been a Jitsugen Samurai, and circumstances have changed much, but I promise I will find some way to begin to repay your efforts. You have the resources of the Imperial House behind you, if discreetly. We would like you to visit both here and Tokyo as often as possible, so that you can get to know the country you protect more fully. We trust your training to the Matsumotos. Masao, as your fathers have done before you, do not fail. Though few will know it, David is now our greatest asset, as was Ninigi and all Jitsugen Samurai after him.

"If we were in the olden days, David, you would have been made a prince of the Imperial Family. As things are today, we hope our meager offerings are enough.

"And do not think we have left you out, Kou, for without you, David would not be what he is. My words were for you as well. We thank you both."

David, overcome, merely bowed. Kou, however had no issues speaking, Crown Prince or not.

"*Thank you, I accept on behalf of David, who is a bit embarrassed,*" Kou said, smiling with David's face. "*He still does not yet believe that he is indeed special. As a Kami, I know better. Neither of us take our position lightly, however, right now, all we wish is to find and help Rie. Please call on us if you need us.*"

"Thank you. My guards would not much like this if they knew, but if you would indulge me... May I see the Seikaku? I have always wondered..." Nakahito's eyes glowed, a bit of boyhood mischievousness breaking through the crafted public mask.

With a smile and a nod from Masao, David closed his eyes and summoned the Seikaku. It appeared before him. Catching it lightly, he demonstrated both forms for the Prince, holding the blade lengthwise in both hands before him.

"Amazing," said the Crown Prince, nearly speechless while he examined the fine sword. "I never thought I would actually see one. This is better than the sword you made me Masao... Though I guess I should expect nothing less."

A few more remarks ended their brief stay in Kyoto. The family was once more dressed as tourists heading home on the train. The guards following were easily apparent to anyone with Matsumoto training.

"How long are they going to keep following us?" David asked leaning in towards Masao.

"Just until Himeji Station. They are mainly there for protocol. Nakahito knows we would not need them in a fight." Masao nodded off to sleep, and David sat back, reflecting on the amazing sites and events of the last few days.

'We need to find Rie.'

'We will. I have some ideas about that.'

二十九
SEARCH

July,

*Although we were emboldened by the trip to Kyoto, Masao-
san's revelations about the ceremony we would have to per-
form once we found Rie weighed heavily on our minds...*

Back at the Estate, the Matsumotos filled Natsuki and Ryohei
in on what they had found during their trip. Natsuki looked
particularly pleased to have the Matsumotos back so it was no
longer just her and Ryohei on the Estate.

Masao's information came from a book written when one
of the Imperial Household became a yūrei. In the days the
book was written, the Imperial Household had been far, far
larger than the constitution restricted House of modern times.

Somehow, the Matsumotos had not been able to record the
incident. It seemed the author had not been aware of the full
story, only that a samurai had used the Emperor's sword, and
a complex ritual to cut the demon out of the Prince, saving
him. The author had been at the ceremony but the story was a
passing anecdote in a longwinded biography.

With everyone back at the Estate, and no problems while
they had been gone, the Matsumotos, Natsuki, and David met

to determine their next steps. Yukiko sat close to Natsuki, giving her a few more details about the Palace and the trip to Kyoto. As with any trip in Japan, the family had also brought her a large quantity of omiyage. Presents and souvenirs, mostly of food, omiyage was a way of thanking Natsuki for keeping an eye on things while they had been away, and also for enduring Ryohei's presence. David finally understood what Yukiko's shopping had been all about while they were in Kyoto.

"I will need some time to study the text and determine exactly what we will have to do once we catch Rie. Luckily, the author was very long winded. He gave a detailed account of everything that happened in the ceremony, including the words he heard used by the Shinto priest. Anyway, that part is clear at least, we have to somehow capture her. Any ideas on how to find the ōkami lair?" Masao was still exhausted and spoke grimly as he looked around the table.

"They will probably need to capture new prey to feed off, right?" Kou asked. "We should be on the watch for any disappearances or people acting strangely. They might be able to lead us to the ōkami. Also, David and I want access to everything you have on yūrei. We need to know how our enemy will be thinking, if we are to save Rie."

"Of course, Kou." Masao sat back thinking, then gestured to Takumi, Natsuki, and David. "I think I would like the three of you to patrol Nakano and the surrounding countryside at night from now on. I will help where I can, but I will have to ensure this ceremony does not go astray. School also starts in just two weeks, then it will be time for the Nakano festival just after. Ryohei, any help you could offer would be appreciated."

"Why don't I take a trip to Himeji?" Ryohei floated closer, the temperature dropping with him. "It will be easier for me to float around there than for any of you to go, and that seems the likely place to find them if they aren't here."

"Sounds fine, thank you," Masao said. "Natsuki, you can take the rest of the day off. We appreciate you watching over the Estate." With a smile, Masao waited for Natsuki to leave before turning to the boys. "David, Takumi, come with me. It is time you know exactly what you are up against."

The meeting broke, with Natsuki heading home, Yukiko off to prepare dinner, and Ryohei on his way to Himeji. Masao led David and Takumi out of the main house and through the garden, heading towards the Dojo.

'Where do you think we're going?'

'Probably to the Matsumoto library.'

'I've never seen a library.'

'They must have one, where do you think Masao and Grandpa always disappeared to when doing 'research'? Or where Takumi got the Book of Swords from?'

'Oh. Right.'

Masao led the pair around the dojo to another outlying building David had never entered. It looked to be little more than a shack. When David entered, his impression was just that. Old tools, broken and rusted, lay organized but untidily around the room. If he had entered before now, he would have left just as quickly from the sheer lack of anything interesting.

Expecting more than meets the human eye, and having been led there by Masao, David attempted to use his training to examine every detail of the room. Frustrated, he finally looked to Masao for answers.

"Nothing? Good, even you and Kou are fooled." Masao nodded to Takumi, who reached behind a pile of rusted and rotting scythes. Not even the dust was disturbed as what had been old floorboards, opened to a steel staircase.

Below, another scanner gave them access to a rotating door. Beyond was a labyrinth of humidity and temperature-controlled rooms. David caught glimpses of spaces that by themselves were much bigger than the shed overhead. In one room, he saw blocks of wood with *kanji* carved into them as an old style of printing. As they passed darkened rooms, he saw books, scrolls, paintings, and even a section of pottery and other artwork. Although each successive room was ever more impressive, all the paper, wood, and earth could not compare to the exhibit on the rear wall of the largest and brightest room.

In separately mounted cases, a copy of nearly every Sei-kaku ever made, along with the name of Jitsugen Samurai and Kami, graced the wall. Some cases were empty, but amazingly, they showed the history and development of the sword over the centuries. From the straight, double bladed to the more tra-ditional katana of later. Each gleamed with a unique design meant to portray their elemental forms. The wall was not overly large, and there was still room for more.

"This vault, for it has been designed to withstand even a direct nuclear blast, contains the most accurate record of Ja-pan's last several hundred years in the world. There are two copies of everything here except the swords, one at the Impe-rial Palace in Kyoto and another in Tokyo. But here, are the originals of the Matsumoto legacy." Masao walked forward, through the cases and shelves, the jewels of the Matsumotos surrounding them.

'So few, yet so many swords in all those hundreds of years.

David twitched in the unnatural air of the place, Kou's feline tendencies surfacing as he reflected on the history around him.

"Why didn't you show me this before?" David asked, as-tounded and surprised by the treasure that had rested beneath his feet the past months.

"The lessons we need to teach you, we learned from the Jitsugen Samurai past. That does not mean you need to learn *all* those lessons, at least not yet. For now, your access will be limited to the knowledge I think you're ready for. You *do* need to know what you are up against. As for the rest… in its own time." Masao explained the room's system to David. In addi-tion to their most used volumes, an un-networked computer kept a database on most subjects. David was given access and shown how to get information on much of the history of the Jitsugen Samurai as well as a compellation of everything they knew of the world's dangers.

David and Takumi spent the next several days down in the library. Although they eventually read everything the system could offer on the ōkami, oni, obake, and yūrei of the last thousand years plus, David was not satisfied.

"This isn't what we need," David said, pushing away from the computer. "I need to know how a yūrei interacts with its host, not at what age it can summon a 'Giant-Horned-Demon-With-Higher-Than-Average-Damage-Potential.' We both know Rie. I need to know if we should be looking for Rie, part of Rie, or something we can't predict." David rubbed his eyes, weary from hours of fruitless search. "The legends and histories don't seem to be doing it."

'I hate being stuffed up in this underground box. Necessity or not, at least outside we can run a bit,' growled Kou.

With a sigh, David resigned himself to spending the rest of his summer vacation days down in the Matsumoto library. While they still trained harder than ever before, and spent their nights prowling Nakano in search of Rie, the library became their second home. They were so focused on the search that, although it would mean many questions and the fierce disapproval of their classmates, David and Takumi both bowed out of the summer badminton competition. Luckily, Yukiko had been able to procure doctor's notes that got them off the hook with their teachers, if not their friends on the team.

On August 26, the second semester of school started with the second years' class decidedly smaller. Those students who had been in town had gone to Misaki's funeral. The kendo team had taken to wearing black armbands in memory of her. Rie's absence was explained away as a transfer to another school. The Jeong brothers' disappearances created a stir among the staff. Chul Soon had been such an outgoing and engaging student that many of the teachers expressed sadness at his sudden departure. Rounding out the disappearances was Enya

Miyagi. A student David had met only occasionally since he was in another class, Enya had lived on the other side of Nakano with his father. In a secluded part of south Nakano, few people knew the family well. The gossip was that his father had suddenly moved without telling anyone. Yonamine was so busy that he had requested a special investigator from Himeji.

'Sounds suspicious to me.'

'Maybe we should check out his house on tonight's patrol.'

David, Takumi, and Natsuki exchanged significant looks at the news. David spent the entire time Moriyama talked to them about dealing with abandonment issues trying to remember everything he could about Enya, but with the age gap, there was little he could think of.

That night after their usual training, they set out to the Miyagi residence. When they arrived, David changed into Kou to give them an extra set of senses. Checking the outside of the house, they found only a few mud prints that could have been from anyone, or anything.

Inside, the house was as empty and quiet as Ryohei when he thought no one was around. Ghosts tended to be so utterly quiet that Ryohei had to make a concentrated effort whenever he spoke. Splitting up, they searched the house. There seemed to be a rudimentary attempt at making it appear as if the family moved out, but little things, like pictures left behind and garbage in the trash can, pointed to a more sinister explanation for the pair's disappearance.

"Rie was here," Takumi said as Kou stalked into the living room. He stood in the corner of the room, his back to the door. In his hands was a box of Pocky, a Japanese snack. "Only Rie would eat banana Pocky. There isn't a single bit of food anywhere in this house, yet here, there's an unopened box with a tag from the supermarket over in the center of town. I mean there's a shop just around the corner that has all kinds of snacks."

Though David was unconvinced, Takumi was sure that Rie had left the banana frosted covered sticks behind for him to find. He took it as definite proof that the ōkami were responsible. Back at the Estate, it was hard to argue with Takumi's unwavering certainty, especially without proof to the contrary. The consensus on the Estate was that the Miyagi family had been abducted, and the ōkami pack had done it.

At school, life continued as if nothing had happened, though the third years seemed split in their feelings and reactions to David. Since returning to school, David could sense the hostility from Koji's friends in the hallways and at lunch. It was a bit surreal for him, living a semi-normal life during the school day, albeit with the threat of being cornered by the school's one bad egg, and then at night tromping through the city as an adolescent tiger. Sitting through a math lesson did not feel like the kind of thing a person who met Crown Princes and could summon a deadly sword at request did. Nevertheless, with school back in swing, David was obliged to spend his time studying and practicing badminton, rather than searching for Rie every minute of every day as he wished he could. Despite all his efforts, his host sister remained elusive. Their only clue, a banana-flavored snack box.

To make matters worse, despite the research during summer break, he was only about half way through the references that Masao had made available. After a particularly frustrating afternoon, he changed his focus to the Jitsugen Samurai diaries. Using the computer to search the censored copies that Masao provided to him, he finally found what he was looking for in one of the texts.

As David's hope began to wane, he came upon an entry that spoke of two men who had been friends and fellow retainers of the same regional governor. When one man became a Jitsugen Samurai, his sudden and unexplained increase in favor and rise to Princedom under the Imperial House drove the friend mad with jealousy. The Samurai's former friend sought out the rituals that eventually allowed him to become a yūrei.

The yūrei wreaked havoc for years before the Jitsugen Samurai finally tracked down and killed him.

In the process, the Jitsugen Samurai noted that the yūrei had systematically targeted people and places that the host had issue with, in addition to the usual rampant destruction of a yūrei. David spent the next several hours delving into the precise and flowing script used by his predecessor and wondered at the mind behind the writing. Not a single word was wasted, yet the entry was long and detailed, answering his every question before he knew to ask.

'This is what we needed. A yūrei isn't completely independent of its host. It's not a full possession, or at least the host can influence the corrupted Kami.'

'We better keep an eye on anyone Rie thinks wronged her, maybe she really did leave that box for us… We need to warn Natsuki and keep an extra eye on her from now on.'

'Thought you would never ask.'

With a grin, David transformed almost immediately. Leaving their clothes in the sword room, Kou jogged up the stairs and out of the library. Takumi agreed to keep an eye on Natsuki so quickly that David was almost unable to keep his mirth from overpowering Kou. Thanks to Kou's pull, it did not take long for Natsuki to show up.

"I'm not going to change how I live my life just because Rie got herself possessed," Natsuki said, taking the news stoically. "If she couldn't get rid of me alone, she won't with help."

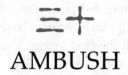

AMBUSH

September,

> *It felt good to fight back against the shadow that had plagued me since I was a still a dependent part of the Zodiac Tiger. I was finally beginning to understand our enemies…*

The next day after evening practice, David and Takumi made a list of all of Rie's potential targets. At the top were Natsuki and the "friends" that had helped create the rift between her and Rie. Ironically, those same friends had been giving Natsuki more and more of a cold shoulder in response to her time spent with David and Takumi. Mizuki, Yuka, and Kaeda seemed especially annoyed that Natsuki had run out on them during summer vacation to housesit for the Matsumotos.

"If your theory is correct, and the yūrei goes after people Rie had an issue with, what's with Enya's disappearance?" Takumi said as they studied the list of names, trying to match them with the situation as they knew it. "It doesn't fit. I don't think they've ever even met. And Misaki…"

"He might have really moved," David said with a frown. "Or it could have been an accident. I don't think we should concentrate just on this list, but maybe keep an extra eye on them."

"As for Misaki, that was before Rie became a yūrei. The Jeong brothers must have gotten to her through Rie," Kou added.

Disgusted, David left the underground vault for some fresh air. His head cleared by the cool autumn night, David withdrew into his subconscious to ponder their findings while Kou ran through the forests, reveling in the wind rushing through his fur. As they twisted among the dark trees, Kou and David formulated a schedule to include their regular patrols, school, training, and a rotation of tracking the people from Rie's list.

A package arrived at the Estate in early September that significantly helped coordinate the increasingly difficult tasks of following Natsuki and her friends, patrolling Nakano, and keeping up the façade that they were normal teenagers. They immediately put the sets of military-grade encrypted radios and other equipment the Imperial House sent to use. The new gear enabled them to cover more distance and stay in contact with Yukiko.

With the Nakano Festival just three days away, David and Takumi returned from their last night patrol of the school week no closer to finding Rie.

"Not in vain," Kou said, replying to David's thoughts and Takumi's expression. *"Every second we are out there, is another second the prey might make a mistake that we can use. Though we cannot sense them, perhaps our presence alone may keep them from more evil."*

They found Masao talking with Ryohei in the main house, luckily, Natsuki had already gone home. Even after her time spent around him while they were in Kyoto, she still avoided Ryohei whenever possible. With him gone, she had been visibly more relaxed at the Estate.

"Good you are all back." Masao motioned for David and Takumi to sit with him at the table, while Ryohei continued to hover just outside the sliding doors. "We have a new problem... Ryohei?"

"I ran into a small group of ghosts in Himeji, not the nice kind," Ryohei said. As always, his voice had the hard-to-name quality that marked him as a creature beyond death. Kou had explained it as a kind of unavoidable side effect, one that Kami did not share because Kami were very much alive. The sound echoed around them though he stayed outside to keep the temperature manageable. "They were discussing whether or not to come to Nakano for the Festival. Apparently, word has gone out about the yūrei, though they do not seem to know there is a Jitsugen Samurai. Another pack of ōkami is on its way. They want to join the yūrei to increase their strength and powers, and plan to attack the Nakano Festival in order to show they are worthy of the yūrei. The obake were trying to decide if they should visit and try to pick off a few souls in the confusion of the attack."

"The last thing we need is the two groups of ōkami combining. We need to attack them before they get anywhere near here," Takumi said, the first to react to the news.

"*Any ōkami attack in Nakano would be bad,*" Kou said, mentally raising his hackles at the thought of another pack of ōkami loose in Nakano. The result was David twitching uncontrollably since his human form could not mimic Kou's natural reactions. "*At least, with nearly the entire town gathered for the festival, we only have to cover one place. It is at the Estate that we will have to hunt.*"

"The townspeople will be on the Estate or along the route for the portable shrines," Yukiko said as she brought in tea. "We cannot wait for them to get that close. The festival includes the entire town, and the portable shrines will parade through most of it. If the ōkami make it into the town they can attack anywhere and we will be too spread out to deal with it before many are injured."

After serving everyone present, she sat to join in on the conversation, but not before sending an apologetic glance to

Ryohei's usual corner. David had often seen Ryohei float along with Yukiko while she tended the Matsumoto's garden, saddened he could no longer eat. Although she could not see him, David knew Yukiko still regarded Ryohei as part of the family. Just as she had been sensitive to David's need when he first arrived, she went out of her way to make Ryohei comfortable as well.

"Yukiko is correct. We are going to have to stop them well outside of Nakano. Ryohei, any idea where they are coming from, or how many there are?" Masao asked, bringing them back to the situation at hand.

"My fellow ghosts neglected to say how many ōkami there are, though they obviously felt there were enough to be dangerous for an entire town. As for direction, apparently they're coming from the north, and will come in through the mountains," whispered Ryohei, staring wistfully at the tea.

"Looks like we have to prepare for another fight," David said, his voice nearly excited. It was a chance to begin undoing the damage he had done with his hesitation before the shrine. It was a chance to make things right. Stretching, he arched his back as luxuriously as a house cat. "The festival is in three days, they'll be stalking the Estate well before they attack."

"*Let's go hunt*," Kou growled.

"I agree," Masao said slowly, "but since the ōkami will have an advantage at night, we should get them in the early morning. I'm wary about leaving the town unguarded, however." Masao frowned, leaning towards the table.

David eyed Masao carefully. In the past, he had been quick and decisive. With Grandpa's death, he seemed to have become far more careful with his decisions. After conferring quickly with Kou, David spoke up.

"Are the traps that you use during Golden Week still out there? Why don't the three of us lead them into an ambush? That would leave Masao-san, Yukiko-san, and Ryohei-san to keep an eye on Nakano. We would also still be close enough to get back quickly in case something happened."

"You're learning," Masao said with just the slightest smile. He leaned over, whispering to his wife before returning his attention to David. Yukiko bowed slightly when he finished. "Your idea is sound. I will get you my maps that outline the traps in the hills. Be careful. Your plan will need to be flexible in case they come from different directions, but I will leave it to you."

"Any reason in particular I'm here at three a.m. and not ten like everyone else?" Natsuki asked as a shadow swept past in front of the main house the next morning.

"*That was just a mouse,*" Kou said. He carefully controlled his voice so as not to startle her. "*I am behind you. You should know by now I will not summon you unless it is important.*" Kou was beginning to get annoyed at the limited time David could spend as a tiger, and it showed in his tone. "*Ryohei is here, be nice, he probably saved a lot of lives. Masao-san will explain inside.*"

With that, Kou brushed by Natsuki's leg and went inside the house. Natsuki followed and soon after they were all standing together again in the garden with full armor, weapons, and their new communications gear.

"Remember they will stalk and hunt as a pack, spread out until you find one, and then call in the others. Do not get caught, do not let any escape," Masao said. "You carry the weight of history with you. Warriors in the tradition of Ninigi. You are Samurai. Don't let Nakano down."

The three students crept out into the forest, each taking their own path. In order to make it easier for Natsuki to patrol her own area without being drawn to Kou, David stalked along in his Tiger Armor. Even with the armor's orange coloring, David was able to blend into his surroundings since it was striped similarly to Kou. They spent several hours trekking quietly through the low mountains surrounding the Estate, hunting for the approaching ōkami.

Connected by radio, they spread out to maximize their chance of spotting the ōkami pack. Since he had more experience with the mountains than the others did, Takumi took the more difficult center approach. Meanwhile, Natsuki and David swung out to the side approaches. A few hours into their hunt, Takumi radioed that he had spotted one of their prey.

The ōkami was a lithe and darkly furred animal that carried a small pack of supplies on its back. It stopped frequently using all of its senses to observe the surrounding area. Obviously a scout, Takumi reported to the others that he figured it would be paving the way for the rest of the pack.

Natsuki and David immediately began converging below Takumi's position. They had already decided on ambush sites, places where they could draw the ōkami in and dispatch all of them easily. David's plan relied heavily on the Matsumoto traps used during their Golden Week trips that were still in place, and simply needed to be armed.

One of the largest sites was almost directly in the ōkami's path. A closed off area of boulders that appeared at first to be a pass through two peaks actually ended above tall cliffs. The area was large and covered with twisting passages between boulders, some larger than trucks. It was big enough for all three to hide while the ōkami explored.

'The trick is getting the scout to enter, instead of going off around one of the sides of the mountains to the real passes,' David thought as he hurried towards the ambush. 'What would draw them in?'

'*Blood. It worked for me didn't it? Lead us right to Grandpa,*' Kou replied from within his mind.

Once David and Natsuki were close enough, Takumi quickly armed the various traps, guided by Masao's map. When he arrived, David scratched himself on a branch just towards the entrance, and then relayed what he had done to the others. Quickly healed, David and Takumi positioned themselves. Ready to drop an avalanche of rock should any ōkami try to escape back out of the enclosure, Natsuki watched and waited from a high hide on the eastern peak.

The dark haired ōkami entered the fake pass cautiously, alerted to the presence of a human by David's trail. To bring the ōkami over one of several concealed pits, David left a wrapper from a food pack. The scout came through the boulders on exactly the right spot. A few loose rocks gave way, pulling the ōkami down into the darkness of a completely blocked off cave. With no way to get out, the ōkami howled in outrage.

While David could have easily finished off the lone ōkami at that point, none of the ambush team showed a hint of themselves. It was not long before a much larger ōkami, again dark, but with streaks of grey came ambling into the rock yard. The larger ōkami found the hole, sniffing around it and listening as the scout howled.

"I should leave you down there," the lead ōkami growled to his tracker. "Who gets stuck in a hole?"

"It's not my fault, the rocks gave way, and I slid in here... Come on, get me out. I got us here all right didn't I? I think there's a hiker around here. I smelled some blood and food." The tracker paced in the hole, his voice a whine that verged on becoming a yelp.

"The other three are keeping an eye behind us. If we didn't need all five of us for this festival, I'd leave you there." The large ōkami howled. A minute later, three more ōkami were there around the hole. With a growl from their leader, two of the ōkami began to search the area for their hiker.

From his hiding spot, David caught the smoke from Takumi's campfire lure, and the subsequent rock fall from the second trap.

Dropping from above silently and with Seikaku drawn, David impaled the third ōkami between the shoulders. The surprised ōkami collapsed below him. Sufficiently weakened by the blow, David instinctually knew he had already won. Without withdrawing the sword, David changed the Seikaku's form and banished the ōkami's spirit. The yelp that came from the ōkami as it turned to wood set off a string of growls throughout the area. Immediately, the leader and a small light furred pup began to back carefully away from the first pit. The scout saw them begin to leave and called to his leader.

Although Takumi and David reacted in seconds, Takumi arrived first. Rounding on him to attack, the large ōkami was stopped by a weak bark of fear from the younger one as David stepped into the open area around the first pit.

One look at David in his armor, with his tiger mask and Seikaku was all the encouragement the large ōkami needed to turn tail and run. The smaller ōkami was faster, however, and nearly made it out of the rock grounds.

"Do it, *princess*." Takumi spoke into his microphone. Along with the advanced communication gear, they had selected call signs. David was *tiger*, Takumi had adopted *shifter* in recognition of his possession, and Natsuki was, of course, *princess*.

A large crash echoed through the mountains as Natsuki triggered the trap and the opening between the two peaks was shut. The large ōkami skidded to a halt before he was crushed. The younger one was not so lucky, stuck beneath a mammoth rock, the ōkami could not move, but remained unhurt.

"You're trapped, you have nowhere to go." Takumi pointed his sword at the lead ōkami.

The leader raged at Takumi's words, growling and spitting. His paws, sporting razor sharp claws, sliced at Takumi's neck. Surprised by the speed and ferocity of the attack, Takumi backpedaled, blocking quickly with his sword, but losing ground with each blow. Feinting high, the leader slashed low, connecting with the back of Takumi's knee. The well-aimed attack caught Takumi in an especially weakly armored section, sending him to the ground. Instead of finishing him, the leader ran, heading for the opposite end of the area.

David flew after the ōkami, catching up to him at the edge of the cliffs. The leader hissed and snarled, turning at the edge as David came to a stop before him.

"Your pack is incapacitated." David stepped closer to the lead ōkami. "Your plans for Nakano thwarted. There's no yūrei in your future. Give up and I'll make it fast."

With a savage growl, the ōkami lunged at his throat. David caught the ōkami's paws with his Seikaku, easily turning aside the blow despite the force behind the attack. The ōkami yelped in pain but continued the attack. Swinging wildly, he tried to force David back from the ledge. David took half a step back, drawing in the ōkami before lunging forward and slicing halfway through one of the ōkami's legs with a move more suited to a badminton court. The ōkami had only a second to look down in shock before David had struck three more times, opening wounds at major joints in order to incapacitate the monster. With the leader still sputtering in his rage, David changed the blade and created yet another ōkami statue.

Takumi was already adding more fuel to the campfire when David found him back near the landslide. With grim determination, David dispatched the three other trapped ōkami. Although David gave them no chance to escape, each encounter took time, as none of the ōkami were willing to go down without a fight. David ended up with several cuts from fighting in close quarters, but by the time he had all the statues sitting in Takumi's fire, he had healed. Takumi had also recovered from the blow to his leg, helped along by the yet unnamed Kami within him, though like his neck, he had another savage scar.

"It's so strange seeing the ōkami statues. They look just like they did in their wolf forms. You know, before, you changed them," Natsuki said as she joined the two boys near the bonfire. She had stayed aloft to ensure no other ōkami escaped or were waiting in the vicinity.

"It's a little less evil in the world, though neither of us relished having to kill them," growled Kou.

"Better them than anyone from Nakano." Takumi threw a lit branch into the base of the fire. As he poked at his new scar, Natsuki sat next to him, looking at the long gashes. Letting Kou take over their body, they crept away as the wood and statues burned. Kou took the opportunity to grind his claws into a nearby tree, sharpening them.

'These ōkami were young, aside from their leader, I'd say they couldn't have been more than a few years old. They must have been new to Japan, or were created here recently… either way it's a bit disturbing.'

'True, but then we already knew danger was on the way… That Evil was back in Japan…'

Kou stopped his sharpening to listen to Takumi and Natsuki talk.

"Already a second one. At least you can't really see it. Now all we have to watch out for are ghosts at the festival," Takumi said. Natsuki shuddered at Takumi's words and slid closer to him.

"I don't care about scars. Ghosts on the other hand…" Natsuki's voice faded as Kou slid further from the fire. David smiled within as the last remains of the ōkami disappeared, ensuring no power could revive them.

When the fire had finally burned itself out, Kou changed back into David and he returned to help clean up the ashes. The three students ensured no coal was left smoking, then scattered the ashes around the boulders and rocks, mixing it into the soil. Finally finished, they used ropes to climb down the cliffs.

Back at the Estate, David, Natsuki, and Takumi hurriedly changed and hid their armor and weapons. Pleased with their success, Masao sent them to help with the festival preparations.

FESTIVAL!

September,

Although we destroyed the ōkami, the ghosts were still a threat. I was proud that David had been able to fight without his previous hesitation, but wished we had fought as a tiger...

David had been to fairs, competitions, and ceremonies, but they all paled in comparison to the Nakano Festival. Early Sunday morning nearly the entire town gathered before the Matsumotos' shrine. For the occasion, trees along the path were trimmed, widening it enough for the massive portable shrines to be brought in and set in the clearing. In addition to the gardening work, bright paper lanterns, banners, and other decorations hung along the entire length of the path and around the shrine clearing.

The villagers arrived singularly and in groups, all wearing the traditional *happi*, blue jackets with swirling designs in white and black. Even toddlers ran around in their miniature versions of the outfits. When almost everyone was present, one of the local leaders began the ceremonies.

The Nakano townspeople stood in long lines before the Matsumoto shrine. After a few words by the Mayor and school Principal, Masao stepped forward in the traditional robes of a Shinto priest. For the first time, he began the festival ceremony his father had always performed before him. The movements of the ceremony were familiar to David. Masao used a combination of bows, chanting, wand waving, and other motions to call the attention of the ancestors and Kami of Nakano town. Unlike previous ceremonies, Masao studiously avoided the summoning chants. Instead of calling for a Kami, he thanked them and their ancestors. He also asked for protection and health for the entire town. Where the metal had rested the day of David's accident, offerings of sake, vegetables, and other goods were presented on small wooden alters. This was a chance for all of Nakano to give thanks for the harvest, and the year.

Unobtrusively, the rest of the Matsumotos, David, and Natsuki wandered around the edge of the clearing and other parts of the Estate, keeping an eye out for obake or any other beings bent on mischief. Takumi had helped Kou don his armor before transforming, so that if they needed to, Kou would be able to fight. The rest of them had to go without since it would be far too conspicuous.

Although it was September, the sun and humidity were still enough to make standing before the shrine a trial. Luckily, despite the speeches and the importance of the ceremony itself, it did not last overly long. After ceremonial drinks of sake were passed around to the adults, a group of young men, mostly college students home for the festival, stepped forward to circle the largest portable shrine and its support of wooden beams. Crowding around it, the strongest of the group lifted the massively heavy shrine, their friends quickly running under it to get a spot. Together the group hoisted the shrine aloft and brought it down on their shoulders, walking forward until they were in the middle of the clearing.

The rest of the festival participants circled around the edges. Then, with a cry of "Wasshoi," the men pushed the shrine up, throwing it so it appeared to be riding an angry river of blue robed rapids. An older man stood apart blowing a whistle. After each whistle, the men responded with another cry of "Wasshoi!" The whistle blower increased his tempo until he suddenly gave a long whistle and the portable shrine was settled back down upon their shoulders. With another whistle, the men began to walk forward through the shrine path. The elementary and junior high students then repeated the process with their smaller copies of the shrine.

The procession walked through the Matsumoto Estate and wound its way towards the city. At houses where the elderly lived the occupants came out to wave and cheer, encouraging the shrine bearers, while the rest of the village followed behind. Once away from the Estate, a tractor pulling a float of drumming *taiko* students led the way. As they entered Nakano, the delicious smells from the various food stalls wafted out from the town's center.

The parade wound its way through the streets of Nakano Town until they reached the supermarket. There, all three groups of shrine bearers took their turns jumping and flinging about their charges in tempo to the whistle.

The shrines stopped at all the major town places... the school, the bank, and finally city hall. Along the way, some of the smaller stores had refreshments ready for the passersby, while the main attraction came at the city hall. After stopping, everyone was treated to performances by dancers and musicians. There were also booths by the local restaurants and bars selling everything from toys to ice cream and drinks.

David fulfilled his obligation and helped carry the heavy student shrine from the edge of town to the store, then retreated to the perimeter of the festivities. Halfway through the festival, it became apparent that a few of the students seemed to be missing. David listened in via his radio as Natsuki discreetly questioned some of the student's parents.

"Oh, I'm sure they're around somewhere," said one slightly inebriated parent. "I'm surprised you aren't with them,

Natsuki-chan. We haven't seen you around as much as usual, you should stop by for dinner next week."

Natsuki found David as the townspeople wandered around the area in front of the town hall, buying, eating, and drinking.

"I can't find Yuka or Yuuto. They were here earlier, but no one's seen them, which isn't that unusual, except neither showed for their turn at the portable shrine after the bank." Natsuki leaned against a building eating a green tea flavored ice cream that dripped in the heat.

"Well Masao-sensei did tell us to be on the watch for anything strange. Go ahead and send him a text. I haven't seen anything odd, though I couldn't really watch before the market, that thing is heavy." David rubbed his shoulder. The portable shrine had bruised his shoulder when it landed during their turn to fling it around. Even with his Jitsugen Samurai powers, the bruise was only just then fading.

"I'll let the others know, any sign of any… obake?" Natsuki asked with such hesitance that David looked up from his observation of the passing crowds.

"You really don't like them do you?" David said, finally beginning to understand just how troubling the obake attack had been for Natsuki. The day in the ruins still haunted her. "Kou's been bugging me for a chance to run around Nakano in the daylight. He's still small enough to pass as a cat, if a large one. If you don't mind taking my stuff and resisting the summons for a bit, we can go take a better look."

"Sure!" Natsuki smiled with relief. Kou growled contentedly at the confidence she showed in his ability to deal with any obake lurking about. After finding a discrete place to change, Natsuki took David's clothes.

"Kou, David, uh, don't tell Takumi about the obake thing will you? He thinks I'm over it," Natsuki said, trying to smile but only managing a troubled frown.

"*Sure, no problem,*" Kou said with a sly smile and twitch of his tail. Running through the shadows and alleys of Nakano

Town, Kou kept his considerable senses piqued for danger and the random festival attendee.

While the majority of the town was at the city hall, many people still had to work or otherwise support the festival activities. Kou found himself dodging to avoid kids carrying candies and drums, adults with instruments and beer, and shopkeepers running for supplies.

All through the town, Kou saw neither spot nor speck of obake, so he headed back along the parade route. Ryohei had tried to find the ghosts again after reporting their intentions, but had returned that morning empty handed. They had no idea if the ghosts had given up or stayed. Near the Estate, a strange sound prompted Kou to investigate further along the main road. Staying in the trees, he trotted towards Natsuki's house.

Just off the road, Kou suddenly spotted three obake crowding hungrily around two fallen people. One of the obake's long fingers stretched down hungrily to the couple, seemingly stroking them. After a few seconds, a short fat ghost pushed the taller one away and reached forward. The third, a cagy older obake of a man stretched forward while the other two fought. Noticing him, the other two obake turned on him.

Sprinting forward, Kou caught the biggest of the three straight in the back of the head, knocking him away from the huddled humans. Before the other two could respond, Kou jumped from head to head knocking them senseless with his clawed paws. Though David felt confident they could have dispatched one obake on their own, with three Kou had a hard enough keeping them all occupied long enough to change and attack.

'I hope Natsuki hasn't gotten much better at resisting you or we are going to be here awhile.'

'*I am sure she will be here shortly...*' Kou managed as he bounded from ghost to ghost.

Kou's sensitive ears just picked up Natsuki's radio call when she could no longer resist the summons. Natsuki laughed when she found Kou jumping from ghost to ghost, smacking them around the head to subdue their entropic energies. Her laugh turned to a scream as she saw who was lying on the ground nearby.

The Ashikawas, Natsuki's parents, were huddled close together on the ground. Their slow ragged breathing the only thing betraying the scant life left within them. Her scream turned from fear to rage as she rushed forward.

"Natsuki! Get them away from here then come back. I need your help again," David called, allowing Kou to concentrate on the obake.

Natsuki looked to Kou. David's blue eyes met Natsuki's dark brown. With a nod, her face hardened into a determined scowl as she carried first her mother, then father away from the scene of the attack. Seeing Natsuki rush back, Kou gave each of the confused ghosts an especially hard smack before jumping behind a tree. Summoning his Seikaku and changing it to its wood form, Kou tossed the wooden blade to Natsuki. Immediately changing back into Kou, they hurtled back towards the obake. Natsuki caught the Seikaku with practiced ease and flew at the closest ghost. Her long black hair billowed behind her in a stormy rage.

Seeing Natsuki approach with a deadly expression and fiery eyes, the largest ghost tried to flee. He never made it. Natsuki thrust the point of the Seikaku right between the suddenly bulging eyes of the ghost. The other two tried to follow the larger ghost's lead but were stopped by Kou. Within seconds, Natsuki had banished the other two ghosts. She stood panting, her shoulders heaving with the sudden release. Natsuki breathed deeply, then, just as quickly, the Seikaku slid out of her hands and disappeared. She sank to the ground, her face in her hands, sobs racking her body.

Kou brushed against her, trying to comfort her, but his armor pulled at her clothing. When that did not work, Kou grabbed Natsuki's bag from where she had dropped it at the edge of the road and came back as David.

"Natsuki, are you alright?" David easily but gently pulled her up. Without warning, Natsuki locked her arms around him in a tight hug. Surprised and more than a little embarrassed, especially since he had yet to put on his shirt, David tried to mumble something comforting. They stood there tightly together as the seconds ticked by, David too embarrassed, too confused to react.

"*Natsuki, we should go see to your parents.*" Kou's words brought them back to the danger Natsuki's parents were still in.

Pulling away, Natsuki was more herself. She turned, and grabbing David's hand pulled him towards where she had left her parents as he struggled into his shirt. They found them in a low culvert, hidden from the road. Trying to rouse them did little, although Natsuki's father did seem to stir, as if plagued by a bad dream.

"Let's get them to Yukiko," Natsuki said, her training kicking in. "She'll know what to do."

"I can be there in about a minute," Takumi called over the radio when David called for Yukiko's help.

"*Shifter*, remember your responsibilities," Masao replied.

With ease born of their training, Natsuki and David gently lifted her parents, then turned and carried them through the forest and across the road to the Matsumoto Estate. Yukiko met them at the Estate entrance. Luckily, everyone was still at the city hall, leaving her free to help the two onto the Estate in secrecy. Once inside, Yukiko examined the pertinent Matsumoto books.

"They'll be alright. It seems like Kou caught them pretty early on, there are not any external marking as there should be if they had been fed on for any length of time. It seems as if they have only been knocked out by the obake's aura. You know what that is like I believe," Yukiko said turning to Natsuki.

"They're alright?" Natsuki asked.

"Yes, I will make them some herbs to sleep a dreamless sleep." Yukiko busied herself around a chest that seemed all too familiar to David. "This will help them forget the attack. Since they are not possessed or Partners, they would not have been able to see the obake that attacked them, yet they will probably be weak for some time if the obake were able to feed on them at all. When they wake, I will laugh and tell them they fell asleep outside and were carried to the Estate. You two had better hurry back to the festival. Do not worry. Your parents will be fine. You both should have some fun. It is David's first festival, after all."

With that, the two returned to the festival, trying to enjoy the sumo matches and other performances. Takumi joined them as soon they returned and immediately began a whispered conversation with Natsuki. Many of their classmates, including all of the third year boys, competed in the sumo competition, so David wandered off to cheer their classmates. Even Kou enjoyed booing Koji. David was happy to see him lose his first match. Apparently, his injured hand had kept him from training. As he left the ring he eyed David dangerously, but the crowds kept them separated.

When the sumo competition ended and prizes were awarded, fireworks marked the end of the entertainment. Shortly after, the shrines were taken back up upon numerous shoulders and the procession of happily oblivious people made their way back along lantern lit streets to the Matsumoto Estate. There at the torii gate before the shrine path, a group turned to face the largest shrine. The two groups met, the young men trying to force their way back to the Matsumoto shrine, while another other group tried to stop them. Natsuki stood with David as Takumi explained the spectacle to David.

"The people are pushing against the shrine to make it more difficult," he said, gesturing along the lamp lit path. "The more challenging something is, the more effort you put into it, the more of an offering it is. They'll struggle all the way back to the shrine in offering to their ancestors and the Kami."

It took more than an hour for the struggling townsmen to get the heavy portable shrine back to the clearing. Once there both sides celebrated together, ending the Nakano Festival.

三十二

LOST AND FOUND

September,

Five ōkami and three obake seemed like good work for a week-end to me, but David could not help thinking back on Rie and Grandpa. Never having had any siblings, I found it harder to be sympathetic. In the wild, you kill your enemies...

Natsuki's parents woke the next day confused and weak, but otherwise healthy thanks to Yukiko's ministrations. With Monday off from school, the Matsumotos, villagers, and students tore down the stages and lights from the festival. Natsuki took the day off to take care of her parents. She especially thanked Kou for finding them just in time. Takumi and David worked together to finish the last of the clean up on the Estate while talking about the events of the previous day. When they finished, Masao had them record everything they remembered about the ōkami and obake attacks, in order to add them to the Matsumoto library.

With Natsuki off, Takumi and David practiced alone together, both attempting to work new techniques and moves into their swordplay. Despite David's months of training, Takumi was still easily the better swordsman.

"How did you beat the ōkami leader, but he got me in the leg?" Takumi asked, lashing out with a practice sword as he spoke, trying to throw David off. Used to this kind of thing, David replied without missing a beat.

"You're better, but I'm more unpredictable." David suddenly dropped to all fours beneath a sideways blow from Takumi and lunged knocking Takumi to the ground. "I used a badminton net slice and got him in the leg. You know your katas well, but we know tiger." David's eyes gleamed orange as he stood over Takumi for a brief second before helping him up.

The next day at school, David was pleased to note both Yuka and Yuuto were in class. Neither seemed to act strangely, but since they were not his friends it was harder to gauge what strange for them was. Part of the class representative's clique, they were included in the group of people who had been enemies of Rie, the same people who had started to shun Natsuki for spending so much time with the Matsumotos and David. As usual at lunch David and Takumi sat together, however, soon after sitting a teary-eyed Natsuki, joined them at their table.

"Hey Natsu, what's up?" Takumi asked.

"Yeah, you never eat with us," David added.

"Apparently I'm not welcome at their table anymore," she said. "I asked Yuka and Yuuto where they were during the festival and they got all mad at me. Then that traitor Mizuki was all 'I think you should find somewhere else to eat.' Then she went on about how of course I wouldn't know what my friends where doing since I never hangout with them anymore. I mean have they always been so mean?" Natsuki wiped her eyes as she looked between David and Takumi. The boys studiously avoided Natsuki's gaze. She stared from one to the other then burst out laughing.

"Yeah, I guess you're right, they have always been like that." Natsuki sighed. "It's what I get..."

After a few days of Natsuki sitting with them at lunch, hanging out during badminton practice, and during free time, Takumi's friends began to include her in their conversations again. Shou seemed to take the longest to warm back up to her, but even he eventually gave in.

If Natsuki had not split with her old clique they might have realized sooner that Yuka and Yuuto were not their old selves. As it was, the second years were left with few leads over the next week. It was not until a science class in another building that the trio had a break. Science, music, and P.E. were the only subjects they did not take in their usual classroom. David and Takumi sat with Natsuki when they overheard Hidemi talking to Daisuke. Hidemi was the only student from the class representative's friends that would still talk to Natsuki, so Natsuki convinced the boys to sit with her.

"Yeah, Yuka quit the track team, and I heard Yuuto quit the soccer team," Daisuke said. "Something about taking care of their families, but that's a load of... well." Daisuke's vehement tones left it clear he was certain Yuuto's family was just fine.

"How strange, they used to be so into those sports, but then they have been acting kind of weird since the festival, haven't they?" Hidemi asked conversationally.

David elbowed Natsuki to get her to ask more, but Minaku chose that moment to start class. David tried to catch Hidemi after class, but Tsubasa caught her attention first. Missing their only chance to talk with Hidemi before the afternoon's badminton practice, they met during a break to discuss what they had heard.

"Well we already followed both of them before the festival since they didn't get along with Rie. Maybe Yuuto and Yuka both want to try something different for a change?" asked David hopefully.

"You don't quit a team once you join it in Japan. It's just not done," Natsuki said simply. "The pressure can be very strong."

"I guess we will have to put them on the top of the suspect list *again*," whispered Kou. Lately he had grown more comfortable in David's body, speaking aloud as often as circumstances allowed. Although David found it just as easy to talk while a tiger, their switching still seemed to throw the Matsumotos and Natsuki off.

David felt a twinge of guilt as Natsuki walked to her court. Just as his sister seemed to be less and less a part of his life, Rie was beginning to fade from his thoughts. She was being slowly replaced by Natsuki and oddly enough, the search. The inability to catch even a rumor of her whereabouts, despite the hours they spent looking every day, was maddening. David found they were spending all their time focused on their classmates and Rie's potential targets, rather than his host sister.

'We need to do a better job of thinking like Rie would,' he though to Kou. 'We need to keep her as the priority in our minds. She may be the enemy, but she is also the victim we have to save.'

'You hope. You hope she is the victim, as does Takumi. But what if she sought them out…'

David, Takumi, and Natsuki spent the next several nights attempting to follow Yuuto and Yuka. As with other tracking attempts, their outings were hamstrung by the requirements of their normal junior high lives and training at the Estate. It was not until the next weekend that they were able to keep an eye on them nonstop. All three faked sick to get out of badminton practice.

Takumi and Natsuki each took one of the suspicious students. Kou took the opportunity to explore Nakano during the day, using his extra senses to help coordinate the hunt. He was careful to stay hidden in case anyone looked too closely. They surely would have found an overly large cat strange enough, let alone one that looked a bit too much like a tiger with armor that made it look fiercer than a dragon, an electronic earpiece, and a microphone attached to its head.

After two days, David grew hopelessly bored with the innocuous doings of the two junior high students. Shopping, eating, talking, and playing were just not as entertaining for the observers. At the end of Sunday night, the only odd things they could piece together were that both went shopping a lot and that although the two were supposedly friends, they never met the entire weekend.

The next day at school, David and Takumi excused themselves from their regular free-time badminton games to bounce a soccer ball around in a secluded section of the school. Though he had been unable to control one just a few months ago, David juggled the ball using just his legs while talking to Takumi. One of Masao's training techniques for David to improve his balance and coordination was to take up juggling, with both his hands and his feet.

"I think we need to find out more. Neither of us were really their friends, we have to rely Natsuki for what they were like before the festival." David suddenly dropped to all fours rolling with the ball between his hands and legs, and then tried to gnaw on it.

"*David!*" hissed Takumi in a low voice.

"*Oops. Sorry,*" said Kou as David jumped back up with orange eyes and a sheepish expression. With a mischievous grin he continued. "*I am only about 5 months old you know… Speaking of Kami, any word from yours yet? It would be interesting to see what kind of Kami a fire type will produce. Masao said so many have been corrupted that fire Jitsugen Samurai and shape shifters are rare.*"

"Well, after your accident you started to feel urges, rare meat for breakfast, things like that right?" Takumi asked, staring off across the open field. David nodded. His eyes returned to their usual blue.

"Well I can't explain it, but I keep getting this paranoid feeling I'm not safe, when I go somewhere high, the feeling isn't as strong," he said, fidgeting. "Also, whenever I see fire, like when we burned the ōkami, I want to stick my hand in it. Don't worry, I haven't, but I think the fire Kami is drawn to it."

"That explains you prowling around the rooftops and trees of the Estate." David laughed, slapping Takumi on the back. Takumi turned a bright shade of red, a feat for someone so much darker skinned than David. "You didn't think we wouldn't keep an eye on the Estate after what happened? Despite all the extra training we've been doing, Kou and I don't need as much sleep. Besides, *I can smell you days after you have been in my trees*," Kou finished.

"You know maybe we've been going about this all wrong," Takumi said. He grabbed the ball from where it had landed, balancing on a finger. "We've searched every bit of the mountains and kept watch on Nakano, why don't we try talking to some of the townspeople. We can see if they've noticed anything. Mom and Dad can help out with that, and it would mean five searching instead of just three."

"Naoto and Shou are starting to wonder why you two 'loners' keep skipping badminton," Natsuki said, cutting in as she arrived from the gym. "You two are going to have to show tomorrow."

David filled Natsuki in on their conversation as Takumi eyed the trees at the edge of the school grounds. When the bell rang, they turned for the gym and fifth period.

Once David and Takumi explained their plan to Masao and Yukiko, they were happy to help. Yukiko was especially effective, since she was able to talk to many of the students' mothers while shopping, or while out and about Nakano.

Within days, they had a list of all the places where both Yuka and Yuuto, not to mention the rest of the class representative clique, frequented. Two of them, the School and local library, were the only places they all went to at around the same time. With a new plan of action, David, Takumi, and Natsuki began to stake out the different locations. The elder Matsumoto helped by making excuses to visit places of interest far more than they normally would have.

On Saturday, the first of another three-day holiday, Kou ran quickly through the Estate, returning from his latest stakeout. As he approached the workshop, Kou paused just long enough to turn back into David.

"Finally." David was just able to catch Natsuki's voice in the still night air. "Kou changed back to David."

Yukiko jumped in surprise as David suddenly appeared in the door. The Matsumotos and Natsuki were arrayed around the Matsumoto workshop. A low fire burning in the corner was the only light. Considering Natsuki's feelings, Ryohei floated as far away as possible, while still staying in the room.

"Sorry I'm late. Kou was distracted by a mouse." David came in radiating excitement. Takumi and Natsuki had returned from their stakeouts earlier that night. Intrigued, David had stayed out a bit later than the others changing into Kou for his better senses at night. Too excited to contain himself, David's eyes showed orange in the flickering light.

"We finally found the lair!" Kou said. *"At least we are about ninety percent sure we found it. We did not want to give ourselves away."*

"Where?" Takumi and Natsuki asked at the same time, jumping from their seats in unison.

"We were snooping around the store when I spotted Tsubasa," David said. "You know, from our class. We talked to him and he said Yuuto asked him to bring a prototype they had been working on in the technology club. Apparently, they had been working on something new, and Tsubasa had just finished it. Instead of asking him to bring it home though, Yuuto asked him to bring it to a warehouse behind the supermarket. I convinced him that Yuuto had gone home and that he would pick up the prototype tomorrow night. I waited and saw Yuuto peak out of a door, but when Tsubasa didn't show he went back in. It's a warehouse with easy access from any number of directions, in a place where a lot of people go and where it would be easy to blend in."

Standing, Masao smiled darkly, a gleam in his eye David had never seen before.

"At last," Masao said. "That must be it. We need to do this carefully, give them no chance to escape. We are going to need a careful plan, but still need to act swiftly. It has been nearly three months and the yūrei will have recovered somewhat from the change. Our goals are clear. Kill the ōkami, save your classmates, capture or destroy the yūrei." A lone tear streaked down his face. Though his voice was strong and determined, he was clearly on the edge. Circling the table the family closed in, ready to find their lost, and bring her home.

THE LAIR

October,

It seemed so obvious after the fact. The lair was in a perfect location for them. I walked right by on many of my patrols and never caught a whiff. The worst part was that we should have realized it earlier. Not only was it where the two students had disappeared during the festival, it was where Jahangir had been arrested…

Masao had been far from idle since the trip to Kyoto. Everything was ready should they capture Rie. They had examined and practiced every contingency they could think of.

As David stood on the top floor of a building next to the supermarket, he struggled with what Masao had told him before leaving. After their final preparations for the attack, Masao had taken him aside from the others.

"You already know how most of the ceremony will go when we capture Rie," he had said. From within the fold of his kimono, Masao had given him the copies taken from the Imperial Treasures so that he could read the ancient Japanese for himself. "The tricky part will be separating her from the yūrei. I can summon the yūrei's spirit but if it holds fast, you may not know which to attack. If your concentration falters, if you are even slightly unsure of yourself, then you could banish both rather than only the yūrei. Knowing it is lost, the creature might seek to take her with it."

"But how will I know?" David still asked himself. "How can I make sure I destroy the right one?"

'Masao-san said he trusts you with it,' Kou thought. *'He trusts you with his daughter's life. Trust in yourself, and the bond you have created with your cub mate.'*

From his vantage point above the warehouse, David could see the others, each in an odd mix of traditional armor and modern assault gear.

'Rie was the first to welcome me.'

They all wore black camouflage under their custom armor. Grandpa had made most of the armor, and although it looked like something from a movie or history book, it contained the latest technologies. Mostly titanium and Kevlar weave, the armor was in the traditional form but painted for camouflage. Each helmet and mask was unique, with David's being the most extravagant.

'She used to smile, even when I made really stupid mistakes.'

'She used to frown too, but only when she caught herself being too happy, what was she afraid of?'

Despite his much lighter skin, glowing in the soft lights of surrounding street lamps, David wore only his armor so he would leave nothing behind if he changed. Kou had also donned his armor before leaving the Estate.

'I won't lose Jessica, and I won't give up on Rie. The Jeong brothers will pay.'

Clicking his radio earpiece, David checked in with the others on the surrounding buildings and alleys.

"I just saw Yuka enter. Yuuto hasn't been seen all day, so we should assume he's inside," David said. Rage boiled within him, tempered only by a desperate struggle to think of a way to ensure Rie would be safe.

"We will attack as soon as it is dark enough." Masao spoke quietly. He was the closest to the warehouse, having already checked the back door for alarms and traps. "If anyone comes out, detain them if you can. Make sure no one leaves. *Tiger*, we will have to leave the yūrei for you. We will do our best to take care of the ōkami, but she is in your hands. Remember... your Seikaku will cut both ways."

After what seemed like hours, Takumi, on one of the flanks whispered, "Everyone ready?"

"*Princess* ready." Natsuki covered the side of the building near a loading dock.

"*Nurse* ready," Yukiko said from the van they were using as a getaway car.

"*Swordsmith* ready." Masao crouched in an alley by the back door.

"*Shifter* ready," Takumi whispered as he moved below David, towards the front door.

David crouched, high up on the roof he was a story above the flat-topped warehouse.

"Let's go then." David ran. With a spring that made Kou roar in pleasure within him, David cleared the gap between the two buildings, and then rolled to a crouch as he landed. He waited, listening for any hint he had been heard.

The only sound was from a passing scooter below. Still crouching, David moved forward as silently as any obake. Reaching the splintered wooden roof-access door, he checked it for any signs of alarm or wiring, and then counted down.

"Three... Two... One... Now! Now! Now!" David called over the radios.

David left a wooden wreak behind him as he sped through the door. If he had not been so focused on his immediate surroundings, following the prepared script for the assault, he would have also heard Masao, Natsuki, and Takumi enter at the same time from the three other entry points. As they converged on the first floor, checking every shadow, David ran like the wind through the upper floor, checking to ensure no surprises waited from above.

As David ran, Kou focused on the surroundings.

'There is not so much as a grain of dust out of place. No one has been up here in years.'

'All the Matsumoto writings said the ōkami would want somewhere cave-like. The second story of just about anywhere wouldn't fit that description too well. They must be below.'

David found the others standing in a defensive ring waiting for him.

"The place looks completely deserted," Kou whispered.

"Which means they are hiding very well, since we know Yuka is here," David added.

Masao nodded, indicating that the lower group had found nothing as well. A sudden dull scraping echoed through cavernous warehouse. One of the large wooden boxes nearby moved across the floor, light spilling from the hole it had covered.

Shadows silently surrounded the box. Yuuto came climbing out of a hidden hole as if he was just walking out of his house or a classroom. Obviously unaware of the four people around him, his shopping bag swung freely from his hand.

A dark wraith suddenly enveloped Yuuto, pulling him the rest of the way out of the hole. Masao had his hands around Yuuto's mouth before he could even recognize he was not alone. Pulling him away from the Lair's entrance, for no one suspected it was otherwise, Masao quickly wrapped his mouth, hands, feet, and knees with duct tape. As added insurance, he taped a hood in place. He stashed the struggling boy in a corner of the warehouse while the others watched over the Lair's entrance.

Masao silently motioned for the other three to follow him as he entered the hole. A flight of steps led down to a long open basement about half the size of the building above it. Although the stairway was well lit, the rest of the chamber was dark, save at the far end where soft lighting reflected off a raised platform and the yūrei sitting comfortably on it.

Rie was splayed on a pile of cushions, tended by Chul Soon. At the Matsumotos' entrance, every pair of eyes snapped to them, all save Rie's. David recognized Jahangir, Chul Moo, and Chul Soon, a fourth pair of eyes blazed from the darkest corner of the room. Seeing David, those unfamiliar orbs went mad with rage. A young male ōkami made it two steps before a bark from Jahangir stopped it cold. Yuka was slumped, a shadow next to Jahangir.

No one moved. Both sides watched the other warily, and then with a sigh, what used to be Rie stood. The being looked as if it might have once been David's friend, except now its skin was nearly translucent. Black shining orbs had replaced Rie's soft brown eyes, the once easy going and friendly face had become a mask of boredom and cruelty. The lips were bloody and broken, the fingers curved into long claws. When it spoke, its voice was otherworldly and sharp, a harsh edge that was only barely reminiscent of Rie's.

"Oh *look*, my family has come to play with me! I was *so* bored. And they even brought dinner. Boys, Natsuki is all yours, but leave Takumi and David to me, we can use them. Kill the old man… just as you killed his father."

With her last word, the yūrei rose off the ground, her hands rising away from her sides in an evil imitation of a Seikaku summoning.

"Stop her!" Masao shouted, springing forward.

Without hesitation, David lunged, changing into Kou on the way. The hallway was too long, David still too slow for anything less than Kou's speed. Jahangir left Yuka limp on the ground. Growling, all but one ōkami ran forward.

Kou easily outstripped Masao, leaving the other three behind. Side slipping Jahangir and Chul Moo, Kou continued straight for Rie. He used the crazed little ōkami as a springboard going airborne towards the yūrei.

The black and white wolf smashed into Kou's side midair, sending them both flying in a tumble of claws and fur.

Rolling, they separated with Kou on the far side of the raised platform, Chul Soon between him and Rie. Kou circled, trying to get to her.

Masao ran toward Jahangir while Takumi veered towards Chul Moo. Natsuki's new sword clanged against the young ōkami's gauntlets. Only Chul Soon was in his wolf form, the others were in loose clothing and their familiar gauntlets. As Chul Moo and Jahangir approached, they pulled pairs of short swords from sheaths at their backs to complement their gauntlets. The black blades were barely visible in the darkness between the entrance and the platform.

On the platform, Chul Soon and Kou growled and bit at each other. Before the yūrei, a dark swirling pit began to form. At first, smaller than a pinprick, the dark abyss began to stretch out and grow, its edge ringed in fire. Kou's fur bristled in frustration, as he was unable to slide past Chul Soon.

"All those days I sat with you in class. Playing games and confiding in you like you were my friend. I should have ripped out your throat right there," David's voice growled out of Kou as they attempted to find a way to Rie.

"Yes, you probably should have," Chul Soon said in his familiar voice. "It was very amusing sitting there, having complete control over Rie without you even knowing. You spent so much time focused on Chul Moo and that fool Koji, you never suspected me! To think my brother was actually trying to help her escape."

Despite keeping so much of his attention on his foe, David and Kou's training allowed them to keep a nearly unconscious record of the rest of the basement. With Kou's extra senses, it was as if they could watch what the others were doing, even as they exerted all of their energy in attempting to get past Chul Soon. At the other end of the basement, Masao and Jahangir met with a clash of steel.

"Your blade won't harm me," Jahangir said, his tone light as his blades connected with Masao's single curve of steel.

"Didn't anyone ever tell you that a fully grown ōkami is nearly indestructible? That's the mistake the old man made."

Masao twirled, cutting off Jahangir's taunts with a swipe of his katana across Jahangir's arm. The sound was like metal against concrete. Jahangir held aloft his uninjured arm and smiled. To their side, Natsuki sent a flurry of blows at the young ōkami. Masao drew back his sword then drove it forward. He struck Jahangir in the side, sending him flying back ten feet.

"You'll have to do better than that, you didn't even bruise me," Jahangir said, laughing as he stood. "Let me show you our new toys. Rie made them, you know." Jahangir attacked with his sweeping short swords.

"You and your boyfriend are going to pay for what you did to Atash," shouted the young ōkami to Natsuki. "We've been together almost twenty years. I didn't survive the old deserts to have her taken away by a few brats."

The crazed ōkami punctuated each sentence with a blow from one of his metal claws. Calm and collected, Natsuki was able to parry each strike, becoming comfortable with his fighting style.

"Twenty years? You can't be over ten," Natsuki said laughing, attempting to make the ōkami angry enough to make a mistake.

"With ōkami, nothing is as it seems." Howling, the young ōkami strengthened his attack.

On the other side of Masao, Takumi fought with Chul Moo, both duelists skilled and fit. The two former classmates created a cloud of dust with the quickness of their blows. Neither spoke a word. Although Takumi's skill was slightly better, Chul Moo's skin protected him from the majority of strikes Takumi was able to make.

While the fights continued in the darkness, ferocious in their own right, the growling spitting slamming mayhem on the platform was the most violent in the basement. Kou did everything he could think of to get past Chul Soon, but it all came for naught. Although slightly smaller than his brother, Chul Soon was far more quick minded and crafty. Kou was also at a disadvantage size wise, though he did have the armor to protect him. All the while, the void grew below the yūrei.

A sudden howl was quickly silenced as Natsuki dragged her blade up through the unknown ōkami. Distracted when Masao finally succeeded in drawing blood from Jahangir, Natsuki was able to drive her point through the ōkami's chest. Slicing upward Natsuki soon had the ōkami in sections, which she kicked aside to keep them from reforming before David could change him to a statue. Turning she ran to join with Masao, barely able to keep the suddenly enraged Jahangir at bay.

Chul Soon cocked his head at Kou after they disengaged from their most recent tumble.

"It's too bad you know? I wanted Natsuki too, but only Rie came running in her little fit of jealousy." Chul Soon's wolven lips curved into a vicious smile, his long white fangs glimmering in the low light. "I should thank you for that. You let enough slip about her in our conversations that it made it almost child's play for me to control her completely. Her one night of weakness, all for a stupid little gaijin. Her soul was delicious."

Under David's power, Kou lashed out with a clawed paw in a forward punch fit more for a boxing match rather than struggle to the death. The punch connected, hitting Chul Soon in the snout, sending him clawing at his own nose in discomfort. Kou used the chance to flip back on his recoil. Halfway through the flip David changed midair. Landing, his armor rustled slightly as David summoned his Seikaku.

"No more games," David said, his hands gripping the handle of the Seikaku more tightly. "This ends now. *You* end now."

David and Chul Soon leapt forward at the same instant. David as a Jitsugen Samurai, Chul Soon as a monstrous wolf, they attacked each other with a single minded, deadly intent.

David raised his Seikaku high, ready to bring everything he had down onto the snarling ōkami before him.

'*Just knock him out of the way long enough to get to Rie!*' Kou thought, trying to break through David's single-minded desire to kill Chul Soon. Brought on by the sense of betrayal, and his own inability to see him for what he was when it could have mattered, David was acutely focused on Chul Soon's destruction.

Millimeters apart, David and Chul Soon were both blown apart like leaves in the wind as an explosion rocked through the basement.

三十四
DEVIL'S DOORWAY

October,

Even with two minds, we were blank in that instant. Flying across the room, despair almost became a coherent thought before the wall drove out it…

'*David… David get up.*'

David slowly opened his eyes. He groaned from the pain coursing through his body. Impacting the basement wall and and landing on something hard and jagged was not a fun experience. His Seikaku gone, David looked around, dazed. The pile of bones he had ended up in sent shivers down his spine. Remembering where he was as the dust settled around him, David jumped up. He re-summoned his Seikaku, seeking Chul Soon and trying to avoid thinking about who he had been laying on. The ōkami laid unconscious, blood seeping from a pile of rubble on top of him.

'*Leave him for later, we have bigger problems.*'

David looked over to where the yūrei had stood before a ring of fire only moments earlier. Rie lay slumped on the raised platform. With the hideous orbs covered by her hair, she seemed almost peaceful. The portal was gone, in its place stood a red bodied, ferocious looking horned demon. David almost laughed at the sight of it.

'It's so small. It might make it up to my waist at best.'

'Don't underestimate it. It's pure evil. Stupid, especially with-out Rie awake to control it, and weak since the yūrei is still weak, but still extremely dangerous.'

The *oni* looked around curiously, a gleam in its eyes as it took in the destruction around it and the fights still going at the other end of the basement.

"David! Use the elemental form… It's small and confused, kill it quickly," Masao yelled, glancing away from his own fight to check on David.

Takumi yelled, receiving a slashed arm from one of Chul Moo's gauntlets. While he tried to recover, Chul Moo took the chance to push Takumi away from the others, further into the darkness.

"Natsuki, go help Takumi, I'll take care of the mongrel." Masao threw a side-glance at Natsuki, battling against Jahan-gir next to him.

With a quick, uncertain glance, Natsuki obeyed, leaving Masao to fend for himself. Masao smiled, changing his stance and grip on his sword, displaying a technique of which none of the other Matsumotos was aware.

On the platform, David approached the oni with his Sei-kaku at the ready. Catching a gleam off the blade, the oni turned to face him, a confused look crossing its sharp face. The Sei-kaku seemed to focus the oni, it small eyes narrowed. Roaring, a flaming sword suddenly erupted in its bright red hand. Run-ning forward, David changed his sword to its elemental form, a growl erupting from his throat to match the oni's roar. Wood and fire met in a furious clash of sound and light as the oni and David collided.

Distracted by David and the oni, Natsuki missed the in-coming blow. Chul Moo caught her in the temple with a hilt, knocking her to the ground. His killing blow was stopped inches from Natsuki's neck by Takumi's blade. He had thrown himself forward to protect Natsuki. Catching the blade left him exposed and Chul Moo took full advantage of it. Taking his other short sword, Chul Moo raked it along Takumi's back. With a look of horror, pain, and fear, Takumi fell.

In the middle of the room, Jahangir's rage at the loss of the young ōkami was far from abated. Still raining furious blows that would have killed Masao if he had not switched techniques, Jahangir snarled and spat, trying to make a blow connect. In return, Masao was a twirling torrent of steel, his features blurring, his blade flashing around him too fast to see. With deadly determination, Masao began to drive Jahangir back, moving towards the oni in case David needed help.

On the platform, David threw his own heavy blows at the oni using his height and reach as much as possible. The oni, like something from an old cartoon, roared and raged at David. Every time his Seikaku connected with the oni's sword, David felt as if someone had dropped a ball of molten lead in his chest. He staggered from the pain, but determined to end the contest quickly fought through it. Passing an old wooden crate David halted his attack, plunging his wooden Seikaku in to the wood. The box exploded in a directed shower of splinters, driving themselves into the oni. As the wooden splinters connected with the demon's scaly hide, they lit aflame, sending the oni running in circles screaming in pain and outrage. David drove forward, his Seikaku held high for the killing blow.

Takumi, covered in darkness and in mortal peril, disappeared in a puff of smoke and flame. In his place, a small grey haired baby bird tried to flap its wings. Wildly trying to escape, the baby Phoenix was hampered by its injury. Chul Moo, howling in triumph swung with both blades. From his side, Natsuki loomed up, slicing completely through one, and halfway through the other of Chul Moo's arms with the force of her blow.

Chul Moo stared first at his missing arm as his swords clattered to the ground around the flapping bird, then to Natsuki. Their eyes met and Natsuki almost hesitated, as if remembering she had once wanted to be held by the very arm she had just severed. With a tear Natsuki pivoted, her blade slicing up, then severing him across his chest.

At the same instant, David's Seikaku cleaved a straight line through the center of the oni. Jumping back, David watched as the oni's sword extinguished. The oni looked stupidly at its empty hand. Suddenly, the Devil's Doorway, the portal of dark abyss and fire reappeared beneath it. With a great rush of wind, the oni was drawn back into the pit, leaving a sudden stillness and silence broken only by Takumi's flapping wings and Masao's flying steel.

Looking back from the platform, David watched as Masao seemed to grow in power and size, his features hazy in the dark distance. Jahangir's body betrayed his fear as Masao moved his sword faster and faster. With a crash like glass, Masao thrust his sword forward, where, just as the old crate had exploded in splinters, Masao's sword, the best of the Matsumotos' craftsmanship, splintered into a million gleaming bits of metal. Jahangir fell, the tip of the once proud sword protruding from the back of his neck.

With all the ōkami disabled, Natsuki reached down to pick up the bird. Still fluttering around with premature wings, its back injured from Chul Moo's attack it squawked weakly in panic. Pulling the bird into her arms, Natsuki suddenly stood erect, a surge flying through her. David's head snapped around to her as he felt for the first time, as if it were a real and physical rope, his connection to her. Instantly the rope tightened and snapped.

"David, hurry…" Masao called. The first to recover his wits in the aftermath of the fighting, the ragged looking elder Matsumoto managed only short gasps. "Take care of the ōkami… We need to grab Rie and get her back to the Estate… before she can wake."

Staggering from the force of the emotional blow, David moved forward, plunging his wooden Seikaku into each of the ōkami he could find. By the time he got to the young ōkami, it had nearly reformed. His Seikaku drew the last piece in as it turned the ōkami into a statue. In under a minute, David had statues of Chul Moo, Jahangir, and the young ōkami piled in the center of the warehouse.

"Where is Chul Soon?" Kou asked, unable to find him. After another look around the basement, Masao met David near the pile of statues.

"David, quickly bind the yūrei, we need to get her back to the shrine if we are going to save her. Natsuki, get Takumi out of here. I will dispose of the ōkami."

David moved forward, binding Rie as Masao began adding small bricks and canisters from a bag to the statues. Carrying Rie, David followed Natsuki up the stairs. Masao followed close behind with Yuka. She was unconscious and limp in his arms. Just after Masao cleared the exit, an inferno exploded from the uncovered hole. Yukiko, alerted by a call from Natsuki, brought the van around to the loading dock. Masao and David deposited their loads before David ran back for Yuuto. They left as flickers of flame reached the first floor, Masao already calling the fire department via a disposable phone.

Back at the Matsumoto Estate, the van raced through a small forest road to the Matsumoto Shrine. During the ride, Masao had bound Yuka, covering her eyes in case she woke. Though she seemed frail, the Matsumotos could not risk letting her go to the hospital until the yūrei was destroyed.

At the Matsumoto shrine, David placed the yūrei gently on the altar. To the side, Natsuki and Takumi, the latter wrapped in a blanket and healing quickly spoke in quick, hushed voices as Masao finished the preparations for the ceremony. Donning the ceremonial garb of Shinto priests, both David and Masao stood before the shrine.

With all prepared, a midnight bell tolled from Nakano as Masao began to chant. Similar to the summoning chants David had heard before, the chant awakened Kou within him. David could feel Kou take notice and caught Takumi jerk in surprise from the corner of his eye. Masao's voice was deeper than Grandpa's had been, more musical than the harsh edge Jahangir had used. Then as if Grandpa's voice had joined him, the chant held a second haunting harmony that seemed to come from Masao, yet could not have. David noticed that, as with the fight in the basement, Masao's features seemed to blur.

Noting a slight nod from Masao, David closed his eyes, concentrating, his arms subconsciously rising from his sides as he summoned the Seikaku. Catching it with his practiced hand, David changed it to its wood form and stood ready for his part in the ceremony. Masao's brow furrowed in concentration, sweat glistening along his forehead. Suddenly rising, Masao's voice and the strange harmony sped up, driving forward with insistent force.

The yūrei awoke violently, thrashing yet locked in place by invisible bonds. David raised his sword above his head, ready to strike. As he watched Rie seemed to blur, two images of her, flashing between her old self and the corrupted yūrei she had become. With two images before him, David had to choose. He held her life in his hands.

"I… I can't do it." David stared into the eyes before him, now dark brown, now evil pits of murder and despair. "I'd rather let this evil walk the land than accidentally destroy you Rie."

David lowered his arm, his eyes never leaving her face. Masao nearly faltered in his chant, his voice breaking, the harmony stuttering. Beside him, Natsuki and Takumi raged words that never met his ears.

三十五
RETURNS

October,

Even being in the same body, I was so surprised I nearly took over and transformed. Though we had talked at length about what to do, we were still too separate, our ideas still too alien for me to comprehend…

The Seikaku's tip fell below David's waist. Then he struck. As he drove the wooden Seikaku into the yūrei, the night was rent with the yūrei's piercing scream followed close behind by an explosion of energy that obliterated the Matsumoto shrine. The closest, David was tossed back into the clearing, leaving only the crumbling foundation of the shrine in his place.

David opened his eyes warily, prompted awake by Kou's urgent pressing. As his eyes cleared, David muttered to himself.

"I'm waking up like this far too often."

Kou's chuckle did nothing to temper the pain in his back. Looking around, he saw Masao, Takumi, and Natsuki all getting up. Rie lay in the rubble of what had been the shrine. David clawed himself to his knees, and then staggered, trying to make his way to Rie.

'Careful, I think you broke… a lot.'

David ignored the pain that seemed to come from his entire body. Oddly, as things began to heal at their faster than normal pace, some parts hurt more than they had only moments before. He could almost envision his twisted nerves and muscles knitting themselves back together.

Although every step was an agony, David made it to what had been the stone steps leading up to the shrine. Pulling himself up, he was just able to catch a glance of Rie's face. Her skin once again whole and real, the dark orbs covered by long lashed lids. She was calm and almost too serene. A deep fear materialized in his mind before Kou pointed out the soft thump of blood through her veins and the gentle pull of her lungs. Then as if the relief broke a dam within him, pain shot through his body, and David slid back down the steps.

It took hours. Unlike his previous experiences, he was conscious through the entire healing process. Unable to speak, think, or hear even Kou through the pain he was only dimly aware that Masao had carried him to the main house and laid him in his own bed. It was nearly as excruciating as the bare memories of his first death, every second worse than the previous.

When he was finally able to move, he rose, stretching gingerly. A few tendrils of pain lanced through his body, but he was whole enough. David made his way through the house and found the Matsumotos sitting around the table, just starting breakfast.

"It never fails… you are always up in time for food," Yukiko said. She smiled broadly and set a place for him. Takumi had a gleam in his eye, and Masao, though he looked exhausted overflowed with a buoyant energy.

"Well?" growled Kou before David could sit. *"How is she?"*

"We… you… did it." Masao smiled widely, gesturing to a nearby seat. "Rie is alive and the yūrei is gone. We have not been able to talk to her yet, but whatever you were thinking at the shrine, it was the right thing. She is sleeping in her room. Her injuries, while not physical, may take more time to heal than yours, even if yours had healed naturally, which is saying something."

"You should have seen yourself after the explosion," Takumi said around a mouthful of rice. "You had rock shards riddling your body, I think your leg and arm were broken though you walked on it, and your back had a gash nearly the size of Kou taken out when you landed on a rock in the clearing."

"I do not know how you made it back to the shrine before you fell back. I assume your injuries are mostly healed now?" Masao asked.

"Yeah, I think so. My back is a bit stiff. I didn't realize... I just had to make sure I got the right one." David's eyes glazed as he drifted back over the events in his mind.

Although Rie finally came around later in the day, every time she tried to talk she burst into tears. It was worse when David came to see her. One glimpse of him sent her into near hysteria, so that David stayed as far away from her as he could. Kou's new freedom made it far easier. During the fight at the warehouse, Natsuki bonded with Takumi's Kami. Their long history and feelings for each other were so much stronger than Kou and Natsuki's that the old bond had broken.

David and Kou were on their own, and while free to change at will, they could not but help feel a twinge of regret at the loss. In the last instant before the bond was broken, David had been able to glimpse just how important it could be. With Rie unable to be in the same room as David, they found solace among the forests and mountains as Kou.

David spent the day off from school on Monday in the mountains, returning to the Estate on Tuesday. At school, the students were awash with the rumors and news of the big fire in town. The rumors only spread further in the coming weeks when fire investigators discovered DNA from Enya and his father. Since the fire was so intense, few remains were left. The firefighters were also baffled when they found a wooden wolf statue completely unharmed by the fire, yet missing a piece as if someone had cut a part of a paw away.

Naoto was sure it was arson, Shou an accident. Yuka and Yuuto returned to school with only a shaky memory of their time as thralls. Both rejoined their respective teams, and even started dating.

It was the third night after David destroyed the yūrei that Rie found him, coming back from the outer forests among the trees at night as Kou. She stood waiting, and although Kou was aware of her far before she could have seen him, he approached slowly. Finally seeing him slink out of the shadows of a tree, Rie shuddered then took a hesitant step forward. Kou and Rie walked together through the forests of the Matsumoto Estate, Rie's hand absently running through Kou's fur where it stuck out of his armor. They walked without speaking, Kou letting her think in peace.

'At least she's not crying right?'

Turning past an especially large tree, the largest in the Matsumoto forest, Rie turned on Kou.

"What did you mean you'd let a yūrei run amok in Japan just to save me?" Rie yelled. Her voice was surprisingly strong with a new edge. "Are you insane? What kind of Jitsugen Samurai are you?"

David was so surprised that Kou's mouth hung open in shock as his body reacted without David's explicit instructions.

"*So you remember that do you?*" Kou chuckled as he recovered from being over ridden by David's emotions. His growling laugh echoed off the trees. "*David needed a way to find out if you were still in there. It was not until he saw your tear at his words that he could strike down the yūrei. It took all our concentration to ensure you would not be banished along with the spirit.*"

Rie's strength left her then, and she shrank, sitting against the tree. Kou sat with her waiting, until finally the words flowed out of her, the dam of silence exploding with nearly as much force as the destruction of the corrupted Kami that had held her.

"It was terrible, far beyond my worst nightmares, worse than I thought possible. I remember *everything*." Rie stared into the forest, her eyes lost in the past.

"I ran into Chul Moo almost immediately after I left that night… I had run into the mountains, almost right to their new lair. I wasn't thinking, I was just so *angry* that Natsuki had… well Chul Moo had always been so nice, he always listened even though everyone else thought he was strange. I poured out all my frustrations, and then I started getting really tired. Chul Moo noticed, he realized he was already feeding off my soul, and tried to stop but right before I passed out, I remember Chul Soon's voice say, 'Nice catch brother,' and then I was gone. I woke up in the cave. It felt like the ōkami were literally eating my memories. I was still there, aware, yet I wasn't there either. It was the most horrible…"

Kou peered up at Rie's face, her eyes turned towards him but instead of looking at him, her eyes still bored into the darkness of her memories.

"All those months, I felt myself get weaker and weaker. Every time David came, I wanted to scream out for help. I saw the suspicion in his eyes, but I couldn't do anything. It killed me, yet what would I have done if Takumi and I had been in opposite positions? The ōkami had me completely, but since I was so useful, they decided to snack on Misaki and use me to make their weapons and learn more about you.

"I wanted you to run, to leave me, yet there you were always willing to help. When you came, I almost broke through. Chul Soon kept a very close eye on me from then on." Rie sagged again, her face dropping into her hands. Her words seeping out, almost against her will.

"Chul Moo was going to let me go that first night, if it hadn't been for his brother… He kept worrying about me, keeping an eye on me. I guess he had feelings for me. He even refused to feed from me."

Rie's voice faded out and she sat quietly for a long time. Kou watched the trees around him, the life that he never would have noticed months before scurrying around the trees.

"Then they made me a yūrei. That was the single most painful thing I've ever felt in my life. It was as if my eyes had been ripped out and dirty oil had been poured in their place. I could feel it seep through my body taking control, warping my thoughts, dragging out my memories, and trying to seduce me with power. Every emotion I had ever felt was intensified. The scariest thing was when I began to agree with the yūrei's decisions." Rie finally looked up again, the fear she had felt etched in every facet of her face. "I couldn't remember why I shouldn't agree with it.

"And then I felt like I was myself again, only powerful. I had complete control over the ōkami and I wanted that control. I made them pay a thousand fold for the time they had spent feeding on my soul. Enya and his father were an accident. They were in the wrong place at the wrong time, but I was weak, and we took them both. I was able to leave the snack pack. By then I had enough control that the ōkami did what I wanted. I think I convinced the yūrei part of me that I was gloating, letting Takumi know I had been there. I wanted to destroy you and everyone else, make you quake at the sight of me. I would have, too. The Kami didn't have enough time, was still too unfamiliar with my body, and hadn't merged completely with my mind. It was so strange to be annoyed at my own body for being so confusing."

Rie finally turned and looked at Kou, sitting next to her in the darkness.

"I couldn't bear to face David, to face you, having felt like I wanted to kill you, having summoned an oni to do it. You never gave up on me, but I betrayed you, I was ready to kill you. And then, looking into your eyes, I wanted nothing but for you to kill us both, but you said… you."

Finally drained of words, Rie buried herself in her arms. David changed, his rough armor the only barrier between them as she leaned into him, taking comfort in his arms.

"After seeing the pain in your face the first night we changed, I promised myself I'd never be the cause of that pain again," David said gently. "I broke that promise because we had to be sure before I struck. Without you, it was like a hole had opened and swallowed a part of them. You're back now, only Grandpa is missing. Everything will be all right. You'll see."

三十六
RECOVERY

October,

Free to run, free to stalk the Nakano valley, yet still, there was that oh so foreign, bitter taste, of regret...

Within days of their talk, David began to overhear Rie asking Masao and Yukiko to let her return to practice. While concerned for her health and mind, she was so insistent that they finally relented at the end of the week. David made a point of cutting his morning run short to ensure he made it back to the house before Natsuki showed. The two girls had yet to see each other since the night at the warehouse, and David was worried. Rie made it back first. Aside from a permanent discoloration of her eyes that she had to hide with contacts, Rie was physically just as fit as she had been before Kou first appeared. The corrupted Kami had healed whatever damage was done by the ōkami feeding off her.

David suspected that part of her desire to return to practice was to get her mind off the memories. She had watched one of her best friends die at the hands of the same monsters that had held her. She had been there when Enya and his father had been devoured.

Rie entered the dojo gasping. She had pushed herself, as if trying to out run the demons that still plagued her. She went to him with a surprised smile after toweling off. If she noticed his eyes constantly flick to the door as they talked, she showed no sign. When she came back from changing, Natsuki was there in the doorway, fresh from her own run. David tensed as the girls stood on opposite sides of the room staring at each other with blank but wary faces. Then Natsuki gave the barest tilt of her head, and the smallest flick of her eyes. Without a word, the two girls left the dojo and disappeared into the depths of the Estate.

Natsuki became a surprise pillar in Rie's life. The girls were able to put aside their old squabbles and pick up their friendship, stronger for having lived on the opposite side of such strange events. David caught the two ex-friends ex-enemies, talking late into the night. Natsuki filled Rie in on all the things Takumi and David did not think to tell her. Yukiko often sat with them late into the evenings.

Despite the end of her Partnership with David and Kou, Natsuki was still as much a part of the secret happenings on the estate as ever before. Although not a Jitsugen Samurai, and thus unable to speak directly to his Phoenix Kami, Takumi had bonded with Natsuki in the ōkami's lair. The baby bird occasionally fluttered around the Matsumoto Estate when Takumi surrendered to its will. Unfortunately, it never stayed to talk. The little bird seemed just as paranoid of the ground as Takumi had felt, and would fly away at the first chance it got.

At her insistence, Rie returned to school the next week, causing a stir among the gossip hounds. Though her story about how cold it was in Hokkaido seemed to explain away her return, many students were still confused over her departure. Although it took time, she was able to reintegrate with her old friends, much as Natsuki had done earlier in the year.

At morning practice, in class, and even with training at night, Rie threw herself at every problem with new determination. Where she had been competing with Takumi before David had ever come, it now seemed as if she battled the dark memories within her. They drove her, and it was the odd person out that did not notice the change in her.

In November, David finally got a chance to compete with the badminton team. As with everything else, Rie practiced with a ferocity that surprised the rest of the team. The team watched ecstatically as she scored third at the Himeji competition. David and Takumi also took spots in the top eight, much to David's surprise.

"You really are getting better," Takumi said after David received his certificate. "By next year you will be giving me a run for first."

"It's just so much easier to move than it was before," David said. "I can put myself where I want rather than flailing around the court and hoping I hit something."

"I don't know," Naoto said coming up from behind him. "I think there was definitely some flailing."

"You're just mad he beat you," Shou added, laughing.

As usual, David shot an email off to Jessica about the competition. As usual, she sent standard congratulations. She no longer bothered asking questions, since David could so rarely answer her truthfully. Surprisingly, she did not even go into a long bit about her latest school gossip or her newest friend.

'Maybe you should look into having her visit. I'm sure the Matsumotos-'

'She's too inquisitive, she wouldn't stop until she found out what was really up here. To invite her would be to welcome her into the Matsumotos' secrets. It's better for her to be off in her own world with my Dad, than bring her into all of this with no protection.'

Rie won over the last holdouts from their friends when she won the one hundred meter dash for their class at the yearly school sports festival. Despite their smaller size, Class 2B won more races than any other class. Their morning runs also got all four a place on the relay marathon team, giving them all a trip to Himeji and then Kobe for the regional competitions.

David and Kou prowled the valley and surrounding mountains around Nakano late into the early mornings. They slept at most an hour or two a night, sometimes as a tiger, sometimes as a human. Although they enjoyed themselves immensely, it was not without regret. David had seen what a Partner could be. An extension of one's self, another person who could grow to know you nearly as closely as David was learning to know Kou.

'There is still so much to learn though,' David thought as their tail swung beneath the tree branch.'

'We have a lifetime to learn,'

'You might have a lifetime, but Koji is still going to try and kill me.'

If other students had been happy about David's successes, David's growing popularity seemed to only annoy his greatest rival at school. Although he had helped defeat two ōkami packs, ghosts, and saved Rie, at school he could not use any of his training or powers. If Koji came for him, he would have little but his own wits and Kou's advice to help him.

'And no, I can't ambush him from a tree,' David thought as the all too satisfying image played through his mind at the tiger's bidding.

Weeks later, Rie sat under the same tree where David had held her while her grief and pain ebbed away. She was the first to every practice, and although darkness occasionally clouded her soft features, she was happy. She had also taken it upon herself to deal with the Koji issue. Slowly, she had begun working on his friends, removing his support system so as to remove the greatest of his strength in an attempt to make it all the more unlikely he would be able to bother David again.

Koji had resorted to trying to humiliate David in front of the school during another open P.E. session. The third and second years had been playing flag rugby together under the semi-watchful eye of Mr. Shima. Thanks to Rie, Koji had been unable to get his fellow teammates to take David down. When he tried on his own, Takumi was repeatedly able to deflect him away from his host brother. Koji had gotten so angry he finally tackled David when he didn't have the ball and got himself thrown out of the game.

"Wow even my sister can tackle the right person," David had said to the laughter of nearly everyone present. Koji's eyes had promised their feud would not end on that field as he was led away by the teacher.

"Boys," Rie said to herself with a laugh as a movement at the edge of her vision brought her out of her recollections. The early winter sun barely filtered down to her through the dense trees, above the grey-feathered phoenix soared overhead. Rie's discolored eyes glinted strangely in the light.

"Did you see the newspaper," she asked in a whisper nearly lost on the wind as she suddenly turned to look directly into Kou's orange eyes.

"About the stolen statue," David said, uncomfortable under her piercing gaze, "sure."

"We expect Ryohei to be around soon with an explanation," Kou added. He stepped out of the shadows and sat by her. Rie eyed Kou with a shrewd glance.

"In that case, we better get back to the house," she said, pushing off from the tree like a sprinter from a block. Kou barely had time to growl at her before David took control. In a blur of armor, they were after her.

As Kou neared the Japanese garden, he slowed, sensing something wrong. Perhaps it was a foreign scent, or a sound barely caught, but they stopped completely, blending into the shadows. They saw Rie burst into the square among the building and stop suddenly. Standing with Yukiko was a tall rangy man. Thin, with a light complexion and brown air, he was staring intently at one of the sculpted trees. Beside him was a young girl with long flowing blond hair, a skirt that was far too short, and a t-shirt that proclaimed her love of Justin Bieber.

Jessica Matthews tossed her hair as she surveyed the old buildings. As soon as they spotted Rie, Kou whipped around the outside of the dojo, running into it as fast and quietly as he could. He was not sure, but he hoped that the movement in the corner of his eyes as he rushed in had not been Jess's curious glance. Inside the dojo, Kou quickly changed back into David. He struggled out of his armor, replacing it with a stash of clothes. He waited until his family's backs were turned again before dashing around the building. He jogged through the forest, and then followed Rie's path out. A squeal broke through the air as Jessica saw him. He was nearly tackled as she flung her arms around him. David's surprise, hit him with all the force of his little sister's embrace.

They spent a week on the Estate, staying in the retirement cottage that had once housed Masato Matsumoto. David showed them around Nakano and filled them in as much as possible about the last eight months of his life. David's father, Dr. Matthews discussed the possibility of David staying another year, which Jessica was completely against.

"If he's going to stay, then I'm staying too," she said.

"But then who would make sure I get to the station on time?" Dr. Matthews asked with a laugh. "There would be no one to do *Crazy Science*, and think of all the projects we have to finish back home."

"*Fine!*" she grumbled.

Kou complained about their inability to transform for a week as all training was stopped. Natsuki was so thrilled by the break that she helped show Jessica around Nakano, even without being able to say much to her. For her part, Jessica chattered away incessantly, as if she was trying to catch David up on a year's worth of gossip. He could not help noticing there was a lot more about boys then he remembered.

Jess seemed particularly interested in David's relationships with Natsuki and Rie. David was extremely thankful the girls did not understand the questions she started throwing at them, and hoped his red face did not give them the right idea.

When Jessica met Takumi, she did something David had never seen her do before. She went completely silent. Throughout the whole week, the only words she was able to mutter when he was around was a stammering "Hi."

Eventually, the surprise visit ended with Jessica standing quietly by their father as he scribbled hurriedly in his notebook. Jess stared widely at Takumi before finally getting in the Matsumotos car with Yukiko at the wheel. David had requested she drive for fear of killing his father with a heart attack at Masao's driving. Together they drove to Himeji so they wouldn't have to navigate the more difficult local trains on their way to the Kansai Airport.

"David," Dr. Matthews said in front of the station, "I'm so proud of you. You really seem to be doing well. Sorry I haven't kept in better touch, it's just so hard to keep things straight. Jess tried to show me how to text you but my phone ended up in one of my experiments."

He gave David a big hug and his usual smile. David was comforted by the half bemused, half-surprised expression that was so *him*. Jess cried, which almost made David cry, something he had not done since the fight. He smiled, and reassured her he would write more. Yukiko invited them all to return anytime.

"I'll keep you to that," Jess said, then smiled. She leaned in to whisper in David's ear. "Don't date Rie. If you get married you'll never come back."

David was so thrown all he could do was sputter until Jess laughed and punched him. Her look of indigent shock at how much it hurt sent David laughing to the point *he* hurt. She had always been able to hit him. Finally, the time came for them to board the train. With another quick round of waves, Jess led David's father through the electronic turnstiles and back to Arizona.

October 31ˢᵗ,

The littlest things, the smallest mistakes can rear up and overthrow every good decision you've ever made. If I had only known... but then who knows? Maybe things would have turned out far worse. Who draws the line between hero and villain?

—*Rie*

An excerpt from the Rie Matsumoto Diary, as seen in the Matsumoto Library

ACKNOWLEDGMENTS

Samurai Awakening is the culmination of more than ten years of Japanese study. From my first introductions in elementary school to the Modern Japanese History course I took with Gail Bernstein, I have sought to understand just what Japan is. A few years ago, I began teaching in Japan and was luckily placed on a small island in Okinawa Prefecture. Many of the names within are borrowed from my students and friends from my time there, though they have been rearranged so personalities no longer match. Although a work of fiction, many cultural aspects of the story contain my personal experiences observing life in the remote places of Japan.

Many people lent me their time, patience, and opinions while writing *Samurai Awakening*. My old friend, Giao was my first victim and reader. Without him, it never would have become more than an idea. Fukiko-sensei, a fellow English teacher and karate-ka helped me perfect my Japanese phrases. Natalie devoted the most time and help in suffering through the multitude of emails and questions I threw at her. Finally, I must thank the people at Tuttle for their hard work and for leaping into the world of *Samurai Awakening* with me.

The Tuttle Story: "Books to Span the East and West"

Most people are surprised to learn that the world's largest publisher of books on Asia had its humble beginnings in the tiny American state of Vermont. The company's founder, Charles Tuttle, came from a New England family steeped in publishing, and his first love was books—especially old and rare editions.

Tuttle's father was a noted antiquarian dealer in Rutland, Vermont. Young Charles honed his knowledge of the trade working in the family bookstore, and later in the rare books section of Columbia University Library. His passion for beautiful books—old and new—never wavered through his long career as a bookseller and publisher.

After graduating from Harvard, Tuttle enlisted in the military and in 1945 was sent to Tokyo to work on General Douglas MacArthur's staff. He was tasked with helping to revive the Japanese publishing industry, which had been utterly devastated by the war. After his tour of duty was completed, he left the military, married a talented and beautiful singer, Reiko Chiba, and in 1948 began several successful business ventures.

To his astonishment, Tuttle discovered that postwar Tokyo was actually a book-lover's paradise. He befriended dealers in the Kanda district and began supplying rare Japanese editions to American libraries. He also imported American books to sell to the thousands of GIs stationed in Japan. By 1949, Tuttle's business was thriving, and he opened Tokyo's very first English-language bookstore in the Takashimaya Department Store in Ginza, to great success. Two years later, he began publishing books to fulfill the growing interest of foreigners in all things Asian.

Though a westerner, Tuttle was hugely instrumental in bringing a knowledge of Japan and Asia to a world hungry for information about the East. By the time of his death in 1993, he had published over 6,000 books on Asian culture, history and art—a legacy honored by Emperor Hirohito in 1983 with the "Order of the Sacred Treasure," the highest honor Japan bestows upon a non-Japanese.

The Tuttle company today maintains an active backlist of some 1,500 titles, many of which have been continuously in print since the 1950s and 1960s—a great testament to Charles Tuttle's skill as a publisher. More than 60 years after its founding, Tuttle Publishing is more active today than at any time in its history, still inspired by Charles Tuttle's core mission—to publish fine books to span the East and West and provide a greater understanding of each.